They were on Katie's side of the car. She glanced over and saw to her horror that one of the men held a gun.

And it was pointing at her head.

"Duck!" the man beside her yelled.

Instead of listening, Katie reacted instinctively, pulling the steering wheel and sending her car crashing into the side of the sedan. There were a couple of wild gunshots and a horrible metallic scraping noise as the two cars rubbed against each other. Katie had a clear view of the other driver struggling to maintain control, but he was driving in softer ground. For one breathless moment nothing happened. Then the black sedan simply dropped off the face of the earth.

"Go! Go! Go! Get out of here!" her passenger shouted, but before she could obey, she heard shrill sirens as police cars swarmed into the quarry.

"Oh, freaking wonderful," Katie whispered. A few seconds later, her car was surrounded by blue uniforms and unfriendly faces.

The man, her unwanted passenger, turned to face her. "I'm really sorry about this," he said.

Somehow that didn't help.

BETSY HORVATH

was raised on MGM musicals, old-school Harlequin books and Nancy Drew, so it should not have come as a shock that one day she'd be writing romantic-suspense novels. The biggest surprise was that it took her so long to actually buckle down and do it.

After mild flirtations with other genres and the completion of her B.A. in English, Betsy took a good look at her bookshelves. She realized that although she owned about a million romances, she hadn't picked up anything by William Faulkner or James Joyce in years (and then only under duress). An epiphany ensued, the scales fell from her eyes and Betsy embraced her destiny as a romantic-suspense author.

Betsy lives in tasteful splendor at the palatial Horvath estate surrounded by four cats and far too much technology. You can usually find her on her website (www.betsyhorvath.com), on Twitter (www.twitter.com/BetsyHorvath) or hanging around Facebook (www.facebook.com/BetsyHorvath).

BETSY HORVATH

HOLD ME

CARINA
PRESS™

For my father.
Indeed, there was always love.

**CARINA
PRESS™**

ISBN-13: 978-0-373-06267-6

HOLD ME

Copyright © 2011 by Betsy Horvath

Recycling programs
for this product may
not exist in your area.

www.CarinaPress.com

Printed in U.S.A.

HOLD ME

A rose by any other name would smell as sweet.
So Romeo would, were he not Romeo called, retain
that dear perfection which he owns without that title.
—William Shakespeare
Romeo and Juliet

Of all the gin joints in all the world,
she had to walk into mine.
—Rick
Casablanca

PROLOGUE

UP AND DOWN.

Up and down.

Katie McCabe stood silently at the office door. Watching.

Up and down.

That really was her fiancé, she thought with a dull sort of horror. That was really Tom having sex with Brandy...his supervisor...

Up and down.

...on his desk. On the leather blotter Katie had given him for Christmas. On the hard copies of the financial reports she'd volunteered to come...

Up and down.

...and pick up in person because it meant she'd have an excuse to see him during the day, which was pretty rare now that the company had moved to a bigger building and their departments were on a different floors. She'd wanted to try and talk things out, but she hadn't expected...

Up and down.

...this. She hadn't expected to walk in and see his white buttocks now rosy pink with exertion. She hadn't expected his designer trousers to be down around his ankles, or the moans or the obvious excitement, or the deafness...

Up and down.

...of passion when she'd intruded, unnoticed. Or the small bald spot on the back of his head glistening with sweat. Or, when he turned to the side, the boyishly handsome features contorted, eyes tightly closed.

Up and down.

Why hadn't he locked the door?

Up and down.

She knew that she should say something, anything, but she couldn't.

Up and down.

She forced herself to move, to turn.

Up and down.

And that was when she noticed the broom. Propped up against a wall.

Up and down.

Probably left there by the cleaning staff.

Up and down.

Forgotten.

Up and down.

And something inside her snapped.

Pause.

"Bastard!"

Things got kind of...ugly after that.

ONE

July...

As he slipped into Joey Silvano's empty office, FBI Special Agent Lucas Vasco just had a feeling that the whole thing was a mistake. Everything felt...off. Wrong.

He wished to hell he could have waited a few more weeks before attempting the break-in. It was still too early in the op for something like this. On the other hand, the timing seemed perfect—he'd been assigned to security detail outside the office on the very night Joey routinely took himself down to Philadelphia to visit his mistress. The man should be gone for hours, so Luc and David Allen, his friend and supervisor, had decided Luc should go for it. They were under increasing pressure to show some kind of results.

Stifling his misgivings, he closed the office door gently behind him and strode over to a massive oak desk occupying most of the room. He rifled through some papers but didn't find anything interesting. He'd just started to work on the computer when he heard movement in the hallway outside the room. Voices. Running footsteps.

Holy fuck.

Hadn't he learned the hard way never to ignore his instincts?

Joey and his goons were back early.

Way, way, way too early.

Cursing, Luc dove for the window.

"YOU KNOW HOW much I value your opinion, Katie. I always did like you better than your brothers and sisters."

Katie McCabe had just gotten into her car after a very long day at work when her mother's daily call had come through on her cell phone. Today she hadn't even made it out of the parking lot. She stifled a sigh.

"Katie?"

"Empty flattery does not become a woman of your advanced years," she said, falling into the expected role. It was just easier that way.

"Advanced years?"

"Besides, I know you like Darren best."

"Well…that's true. But don't you think it's a good idea? A really good idea. Come on, tell me you think it's a good idea."

Katie was silent for a minute, watching the traffic race back and forth on the highway beyond the parking lot. Was her mother serious, or just trying to distract her? "Okay, I can handle the karate, but the police? Are you sure?"

"Can't you see that this is all a part of my fiendishly clever master plan? Besides, I'm going to be a volunteer counselor attached to the police department, not Dirty Harriet. Your father thinks it's a good idea, don't you, Sean?" The cell phone crackled. "He said he does."

"I didn't hear anything."

"He humphed. But it was a positive humph."

Katie took off her glasses with her free hand and, holding the sidepiece, rubbed her eyes before jamming them back on. Boy, she was tired. Beyond tired. "Mom, I know you hang on my every word, but can we possibly talk about this tomorrow? I really want to get home."

"Get home? It's after seven. Why are you just going home now?"

"I had to work late. I didn't mind."

"Katie." Darn. She never could fool her mother. "You're turning into a hermit and, honey, you didn't have all that far to go in the first place. It's Friday night. You should be out with friends."

"Right now the only friend I'm interested in is the half-gallon of Rocky Road ice cream I have at home in the freezer."

"So call some of your brothers or sisters and ask them to come over. God knows you've got enough of them."

"Mom." Katie sighed and rubbed her eyes again. "I don't need anyone to come over."

"But—"

"Mother, Darren and Brandon both have dates, the rest of them are busy living their own lives and Melanie's away for a couple of days."

Again. Somewhere. Years ago, she and her foster sister had been inseparable, more like twins than two girls who happened to be the same age. Now, they were still friendly, but it was…different. Life had made it different.

Katie's throat ached with her sudden sense of loss. Of guilt.

"I'm worried about her." Her mom sounded sad.

"So am I."

There was a short silence during which Katie hoped that maybe her mother's focus had switched to Mel. But when she spoke again, her voice was determined.

"On the other hand, I'm worried about you, too, and you're the one I'm talking to. I'll deal with the problem of Melanie later."

Katie tried not to groan. Wonderful.

"You've been at this new job for over a month," she continued, blissfully unaware of her daughter's thoughts. "You need to, you know…meet somebody. Move on."

"Mom."

"Katie," her mother said in exactly the same tone. "You have to put the whole Tom incident behind you, sweetie. You can't keep—"

"Mother," Katie interrupted with more sharpness than she'd intended. "I love your lectures, but I am really too tired to talk about this now."

"Oh. Well. Okay."

Katie grimaced and rubbed her hand across the steering wheel. "I'll call you in the morning," she promised by way of an apology.

"Actually, you can't."

"I can't?"

"Don't sound so excited. I'm going shopping with Barbara tomorrow."

"All day?"

"All day. All frigging day."

"Now who sounds excited?" Having met Barbara many times over the years, Katie was surprised that her mother had agreed to spend even an hour with her. Especially since the woman was, quite simply, an arrogant bitch.

"Yeah. I'd rather stay at home and work in the garden. Or dig ditches. Or wash the car."

"Well, you could have told her no. N. O."

"You try telling Barbara no sometime and see how far it gets you. And she's got a lot of money and important connections. You know she put in a good word for your father and helped him get a big contract with that developer." Her mother hesitated. "Besides, Sean leaves with the boys in the morning. This is the week they all go away. I thought I might as well do some P.R. work."

"Ah." Well, that explained it. For as long as Katie could remember, McCabe men of all ages had gathered once a year at a rustic cabin in the Poconos to spend a few days away from the McCabe women. It was a strange and incomprehensible male bonding ritual, and her mom hated it, hated to be without Katie's father. It had only gotten worse after the children had all moved out.

Katie couldn't understand being tied so tightly to a man that you practically died from loneliness when he was gone—especially when that man was Sean McCabe. But there was no accounting for taste. She'd learned to keep her opinions to herself on that subject.

"I hope you have a good time anyway," she said, referring to the impending shopping trip.

"Thanks."

Katie laughed in spite of herself. "I'll call you to see how it went."

"Just pray that I can hang on to my temper, or you'll be visiting me in the slammer."

"Not a good career move for a budding volunteer police counselor."

"Tell me about it." Her mother hesitated. "I really am worried about you, Katie."

"I know."

"I want you to start acting normal again."

"I know. I appreciate the fact that you're concerned. I really do."

"So we'll talk in a day or two?"

"Oh, absolutely."

"Promise?"

"I promise." Katie smiled out through the windshield. "I love you, Mom."

"I love you too, baby."

THE ROAD CURVED, forcing Luc to squint into the late afternoon sun. By some miracle, he'd made it all the way from Joey Silvano's office to his Corvette parked in front of the mansion without getting shot, but he'd twisted his ankle pretty good when he'd taken that swan dive off the balcony. It throbbed like a son of a bitch. Fortunately it was his left ankle, but the pain still exploded into spikes of agony every time he used the clutch to shift. Probably ripped some ligaments or tendons or something else he hadn't noticed in the initial adrenaline rush.

He ignored the pain. The 'vette's gears whined when

he sent it speeding around yet another corner and out onto the highway.

The road behind him was clear, and he almost let himself believe that he'd gotten away. That he'd lost them in the chaos of his escape.

Then a black sedan flowed into sight in his rearview mirror and he heard the first gunshots.

Shit.

Luc focused on driving. And on trying to stay alive.

KATIE TUCKED THE cell phone back into her overloaded purse, then dropped the purse on the floor of the passenger seat. She sat, hands limp on the steering wheel, staring at the traffic beyond the parking lot. The cars were full of people intent on getting somewhere else.

What were their lives like, all of those faceless drivers? Were they rushing to get home to their families? Or were they trying to get away from them? Were they taking the kids out to the movies or meeting a loved one for dinner? Were they alone?

She was.

God, she'd been stupid to stay with Tom for two and a half years. To be engaged to him for two of those years. She hated remembering how he'd played her.

She swallowed against the sudden lump in her throat and gazed blindly out at the highway. Oh, yeah, she'd been vulnerable, miserable after Melanie's brother had stood her up at that party. A prime target.

Still, she had no excuse. She'd been dazzled by Tom, by how handsome he'd looked in the low lights when he'd asked her what was wrong. That kind of thing just didn't happen to girls like her. Then, when she'd found out that he'd been hired in the controller's department of the same company she worked for, it had seemed like fate. Destiny. Kismet.

"Romantic bullshit," she muttered.

She could not believe she was the only one who hadn't known what he was like. It wasn't as if she hadn't had warnings. Even in the beginning when he'd paid attention to her, when he'd seemed to be every woman's dream, there'd been signs. He'd watched other women all the time and made crude sexual remarks about them. When Katie didn't act the way he thought she should, his anger had been a frigid slap of disapproval.

But she'd ignored the problems, rationalized them away. Trusted. She'd always thought their issues were her fault. That if she changed a little more, was a little more, she could make everything all right. Even on those occasions when he'd turned on her, she'd made excuses for him. Accepted the apologies.

And all the time he'd been doing the horizontal mambo with everything that had a pulse. Maybe even some things that didn't.

She was such a moron.

Stop! Katie shook her head so hard that her red-brown curls bounced wildly and her glasses slipped sideways.

Enough, enough and more than enough. Her mother was right about one thing. It was definitely time to move on.

Now, how did one do that?

Katie shoved her glasses up her nose and started her car. She waited until the ancient Chevy Nova had gotten over a few initial hiccups before pulling out into the never-ending stream of traffic.

She had to get away. Move somewhere else. Maybe she should have thought of that before she'd found her new job, but it didn't change the facts. She had to get out of this part of Pennsylvania. Make a clean break, maybe move down closer to Philadelphia. Around here she saw people all the time who knew her, or Tom, or both. She could never tell who she'd bump into. These small-town people tended to remember Tom's glory days as a second string quarterback for a third-rate football team and overlook his many less charming qualities.

Witness the consequences of The Tom Incident. She'd been fired; he'd been promoted. After all, he'd been the wronged party in the whole thing. Never mind that it turned out Brandy had been taking his…reports for months. Never mind that his escapades had been common knowledge to everyone in the company.

Everyone but Katie.

She shook her head. Bitterness wasn't going to help.

What would help was a new beginning, she thought. A new life. A new attitude.

Yeah.

She brought the Nova to a shuddering halt at a red light. It was a lovely evening. The warm July sun was still bright and the birds were singing their songs from nearby trees and telephone wires. Katie massaged her temples.

She'd be fine, she told herself. Everything would be fine. It was just the end of another hard day at the end of another long week, but now it was over. She'd be home soon. Surely nothing else could go wrong before she got there...

As if it read her mind, the Nova gasped and stalled.

TWO

LUC SLAMMED ON the brakes when the line of cars stopped for a red light. One of the 'vette's tires was shredded, thanks to a lucky shot by the assholes chasing him, so he lost control, went into a slide and ended up nose down in a drainage ditch on the shoulder. He tried to reverse, but the abused tires just spun in the loose dirt and gravel.

He jumped out. He'd managed to put a little distance between himself and the black sedan, but it was moving steadily closer now, pushing its way through the traffic. He tried to run, but his ankle was weak and didn't support him. It slowed him down. Luc knew that he couldn't escape on foot. He needed help. But to involve a civilian...

An old, green Chevy Nova suddenly roared beside him. For one brief, delirious second he even thought he recognized it, but then all old Novas looked alike, didn't they? Still, Mama Allen would have said it was a sign. And, when it came right down to it, he didn't have much of a choice. He put the rest of his energy into the final few steps, trying to think how he could convincingly ask for assistance.

The Nova's driver gunned the motor again. It sounded fast.

He hoped it was.

Katie finally got the car started, holding her feet on the gas pedal and the brake at the same time so the thing wouldn't stall out again. Then, without any warning, the passenger door opened and a disheveled, dark-haired man slid in next to her.

She stared at him, shocked.

"Hi," he said.

"What do you think you're doing?" The fear slammed into her. Her car doors. She'd forgotten to lock her car doors. "Get out of my car!" Everything her mother had ever told her about serial killers and rapists and carjackers raced through her mind so fast they burned it out and left it blank.

"Yeah. Well, see, I'd like to, but—"

"You'd like to? Get out or I'll call the police." Call the police. Yes, yes. Call the police. Katie fumbled for her purse and her cell phone, but he grabbed her wrist.

"Damn it, don't panic! I'm not going to hurt you."

"I'm not panicking." Okay, so that was a lie, but he didn't have to know it. "Just get out!" She struggled to unhook her seat belt. The buckle, naturally, refused to budge. Oh, God, she was trapped in the car with a stranger. The light turned green, but she ignored it and the car horns that blared behind them as she fought with the belt. "Take the car," she panted. "You can have the car. Just let me go."

"Would you listen to me?" The man tightened his hold on her arm and glanced back through the rear window. "Please. I swear that I'm not going to hurt you. I swear. Honest. I'm with the FBI. There are people chasing me who want to kill me. They're almost here. I need your help. Please."

Katie hesitated and looked right into the man's beautiful dark eyes. He seemed sincere. This could be a scam, though. Her mother's voice in her head was screaming at her not to be stupid. This could all just be a way to lull her suspicions. But his voice was deep and musical, and she thought she heard some real desperation in it.

"If you—"

There was a sharp sound like a firecracker. The mirror on Katie's side of the car exploded.

She screamed. Loudly.

"Go!" the man yelled. He let go of her arm and she didn't think, she just reacted. She grabbed the steering wheel, let up on the brake and hammered her foot down on the gas pedal. The Nova screeched and faltered, then careened through the intersection.

"What…but…somebody's shooting at us." Katie sputtered almost as much as the car. Somebody was actually shooting at them.

"Yeah. Shit."

Katie looked in the rearview mirror. A black sedan had appeared on their tail, gliding after them like a big shark. The supposed FBI agent moved, drawing her attention.

"Oh, God, oh, God. That's a gun. You've got a gun!"

"Yeah." He sounded distracted.

Well, duh. Of course he had a gun. Katie swerved around a propane tanker and ran a yellow light. The black sedan stayed close and one of its occupants shot at them again. Okay, those people chasing them were freaking nuts to shoot a gun around a propane tanker. She tried to go faster.

The FBI man rolled down the window and leaned out, apparently thinking that he'd shoot back at the other car, which meant he was nuts too.

Katie had to brake abruptly as she wove between two slower moving vehicles. The man grabbed at the window frame to keep from flying out onto the road.

"Would you be careful?" He jerked his upper body inside. "There's too much traffic to get a good shot. You'll have to lose them."

"Trying!"

"Because if you can't, we'll both be dead soon."

"We'll be dead? How did this become a 'we'? You're the one they're after, not me."

"They're shooting at you, too, aren't they? Drive faster."

"But… I can't believe… Oh, jeez."

Katie took a deep breath and tried to calm down. Okay, okay, okay. Two things were obvious.

One: whoever was in that black sedan wanted to kill somebody.

Two: whatever was going on, she was right in the middle of it.

She had to stay in control. If she did what she wanted to do and collapsed into a weeping pile of hysterics, the car accident alone would kill them. She concentrated on zigzagging like a maniac through the maze of traffic. The sedan stayed on their tail.

"I think they're stuck to my bumper," she muttered.

"This isn't working." The man grabbed her arm.

"No? Really?"

"Turn down a side street or something."

"I hope you know what you're doing because I sure don't." Katie saw a likely looking road up ahead. "Hold on."

The man obediently clutched at the door and braced himself against the dashboard.

She waited until the last possible second, then jerked the wheel. Tired squealed and scattered as the Nova darted across three lanes of the highway to make the hairpin turn. For once the driver of the black sedan couldn't seem to react in time because the other car kept going, hemmed in on all sides.

When she saw that she'd lost them, Katie sagged in her seat, trembling. Her hands ached from gripping the steering wheel. Jesus, Mary and Joseph.

"They're gone," the man reported after a moment. "You, um, can slow down now."

It was only then that Katie realized she was still driving like a lunatic. She also saw that her unwanted passenger had a tight hold on the door handle and was looking more than a little queasy.

The surge of adrenaline pumping through her system made her feel reckless, powerful and pissed off. Instead of slowing down, she actually sped up. The man slid lower in his seat, jiggled the door handle and looked like he wished he could jump for it.

She smiled. Served him right. Jerk. Big, huge, hacking jerk.

"Do you do this sort of thing often?" she asked, admiring her own casual tone.

"What sort of thing?"

"Oh, you know." She waved a hand, then grabbed the wheel again as they bounced over a pothole. "Shooting at bad guys, car chases through small towns, etcetera, etcetera."

"Oh, that." He shrugged and twisted in the seat to face her. "I don't know. Pretty often."

Katie glanced at him and saw that his eyes were twinkling. She blinked. The jerk really did have beautiful eyes. They were a rich, deep shade of chocolate brown, framed by incredibly long, dark eyelashes. Never in her life had such eyes actually twinkled at her. She almost steered the car into a ditch and the bump drew her attention back to the road.

He didn't appear to notice anything unusual. Probably women drove into ditches whenever he walked by.

"Besides," he said, and grinned, "how do you know I'm not the bad guy?"

Katie swallowed. The giddy high washed away, leaving her weak and shaken. This wasn't a game, she reminded herself. She didn't know this guy. She didn't know the first thing about him. Thoughts of murderers and rapists raced through her mind again. What if she'd been running from the police all this time? Of course, she'd never seen the police driving black sedans, and one would hope they wouldn't shoot at a car on a busy highway, but who knew?

As soon as possible, she pulled over to the side of the road.

"Get out. Now." She tried to sound hard and powerful but didn't think she'd pulled it off. That was the problem with being short—no authority.

"Hey, come on. I'm sorry. I didn't mean it," he said, his voice soothing. He didn't even try to move.

She swallowed and shoved her glasses higher on her nose with a shaky hand. What was she going to do? He was a lot bigger than she was and seemed to be in pretty good shape. His shoulders stretched the material of the black T-shirt he wore and his biceps bulged quite nicely, even though he wasn't doing anything special with them at the time.

Now that she really looked at him, she noticed he had a long scar across his left cheekbone. She didn't know how she'd missed it before. He had a tattooed band of Celtic knots wrapped around the arm closest to her, peeking out under the short sleeve of his shirt. And there was another tattoo of a snake farther down on his forearm. He looked dangerous.

All right. So, she probably didn't have any hope of forcing him out of the car by herself. A surreptitious tug on the seat belt confirmed that the buckle still wouldn't move. But if she could reach her utility knife in the glove compartment, maybe she could stab him...

"Come on, I was joking," the man said into the thick silence. "I'm not one of the bad guys. I swear. I didn't mean to scare you."

Joking? And he expected her to believe that? How stupid did he think she was? She crossed her arms over her chest and glared at him.

"You're with the FBI?" she asked.

"Yeah."

"Don't you have to show me some kind of a badge or something?" She'd seen enough cop shows on television to know that much.

"I don't have one with me." He squirmed a little in the seat. "I am, was, working undercover."

"Okay." She raised her eyebrows to show him she didn't buy it. "Then just tell me what's going on."

He coughed. "I can't."

"All right." Katie studied him, refusing to let his beautiful eyes distract her, refusing to notice how he took up most of the room in the car. "So, let me see if I've got this straight. You're telling me that you're with the FBI, but you can't prove it. You've carjacked me, gotten me shot at and generally scared the heck out of me, but you're not going to tell me why. About cover it?"

He hesitated, then nodded. "Uh, yeah."

"Buddy, if you think—"

"You really did save my life. I can tell you that much." He smiled at her fully, and the temperature in the car went up about ten degrees. His face had a fierce quality that, combined with the scar and his obviously once-broken nose, saved him from being merely handsome. But when he smiled, these attractive brackets showed up and framed his long, full mouth. In a softer face they might have been called dimples, but it was ridiculous to call them dimples on this man. They bothered her.

Katie looked quickly away, but that just made her more aware of the warmth of his body in the seat next to her. She felt him shift, saw him glance out the rear window. Then he stiffened and cursed.

"What?" She looked, too, and her eyes widened when

she saw a very familiar black sedan speeding up behind them. "Oh, no."

"Move!"

Katie didn't think. She didn't stop to wonder whether the people in the black sedan really were the police. Somewhere, deep down inside, she knew that they weren't and that whoever was chasing them wanted them dead. So she grabbed the steering wheel and stomped her foot on the gas pedal. The Nova spun gravel, hesitated a split second, then took off.

"We've got to lose them again," the man told her.

"Hello! Figured out that much, okay? You're making me nervous."

"Great. At least there isn't any traffic around here." He leaned out the window and shot repeatedly at the sedan. His face was grim when he ducked back inside. "The car shakes so much that I can't keep my aim."

"Well, I'm sorry!" They were out of town now, and the road was narrow and winding. "Maybe you should have thought about that before you jumped into it!"

"You don't have to shout," he muttered.

"I AM NOT SHOUTING!"

"Sorry, I must have mistaken you for the other screaming banshee in the car." He paused and looked at her. "Are you all right?"

"All right? Oh, yeah, yeah. Sure. Fine." She tried to rein in her hysteria.

"Just hold it together." He leaned back out the window.

The countryside was becoming increasingly rural. With no real logic other than panic, Katie made a sharp turn at a crossroad in an attempt to lose the sedan. She almost succeeded in dislodging her passenger, but the sedan stayed on their tail.

"Would you give me some warning before you do that?"

"Sorry." Katie swept around another curve and practically unseated him a second time. She cleared her throat. "Um, I don't suppose this is a good time to mention I don't have the slightest idea where we are."

"What?" He jerked himself back into the car just as there were more gunshots from behind them. The mirror on his side shattered. "What do you mean you don't know where we are?"

"I mean that I don't know where we are." They spun around another sharp turn and teetered on the edge of a ditch. "So sue me if I don't have a great sense of direction."

Katie saw a wooden barricade across the road. She jammed on the brakes and the car pulled up in a cloud of dust. They were at the entrance of a stone quarry.

"Why are you stopping?" the man next to her shouted. "Go in! Go in! Crash the gate!"

"But—"

He said something and shoved his foot over hers on the accelerator. The Nova flew, burst through the barricade, splintering the old wood while Katie clutched the steering wheel and tried to avoid hitting quarry trucks and gaping workers.

He removed his foot and grabbed her arm.

"Just drive as fast as you can, okay?"

"Do I have a choice?"

"No."

"Okay."

He started shooting at the sedan again. Katie crouched down as far as she could, shoved the pedal to the metal, and sent the car racing up one of the narrow trails winding around the quarry pit.

The black sedan steadily gained ground until their pursuers had forced their way between the Nova and the lip of the pit. They were on Katie's side of the car. She glanced over and saw to her horror that one of the men held a gun. It was glinting in the afternoon sunshine.

And it was pointing at her head.

"Shit! Duck!"

Instead of listening, Katie reacted instinctively, pulling the steering wheel and sending the Nova crashing into the side of the sedan. There were a couple of wild gunshots and a horrible metallic scraping noise as the two cars rubbed against each other. Katie had a clear view of the other driver struggling to maintain control, but he was driving in softer ground. For one breathless moment nothing happened. Then the black sedan simply dropped off the face of the earth.

"Go! Go! Go! Get out of here!" her passenger shouted, but before she could even hope to obey, she heard shrill sirens as police cars swarmed into the quarry.

"Oh, freaking wonderful," Katie whispered. A few seconds later, the Nova was surrounded by blue uniforms and unfriendly faces.

The man, her unwanted passenger, the bane of her

existence, sighed and turned to face her. "I'm really, really sorry about this," he said.

Somehow, that didn't seem to help.

THREE

NOBODY WANTED TO listen to Katie. Which was, she admitted, pretty much the story of her life.

"You've got to believe me." She grabbed a policeman's arm after he'd cut her seat belt strap, hauled her out of the Nova and patted her down for weapons. He stared at her, his face earnest and young and not exactly intelligent. Great. "I don't know what's going on. I was just sitting there and this…this guy jumps into my car…he said he was with the FBI…they shot at us…they chased us. Would you say something?" she yelled at her passenger. "Tell him I don't know anything!"

The man was flattened across the hood of the car being handcuffed, but he glanced up and shrugged as best he could.

"She doesn't know anything."

"There! There! See? This is all a mistake!" Katie gestured wildly. The police officer jumped back to avoid her purse.

"With all due respect, ma'am, I've heard that one before."

"Tell him you're with the FBI." Katie snapped at the man.

"I'm with the FBI," he repeated.

"I don't believe him," the police officer said.

"He doesn't believe me," her passenger reported. His voice was muffled because one of the other cops had pushed him down on the car again.

"Oh, be quiet." Katie was thoroughly disgusted.

"Make up your mind."

Katie took a deep breath to tell the man that she knew exactly what she wanted him to do, but was interrupted when the young policeman's significantly older partner walked up to the car.

"Now, now," he chided. "None of that. And may I say what a pleasure it is to see you again, ma'am."

Katie looked at him more closely and bit back a groan. Oh, no. No, no, no. It wasn't possible. It was the same guy who had questioned her after the Tom incident. How had they ended up in his jurisdiction? She thought about denying that she knew him, but realized it would probably be a waste of effort. The young cop might be more than a little dull, but this man definitely was not.

"Officer Jenkins," she muttered, excruciatingly aware of the so-called FBI agent's interest as Jenkins took her purse and rummaged through it before handing it back.

"It looks like we have a lot to talk about. Again." He seized her arm. "So why don't we go to the station and have ourselves a nice little chat?"

Katie had enough brains left not to say what she really thought about that idea and let him pull her over to another patrol car while he recited her rights. He tried to open the door, but it was locked.

"Oh, for the love of…" He took a deep breath and let it out slowly before giving her a crooked half-smile.

"Rookies. Gotta love 'em. I'll be right back. Don't move." He pinned her with a glare until she nodded, then strode off.

Katie hugged her purse to her chest. Oh, God. Oh, man. What a day. What a horrible, horrible day.

The sound of voices nearby caught her attention. She saw that the two men from the black sedan had been handcuffed and were being dragged out of the quarry pit by several policemen.

The man who'd been driving the car didn't look too threatening, she decided as she watched him stagger along between his escorts. He was stuffed into an ill-fitting suit and had a heavy, almost stupid face. But the other one, the one who'd been holding the gun...

He stared at her with a fixated expression, hatred in his eyes, in every line of his body. He was a little man. Short. Not too much taller than she was, but he had an almost kinetic energy, the illusion of both strength and madness. Not really aware of what she was doing, she took one step back and then another, stopping only when she came up against the police car. The man saw her retreat and laughed, an eerie, high-pitched sound.

Suddenly, one of the two officers restraining the little man stumbled in the soft dirt and fell, losing his grip. With an abrupt, violent move, the man twisted free from the other cop and shoved him into the group behind them. Then he turned and ran right at Katie.

The policemen scrambled to regain their footing, but the little man was quick. They'd handcuffed his hands behind him, but that didn't seem to matter. He leapt at her, mouth open, teeth gleaming as if he would bite her.

As if he wanted to rip her apart. Katie stared until she realized that he was only a few steps away. She panicked.

Grabbing the handle of her purse with both hands, she swung it at his head. It missed his temple but caught him on his cheekbone and knocked him off balance. He launched himself at her again, and she kicked him as hard as she could. She aimed for his groin, but got his thigh instead.

He went down on his knees, teeth bared. He would have gone for her a third time, but the policemen finally reached them and tackled him back to the ground.

Then Officer Jenkins was there. He unlocked the car, grabbed her purse and pushed her into the backseat, slamming the door shut behind her.

Katie sat, stunned. What had just happened? What was happening here?

Through the window, she saw the police officers subdue the little man, but it was hard because he seemed to be very strong. Like a wild animal. He was spitting, his eyes were rolling, and all the while he was shouting obscenities. Obscenities directed at her.

Katie stared at him, watching his mouth move. She heard his curses through the closed window. So many words. Such foul words. She wanted to put her fingers in her ears, but wouldn't give him the satisfaction.

He strained backwards as the policemen pulled him away. "I'll find you, you fucking little bitch!" he yelled. "I'll find out where you live. You'll pay for this!"

She wrapped her arms tightly around herself and tried not to shake.

It was almost a relief that Officer Jenkins and his

young associate immediately slid into the front seat of the car and drove her to a small, local police station where she was fingerprinted and photographed. When Jenkins finally led her into the squad room and seated her at his battered desk, the two men from the black sedan weren't around. But her passenger, the jerk, the cause of all of her problems, was.

He was slumped in a chair across the room being questioned by another policeman, his long legs sticking out in front of him, his dark hair rumpled. He saw her looking at him and scowled, which drew his face into even fiercer lines. He appeared to be so thoroughly annoyed that Katie couldn't suppress a small smile of satisfaction. Good, she thought. Good. You suffer too.

"What's so funny?" Officer Jenkins asked, looking up from some paperwork he'd been busy perusing.

"Nothing." She sat straighter and quickly brought her attention back to him. "Um, where are the other two men?" Because, God, what if they brought that little man into the squad room too?

"Hmm? Oh. Don't worry. They're in the holding cell. The one guy seems to be kind of…agitated."

"Yeah." That was one way of putting it.

Jenkins put down the papers and took off his reading glasses, folding them carefully before he spoke.

"You're in a heck of a lot of trouble, ma'am."

Katie stared at him. She tried to hold on to her composure, but she suspected it was a losing battle.

"More than before? With the broom…?" Her voice cracked.

"More than with the broom." She thought he might have been hiding a smile, but it was hard to tell.

Her temples throbbed and she rubbed them. "But I didn't do anything wrong. What kind of a person do you think I am anyway?"

Officer Jenkins just looked at her for a moment, then showed her a stack of reports detailing a variety of traffic accidents caused by a crazy woman driving a dark green Chevy Nova.

"Frankly," he said, "after seeing the amount of damage you can do with a broom, I'm not at all surprised that you can cause this much of a mess with a car."

Katie tried to summon up the old McCabe bravado. "Those guys in the black sedan were shooting at us. What did you expect me to do?"

"The question is why were they shooting at you? And how did you end up in that quarry?"

She swallowed. "Don't I get to call a lawyer or something?"

"Sure, sure. But maybe we can talk a little first. Besides, I need you to tell me what really happened in your own words."

Katie looked at him, looked into those astute cop's eyes, and sighed. "Okay. My car stalled at a traffic light…"

A long time later, Officer Jenkins shepherded her into a small office where he gave her a cup of coffee, a box of tissues and the chance to make her phone call. She'd told him what had really happened about a thousand times, but he obviously didn't believe her. He knew her past record, after all. Heck, she'd be lucky if she didn't end up in a psycho ward with anger management issues.

After he left her alone, closing the office door with a solid "thunk" behind him, she sat down at the cheap metal desk, blew her nose and tried to pull herself together. She'd probably talked too much and should have insisted on being able to call someone first. But at least he hadn't put her in the holding cell with the men from the quarry pit.

No, he'd just locked her up in an office. Sure hope he'd checked it for brooms first. Maybe she'd lose it and run wild. You won't get me, you lousy copper!

Katie shook her head and blew her nose again.

What the heck was she supposed to do now? Calling a lawyer would probably be good. If she knew any other than Harry, that friend of her mother's who'd represented her for the Tom incident. Harry didn't want anything more to do with her because he thought she was nuts.

And the way the day was going, choosing a lawyer out of the phone book would definitely be a mistake. It was a little late now anyway after the way she'd spilled her guts to Officer Jenkins. She should call her mother, who knew everything. After this mess was over, the calls to check up on her would be coming hourly instead of daily.

Katie bit back the tears she'd been fighting for hours.

Reckless driving. Reckless endangerment. Maybe worse. Maybe assault with a deadly weapon after the way she'd whacked that little man with her purse. Of course, he was a bad guy and it had been pure self-defense, so maybe she'd be able to beat that rap.

She slid lower in her chair.

Against her will, her thoughts drifted back to her passenger. She wondered if he'd been telling her the truth. She should have pushed him out of the car when she'd had the chance. On the other hand, he'd obviously needed her help. Whoever he was, no matter what the police believed or didn't believe, those men had definitely been after him. Maybe he'd be dead right now if he hadn't jumped into her car. Somehow that thought wasn't as appealing as it should have been.

Katie shook her head at her own pathetic state of mind. She was scared. She was angry. She'd bloody well kill him herself the next time she saw him.

She'd call someone after she found out what was going to happen to her.

Luc Vasco swirled the dregs of his coffee around in the bottom of the paper cup. They'd left him to wait in the police station's tiny conference room, but he knew they weren't done with him yet.

He drained the last of the coffee, then crumpled the little cup into a ball with a sudden, angry gesture and lobbed it at the trashcan.

He missed.

The door opened and a tall, well-dressed African-American man of an indeterminate age stepped inside. About damn time.

Luc leaned back in his chair and looked up at him. "David."

"Lucas."

David Allen, his long-time friend and FBI squad su-

pervisor, walked farther into the room and pulled the
door shut behind him. He was carrying a purse under
his arm like a football.

"That's new." Luc gestured at the handbag. "Clashes
with the suit."

"Don't get any ideas. I got this back for the young
lady you manhandled. I do believe she carries rocks in
this thing." David slid into a chair on the opposite side
of the conference table and dropped the purse to the
floor with a thud.

"Did you talk to the police chief?" Luc rubbed the
back of his neck. God, he was tired.

"Yes. I hit construction in Philadelphia, so you're
lucky I got here in time. They were just about to bundle
you off to another police station."

"Well, now, wouldn't that have been lovely? What
did the chief say?"

"I gave him an idea of the situation. He understands
now."

"Swell. They didn't believe me."

"They wouldn't. You did cause quite a stir. And the
chief wasn't exactly thrilled to hear that the FBI has been
in his territory for weeks and he hadn't known about it."

"Yeah? Who's fault was that?"

"Glitch in the paperwork."

Luc laughed because he couldn't help himself. "Perfect."

"I calmed everyone down." David put his elbows on
the table and steepled his long fingers together, gazing
at Luc with a calm, watchful expression. "Tell me what
happened."

Luc groaned. He wished his ankle didn't hurt so much because he would have liked to have gotten up and paced around the room.

"You could say things didn't go as planned."

"They caught you."

"Might as well have." Luc told David about the botched office break-in and his escape from Joey Silvano's mansion.

When he finished, the other man was silent for several minutes. "I'm surprised you got away."

"Don't worry, there wasn't another Marie on this job. Nobody died for me this time." Luc pushed back the memories with an effort. "As far as this op goes, we're done. My cover's blown, and they sure as hell won't let me back in there again."

"Yes." David nodded and considered. "The powers that be are going to be royally pissed off when they find out what happened."

"Tell me about it."

David smiled briefly, then sobered. "Okay, so let's talk about the lady down the hall."

"My chauffer? With this ankle, I couldn't run very far. It seemed like a good idea at the time." Luc drew a hand through his hair and tried not to think about what he had done to her. About how he'd felt when he'd seen that gun aimed at her head and its halo of wild red curls.

He frowned. Why did she look so familiar? It had been nagging at him since the time he'd jumped into her car. With an effort, he forced his mind back to the matter at hand. "You know who's in the holding cell, right?"

"Frankie Silvano." David's face grew hard. "And we've got a problem."

"You mean the woman has a problem. Thanks to me. Any chance of holding him?"

"Not for long. No outstanding warrants, remember?"

"Don't remind me. And the driver?"

"Just some hired muscle. Goes by the name of Arlo. No warrants out for him either, which is kind of amazing. He seems to be on one of the lower rungs in Joey's organization."

Luc nodded. He'd met Arlo Kravitz a time or two during his months on the Silvano estate. The guy wasn't much of a threat. But Frankie, well, he was another story.

"How much time do we have?" he asked.

"Their lawyer's here already." David's lip curled. "He took a lot of pleasure in telling me that the judge is coming in for a special arraignment so they won't have to spend the night in jail. They'll be out on bail in a couple of hours."

"I love small towns." Luc was too tired to be angry. That would come later. "I swear to God I didn't know it was Frankie. It all happened too fast, and I was concentrating on getting away. I never saw who was chasing me."

"I figured."

"I didn't see him until they pulled up next to us at the quarry pit. I never would have jumped into her car if I'd known. I would have taken my chances on foot."

"And you'd be dead."

"Maybe. Maybe not." Luc absently fingered his scar. It was long, cutting from just over his left ear all the way to the top of his cheekbone. Another mistake. One of too fucking many. "Does she know?" he asked.

"No. I thought it would be better if you told her yourself."

"Oh, yeah. That's much better. She'll probably finish me off and save everyone the trouble."

"A nice young woman like that? You must be losing your touch."

"You've never met her."

"You talk like she's going to beat you up. I've heard she's a short little thing. You can probably take her."

"Funny." Luc hoisted himself to his feet and hobbled to the door. His ankle hurt like hell. It would probably swell up like a watermelon as soon as he took off his shoe.

David chuckled and grabbed the woman's handbag before following. "She's right down the hall here. Tell her we'll cover all of the costs for the damage she inflicted saving your ass," he said as they walked, moving slowly to accommodate Luc's limp. "The chief has dropped the charges and rescued her car from the quarry. That should make her feel better."

"Great."

"Maybe she won't knock you around too much."

Luc cursed and let the other man prod him toward an office. They paused at the door.

"Here. You can give her this." David handed Luc the purse.

When he grabbed the strap, he thought his arm was being pulled out of its socket. "Christ."

"Tell me about it. I'm surprised she's not a hunch-back."

Luc looked at his friend. "So, what do I say to her?"

David shrugged. "I guess you might as well tell her the truth."

"Um, then you should probably give me a few minutes."

"Sure."

"And if you hear the sound of furniture being thrown around, come rescue me."

David's only reply was a deep laugh as he walked back down the hall.

FOUR

SHE WAS SITTING alone in the room, behind a metal desk. Her head was bent, her eyes on her clasped hands. She looked as if she was praying.

Once again Luc found himself fascinated by her hair. Those rebellious red curls were like living things, each one stretching up to make itself known, like new little seedlings reaching for the sun. He shook his head at his own foolishness, put her purse on a chair by the door and limped farther into the room.

She stared up at him then, the expression in her blue eyes unreadable behind her glasses. She had freckles splattered across her cheeks and nose. "I've been trying to forgive you," she said. He noticed that her voice was low and clear when she wasn't screeching at him.

"That's nice." He didn't quite know how to begin.

"It hasn't been working."

"Ah." Luc decided that the best thing was to start with an apology. "Look, I'm sorry for all of the trouble I've caused you—" He cut off when she exploded out of the chair like a small, red-haired hurricane.

"Sorry! You destroy my life and then tell me that you're sorry?"

"Yeah. Now don't overreact, but—"

"Overreact! Over react!" She threw up her hands and stomped around the desk.

"Everything will be all right—"

"All right! All RIGHT!"

"Do you have to repeat everything I say?" Luc snapped, angry because she wasn't even trying to listen to him.

"No." She came to a halt and glared up at him, her small, animated face flushed, her eyes sparkling behind the glasses. "But the other things I want to do to you can't be done in a police station."

Luc stared at her and then, in spite of the deadly seriousness of the situation, laughed. "Gosh, and here I didn't even think you liked me very much."

"Aargh." She marched away, then whirled around and clapped her hands to her face, her expression now one of complete dismay. "Oh, my God," she cried. "I forgot all about Kato!"

Luc frowned because somewhere along the way, he'd missed something. "Who the hell is Kato?"

"You probably killed him. What am I supposed to do now?"

"Killed him! I don't even know who you're talking about." He hadn't thought he'd hit anyone, but maybe one of his shots had gone wild. He tried to remember the chase.

"My father and brother babied him for years and years and now in one afternoon, his side is all crushed in and the mirrors—"

"Wait a minute." Luc found that he could breathe

again. "Wait just one damn minute. Are you telling me that Kato is your car?"

"Yes." She scowled at him. "And I can't afford a new one."

Luc smiled. She was just about the cutest thing he'd ever seen. He folded his arms, leaned heavily back against the desk to take some of the weight off his bad ankle and regarded her in silence for a moment, enjoying the play of emotions across her mobile features. Kato. Of course.

"When I was a little kid," he told her conversationally, "I read every comic book I could get my hands on. I would read them from cover to cover until they fell apart. Didn't matter what they were about."

"How nice for you." She looked a little uneasy. "And I care because…"

"Kato was the Green Hornet's sidekick."

She stared at him, then blushed a bright, fiery red. "I don't know what you're talking about."

Luc burst out laughing a second time. It was good to laugh. "What? No sense of humor, Hornet?"

Her blush disintegrated into a fierce glare. "You are an ignorant pig," she said. "And if you ever call me Hornet again, I swear that I—"

"Eh-eh." He waggled a forefinger at her. "Don't swear."

"Oh!" She started to pace. Luc watched her move. She was pretty, he decided, but not in an obvious way. He liked that. Not beautiful, but definitely appealing. Cute. Especially when she glared at him, with her eyes flashing and her chest heaving.

Come to think of it, that was a pretty nice chest, and the rest of her wasn't bad either. She might be short, but she had curves in all the right places.

He watched her until he realized the direction his thoughts had taken, then frowned. God, she was right to call him a pig. This was not the time, not the place and she was definitely not the girl. Besides, she really did look upset. She was blinking and while he watched, she took off her glasses with one hand and wiped her eyes with the other.

Oh man, she was crying. Here she was, most likely terrified and he was laughing at her, leering at her.

Way to go, asshole.

"All of the charges have been dropped," he offered.

She stopped and, still holding her glasses, turned to face him. Without the distortion of the lenses, her eyes were blue like the sky and shiny.

Holy…

Luc drew in a sharp breath, stared at her. He felt like he'd just been sucker punched because, God, he knew her. He knew her. Without really willing it, his hand dipped into his pants pocket, his fingers brushed the photograph he always carried with him. He was crazy; it couldn't be her. It couldn't.

Could it?

"The charges have been dropped?" She sniffed and jammed her glasses back on, breaking the moment. He tried to relax and focus on what she was saying.

"Uh, yeah. You're clear. And we'll pay for all of the damages caused by the chase this morning. Including the repairs to, um, Kato."

"There won't be an arraignment?"

"No."

"I won't have to post bail?"

"No."

"I won't have to call my mother?"

"Only if you want to."

"Oh." She was silent for a bit. "Well, why didn't you tell me about this when you first came in?"

"I don't know." He forced a smile. "It must have been the warm welcome."

She snorted and turned away.

"What's your name?" he asked abruptly. He didn't want to know. He had to know.

"Katie McCabe. What's yours? Not that you'll tell me."

He felt a sharp mixture of relief and disappointment and confusion. The woman he'd thought she was would have been named Annie. But the last name was still the same, and that in itself was a big coincidence. What the hell was going on?

He realized she was watching him and struggled to pull himself together. He couldn't think about this now. Wouldn't think about it. Would put it away until he was alone again and could work it out. And whatever the truth was, it didn't change anything anyway.

"I'm Lucas Vasco." He was pleased when his voice just sounded a little gruff. "Luc."

"Thanks for getting me arrested, Luc."

"Katie—"

The office door opened and David poked his head around the corner.

"How are you both? Doing okay?" Luc turned aside, glad for the interruption. David stepped into the office, walked over to Katie and took one of her hands in both of his. "Ms. McCabe, it's so nice to meet you."

"And you are?"

"I'm David Allen, Luc's squad supervisor."

"And that means something to me because…"

David smiled as he let go of her hand, but Luc saw the glint of steel in his eyes. The people who underestimated David were the people who didn't know him. "You didn't tell her."

"Yeah, well, I was getting around to it," Luc mumbled.

Katie looked from one man to the other. "Tell me something? God forbid that he should actually tell me something."

"When did I not tell you something?" Luc demanded.

"In the car." She tossed back her hair. The curls bobbed and weaved like little red springs. His hand twitched, wanting to touch them. He concentrated on his exasperation to make sure he didn't.

"That was before. I couldn't tell you anything then. Things are different now." God, she had no idea how different.

"Very comforting." Katie crossed her arms. She stuck out her chin in a clear challenge. "Okay, then. Talk."

Luc noticed that David was still hovering near Katie and it bothered him. "First of all…" He hobbled over to her and pulled her away. A sharp, lancing pain shot up his leg when he moved, and he muffled a groan. "First of all, let's sit down."

"Why?"

"Because my damned ankle hurts like hell, that's why."

"Oh." She appeared to see his limp for the first time. "You're hurt."

"Yeah, well. I noticed." As if on cue, when he turned to lead her to two chairs, his leg finally buckled and caved underneath him. He would have pitched onto his face on the floor, except for the small hands that gripped his arm with surprising strength and steadied him until he could regain his balance.

"Shit."

"I'll help you." Her voice held a mixture of resignation and embarrassment.

Almost against his will, Luc's arm went around her shoulders. It might have been the wrong thing to do, but he couldn't have stopped it if he'd wanted to. And he didn't want to. Her body tucked under his arm perfectly, like she'd been made exactly for that spot. She smelled like flowers.

She was obviously uncomfortable, but she stayed with him until he dropped into one of the chairs. Then she backed away a little bit, face flushed.

Luc smiled and reached out, pushing aside one of the living curls that had fallen over her forehead.

"Come on and sit down."

She glared at him, but perched on the edge of the other chair anyway. Luc ran a hand through his own hair and tried to think. He didn't know how to begin. He didn't know where to begin. Focus, damn it.

"Katie, you saw those men in the black sedan, right?" he finally asked.

She shivered and crossed her arms over her chest. "You know I did."

"They're dangerous men."

A hint of amusement flickered across her face. "Believe it or not, I'd already figured that much out for myself."

Luc grinned briefly.

"Just get it over with, Luc," David said. "Tell her already."

Luc glanced at him and saw he was leaning against the desk, his bland expression not quite hiding his impatience.

"Tell me what?"

Katie looked at the two men, her heart pounding. The tall black man was sober, his weathered features grim, and Luc was acting weird. His face was taut, his cheekbones prominent, the scar white against his tan skin. His dark hair was tousled because he'd run his hand through it so many times. She knew she wasn't going to like whatever he had to say and was almost glad to be distracted from the memory of the warmth of his body against hers.

"You're in trouble."

Luc said it simply in his deep, musical voice, but all at once she was terrified, so much different than when Officer Jenkins had said basically the same thing. She latched onto his gaze like it was the only real thing in the room. He had a solidness that she found incredibly comforting at the moment. Stability. Confidence. Assurance.

"Like I told you in the car, I'm with the FBI. Show her our creds, David."

David leaned forward and flipped open their badges, but she barely spared them a look. Her focus was on Luc.

"I was working undercover in the household of Joey Silvano, one of the capos for a large crime family," he continued. "He has a house nearby where he stays a lot of the time. It's close enough to Philadelphia and Atlantic City to be able to conduct business, but because the town's small there's a lot less heat from the cops."

"Crime family? As in the mob?" Katie couldn't believe she'd heard him correctly, but Luc nodded.

"Let's just say that I got caught in the wrong place at the wrong time." He stared at her. "One of the men who was chasing us is named Frankie Silvano. Frankie is Joey's only son. His only child, in fact." He took a deep breath. "And he's a stone killer. He's crazy and mean and holds a grudge until the end of time."

Katie was silent while she tried to absorb everything he was telling her—and everything he wasn't. She thought about the little man with the wild eyes, the one who had shouted curses at her. Frankie Silvano. It had to be him.

"A killer?"

"Very much so."

Silence.

"And I pushed him into a quarry pit."

"And you pushed him into a quarry pit."

Luc inched forward in his chair and took her hands. His were warm. Hers were not. "Katie, please believe me. I never would have jumped into your car if I'd known who the men were. I would have made a run for it." He frowned. "Joey Silvano knows that I didn't find anything at the house. He wouldn't see the need to get involved with the Feds. But Frankie...well, I don't know about Frankie. See, he had a perfect record before this. No arrests, no warrants. But that's broken now."

And he'd blame her.

"He threatened me." She found it difficult to talk, realized she was gripping Luc's hands so tightly that her nails were digging into his skin. She forced herself to relax.

Luc tensed, his face forbidding. He held her firmly in place when she tried to pull away. "When did he threaten you?" He growled the words.

"At the quarry pit. You must have seen it."

He shook his head. "After the cop pulled you away, another one shoved me into a patrol car and brought me here. What happened?"

"One of the men attacked me. I knocked him down. It sounds like he was that guy. Frankie Silvano."

Luc blinked and let go of her hands. He sat back in his chair. "You knocked him down?"

"Well." She cleared her throat delicately. "I hit him with my purse. I tried to knock him out, but I couldn't quite get the right angle. But he went down when I kicked him."

Luc and David were both silent for a moment.

"Your purse?" Luc asked, seeming to need confirmation. His voice sounded a little strangled. "You hit him with your purse?"

Katie just looked at him, which was apparently answer enough.

"It really is full of rocks," David muttered.

Luc glared at his supervisor. "Why didn't the cops
just freaking shoot him when he attacked her?"

"Apparently there was the slight problem of hitting
Ms. McCabe. They seemed to think that would be a
bad idea."

Ms. McCabe tended to agree.

"You realize what this means, don't you? Frankie is
really going to be out to get her now."

Katie's eyes widened.

"You don't know that," David said.

"Of course I know that. She made a fool out of him
in front of the police. You know as well as I do how
crazy he is. And now he's been humiliated in front of
these small town cops. He'll never forget that. Never."
Luc's face blanked, hardened, concealed his thoughts
for several long seconds.

"She's coming home with me."

"Excuse me?" Katie squeaked.

"Luc—" David's voice held a note of warning.

"Don't give me any crap about this, David. You know
it's the right thing to do."

David straightened. "I agree that she can't go
home—"

"What do you mean I can't go home?" Katie's voice
rose as she turned to the other man.

"—but there are other safe houses. What's the deal?"

"Yeah, what's the deal?" Katie demanded, facing
Luc again.

Luc continued to ignore her, his sharp, dark eyes on his squad supervisor, his body taut beside her. "Joey Silvano has never come back early from visiting his mistress. Never. It takes him over an hour just to get to the woman's house. And he comes back unexpectedly on the one night I planned to break into his office? I don't think so. I think we have to face the possibility that we have a leak. I think our safe houses might not be so safe anymore. I'm not going to risk Katie's life to find out."

"I think you're overreacting."

"You do, huh? Come on, you know what Frankie's like. If there's a leak, he'll find her. Remember the waitress in Glenside? He's got to be a lot more pissed off at Katie than he was at her. A lot more."

"Luc—"

"Do you want to take the chance?" Luc demanded. "Well, do you?" David didn't answer. "She needs to come home with me until we can work something out. You know the Museum's perfect."

"I'll have to keep Liza from finding out."

Luc's lips twisted. "I don't give a shit about Liza. Just don't tell her anything, boss man."

"Shows you've never had an admin."

The two men had forgotten she was even there. She sat straighter, listening to them bicker, fighting down the claustrophobic, panicked sense that her whole life was being swept away, that it was being erased even as she watched.

She stood. Okay, so she didn't have to stay in her apartment. She could crash with one of her brothers, or with her sister Brenna. Or she could go to her parents' house. She had plenty of alternatives. She had options she could control. And these two men could—

"Where are you going?" Luc struggled to his feet. He grabbed her arm before she moved away.

Katie lifted her chin. "It's none of your business."

Luc's dark eyes glittered. His jaw hardened so much she thought it might crack. "The hell it's not."

"Okay, then maybe I'm just going to leave. You can't stop me."

"The hell I can't."

"Luc, ease up," David said, taking a step forward.

Katie glared at each man in turn, her body rigid and brittle. "Frankie Silvano won't find me. He was just bluffing." This made no sense; she knew it made no sense. Fighting made no sense. If Luc was right, going home with him was a good plan. But she just couldn't seem to stop herself. Couldn't just let herself get…swept away.

"Katie." Luc sounded exasperated. "Don't be stupid. He has your license plate number. He saw it, remember? He can find out who you are in a heartbeat."

"Oh." She froze. Oh, God, she'd forgotten. Her license plate number. Right there on the back of her car.

"Yeah. Oh. With his connections, I wouldn't be surprised if he already knows your name and address."

Katie couldn't control a shudder. "I don't even know you." The words were ripped out of her.

Luc stared down at her, his eyes dark and brilliant. "I won't hurt you. You're safe with me."

"I don't want to go."

Luc took a deep breath, but when he spoke his voice

was almost gentle. "Katie, I don't give a damn if you freaking hate the idea. You're coming with me anyway. You don't have a choice because I'm not giving you one."

FIVE

"WE'LL TAKE THE Bureau car," Luc told Katie later that night as he escorted her out of the police station. The idiot had refused medical treatment for his ankle, so she wasn't sure if she was walking with him or propping him up, but either way his hand was large and warm on her arm. It was still a manacle.

Katie didn't say anything. She had to go wherever they wanted to take her anyway now that Luc had arrested her again. No, no, wait. Put her in "protective custody." That's right. That made all the difference.

But she didn't especially want to die. And, according to Luc, he was trying to save her life. So she should probably be grateful.

God, she was tired.

"You mean the Corvette?" David asked from behind them.

"Of course I mean the Corvette. How often do I get to drive one of those babies?"

"Hmm."

Luc stopped, which meant that Katie had to stop, too, and turned to look at the other man. "You got the tires replaced, right?"

"Well…"

"You're freaking me out, David." Luc towed her toward the parking lot again.

For some reason, memories of her ex-fiancé, Tom, popped into Katie's mind. How he'd always chosen the restaurants and the movies. How he'd always wanted to make the decisions. How he'd never really thought she knew what she was doing.

Until she'd taken a broom to his ass.

Luc pulled them both to a stop again at the edge of the police station's parking lot. It was surrounded by a high stockade fence and dark, lit only by a few old, crackling spotlights and the full moon rising above the trees. David sauntered up beside them and stood, his lean body loose and casual with his hands in his pockets. Katie saw his eyes glittering in the moonlight.

"I don't see the 'vette," Luc said. "Didn't the chief have it towed here?"

"Oh, it's here."

"So…?"

In answer, David gestured at an object sitting in a pool of light. It took a bit before Katie realized she was looking at the mangled remains of a red sports car.

"No! God, no!" Luc dropped her arm and hobbled to the car with surprising speed.

Katie followed more slowly with David. The Corvette, if that's what it had been, looked like it was in pretty sad shape. Not only was it riddled with bullet holes, but it seemed to have been vandalized. Probably stripped clean. Pity.

"They've killed it." Luc laid his palms on the roof and lowered his head. For a moment Katie thought he might even cry. Brandon sure would have been sobbing right about now.

Thinking about her second-oldest brother made her remember what was happening to her, so she deliberately blanked her mind. Later. There'd be time to think later.

David walked up to the car and kicked it. Something metallic fell off and hit the ground with a clang. "I, uh, didn't bother to replace the tires since parts of the engine seem to be missing."

"The engine?"

"Well, just a few of the more important parts."

"Holy shit." Luc laid his forehead on the roof between his hands for a minute. "I gave my word that I'd return it in one piece. I promised this time would be different."

David shrugged. "They should know you by now." He leaned to Katie. "Luc has kind of a rep in the motor pool."

Katie crossed her arms and shifted away a little bit. She didn't really care about Luc's rep.

"Yeah, well, this time I promised Vinnie," Luc said. "The bastard wanted to make me sign my name in blood. Blood!"

"Okay, you're right," David agreed. "You are so screwed."

"They'll never give me a decent ride again," Luc groaned. He looked at David, face gloomy. "Maybe they'll make me drive my car. All of the criminals will just laugh at me."

David chuckled. "I'll see what I can do to help you out."

"Good luck."

"I didn't think we should risk renting a car, and if you borrowed mine it might raise a flag with someone at the Bureau since I usually return my vehicles on time."

"Bastard," Luc muttered. He was still smoothing the Corvette's roof with his hands. Katie wondered if he'd start cooing at it.

"So it looks like you're going to have to use the Nova."

She perked up at that. The Nova? *Her* Nova?

"The Nova?" Luc turned abruptly. "Are you kidding me?"

"The chief said it ran fine when the cops brought it back from the quarry. It's supposed to be out here somewhere."

"Oh, sure. A car that's older than God 'runs fine' and a new Corvette is a giant planter. Jesus."

Katie didn't defend Kato's honor because she'd just spotted him on the other side of the parking lot. He actually didn't look all that much better than the Corvette, but he was a tough and scrappy little car, handed down from her father to Darren to her.

Without waiting for the men, she walked over to him and patted his hood, then found herself blinking back tears. Ridiculous to get weepy over an ancient car. Pathetic to believe it was her only friend. Sad. Very sad.

She got her keys out of her purse, but Luc, who'd come up behind her with David, immediately snatched them away.

"Hey!"

"I'm driving," he said.

"You are not." This was one area where she thought she was entitled to have a little input.

"Am too."

"You can't drive. You've got a broken foot."

"Sprained."

"Whatever. Don't be stupid."

"I'm driving."

"Sure. Why should I even be able to say who can drive my car." She knew she sounded like a three-year-old. She didn't give a damn.

"Just get in. Please." Luc pushed her aside, opened the door, and fell into the driver's seat.

"Don't mind him. He's sulking," David told Katie. He pulled her around the car and opened the passenger door.

"Am not," Luc said. "I just want to get out of here." He turned the key in the ignition. After a measure of thought, Kato agreed to start.

"He'll get over it," David whispered to Katie and smiled.

She met his eyes and saw him watching her around that smile. She turned away; she thought David Allen saw a whole lot more than he let on.

"I have to go back to the office to hide some paperwork," David told Luc while Katie slid into the car. "I hope you'll be okay until I can contact you."

"We'll be fine," Luc said.

"I think we kept word from getting out for now. Silvano didn't have a cell phone on him, and neither did Arlo. We monitored their phone calls from the police station. Their lawyer's been screaming because we didn't let them go right after the judge left."

"Right."

"When I saw the Corvette, I assumed you'd have to take the Nova, so I changed the plates. I think we were able to fix the taillights, but we couldn't do too much about the mirrors. I hope nobody recognizes it."

"Hey, Mom, quit worrying." Luc revved the engine.

"Would you be careful?" Katie didn't think he was treating Kato with the proper respect.

"Relax. I'm a professional." Luc leaned back and squinted down at the floorboard. "Where's the clutch on this thing?"

Katie stared at him. "It's an automatic."

Luc grinned. "Ohhhhh."

She closed her eyes briefly.

David laughed. "Try not to kill each other. I'll be in touch soon."

"Adios." With a little nod to the other man, Luc reversed out of the parking space and put the car into gear.

"You're going to have to lay down on the seat," he told Katie.

She blinked. "Excuse me?"

"There might be somebody waiting for us outside the gate. They'll either be expecting a woman alone or both of us. Maybe it will confuse them if they only see me."

Katie hesitated. "If this is a joke—"

"Just do it, okay?" He sounded tired and irritated.

Ironically, that reassured her and she curled up on the bench seat next to him. She was short, but the space was small so her head was almost in his lap, her cheek resting very close to his jean-clad leg. Close enough that she could feel the heat of his body through his clothes.

She would have edged away, but there wasn't anywhere to go, so she made herself lie still and tried not to notice how his muscles shifted when he drove.

It seemed to Katie that it took forever to leave the police station parking lot, but she finally heard the gates close behind them. Then they were out on the road and moving along at a pretty good clip. She started to sit up, but Luc gently put his hand on her head and held her down.

"Not yet."

"Is somebody following us?" She tried to ignore how his fingers sank into her hair, almost as if they were burrowing into it of their own accord. They were strong and warm and soothing as they tunneled through the curls.

"I just want to make sure no one's back there. I'm going to take a few side roads."

"You'll get lost."

"I can find my way back to the highway." He sounded amused.

"Really?" she asked, unwillingly distracted. People who had a sense of direction always impressed her.

"Really." He was silent for a few more minutes, then moved his hand back to the steering wheel. "Okay."

"Okay, what?"

"You can sit up now."

Katie pulled herself upright, realized she was practically on top of him and shifted quickly to the other side of the car.

"I'd better tell you how to get to my apartment," she said to cover her embarrassment.

"Why?"

"So I can get some of my things." That should have been pretty obvious.

"No."

"No?" She stared at him and, although she couldn't make out his features in the dim light from the dashboard, thought she saw his jaw clench. "But...but I at least need a toothbrush and some clothes."

"You'll have to make do with what we can find at my house." The silhouette of his head turned to her and then away again. "It's too dangerous, Katie."

"David said the guy didn't have a chance to talk to anybody."

"No offense, but I don't put anything past Frankie Silvano."

Frustration, anger and the fear that had been building since he'd jumped into her car, boiled together in a caustic mix that tasted bitter in her mouth. She tried to remain calm.

"Come on, Luc," she said. "You're already making me go with you. I want some of my own stuff."

"I said no." His voice was rough and what little control Katie had left snapped.

"Don't I get a say in this at all?"

"No. Sorry."

"Okay, then, tell me this, Mr. FBI agent—why didn't you just leave me in jail if I'm under arrest?"

"You're in protective custody, in case you hadn't noticed."

"Oh, so sorry. I guess it's the lack of freedom or control over anything that confused me."

Luc glanced at her. "What's wrong with you?"

"What's wrong with me? What's wrong with me? I'm angry, that's what's wrong with me!" It was either be angry or cry again, and she was far too close to the second option for comfort.

"Why?" He actually seemed puzzled. Ass.

"Why? Why?" For a moment the utter denseness of the question robbed her of speech. "Because…because you jump into my car…no, no, wait, you destroy my car—"

"It still runs, doesn't it? That's more than I can say about my car."

"—I'm forced to cause hundreds of traffic accidents—"

"Only twelve."

"—and now you're kidnapping me and taking me God knows where and I can't even get my own TOOTH-BRUSH! Men. I'm so sick of men telling me what to do, I could spit. None of you listen when other people try to talk, you just sit around and bark orders and think you're right."

"Hey, lady." Luc was losing his temper too. Good. She didn't want him to be calm and reasonable when her life was out of control. "Don't thank me or anything. After all, I'm just the man who's trying to keep you alive."

"Yeah, don't do me any favors. If this is the way it's going to be then I might as well let Frankie Silvano get me."

"Well, the door's right there. Feel free to jump out any time. This isn't a goddamned picnic for me either.

It's not like I don't have plenty of other things to do with my time."

"Fine. Aren't you even going to slow down?"

"No."

"Fine."

"Good."

"Fine."

Katie crossed her arms and looked out the window at the dark scenery.

"So? Aren't you going to jump?" Luc asked in that snidely superior male voice she'd always loathed.

"No." Of course she wasn't going to jump and he knew it. She wasn't that stupid. "I should have pushed you out of my car as soon as you got into it," she muttered.

"Yeah, well I wish you had."

"Yeah, well I didn't, did I? So now here I am. Oh, I forgot. Thanks a lot."

There were no streetlights on the little road, just the occasional porch light and the silvery glow of the moon. The warm summer night was filled with heady smells drifting in through the slightly open car window along with the noise of singing bugs from the brush and trees.

Katie wrapped her arms across her chest and blinked away sudden moisture. Oh, crap. She refused to cry in front of him again. There was no way she would let him see how vulnerable she felt. And stupid. And utterly terrified. What was going to happen to her now?

"Jerk," she whispered and sniffed. She didn't care if he had beautiful eyes and broad shoulders. He was a

big, huge, hacking jerk and a control freak, and she'd
better not let herself forget it.

She thought that maybe Luc heard her soft comment,
but he didn't say anything. Then, miraculously, there
was a traffic light and a four-lane highway with cars
endlessly speeding back and forth.

"Which way?" he growled without looking at her.

"Which way where?" How was she supposed to know
where he was taking her?

"To your apartment. Which way?"

"What?" Katie started and tried to pull herself together. Her apartment? He was taking her to her apartment? He'd changed his mind? It was so unexpected that
it almost didn't register. She looked around, anxious not
to miss the opportunity, but nothing seemed familiar.
Her sense of direction really was pitiful. At that point
she might as well have been trying to fly to the moon
hanging so low overhead.

Luc waited, his impatience palpable. "Well?" he demanded.

"I don't know where we are," she admitted. Her voice
broke a little bit in spite of her best intentions.

Luc rubbed the back of his neck, then sighed. But
now it wasn't an angry sigh, just a tired one. "Look,
why don't you tell me your address?" he asked in a
kinder voice.

Taking a deep breath, Katie did.

Strange as it was to believe, that little bit of information seemed to be enough. Within moments they were
speeding down the highway, and Luc seemed confident

that he knew where they were going. A part of her brain marveled at that. Amazing.

"I really think this is a mistake," he grumbled.

"Yeah, you've made that pretty clear."

Silence. Katie held herself rigid, trying not to touch him in the tight space of the car.

"Don't blame me if we run into trouble."

"I won't."

Silence. Longer this time. He could have been a rock sitting next to her, except that she could feel his heat and smell the scent of soap, sweat and man. "We're just going to get in and out. No fooling around," Luc said.

"Okay."

The car hummed on the road. His hands clenched and relaxed on the wheel. "I'm sorry," he said.

Katie looked at him in surprise. She could see more of his face now in the reflected lights of the highway.

"I shouldn't have yelled at you." Luc sounded uncomfortable, but he kept talking. "I don't know why I did. I guess I'm…geared up too. I know you're scared."

Katie didn't answer. The words were nice, but they didn't change anything, did they? She stared out the window at the cars flashing by. She knew where they were now—they were getting closer to her apartment complex. Funny how he had found it with so little effort.

"Katie?"

She glanced over at him again and saw him watching her out of the corner of his eye. His shadowed face looked concerned and tired, and he appeared to be a man who'd had a very bad day.

She stifled a sigh. Well, what choice did she have anyway? Being angry and upset about this situation might be normal, but snapping at him wasn't going to help her. He was, when everything was said and done, going out of his way to do what he considered the right thing. He might have gotten her into this mess, but at least he hadn't left her there alone to deal with it. He seemed to believe that he was her protector. And he probably was.

"I'm just tired," she said finally, extending an olive branch of her own. It was true enough. She was mortally tired. "Thanks for bringing me to my apartment."

Now it was his turn to be quiet.

"We're almost there," he said after a minute.

"I know." She smiled a little. "I actually recognized some of the houses."

"Oh. Sure."

"You don't know me well enough to realize what a miracle that is."

She was rewarded with a grin. They were back in town so she could see his face pretty clearly now. She also saw the road that led to her apartment complex.

"Make a right here."

Luc's smile faded. "I'm going to drive past it to make sure everything's okay first."

The apartment complex was relatively small, just a few buildings with some parking lots and a little pond in a stand of trees management had put in so they could justify raising the rent. Luc drove slowly down the road, his whole body stiff, broadcasting his alertness.

"I'm in C," Katie told him, her voice tight. His tension was rubbing off on her.

He nodded. They drove by her building. Everything

appeared to be in order. The appropriate cars were in the appropriate places. Everyone always seemed to take the same spots. The floodlight was blinking off and on like it usually did. A few old crabapple trees grew around the dumpster on the far side of the biggest parking lot.

Katie glanced at them and froze. "Luc." She grabbed his arm and pointed. "Look there." The front end of a dark car was just barely visible next to the dumpster.

"That's not normal?"

"No." She was whispering, but she didn't know why. "Nobody ever parks there. The birds like to sit in the trees and stuff gets all over your car. Besides, there are plenty of other spaces open. Why park so far away?"

Luc cursed. "I'm sorry, Katie. We can't stop. We can't take the chance."

"You think it's—"

"Lay down on the seat again. Quick, before they see us. We'll just keep driving and hope they don't follow."

Katie curled up on the seat in a fetal position. "David said that he'd changed the license plate."

"Yeah, well, they might be curious anyway."

"David said he thought nobody knew," she whispered.

Luc was silent for a moment. "I guess he was wrong."

He kept the Nova traveling at a sedate pace. To Katie, they seemed to creep down the road. She could tell Luc was restraining himself when he really wanted to speed off. But that would have been a dead giveaway.

Dead.

Somebody wanted her dead.

It was a long time before Luc finally relaxed. "I don't think they followed us. You can sit up now."

Katie sat and stared at him. He kept his eyes on the road.

"How many times do I have to say that I'm sorry?" he asked softly. Bitterly.

She couldn't answer because the full reality of her situation had finally hit her. Someone had found her apartment. Someone hated her. Someone wanted to hurt her—to kill her.

This was real.

"Do…" Katie cleared her throat and started again, desperate for some normalcy. Desperate to turn the clock back to this morning. "Do you want me to drive for a while?"

"No." He paused. "I don't want to get lost." It was a feeble attempt at humor.

"Where are we going?"

"New Jersey. It's going to take a little while to get there. Why don't you try to get some sleep?"

Katie nodded and looked out the window again. Her mind was blank. Numb.

"Katie, go to sleep."

She smiled a little bit in spite of everything. Definite dictator tendencies.

"It's not something you can force, you know." She rested her head on the back of the seat and watched the lights and the darkness slide past the window. She was tired, but there was no way she could sleep. How could anyone sleep when life was so uncertain?

"Luc?" she asked.

"Hmm."

"What's going to happen to me now?"

He didn't answer right away. "You're coming to my house. You know that."

"I mean after that."

"We'll have to play it by ear."

He was trying to be evasive, but she couldn't let him. He probably didn't want to frighten her, but it was too late for that. She turned away from the window and tried to see his face.

"He's not going to go away, is he?" she asked.

"Katie—"

"Don't lie to me." Her voice rose and she forced herself to calm down. "Please don't lie to me. I saw his face. I saw his eyes. He already found me. He already had people at my apartment."

"We're not sure—"

"Luc!" She straightened and put a hand on his forearm. The muscles tensed under her fingers until they were like steel. "It had to be him. He must have gotten word out somehow."

"Maybe he had a cell phone he ditched at the quarry," Luc said reluctantly. "Or it was the lawyer. Maybe even the judge."

She shuddered. Powerful, well-connected people could be dangerous. If nothing else, her experience with Tom had taught her that much. "Tell me the truth," she said. "Frankie Silvano is not going away, is he?"

He was quiet a long time. "No," he finally admitted. "No, most likely he won't go away."

"Then this isn't going to blow over." She was talking as much to herself as she was to him. "This is long term."

"Yes. Until we get Frankie, you will be at risk."

Katie nodded and dropped her hand. It was what she had expected him to say, but hearing the words was still a shock. She thought of all of the loose ends, all of the things she wanted to do, needed to do, all of her responsibilities. She was supposed to help her boss prepare for a presentation to the board of directors on Wednesday. Kato was due for his inspection. Her parents' thirty-sixth wedding anniversary was coming up. Her baby sister, Fiona, might actually get a college degree at the end of the fall semester. Melanie had asked her if she'd wanted to go shopping in Philadelphia. So many little things...

"My family?" she asked. "What about my family?"

"David will work on what to tell them," Luc replied. "They should be safe enough for the time being. I think Joey will be able to control Frankie at least that much. He really won't want to put his organization at risk for the sake of a personal vendetta."

Katie drew in a breath. "You think?" It hadn't occurred to her that her family might be in danger. Her sense of helplessness intensified. She couldn't do anything about it. She couldn't do anything to make it better.

"They'll be fine." Luc seemed to realize that he'd probably said too much. "We'll watch out for them."

She nodded, but she wasn't sure she believed him. Her family. She cleared her throat.

"My job?"

Luc's voice was soft, as if he was reluctant to give her any more bad news. "We'll get you another one wherever you end up."

Wherever she ended up? "My life?" she whispered.

Luc didn't answer. Which was answer enough, she supposed.

She leaned back against the seat again.

"I can't..." She swallowed. "I can't do this."

Luc glanced at her, then reached over and touched her cheek gently, rubbing the backs of his fingers against her skin before he drew away. "You have to."

Katie looked out the window. Just her purse, the clothes on her back and Kato, unless someone could eventually clean out her apartment. Because of Frankie Silvano. Because of one man. Because of an evil little man.

Now she really was alone.

"Luc?"

"Yeah?"

"Do you think everything will work out?"

He didn't answer right away. The car hummed, the wind whistled by the window. "I'll make sure it does," he said finally. "Go to sleep."

SIX

SHE'D THOUGHT IT was impossible, but eventually the hypnotic movement of the car, Luc's hands strong and sure on the wheel, the silence between them and her own utter exhaustion did indeed lull Katie to sleep. She didn't wake up again until Luc touched her on the shoulder and startled her so much she practically jumped through the roof.

"Sorry." He sounded like he might have been smiling. "I just wanted to let you know we're here."

She blinked, disoriented. They weren't on a paved road anymore; she could hear gravel snapping against the undercarriage of the car.

"Here?" She was groggy with sleep. Aw, man, please don't let her have snored. Or drooled...

"My place."

Katie glanced out the window and drew in a sharp, shocked breath as she came abruptly back to full awareness.

Bathed in the strong silver light of the moon and nestled into tall, dark trees was a castle. A real medieval castle complete with a maze of turrets and towers jutting haphazardly from thick stone walls. In the soft light it had a fairy tale quality, as if it would vanish at any time.

"Your place," she murmured. Oh, sure. Here she'd

been picturing a grungy apartment or, at best, a split-level in the suburbs, but he lived in a castle.

Luc chuckled and pulled the Nova to a stop in a gravel parking area. "Yeah, well, it's a roof over my head, you know? Welcome to the Museum. It's something else, isn't it?"

"You can say that again." Katie grabbed her purse and jumped out. She stood staring up at the walls looming over her, massive and impenetrable. For a moment she forgot about evil little men and just enjoyed the magic of it all. Let the moonlight and the castle draw her away from the madness.

There was a muffled grunt behind her. She turned to see Luc struggling to get out of the car. She rushed to help him, ignoring his grumbles, and took his arm until he found his balance.

He leaned on her, his body warm and solid against hers. When she tried to step back, he didn't let her. Instead he kept his arm around her shoulders, and looked up at the castle, smiling, his black hair shining in the moonlight.

"It's just a folly," he said. It took her a second to realize he was talking about the house. "Stupid. Should never have been built in the first place. One of my crazy relatives had it constructed in the nineteen twenties, and apparently it's been a curse on the family ever since. I probably couldn't unload it if I tried. More than half of the thing is closed up, there aren't any closets and it's as drafty as hell. I don't know why I just don't have it torn down."

"No!"

Luc glanced at her. "Well, even if the lawyers would let me, I'm really don't think I could," he admitted.

"Lawyers?" she asked before she thought better of it.

He shrugged. "The whole place is in a trust. When my great aunt Isobel died, she didn't want it to leave the family, but she didn't appreciate my gene pool. Bad blood and all that."

She didn't know him well enough to ask more questions. But before she could think of how to change the subject, something black and as big as a Volkswagen came baying out of the night, lurching across the lawn.

"What's that?" To her complete disgust, Katie actually found herself moving closer to Luc for protection.

He gave her a cheeky grin. "That's the dragon at the gate." He managed to push her aside just as a he was assaulted by some kind of a huge animal. Katie backed up, watching the beast snuffle and slobber all over Luc with evident delight while he ruffled large ears and muttered affectionate nonsense. Finally the thing stilled, raised its head and sniffed the air. Katie took another step back. She wasn't exactly scared, she was just…cautious.

"So…um…is that a…bear?" she asked.

Luc laughed. "No, a dog. A Newfoundland."

"Ah. Uh, big."

"Relax. Spot won't hurt you." Luc pulled the animal's head up so he could give it a loud, smacking kiss between the ears. The gesture was surprisingly sweet.

Katie shook her own head. "Not that I don't believe you, but this hasn't exactly been my day," she said.

"Trust me."

"Yeah. Sure." The monster seemed to be as big as a

horse, but now that it had settled down a bit it looked like it could be friendly enough. Katie edged her way around Luc until she and the "dog" were staring at each other.

"Hello…boy?"

"Spot is a girl," Luc corrected. "Lady Guinevere of the Round Table if you want to be formal, but Spot for short and no particularly good reason. Just don't call her boy again, or she might get mad."

"Oh, no. Spot mustn't get mad," Katie murmured.

Luc laughed.

Spot walked over to her, tail waving like a great flag, and Katie finally got up the nerve to hold a hand out to the very large, incredibly wet nose. She half expected to pull back a bloody stump for her trouble, but the dog merely sniffed her fingers and sat, tongue lolling as she panted.

"Good girl," Luc said. Katie wasn't sure which one of them he was talking to. "Let's go in."

His ankle had stiffened up during the drive, so Katie was drafted into service as a human crutch. Even so, by the time they reached two gigantic carved oak doors that seemed to be the front entrance of the castle, he was holding his breath every time he took a step.

"Are you okay?" Katie asked.

"Fine."

Yeah, right, she thought.

After maneuvering around a security panel, the heavy oak doors and Spot, who was intent on entering the house before anybody else could, they finally got inside. Luc flipped a switch on the wall. Light flooded a long hallway.

Katie's mouth dropped open.

Stone walls decorated with tapestries rose at least three stories before ending in vaulted ceilings high above their heads. Chandeliers on long chains hung suspended from the vaults every six feet or so. On one side of the hall, successions of curved arches opened on each floor. On the other, the outer walls were cut with tall, narrow windows, most of them made of stained glass. A series of round windows, also stained glass, ran along the roofline.

In the daylight, the space would be absolutely magnificent.

"Ho-ly crap." She couldn't help staring before turning to her companion. "Even if this place is in a trust, you must be freaking rich."

Luc's laugh was a bark that didn't have a whole lot to do with humor. "That would be a big fat no. I'm nothing more than a glorified caretaker."

Katie was a little startled by the bitterness in his voice, but he was already hobbling away so she decided to let it drop, running after him.

She knew he'd never admit it, but it took both of them to get him down the hall and into a lovely modern kitchen containing yards of countertop, a large, rectangular table and a bunch of ladder-back chairs. Katie grabbed one of the chairs and shoved it under Luc's butt. He didn't so much sit in it as crash.

"Ugh," Luc said.

"I hate to say I told you so, but—"

"I'm fine."

"—you really should have let me drive. Then you

could have been in the backseat with your foot elevated and maybe it wouldn't hurt so much."

"Yeah, well, thanks for mentioning it."

He looked at her then and a sudden, unexpected tremor of awareness shot through her. He was tired and grumpy and in pain. His rather shaggy hair had fallen over his forehead and his chin was dark with the start of an impressive beard. He looked dangerous and…something else. Something that made her stomach clutch and roll just the slightest, delightful bit, even now. Even in the middle of everything.

Boy, oh, boy, she thought. Talk about trouble.

Clearing her throat, Katie tried to pull herself together as she dragged another chair over to him. "Put your foot up on this."

His hooded eyes grew wary. "Why?"

"Because I'm going to try to help you, you idiot."

"I'm okay."

"No, you're not, so shut up."

"That's nice."

"Your ankle needs some attention."

"My ankle needs brandy."

"No it doesn't." She gave up waiting and tugged at his leg.

"Fine, fine, fine." With obvious reluctance, he propped his foot on the chair.

Katie knelt beside him. She carefully removed his worn running shoe and sock, feeling a little bit like Androcles with the lion. But one look at his ankle pushed everything else out of her mind. It was bluish-purple and swollen two or three times its normal size. She touched it, and he flinched involuntarily.

"This is really bad." She looked up at him, resting on her heels. "You should go to the hospital."

"No hospitals." His harsh face was a little pale under the five o'clock shadow.

"But—"

"I mean it, Katie. No hospitals. Especially not for some piddly-ass thing like this."

"It's not piddly-ass, and it must hurt like heck."

He shrugged.

She sighed. Deeply. Men. Still, she couldn't drag him out of there by force, so she contemplated his foot again, anxiously chewing on her bottom lip while she tried to figure out what to do.

She wished her mother was there. Her mom could handle any situation. Even sitting in a strange man's kitchen looking at his large, well-shaped foot and swollen ankle wouldn't have fazed her.

Katie, on the other hand, was beginning to be just a little faint. Absently she touched his foot again down near his toes, where it didn't seem to be quite as puffy. His skin was warm and elastic under her fingers. She smoothed it, unconsciously trying to ease the pain.

"Does it hurt when I touch you here?" she asked. There was a pause.

"Um, no." His voice sounded strange.

She glanced up to find him watching her with inscrutable eyes. Abruptly she was aware of the intimacy of their situation. His foot seemed vulnerable, unguarded. It was strangely wicked of her to be touching it.

She snatched back her hand and caught her breath.

"Does it smell?" he murmured.

"What?"

"My foot. Does it smell? You look weird."

Katie found herself laughing, grateful that he'd broken the oddly tense mood. "No. I was just thinking about what to do." She hauled herself to her feet and frowned down at him. "Ice, I think. We need to bring down the swelling." She should probably get some for herself while she was at it; she was kind of overheated.

He sighed and tilted his head against the high back of the chair. "Freezer."

When they'd first come into the kitchen, Spot had spent some time slurping from a huge water dish on the other side of the room. But now she was a large black mountain sprawled right in front of the refrigerator, which meant that Katie had to stand on her tiptoes and stretch over her to see inside the freezer.

Not that there was too much to see. Just two frozen pizzas and about thirty ice packs. Sheesh. The man sure must get hurt a lot.

When she'd snagged a couple of the ice packs and turned around, Luc was watching her, his expression strangely shuttered.

"What? What's wrong?"

"Nothing." His voice was clipped and as frigid as the air in the freezer. But then again, Katie couldn't blame him for being in a bad mood. He must be in a lot of pain, even if he was too macho to admit it.

Grabbing a dishtowel she'd spotted hanging next to the sink, she wrapped the ice packs up in it, and knelt down again next to his chair, applying the bundle to his ankle.

Luc stifled a groan and closed his eyes.

"Do you have any aspirin?" she asked while she held the pack in place.

"I'm out down here, but there's some in the medicine cabinet in my bathroom upstairs."

"And an elastic bandage?"

"Yeah, there's a couple of them up there too."

"Well, that's something anyway. Why don't you hold this, and I'll go get them for you."

Luc leaned forward to do as she asked. For a moment their hands touched. She looked up and he was much closer than she'd expected. His hair fell over his forehead, just begging her to push it back. His scent teased her, subtle and male.

Katie swallowed. She must be more tired than she'd thought. "Where?" Her voice was a choked whisper.

"Where what?" His beautiful eyes were dark and intense.

She stood abruptly and backed up. "Where is the medicine cabinet?"

"Oh. It's in the master bath attached to my bedroom. Go down the hall to the end, take the first stairwell to the second floor and it's the third door on the right. The bathroom is through the bedroom."

Katie frowned. "That's pretty complicated."

"It's practically a straight line."

"The second stairwell and the first door to the right?"

"No, the first stairwell to the second floor to the third door on the right." He sounded exasperated.

Katie shrugged. "Hey, you know I have a bad sense of direction."

"Wonderful. Maybe I should—"

She pushed him back into the chair when it looked like he was going to try to get up. "You, my friend, are going nowhere and doing nothing. I'll be back before you know it."

"Are you sure?"

"Positive. But maybe I should take my cell phone just in case…" Katie shook her head when she saw him stare at her. "Nah. Um, just kidding. I'll be right back."

Luc watched her leave, then settled back in the chair with a heavy sigh. He took the dishtowel full of ice packs off his ankle and put it on his forehead.

"Shit," he muttered.

Shit, shit, shit, he was in trouble. He thought about how she'd looked leaning into the freezer, her light summer pants stretched over her truly lovely ass, and pressed the ice harder against his head. Maybe he should put it on his crotch instead.

"Get yourself under control, Vasco, and I mean now."

Wild auburn curls, blue eyes that could look so sad they broke his heart. A mouth he couldn't stop thinking about. He was supposed to be guarding her. And she couldn't leave.

Oh, yeah. He had a big problem.

He sat for a few more minutes until his ankle started to throb. His leg was falling asleep, and he knew he should probably move to the sofa in the family room where he could stretch out. Maybe get a little perspective.

He rubbed the scar on his face and drew in a deep breath. Then he hoisted himself out of the chair and hobbled over to the freezer to get some more ice packs.

He wondered if she'd gotten lost.

SEVEN

It took a little while, but Katie eventually found the first stairwell and the second floor and the third room on the right. Unfortunately, she wasn't entirely sure that she'd be able to make it back to the kitchen. Maybe if she'd brought along a loaf of bread and left a trail of crumbs... except that bear Luc thought was a dog would probably have eaten them. She definitely should have brought her cell phone so she could call for help, though. *I'm in the study. I repeat, the study with Professor Plum and a candlestick...*

She shook her head. She was rapidly losing what was left of her mind. What had that been all about, massaging his foot? His foot, for sweet Christ's sake. She'd never even thought of touching Tom's feet.

And that begged another question—how could a man have been through everything Luc had been through that day and still manage to have good-smelling feet? He wasn't even freaking human.

Katie stopped at what she thought was the right door and grabbed the knob with frustrated violence, then hesitated when it belatedly occurred to her that this was Luc's bedroom. His private space. His inner sanctum.

Hmm. What would she find? Red velvet? Spartan cloister? Blow-up dolls with fish tanks for breasts?

She opened the door and peaked inside, then blinked and stepped over the threshold.

"Jeez."

Of course, the first thing she noticed was the bed. It was kind of hard to miss. It was massive, as big and impressive in its own way as the house. Four giant posts reached almost to the ceiling, and the mattress seemed to go on forever. It faced a large stone fireplace that took up most of one wall, and there was a very attractive bay window off to the side with a small sitting area. She wouldn't have imagined Luc sleeping someplace so, well, pretty.

But she had to admit what really surprised her were the books. Not only were there bookcases full of books, there were piles and piles and piles of books in every position, covering every surface, seemingly on every topic. She wandered farther into the room, intrigued and, in a way, enchanted. There were books on the floor, books on the dressers, books on the nightstands and an impressive stack of volumes teetering next to the bed. It was just so completely unexpected that if the space hadn't been so obviously occupied she would have thought she'd made a mistake.

After a moment, she walked through the bedroom to the attached bathroom and stopped short again when she saw a whirlpool tub and walk-in shower. Her apartment had a cramped shower stall barely big enough to stand in.

Her apartment. Would she ever see it again?

Just like that, the fear came back. The uncertainty.

She wouldn't think about that now. She couldn't deal with that now.

Keeping her mind on her mission, Katie found the aspirin and the elastic bandages, then headed back downstairs to her patient. She only got lost twice. But when she eventually made it to the kitchen, it was empty. Even Spot was missing.

"Luc?" She was surprised by an irrational spurt of panic.

"In here."

Following the sound of his voice, Katie went through swinging doors into a well-appointed family room. There was a large fireplace at one end, flanked by several comfortable-looking armchairs. A wide flat-screen television took up most of another wall. Luc was stretched out on an old sofa in front of it.

"Welcome back. I was just getting ready to send out the hounds. Or, I should say, hound." He nodded at Spot, who was lying on a nearby rug, snoring.

"You moved," she accused and walked briskly around the sofa to check on his ankle.

"I had to. That kitchen chair was torture." He took a long sip from a glass filled with clear amber liquid, saw her look and smiled as he set the glass down. "Don't worry. It's just ginger ale."

"Oh. Okay." Embarrassed for no good reason, she put down her loot from the master bath and studied his ankle. He'd wrapped it in the dishtowel and piled ice packs around it. "Good idea," she admitted, gesturing to the mountain of ice.

"I have them every once in a while."

"The couch will get wet when everything melts."

"So?"

She just barely resisted rolling her eyes. But she'd had more than enough experience with the male of the species to restrain herself and shrug, hands in pockets, one hip cocked.

"Hey, up to you. Personally, I'd think it would get kind of uncomfortable when the whole thing is soaked with cold water, but that's me."

He grimaced. "Uh, yeah. Good point."

"I have them every once in a while."

"Smart ass." His lips twitched quickly as if he was hiding a grin.

"I'll get another towel. Stay."

"Staying."

Luc let her fuss. To tell the truth, he was more than a little flustered by the whole thing. His mother had fussed over him when he'd been small. Before the ovarian cancer had come and swept her away like a sudden hurricane. But that had been a long, long time ago. And since he'd met David, Mama Allen brooded over him, treating him like a chick she was determined to hatch. But none of the other women in his life had ever cared much about what he did, as long as he could, um, perform.

To have Katie McCabe bustling around knocked him completely out of whack.

It took a few minutes, but eventually she had him settled on the sofa, towels under and around his ankle, which was once again smothered with ice packs. She gave him a few aspirin and buzzed over him, watching sternly while he took them. Then she plumped up the sofa cushions, put another pillow behind his back and placed the remote control where he could reach it.

"There." She stood back, beaming down at him. Her hair was a springy auburn halo in the soft yellow lamplight.

Luc could only stare at her while something shifted inside him.

Then her stomach growled, long and loud, and she grimaced, rubbing it. "Sorry. Those crackers David bought me at the police station just didn't cut it. Should I get out one of those frozen pizzas? Or do you want something else?"

"Food." Luc groaned. "I forgot all about food. Uh, yeah, a pizza would be good, or I might have a few cans of soup…"

He could have kicked his own ass. He hadn't been able to get home in over a week. The neighbor who cleaned the place and watched Spot for him while he was gone usually left a casserole or something, but she hadn't expected him back for a couple of days.

"Soup," Katie decided. "Pizza will take too long. I'll see what I can do."

She did pretty well. Luc didn't know how she'd made canned soup taste so good. Of course, it could have been that he was hungrier than he'd thought. Food hadn't exactly been his top priority of the day.

When they were finished, Katie carried the bowls back out to the kitchen, then returned and started taking the ice off his ankle.

"We should probably let it rest for a little while and give the packs a chance to refreeze," she told him as she efficiently wrapped his ankle in an elastic bandage for support.

Luc, who'd had more experience than he wanted in tending his own injuries, knew he should tell her that she'd done enough. That he could handle things now. But he just couldn't bring himself to make her stop.

"You sure seem to know what you're doing," he said instead.

"Appearances can be deceiving." Katie took the ice packs to the freezer. When she came back, he watched with some amusement as she ignored three perfectly good chairs in the room and plopped herself down to sit on the carpet next to the sofa. She settled back against it with a sigh. "Boy, am I tired," she said.

"You should go to bed. You can use my bedroom. None of the others are in shape anyway."

"Thanks." She glanced at him, then away. "Um, what about you?"

"Believe me, I'm not going anywhere tonight. I'll sleep down here."

"I'm afraid I'll drown in all of the books," she said, then looked at him, her expression sharp with sudden curiosity. "Those belong to you, right? Or are you just a caretaker for them too?"

He shrugged, a little embarrassed. He'd forgotten about the damn books. "They're mine. I like to read."

Katie stared at him, obviously waiting for him to add something.

"That's it? Just, you like to read?"

"Yeah."

"Well, heck, I like to read, too, but I don't have an

entire bookstore in my bedroom. It must have taken you years to collect them all."

"A few. I got most of them after I got out of the Army."

"Because you like to read."

"Yeah."

"There's this thing called a library, you know."

"I like to own them. Then they're mine. Pain to move, though."

"Hmm." She continued to stare at him before turning away again. "I think you're an addict."

"Probably."

"Bordering on an illness."

"No doubt."

Her wonderful hair was stretching toward him. Luc touched it with gentle fingers. It felt so soft and vibrant. Alive.

She stiffened a little, but didn't move away. "I'm tired, but I'm not sure I'll be able to sleep," she said. "Do you know what I mean?"

"Yes."

Luc looked at his fingers in her hair and smiled when the red curls insisted on wrapping around them. All parts of her were determined. "Why don't you tell me about your family," he said. He didn't know if it was a good idea to bring them up, but the thoughts, the doubts, the uncertainty were whirling around inside him. He couldn't wait any longer. He had to know once and for all.

"There's not much to tell. I have three brothers, two sisters and a foster sister."

"Foster sister?" he repeated slowly. His stomach clenched, he pulled back his hand. Foster sister.

Katie didn't seem to notice. She was looking at the wall, her head slightly tilted, wild hair falling to reveal the graceful curve of her neck.

"Melanie and I met in middle school when we were both twelve or thirteen and having a bad time. Some of the other girls were making fun of her in the cafeteria because she didn't wear new clothes or something stupid like that. I defended her." Katie laughed. "I had kind of a temper back then."

"Hard to believe." He was surprised he could speak. He'd heard this story before.

Oh, hell. Melanie.

"Those girls were jerks anyway, and they already hated me. Cheerleaders." Katie snorted. "Well, I think they were cheerleaders. Anyway, Mel and I banded together out of self-defense, but it was more than that. It was like I'd always known her, if that makes any sense."

Luc nodded.

"I realized she was in foster care and that she was in a bad situation. Really bad. I went to my parents and convinced them to take her in. Mom and Dad went to court, and somehow they were able to get her moved into our care. My mother has connections."

She looked back at him and he saw she was smiling. "Mel's like my real sister. I forget that we didn't grow up together." The smile dimmed. "She was hurt in a car accident when we were eighteen, but she's pulled herself together. I admire her."

Luc couldn't think of anything to say. Didn't know how he felt. His mind was blank, as frozen as his ankle.

Her eyes sharpened as she continued to watch him. "Are you okay?" she asked.

No, Luc wanted to say.

"I'll bet she calls you Annie," he whispered finally, needing to fit in the last piece of the puzzle.

Her eyes widened with surprise. "How did you know?"

Luc was silent for several long seconds. Then he forced himself to smile and reached down to tug her curls. "Little Orphan Annie from the comics. It's obvious."

"Yeah, well, everyone in my family seems to find it quite amusing. I've never really thanked Mel for that little gift."

Katie didn't know how much she'd given Melanie in return, Luc thought. He realized she was watching him closely, her blue eyes intelligent and aware behind the glasses that hid so much of her face. She had soft, soft, skin. Freckles. God. It was her.

"You look strange. Are you sure you're all right? Do you need me to do something for you?"

Yes!

"No." He cleared his throat and straightened a little against the cushions. "I'm tired. I need to rest now." His voice was harsh.

"Oh. Okay. Well, uh, I'll just go to bed then." Katie stood. He could tell she was trying to understand what was going on. He couldn't do anything to help her. "Do you, ah, need a change of clothes? Or something?"

"No, I'm fine."

"The ice—"

"I said I'm fine. Go to bed."

He saw her quick temper flare, but she nodded.

He was going to let her go, let her be angry with him and think he was being patronizing and insensitive, but when she turned away he found himself grabbing her hand.

"Pleasant dreams." He placed a gentle kiss in the center of her palm before he could stop himself.

She looked at him, startled, and pulled her hand away. He was too surprised by his own actions to stop her.

"Goodnight," she said and fled the room.

Luc closed his eyes. "Goodnight, Annie," he murmured.

Her hair. He should have known her right away. He should have recognized her hair.

Jesus Christ, he thought. Sometimes life was pretty damn ironic.

EIGHT

KATIE THOUGHT SHE probably wasn't going to need to worry about having many dreams, pleasant or otherwise. With a little luck, she'd been able to find her way back to Luc's bedroom, but once there she just couldn't seem to settle down. The nap in the car had taken the edge off her tiredness, and now her mind was racing, thoughts flying back and forth so quickly she was afraid she might be going insane. And Luc wasn't helping.

Why had he kissed her hand? Why had he sent her away when he could tell she needed to talk to somebody?

Katie prowled the bedroom, picked up books, looked at them, put them down again. She was full of a restless energy that only intensified when she tried to be calm.

"This is ridiculous."

She needed sleep, and she needed something to wear because she was not going to get into Luc Vasco's huge bed stark naked. So she had no choice but to paw through his dresser drawers. And wasn't that…intimate.

"Well, he's the one who said I would have to make do with what I could find," she muttered. But she still felt herself blush when she opened a drawer and found his underwear. Briefs. Quickly she shut that one and opened another. T-shirts. Much better.

In typical man-fashion, most of the shirts on the top

were, well, ratty, so Katie started digging through the pile. If Luc was anything like her brothers, there would be a couple he didn't wear because they were too far down to make them worth the effort of retrieval.

Then her fingers touched something silky.

Silky?

She shouldn't look, Katie thought. She really shouldn't. She should respect Luc's privacy, get out a T-shirt and walk away.

She wasn't going to do that, but she should.

She grabbed the silky slip of cloth and pulled out an incredibly small pink teddy. She held it up and stared. Some nastier minds might have assumed that Luc was trying to hide a habit of cross-dressing, but Katie had no doubt at all this tiny scrap of fabric didn't belong to him. Wrong size.

There was a name embroidered on the tag. She twisted it around so she could read it. "Liza."

Liza. Where had she heard that name before? Oh yeah. They'd mentioned her at the police station.

Luc and Liza. Cute.

Katie stuffed the teddy back in the drawer and pulled out a T-shirt that was old, but clean and relatively hole-free.

She'd gotten what she deserved. If she hadn't looked, she wouldn't have known. She went into the bathroom, took off her clothes and put on the shirt. It fell to her knees. Of course she could have worn the teddy, but that was *so* not going to happen.

She found a new toothbrush in the medicine cabinet and brushed her teeth vigorously, then washed her face and headed back to the bed. Placing her glasses carefully on one of the nightstands, she climbed under the sheets and, engulfed in a sea of mattress, leaned back against the headboard.

Liza.

All at once, Katie felt very, very much alone. She sat straighter and pulled her knees up to her chest, hugging them tightly until she was a little ball in the big bed.

Well, of course Luc had a girlfriend. Stupid to think that he wouldn't. A guy who looked like he did wouldn't be walking around loose. And it really didn't make much of a difference to her one way or the other. She needed him because he'd gotten her into a frightening mess, and now he had to help her get out of it. She was just a job to him anyway. A mistake.

And what was she doing worrying about Lucas Vasco's love life? She had a few bigger problems on her plate. Such as whether she'd be murdered. Whether she'd ever see her family again. Whether she'd ever have a life again.

Yeah, that was a good one.

She thought about the future, struggled to see something to indicate there was going to be an end to this nightmare. It was blank. She couldn't even see herself.

"Is this it?" she asked the question out loud. "Is this my life now?"

Then, almost unwillingly, she began to cry. The tears were wrenched out of her. As if they were hard. As if she was vomiting them out of her system. She cried because of today. She cried because of the days and years before today. She cried because of Frankie Silvano. She cried because of her father. Because of Tom.

Mostly, though, she cried because she was just so alone. So scared. So powerless.

In the privacy of Luc's bedroom, in the quiet of the abandoned second floor of his castle, all of Katie's pain and fear poured out of her, and she couldn't stop it.

All she could do was grab Luc's pillow, hold it tightly against her chest, bend her head and cry.

Luc knew it wasn't a good idea, but he couldn't seem to stop himself. Twisting, he pulled the photograph out of his pants pocket. He looked at it, smoothing it absently, even tenderly. It was faded and old. Twenty years old, in fact. It had been halfway around the world with him. Gotten into fights with him. Saved him more than once. He'd never shown it to anyone, not even to David. Not even to David's mother.

Two thin and gawky girls were standing with their arms wrapped around each other's shoulders, grinning into the camera like imps. The girl on the right appeared to be as delicate as a fairy, but was really stronger than anyone he'd ever known. She had soft, straight brown hair and eyes he knew were hazel.

"Hello, Melanie." He smiled and touched her young face in the photo. That sweet face held shadows now. He'd been sick with worry and guilt when he'd found out about the car accident because he should have been there to help her. But he'd been off doing his stint in the Army and hadn't even known something was wrong until she'd already recovered.

Later, when he'd finally seen her, he'd confirmed for

himself that her leg was okay. The scarring wasn't too bad and the limp was minor. In fact, it wasn't nearly as noticeable as the limp he had right now. But it bothered her. Had damaged her. It was a girl thing, she'd said. He knew better.

As much as he loved to look at Mel and remember her, he loved looking at the other girl in the picture even more. Something about her had always made him smile, even when he'd been exhausted. Even when he'd been in hell.

She was a spry little elf with a cap of wild, curly red hair and an expression that announced to the world she had arrived and was ready to take over.

"Hello, Katie." Always before he'd called her Annie, but now for the first time he called her by her real name as he gently touched the image of the soft, round face. How many times, in how many places had he sat staring at this picture and thinking about this girl? Annie. Katie. He had looked into her young face and wondered about her. Wondered what she was like, how she'd grown up. Wondered what it was about her that drew him.

Well, he sighed. Well.

Her hair was shorter in the picture than it was now. As if someone had tried to tame it. He laughed a little because that hair was never going to be tame. It had too much life trapped in the wild curls. And now he knew that he'd been right about the color of her eyes. He hadn't been able to tell from the picture, but he'd always thought they'd be blue. He just hadn't expected them to be as clear as a summer sky.

The cocky pre-teen confidence of the young girl's

smile had dimmed in the adult, her mouth still sweet but wistful. What had happened to her? What hadn't Melanie told him?

Luc forced a deep breath and turned over the photo, tracing Melanie's scrawled handwriting on the back. The ink had almost worn off, but it was still clear enough to read. "Me and Annie."

Well, grammar had never been Melanie's strong point. She'd been ten years old when they'd been thrown together at that god-awful foster home and barely able to read her own name. The only way he'd been able to get her to learn at all had been by letting her look at his precious comic books. He wished she'd told him that Annie wasn't the girl's real name, but then again he should have remembered how she named everyone she met after the comics.

Luc sighed, closed his eyes. The box holding his memories had opened now, and they flowed through him like water. Like a flood. He knew from experience that the best thing to do was just let them run their course and then lock them up again.

Melanie had cried the night he'd left, but he'd known that he was doing the right thing. He couldn't stick around because if he'd gotten caught it would have been really bad. He'd waited as long as he could to make sure she was finally in a decent situation before he took off.

He rubbed the scar, then the side of his face. God, he really needed to shave.

She'd shoved the photo at him as he'd climbed out of her bedroom window and cried and asked him to remember her. As if he could have forgotten.

He thought about how impressed he'd been that she'd been given her own bedroom in the old farmhouse where she'd gone to live, because he'd known that the Mc-Cabes already had a ton of kids. It was only temporary until she'd settled in, but still. He'd been tempted to ask if they'd notice one more boy hanging out in the basement, but he'd known that he couldn't stay.

Was Katie the one who'd eventually moved in with Mel? Probably. Maybe he'd have been able to see her if he'd stuck around.

Luc shook his head. Stop.

He didn't have any more pictures. Only this one. There'd been letters and phone calls and Mel had visited him in Philly after he'd gotten out of the service and finished college, but she didn't send him any more pictures. She hated having her photograph taken, and he hadn't had enough guts to ask for a new one of Annie.

Jesus, it had been stupid for a grown man to feel the way he did anyway, so he'd done his best to ignore it. But he'd gotten Mel to talk sometimes. And, as ridiculous as it was, he'd hung on the little snippets of information casually tossed out here and there.

If he'd listened to Mel three years ago, he'd have met Katie then. Annie. Katie. But he'd chickened out. Big time. He couldn't quite believe how freaking terrified he'd been at the thought of actually meeting Melanie's foster sister. He'd been afraid she would look at him with those clear eyes and see right through him. That she'd see him for what he was, a fraud and a coward. That she'd see the violence and the mistakes and turn away from him. Then the dream would be over, and he'd be left with nothing and he couldn't handle that. So he'd run.

And now, here he was. Forced to deal with the reality of her anyway. Forced to live with her. Forced to try to hide the truth about himself so he wouldn't lose all of her respect. Sworn to protect a woman he'd thought he would never meet. She fucking terrified him. And she was trapped, and he trapped with her.

He'd been wrong. Life wasn't just ironic. Sometimes it was downright twisted.

Christ, what was he going to do now?

NINE

K<small>ATIE WOKE UP</small> in a large, unfamiliar bed. Her mind still bleary with the remaining edges of sleep, she reached out, but didn't touch the bedroom wall of her undersized apartment. She frowned, confused. Then she remembered.

His bed. His room.

Her eyes snapped open.

Because she was as blind as a newborn puppy without her glasses, everything was a big light blur. Since it had been a big dark blur before, she assumed it was morning now.

Groaning, she sat up, leaned out to the nightstand and groped for her glasses. Once she'd slid them into place, the world came back into focus, and she felt a little bit more in control.

The graceful room was gilded with sunshine. Long beams of it spilled through the bay window, danced patterns across the stones of the fireplace, the multi-colored spines of the books, bounced against the ceiling and the walls. The space literally glowed.

For a few minutes, Katie sat watching the light strengthen, comforted by the reminder that not everything in her life was ugly now.

When she pulled her knees up to her chest and

hugged them, she winced, surprised at how much the small gesture hurt. She felt kind of beaten up, like she'd been fighting. Maybe in a way she had been. It was hard work wrestling with the demons when they chose to make an appearance.

She smiled at her own thoughts, then grimaced because even her face hurt. Which shouldn't have been a surprise, considering how much she'd cried. But maybe the indulgence had actually helped because inside she felt better. Definitely confused. Still very frightened. Absolutely bruised and battered. But underneath it all... better. Maybe her mother had been right after all when she'd said that McCabes were a resilient lot.

The smile faded. God, she missed her mother. She wanted to tell her what was going on. She wanted to get her advice, listen to her lecture, have her voice opinions about things that really didn't concern her. She missed all of her brothers and sisters, even Fiona. And her father, well. She wouldn't think about him.

Although the clock on the nightstand showed that it was still pretty early, Katie didn't think she'd be able to go back to sleep, so she climbed out of the bed and stood staring at her reflection in the mirror hanging over Luc's dresser. Her hair was a jumbled mass of curls sticking out in all directions like Medusa. She was pale, her nose and cheeks red. Her eyes were wide and dark behind the glasses. Attractive.

What was going to happen now? Katie found herself looking at the shirt she'd worn to bed, remembering the silky pink teddy she'd found.

She pressed the shirt against her stomach, then shook her head and headed for the shower.

After she'd bathed, it occurred to her that one way she should have worked off some energy the night before was by washing out her clothes. Her twill pants would be okay, but the rest of her wardrobe was definitely not, uh, fresh as a daisy. She supposed extreme amounts of stress did that to a person.

Sighing, she rinsed out her blouse, bra and underwear in the bathroom sink and hung them in the shower.

Further investigation of Luc's dresser drawers produced a soft, brown shirt that was a little warm for the season, but clean and in reasonably good shape. Certainly decent enough for breakfast. Which left only the problem of feminine unmentionables. Maybe Luc would let her use his washer and dryer. Surely he had one somewhere in the place.

In the meantime it looked like Katie McCabe was going out commando style.

LUC SHIFTED HIS POSITION at the stove when the door behind him opened, and Katie slid into the room, Spot following closely at her heels.

"There you are." He tried to keep his voice neutral, but it was hard.

She was carrying a book and looked more than a little uncomfortable. Her hair was damp from a shower and, for the moment, relatively subdued, but it had already started to spring into curl around her face. She had on his favorite old shirt. It hung on her like a tunic. She'd had to roll up the sleeves several times so her hands could peak out. She was adorable.

It just wasn't goddamn fair.

"I hope you don't mind that I borrowed your shirt."

"Uh…no." Luc's mind felt like the batter he'd stirred up for some pancakes. He struggled to pull his thoughts back together. "It never looked so good."

"Flattery will get you nowhere." She smiled and sat down at the kitchen table, facing him.

"I wondered where Spot had gotten to," Luc said. He grinned when the dog took up a position next to the stove, staring with fixed interest at the pancake griddle as if willing it to fall.

"She was waiting for me in the hallway when I came out of the room. I guess she's appointed herself my official escort."

"She likes you," Luc said. We both do.

"That's good. I, uh, brought you a book," she said, putting it on the table. "It was on the nightstand and looked like you were reading it, so I thought you might want it." She wrinkled her nose. "Although why in the world anyone would voluntarily read *The Illiad* is beyond me."

"Heathen." Luc was disoriented. She smiled again and he cleared his throat. He wasn't going to get distracted just because she wore his shirt and brought him a book.

He wasn't.

"Is your ankle okay?" she asked. "Should you be on it?"

"I heal fast. It's better this morning." More importantly, he couldn't stand the thought of lying helpless on the sofa for one more minute. "How are you?" He looked her over carefully. She was pale, but at least she didn't seem to be quite so fragile today.

"Better." She inclined her head. "Less breakable."

"Good."

"Where did you get the crutches?"

Luc glanced at the old crutches leaning against the stove and shrugged. "A closet. I forgot I had them last night." He hadn't been thinking too clearly.

Katie nodded soberly. "Good man. Prepared for all emergencies."

"That's me. The proverbial boy scout."

"What's for breakfast?" There was a smile hidden in the corners of her mouth and in her blue eyes behind the glasses. Hidden was a good word to describe her, Luc thought. If you just looked at the surface you would miss the intelligence in those eyes, the soft roundness of her features.

"Luc?" Her eyebrows were raised. Had she asked him a question?

"Pancakes," he said, shaking his head to clear it. "I found a few things around and my neighbor brought me some milk. She dropped it off on her way to work at the diner…" He forced himself to stop talking when he realized he was babbling. Christ, he never babbled.

"Again, very resourceful."

"Thank you. I try."

"They're burning."

"What?" Luc turned back to the stove and frowned when he saw she was right. "Crap." He hated burned pancakes. They always reminded him of his and Melanie's time as foster kids at the god-awful Winston house and how the bitch who ruled there had insisted that they call her "mother", and the beatings, and... Grumbling, he flipped the pancakes off the griddle to cool for Spot and stirred the batter again.

"Are you sure you should be standing?"

"I'm fine." Actually, his ankle was killing him, in spite of the fact that he'd been a good boy and wrapped it tightly in an elastic bandage. But he wasn't going to admit that to her or she'd want to come over and help. Then she'd be too close. He was trying to cut down on temptation, not ramp it up.

Katie was silent while he carefully poured the batter onto the griddle in perfect little circles. "Do you have a washer and dryer?" she asked suddenly.

"Sure. Why?"

"Because I need to throw in a few things."

"What?" He glanced back at her and saw her blush. Deeply.

"Um, well, I only have one, uh...okay." She sat straighter. "Here's the deal. I washed out my underwear and my bra upstairs, but they're still kind of icky, and it's going to take them a while to dry anyway." She fidgeted around on the chair. "And these twill pants really itch when you aren't wearing underwear."

Luc's hands jerked. Batter flew all over the griddle. "Shit!"

"What's wrong?" Katie jumped up and rushed over to him. He looked down at her, into her wide, concerned eyes. She really had no idea...

"We'll go to a mall and buy you some clothes." He hesitated, watching as she pushed up the sleeves of his shirt only to have them flop back down to cover her hands again. "Now," he added.

Katie blinked. "Now?"

"Now." Sure. Why not now? Get them out of the house. Christ, had the kitchen always been this warm? He tugged at the collar of his T-shirt. "Besides, we really need to get some food," he added desperately.

Her things would dry, of course, but he wasn't going through this every morning while she was here. He was under enough stress as it was. They could take her car; his Volvo station wagon still had the unfortunate tendency to lose all of its fluids at inappropriate times. They could do some grocery shopping while they were out, buy her clothes, get gas for the Nova. Yeah, this was a good plan.

He turned off the griddle and dumped the entire mess into the sink, then tossed the burned pancakes to Spot, who caught each one in mid-air like little Frisbees.

Katie seemed puzzled. "But what about breakfast?"

"We'll get something while we're out."

She hadn't moved. He wished that she would. She smelled like his soap. Like warm, clean woman. "Won't it be, uh, dangerous?"

"We'll be okay." He hoped that was true. But he couldn't leave her alone here at the house and he wasn't going to shop for her clothes and underwear by himself. That would mean he'd have to figure out her size, decide what would look good... "There's a big mall about an hour away," he said on a surge of panic. "We'll go there. We'll be fine. Really."

"I look like a bum." Katie pulled at the shirt.

"Who the hell cares what you look like?" Luc snapped. "You look good." More than good.

And then, God have mercy, she blushed a bright scarlet red again.

"But I'm not wearing—"

"Would you just shut up about the underwear?" Luc banged his hand down on the edge of the countertop and made both Katie and Spot jump. "I'll buy you a whole freaking pile of underwear. Just go get your purse and I'll meet you at the Nova. Move!"

He grabbed the crutches and hobbled off, trying to ignore how she stared after him, her mouth hanging open with surprise.

TEN

WHEN THEY GOT to the mall, Luc insisted on buying all of Katie's clothes with cash so there wouldn't be a paper trail. The whole time they were shopping, he was funny and charming and obviously out to prove that he was the one in charge.

But later in the afternoon it was Katie who drove back to the Museum. Of course, she knew the only reason she'd been given the privilege was because after they'd stopped at a grocery store for provisions, Luc had been in so much pain even he couldn't ignore it. He'd finally given in and agreed to sit in the backseat where he could stretch out his leg, providing shouted directions whenever she went astray. Fortunately, there weren't that many turns.

"How are you?" she asked after they'd been driving turn-free for a little while, breaking what had become a rather companionable silence. She glanced at him through the rearview mirror and saw him straighten a little bit.

"I'm okay," he said, but she knew he was lying.

"That ankle isn't going to heal as long as you keep walking around on it."

"I have to. Spot doesn't take well to a saddle."

Katie laughed in spite of herself. "We could always

hook up a cart." When she looked at him again, Luc smiled at her in the mirror. The brackets appeared around his mouth for one tantalizing instant, then were gone.

"Obviously her training has been sadly lacking."

Katie looked away and focused on driving. She was suddenly breathless, caught by his smile, by the way his dark hair fell around his face, the way his skin gleamed a lush golden brown against the old black T-shirt.

"You really should have let me pay for something," she said. Even if he was filthy rich and hiding it for some reason, she had her pride. She could support herself.

"I've never met a woman who could argue so much about not spending money."

"I'm taking advantage of you."

"For the last time, will you quit worrying?" He sounded amused. "I'm just going to put it on my expense report anyway. David will love it."

"I do have some cash with me. I could have bought something without using my credit card." She flexed her hands on the steering wheel. She knew she was talking much too quickly, but she knew he was watching her. She wished she could tell what he was thinking.

"Drop it, Katie. You're not going to win this one. I got you into this. I'm buying your damn clothes."

She risked another glance at him in the rearview mirror. His mouth had a stubborn set to it, so she decided to let the clothing issue go. But another worry was still niggling at her, the reality of her situation constantly hovering on the edges of her thinking. She turned her attention back to the road. "Are you sure you didn't see anyone you knew?"

"Yes. I'm sure." Luc sounded impatient. Which could be because she'd already asked him that same question about five times already.

"You really don't think people noticed me?"

"No. I don't think anybody noticed the way you were dressed. Besides, you changed right away." He had insisted that the first thing they did, even before they ate breakfast, was buy her a shirt that fit. And underwear.

Katie smiled. "The saleswomen sure noticed you, though," she teased. "I saw how they looked at you. Fresh meat without the ability to run." Bunch of barracudas.

Luc, to her surprise, did not laugh at the small joke. When she glanced at him, he was frowning.

"Yeah. I hope they don't remember me," he said. "The scar, you know? It's a little hard to miss." He drew his hand down the side of his face.

"I like it," Katie spoke before she thought, then felt herself blush a bright, fiery red. "Um, I mean it suits you. How did you get it?"

Luc didn't answer.

"Forget it. I don't want to bring up any bad memories," she said quickly. She gripped the steering wheel tighter, intent on the road so she wouldn't look at him.

"No, no. It's all right." He paused again. "It was a mistake. I was in the middle of a situation I didn't know how to handle. I was young and stupid. I messed up. I paid. Everything worked out for the best in the end."

Katie found that she wanted more details, but was

afraid to ask. What had happened? Why hadn't he ever gotten the scar fixed?

"Here's the driveway," he said, interrupting her thoughts. "Congratulations, you made it."

"Hallelujah. I don't know why in the world New Jersey thinks traffic circles are better than good old-fashioned stop lights." She turned into the familiar gravel lane and soon Luc's castle loomed into view.

"Museum, sweet Museum," Katie sighed, charmed by the building all over again.

Luc didn't respond. When she glanced back at him, she saw that he was sitting straighter, looking out the window, the tight line of his wide shoulders radiating a fine tension.

"Is something wrong?" she asked.

"No, I just wanted to make sure—"

"Did we leave on the light over the front door?"

"We must have," he said.

She was a little puzzled when she sensed him relax.

As soon as she pulled the car into the parking area and stopped, Spot came running out to greet them with loud barks and enthusiastic waves of her black tail.

"She's pretty lively," Luc commented. "Guess she was lonely."

"Think you can make it inside?" Katie asked, twisting around in the seat to face him.

"No." Luc tried to move his leg with limited success. "But I don't have much of a choice, do I?"

"Not unless sleeping in a Nova appeals to you." Katie jumped out of the car and hurried around to help him extract himself. It took some effort and a great deal of cursing, but eventually he was standing, balanced precariously on one foot. Spot playfully leapt at him.

"Hang on a minute." Katie let go of Luc's arm and went to get the crutches out of the car while he tried to fend off Spot.

"What is your problem?" he yelled at the dog. "Stop pushing me. Stop it! Sit! Stay, goddamn it!"

Spot ignored him and nudged him toward the house by pushing her large head against his thigh. The nudges didn't look gentle either. Before Katie could hand Luc the crutches, Spot gave him a particularly eager shove.

"Oh, hell," he said.

He teetered. It was like watching one of those films of a building swaying in an earthquake. One where you just knew the foundation wasn't going to hold.

She dropped the crutches and made a grab for him, but it was too late. He fell, pulling her down with him, managing at the last minute to twist his body to cushion hers.

The next thing she knew she was lying on top of him, face to face in the driveway next to the Nova.

"Ouch," Luc wheezed.

Spot moved to straddle them both. Katie felt the dog snuffling at her hair. She refused to speculate if there was drool involved.

"Oh, my God, are you hurt?" She tried to get off Luc, but the dog wouldn't budge.

"Yes." He sounded pathetic. "This just hasn't been my week."

Katie realized she and Luc were nose to nose, and she was looking directly into his beautiful eyes. Her breath caught in her throat with a slight squeak. They stared at each other in silence for a moment.

"Katie?" Luc lifted a hand, pushing back the curls that had fallen forward into her face.

"Yes?" Her voice came out as a whisper. It didn't sound like her voice at all.

"I'm going to kill that dog."

Katie laughed softly. Before she quite knew what she was doing, she touched his hair. She'd been aching to touch it from the moment he'd jumped into her car, she realized. It was smooth and silky and slid through her fingers. Midnight black. Soft and sensual. His body was big and warm and all hard muscle under hers, their legs intertwined. So different. So exciting. She stared at him, stared into those deep, dark eyes. Saw them watching her.

She didn't know if she moved first, or if he did. Maybe they both did. All she knew was that they were closer. His lips skimming hers, his mouth light and warm, but firm. Testing, tasting, questing, asking for more but not demanding it.

He nibbled on her lips, ran his tongue along the seam between them, acting as if he had all the time in the world, no desire beyond discovering the shape of her mouth, its texture, how it molded to his. His scent wrapped around her, his whiskers scraped her skin, his hands hot and insistent as he pulled her even closer.

Spot moved, and Katie knew the dog had ambled away, but it barely registered. It was probably a mistake, but God help her, she wanted this. Wanted him. Her lips were impossibly sensitive as he teased them. She found herself softening against him.

He sucked on her bottom lip, and she couldn't control a little gasp. Immediately he seized the opportunity to plunge into the warmth of her mouth, sliding them deeper into the kiss, his tongue probing, wrapping around hers, coaxing, savoring her. She was being pulled under by the sensations. He tasted of sweetness and Luc and pure sex. She couldn't breathe, but breathing was definitely overrated.

Almost abruptly his strong fingers threaded through her curls. He changed the angle of the kiss, bringing her impossibly closer. She couldn't seem to do anything but respond and melt against him.

She shifted slightly, restless for more, and experimentally rubbed her body against a very hard part of his, making demands of her own.

He groaned and muttered something, then his mouth hardened, quickened. He wasn't gentle anymore, but, God, she didn't want him to be. He ate at her mouth, devoured it. Consumed it. Fed on it, on her.

She moaned deep in her throat, gripped his dark hair in both hands and gave.

She'd never been kissed like this. The passion took her by surprise. His passion. Hers. Theirs. She hadn't realized she could feel this way. She didn't know how she was feeling.

His mouth slanted, slid across hers again and again. Hotter now. Wilder. Wetter. He tasted so good. He smelled so good. She drank him like he was cool water. She thirsted for him. She hungered for him. She—

"Everyone okay?"

At the sound of the masculine voice, Katie's eyes flew open. She jerked away from Luc, rolled and jumped to her feet, even as Luc shifted and his hand moved behind his back. Through the haze of her now crooked and foggy eyeglasses, she saw David Allen. He was standing a few feet away from the Nova, arms crossed, watching them, Spot sitting at his feet.

Uh oh.

Katie felt her whole body heat up in one big flush.

"It's not what it seems." She tried to clean off her glasses with her shirtsleeve and put them back on just in time to see David arch a dark eyebrow.

"Then what is it?" he asked politely.

ELEVEN

Luc struggled to get himself back under control, but it was hard—in more ways than one. He tucked his gun back into the waistband of his jeans under the T-shirt and shifted so his arousal might be a little less obvious. But he didn't hold out much hope that David hadn't noticed his condition. It would have been kind of difficult to miss, considering how he was pushing out the zipper of his jeans. Fuck.

He tried to think and couldn't. Holding Katie McCabe had been like setting himself on fire, and right at the moment he couldn't concentrate on anything but the burn.

And wasn't that just fucking great?

Somehow he managed to crawl to his feet, then took the crutches Katie handed him. He tried to read her expression, but she backed away, studiously avoiding his eyes, so he sighed and looked at David. The other man's face didn't give anything away, his features like burnished mahogany, unmoved and unmoving.

"What the hell are you doing here?" Luc asked.

"I told you I would check in."

"Yeah, but I didn't expect the pleasure of your company."

"That much was obvious." David's eyes glittered with

some suppressed emotion. Disapproval? Irritation? Luc couldn't tell.

Luc pushed down his own anger. "I knew you were here, but you're lucky I didn't shoot you anyway when you snuck up on us like that. Where did you park?"

"I'm out by the barn. Next to that wreck you call a car."

"You knew he was here?" Katie's voice was an embarrassed wail, and Luc winced.

"I, uh, yeah. The light. It's a signal, you know?"

"Oh, my God!" She didn't sound pleased.

Wonderful. Now she probably thought he'd wanted David to catch them making out like a couple of hormonal teenagers. Rolling around in the driveway for sweet Christ's sake. If she'd believed he was a jerk before, what did she think of him now?

"Sorry," he muttered.

"Go. Go now. Just go inside and talk to David. I'll get the bags out of the car." Katie's voice sounded strangled. He could practically see her willing them both to leave immediately, if not sooner. She still refused to look at him, but he noticed a deep blush of pink under her soft skin. Soft skin with freckles. Softer lips.

Damn it. Goddamn it. He hadn't meant to touch her, let alone kiss her, but when she'd landed in his arms he'd forgotten everything. Everything. Forgotten that she was under his protection and in his care. Forgotten that David was in the house and would undoubtedly come out to see what was taking them so long. He hadn't given a damn about anything but kissing her.

Now here he stood, so hot he was ready to spontaneously combust and wishing like hell that he could just ignore David, pull her inside and not let her out of his bedroom for a week. Shit, shit, shit!

Needing the space as much as she did, he turned abruptly, swung the crutches under his arms and limped past David. The other man hesitated, then followed without a word. Luc let the silence stretch, knowing he'd eventually get a lecture, but what the hell. It wasn't like he could fucking run away. He couldn't fucking run away from anything.

"Let's go to the kitchen and talk," David said once they were finally inside the house.

"It's going to take me half an hour to get to the kitchen." Luc hobbled down the hallway, his crutches scraping across the mosaic tiles he'd restored last year. "You might as well say what you have to say while we're walking."

David didn't answer. They moved slowly to the modern wing. Spot had stayed with Katie, which was just as fucking well. Luc grimaced. Yeah, right. Like it had all been Spot's fault. He wanted to throw something, to break something, to yell because he'd screwed up so badly, but instead he concentrated on moving the crutches.

"Care to explain yourself?" David asked, a pulse of anger vibrating in his voice. Apparently he was even more pissed off than Luc had assumed.

"It was a mistake," Luc said, managing to sound relatively unemotional.

"A mistake, huh?" They walked for another minute

or two. "I have to be able to trust you. I need to know Katie will be okay here alone with you."

This was not the friend talking, not the surrogate older brother. Luc understood that. This was the squad supervisor. Still, friendship could never be completely stripped away between the two of them, and David's words hurt.

"Last time I checked we were both adults. She doesn't need you to babysit her."

"She's under your care. She can't leave. We have a responsibility to her," David snapped.

"You know what? I kind of figured that out all by myself." Luc's own temper flared. He looked at the other man. "You don't trust me?"

"I don't know." David returned his stare. "You're obviously attracted to her. Under these circumstances, that's dangerous."

Luc agreed. Katie McCabe was very dangerous to his peace of mind. But he knew that wasn't what David meant. The man thought he would take advantage of the situation.

Was he right?

What would have happened out in the driveway if David hadn't been there?

It is human nature to think wisely and act foolishly.

He couldn't remember where he'd read that, but he knew without a doubt that it was true.

They finally made it all the way to the kitchen. Luc eased himself down onto one of the chairs. It was good to get off his feet. Foot. David, however, did not sit. Instead he paced with a rare restlessness. Luc wondered if Katie was sitting outside with Spot cursing him.

"You get involved with that girl and you're going to hurt her."

Luc raised his eyebrows. "Oh, yeah? Sure about that, are you?"

"I know it won't be intentional. But you will."

For a moment, Luc struggled with annoyance and anger. He forced himself to take a deep breath. "Was that your only reason for coming out to check up on us?"

David glanced at him, then away as he continued to pace. "I'm clearing my plate. I'll be able to come out here tomorrow," he said.

"Tomorrow?" Great.

"You need help." David stopped and turned to face him. "If somebody found this house you wouldn't be worth a damn right now."

"God, David, I sprained my fucking ankle. My leg wasn't amputated."

"How fast could you move if you had to run?"

"Fast enough."

David just snorted.

"You want to keep an eye on me," Luc accused.

"Hell yeah."

"Jesus Christ, David, Katie's going to be fine. I sure as hell don't want to touch her again!" In his frustrated rage, he practically shouted the words.

They both saw the kitchen door swing open and Katie herself hesitating on the threshold. She was holding her purse and a number of shopping bags. Luc could tell that she'd heard his last outburst.

"Perfect," he muttered and turned away.

KATIE WALKED into the room, schooling her features so Luc wouldn't know how his words had sliced her. She shouldn't want him to touch her again, right? Wasn't that why she'd just wasted so much time out at the car? Hadn't she pretty much come to the conclusion that he was another loser like Tom? Someone who didn't care who was watching as long as he got what he wanted? Someone who hadn't even seemed to give a passing thought to the mysterious Liza of the flimsy teddy?

It should have been a relief to know he wasn't going to try anything else, especially since she'd be alone with him again after David left. So why had hearing him reject her so baldly been such a kick in the gut? Why did it make her feel somehow…lacking?

Again.

She was overwhelmed by sudden fury. Yeah, okay, she shouldn't have kissed him in the first place. And yes, knowing that he didn't want to touch her again should have made her feel better, but it didn't, all right?

What? She seethed. Couldn't she compare with the woman who could fit into that tiny little scrap of a silk?

She took a deep breath. "Of course Luc won't touch me," she said when she thought she could speak normally. "Don't be ridiculous. I'm not going to give him the chance. What you saw outside was purely the result of proximity."

"Proximity?" David asked.

"Caused by a very large dog." The dog in question padded into the kitchen and lay down next to her food dish, clearly waiting for it to be filled. "And let's just say there was a whole lot of stupidity thrown in for good measure." Katie carefully avoided looking at Luc. "Anyway, David, I wanted to ask if you'd carry in the groceries. I'm going to take my clothes upstairs."

"Sure," David said. "Why don't you rest for a few minutes." His voice was so gentle that she wanted to strangle him and scream at him not to patronize her.

She forced herself to smile politely instead. "Thank you."

"Katie—" Luc started to say something, but she ignored him and stalked out of the room.

TWELVE

DAVID STAYED FOR a while, but he finally left because he had places to be. For once, Luc was glad to see him go. They'd both calmed down some after Katie had stormed out of the kitchen, but the ensuing conversation had been stilted and excessively polite.

On the other hand, at least dealing with the other man had kept him from thinking. The house seemed awfully quiet after he'd gone. There'd been no further sign of Katie, which wasn't too surprising. Luc figured he'd be lucky if she didn't start having takeout delivered to his bedroom so she could avoid seeing him altogether. What with one thing and another, he'd managed to come off as quite the asshole this afternoon. Great. Just great.

He leaned his head back against the cushions of the sofa where he'd stretched out after David had gone. Spot was lying in the middle of an antique oriental rug, snoring. Shifting, Luc grabbed his wine glass, took a sip of the ruby-red liquid. When he put the glass back on the table he saw the book Katie had brought him that morning. He touched the binding gently, although he didn't open it. He wasn't in the mood for capricious Greek gods at the moment. He had enough troubles of his own.

Katie. Annie. Katie. Funny how he didn't think of her as Annie anymore after so many years spent wondering about the girl with that name. The reality of Katie had pushed aside the dream of Annie.

He wouldn't think about that amazing kiss.

Who the hell was he kidding?

"How are you doing?"

Luc jumped and pulled himself to a sitting position, turning his head to see Katie standing in the family room doorway. She'd come in so quietly he hadn't even heard her. He shot Spot an accusatory look, but the dog had her head up and was wagging her tail. He'd just been too preoccupied with his own thoughts to notice.

He forced a smile. "Uh, I'm fine."

He ran his gaze over her face as she moved farther into the room. The young girl's features from the photo were more mature now. Not hard, though. Soft. So soft. Her cheeks were slightly rosy, but that was probably because he'd given her whisker burn. She seemed composed and distant. He could have dealt with it better if she'd still been angry.

He hesitated, awkward and unsure of himself and hating it. He wished he knew what she was thinking. "Sorry about not getting up." He gestured down at his ankle buried under its mountain of ice packs.

She waved a hand. "Don't worry about it."

Silence.

"Where's David?" she asked.

"He left. He had to go to a dinner or something. Why?"

"No reason." Katie walked over to Spot and sent the dog into rolling ecstasy by scratching her head and chest. Luc cleared his throat as she straightened and faced him, meeting his eyes directly for the first time since she'd come into the room.

"Katie—"

"Luc—"

"—we need to talk."

They both said it at the same time, realized it, and fell silent, staring at each other.

"Um, you first," Luc said, knowing he was being a coward.

"Okay." She seemed to gather herself. "Look, we can't change what happened out there on the driveway, but it was nothing."

Nothing?

"Katie, I—"

"Just let me finish," she interrupted, her voice flat. "I know you're involved with someone else. I know we both got, um, carried away."

Luc rubbed his forehead to ease a sudden headache. "We did?"

"Sure. I've made enough mistakes to recognize one when I see it."

Mistake? Well, yeah. Of course it had been a mistake. He just didn't like her calling it one.

"It wasn't that big a deal, so just forget about it. I have." Katie clapped her hands together and gave him a bright smile. "Now," she said, her voice fucking cheery. "I'll cook dinner. How about chicken and vegetables? Or do you want something else? We bought plenty."

Luc blinked at her.

"Uh, no. Chicken and vegetables sounds fine."

"Great. I'll get it started and you just stay there and rest your ankle." She glared at him. "Don't move."

Still smiling, she left the room, Spot close at her heels. Luc watched her go, wondering what the hell had just happened.

She thought that kiss in the driveway hadn't meant anything? Well, it hadn't. Just a mistake.

Fucking hell.

He shoved the ice packs away, got up and hobbled after her, not bothering with the damn crutches.

"Wait, what do you mean that you realize I'm involved with someone else?" he demanded as soon as he got into the kitchen. He didn't know why he was asking about that, since it apparently didn't matter at all. Maybe because it was the one thing he could actually answer.

Katie was standing in front of the stove, hands on her hips as she studied it and the cabinets surrounding it. She turned to look at him and he saw the surprise on her face. Across the room Spot raised her head from her water dish.

"I mean your girlfriend, of course," she said, then frowned. "At least I assume she's your girlfriend."

"My girlfriend?" What the hell was she talking about?

She nodded, as if that explained everything.

"Liza," she added when he still didn't respond. Now it was his turn to frown.

"How do you know about Liza?"

Katie crossed her arms in front of her chest as she glared at him. "Why do you keep thinking that I'm stupid? You guys mentioned her at the police station. And

then I found her, uh, teddy. In your dresser drawer upstairs," she clarified when he knew he looked confused.
"Last night. You said I was going to need to wear whatever I could find, so I had to look through your stuff.
It's your own fault."

"Teddy?" What was a teddy? "What the hell are you
talking about?"

She sighed. "There is a really, really tiny pink teddy,
um, lingerie, in your T-shirt drawer. It has the name
'Liza' embroidered on the tag." She laughed scornfully.
"God, is that pretentious or what? Does her underwear
have the days of the week on them so she won't get confused?" She paused. "It really isn't yours, is it?"

"What? Shit, no, it's not mine."

He must have sounded horrified because she almost
laughed.

"Well, good, because there's no way it would fit."

"Oh, God, I didn't know that was there," he muttered.
"Doesn't that just figure? It's the way things have been
going lately." He limped over to the kitchen table and
sat down heavily in one of the chairs. "Liza is David's
administrative assistant, and my former fiancée."

"Former—"

"Former as in I broke it off a year ago. There were,
um, issues." And that was putting it mildly.

"Issues?"

Luc forced himself to keep eye contact, but it was
hard. "She, well, it just wasn't right between us, and it
turned out that she was with other men when I was out
on assignment, so I ended the engagement. I, uh, when
we were engaged she, um, stayed over…sometimes."

Great. Now he sounded like he was in eighth grade. "I guess she left the thing behind when we broke up."

"Well, it was at the bottom of the drawer," Katie said. "I can see how you missed it."

"And just so you know, you're the only other person who's had an opportunity to find that…teddy in, um, months," he said, wanting to be clear, but Christ.

"Oh." She blushed.

"I wouldn't have kissed you if there'd been another woman in my life, Katie." He needed her to know he had at least that much integrity. "I wouldn't have done that."

She didn't answer for a full minute. "Good to know."

"I should have said something in case you, you know, came across some of Liza's…stuff. It didn't even occur to me that you might find something in my room."

She shrugged. "It's okay. I sure don't go around telling a complete stranger about my crappy engagement either."

Luc paused for one long heartbeat, then two. "What?"

Katie looked like she wished she could have bitten off her own tongue, but she shrugged again with a studied casualness. "It's no biggie. It ended about six months ago."

Luc was still trying to wrap his mind around that little bit of information. His elf? His imp? Katie had been engaged? Why the fuck hadn't Melanie told him?

He fought back his emotions and tried to appear merely interested. "So, um, how long were you engaged?"

She turned to the sink and busied herself with what he

assumed were the preparations for dinner. "Two years. Frying pan?"

He pointed absently at a cabinet. Two years? Two years? He was going to kill Melanie the next time he saw her. "What was he like?"

"Oil?"

"He was what?"

"Do you have any cooking oil?"

"Oh." He pointed at another door. "I mean two years is a long time to be engaged." Hell, he'd been engaged to Liza for eight months, and that had been plenty long enough.

"So they say."

"What happened? Was he a complete slime? Or did you just find out that you were, uh, incompatible?"

Katie sighed and turned to face him. "You're not going to let this go, are you?"

"I'm just curious."

"I'm sorry I mentioned it."

"It was just a question."

"I don't think I want to answer it."

"I'm trying to learn more about you. So I can protect you better." He gave her his most winning smile.

"Yeah, right. Do you want to eat or not?"

Luc thought about it. He could tell by the stubborn set of her chin that it wasn't going to be easy to get her to talk about this. But he had time. He didn't have to push.

Yet.

"Eat," he decided.

"Good." There was some relief in her eyes. "Then change the subject."

"So." Luc cast around in his mind for a different topic of conversation. "How about those Phillies, hey?"

Katie grinned for the first time since she'd come downstairs. She opened a cabinet, found the cooking oil then took it and the frying pan to the stove. "Please. Anything but sports."

"You don't like sports?"

"I grew up with three brothers who, in their prime, gave a whole new definition to the word fanatic. They even made up flashcards so I could memorize the stats of all of their favorite players."

"Yeesh, that was a little over the top. Did you?"

"Did I what?"

"Memorize them?"

"Well, sure. Brothers, you know. Besides, Michael pinched me every time I got one wrong."

"Ah, the whole Pavlov's dog theory."

"Or the bratty little brother theory."

Luc realized he was smiling. "So what's the problem? Sports should be your middle name."

"Yeah." She turned away from the stove to look at him. "See, here's what happened. One fall they decided that I needed to learn how to play touch football."

"Touch football?"

"Darren had been studying the Kennedys at school, and he realized we had our own team. Frolic in the fall leaves, that sort of thing."

"What happened?"

"I, uh, accidentally kicked him in the groin."

"Ouch."

"Um, pretty hard too. They had to take him to the hospital."

Luc couldn't control a purely male shudder of horror at the thought.

"They never let me play with them again," she continued. "So now, alas, sports hold only bitter memories for me."

"Scarred you for life, huh?"

"Naturally."

"Well, can you blame them? They were probably terrified of you after that."

She shrugged and turned back to the stove. "Well, Darren never forgot to wear a cup again."

"I'll bet. Okay, no sports." He thought for a moment. Unfortunately the only subject he really wanted to discuss was her mysterious fiancé. Ex-fiancé. And the reason for the "ex."

No. Not now. He wouldn't ask now.

"How about medieval morality plays?" he suggested.

"Oh, yeah, that sounds exciting." Whatever she was cooking sizzled and popped and smelled really good, like onions and garlic in oil. He didn't believe a woman had ever actually cooked in this kitchen before.

"What's exciting? Oh. Yeah, the morality plays are pretty freaking exciting. Do you know all about them too?"

"Very funny. I don't even know what they are. Pasta?"

He pointed. "Then, see? It's a good topic."

"Maybe if I wanted an English lecture." She turned to face him and crinkled her nose in a delightful and unexpected way. Jesus God, when had he gotten so sappy? "And, no offense, but it's a little late in the day for that."

"Humph. Cretin."

"I don't believe you've even read one. I don't care how many books you have upstairs."

"I've read one," he protested.

"Yeah? Then tell me the plot."

He paused. Well, now that he thought about it, he wasn't entirely sure. Maybe he'd fallen asleep in the middle of it.

"It's very complicated," he said loftily.

"See?" she said, pointing the spatula at him. "I'll bet you don't know what they are either."

Luc watched her cook for a few minutes, watched her move gracefully around his kitchen. The silence wasn't strained now, just companionable. It was good to have her there. In his house. In his space. In his life.

Damn.

He knew he wasn't right for her. She didn't know the things he'd done, the way he'd lived, what he'd had to do to survive. She needed someone…someone…well, just someone better.

Jesus. He dragged a hand through his hair and briefly wished that he hadn't quit smoking a couple of years ago. He knew no matter what he did, no matter what he said, he was going to mess up, and that made him feel both pathetic and vulnerable.

Suddenly he was angry. If there was one thing Lucas Vasco was not, it was pathetic. Or vulnerable. He stood on his own two feet. He made his own way in the world, and to hell with everyone else. He'd never been pathetic, not even when he'd been a powerless kid.

How did this one woman manage to turn him upside down? She made him needy and he didn't like it.

He glared at the back of Katie's head while she continued to chop and stir and make his house a home merely by her presence.

"I didn't act very professionally this afternoon," he said abruptly. "I'm sorry if I made you uncomfortable."

Katie turned and looked at him, her expression cautious and a little surprised at his abrupt change of mood.

"David called me on the carpet for it," he continued, "and he was right. I don't have any excuse for my behavior. I hope that you won't let it influence how you feel about being forced to stay here or your opinion of the FBI."

Katie didn't say anything.

"You're under my protection. I take that very seriously," he said.

"I know."

Luc wanted to shout with frustration. He didn't even know what the hell he was trying to say to her. How could she look at him that way? As if she saw right through him? It was exactly what he'd thought would happen if he'd ever met the girl in the picture.

"You won't be here for very long," he said. "We'll have a better place for you soon."

Katie studied him with large, clear blue eyes for a long time. "Let's eat," she said.

THIRTEEN

KATIE WOKE ABRUPTLY to annoying music playing very close to her ear.

"Wha...?"

Still groggy and half asleep, she fumbled for her glasses and jammed them on. It was morning again. She was in Luc's bedroom. In his bed. Again.

The music stopped, then restarted, and she finally realized it was her cell phone ringing on the nightstand. She checked the caller ID, and—oh, God. It was her mother.

Should she answer it?

Katie's mind whirled, sleep vanishing. Could cell phone calls be traced? What if Frankie Silvano had her mother's phone lines tapped or bugged or something? Answering might not only give away her own location, it might put her mother in danger.

The little phone went silent, paused, then started its endless tune again. She wanted to turn it off, but she didn't dare because her mother would start getting bumped directly to voice mail and think there was a problem. But if she didn't answer at a time when she should have been available...

Well, her mom wasn't exactly known for just sitting around.

"Crap! Crap!"

Leaping out of bed, Katie haphazardly threw on some clothes and bolted for the door, the still-ringing phone clutched in her hand.

She found Luc stretched out on the sofa in the family room, reading and looking all dark and attractive in a white T-shirt with his hair still wet from a shower and his chin freshly shaved. He glanced up and smiled when she raced in, Spot jumping at her heels. But his smile faded as soon as he saw her expression. He put down the book and swung into a sitting position.

"What?"

"My mother." Katie skidded to a halt in front of the sofa, completely out of breath thanks to her mad dash from the bedroom. Man, this house was big. "She called…on my cell phone… Jeez." She put her hands on her knees and hung her head, panting for a moment before she recovered. "It's stopped now, but she'll call back again."

"Shit. You didn't answer, right?"

"No."

"Good."

"I have to talk to her, Luc. If she's trying to find me, she's not going to stop with a few phone calls. She'll probably go over to the apartment."

Luc cursed again. "David didn't want to tell your family anything until we know more about what's going on and can get you somewhere safe. I didn't think that would work." He looked at her. "How long can you put her off without calling her back?"

Katie snorted. "No more than an hour if we're lucky. Unless she's really freaked. Then all bets are off."

"Okay. Okay." Luc stood, pulled up the crutches and paced around the room. "Okay, here's what we'll do." He grabbed another cell phone lying on the small table next to the sofa. "You call her, but use this phone instead of your own. It's a secure line with caller-id blocked. I just got the number changed so only David has it. We don't know if her lines are tapped—they weren't as of last night. Something could have happened in the meantime, but using this should minimize the risk they'll find us."

It was like James Bond. It would have been fascinating if it hadn't been so very frightening.

"What should I say?" Her voice came out as a croak.

Luc ran a hand through his dark hair, rumpling it. "I don't know. Something to make her think it's okay that you'll be out of touch for a little while. We don't want her filing a police report and drawing attention to herself until we have you safely stashed away and can put the word out that you've disappeared."

Katie swallowed.

"How about saying that you've been sent out of town unexpectedly for work?" Luc suggested.

She pulled a face. "Hello, I'm an admin, okay? I've never been sent out of town for work in my life and my mother knows it." She frowned, thinking. "But…"

"But what?"

"Well, they were talking about a corporate retreat the other day. It would only be for the big guys, but Mom doesn't know that."

Luc nodded. "That's good. Use it." He handed her

the cell phone and she took it, stuffing her own into the pocket of her new khaki shorts. "Keep the call as brief as you can without being obvious. And don't forget to let her know that you'll be out of touch. And don't give her any clues about where you are."

"Jeez, would you shut up? I'm starting to hyperventilate." Katie looked down at the phone, her finger hesitating over the buttons. "I don't think I've lied to her since I bought scalped tickets for a concert back when I was twenty. Even then she knew about it almost as soon as I got home."

"Just stay calm and you'll be fine."

"She's psychic or something."

"She's not psychic. If you keep your story straight, she won't have a clue."

"Shows what you know. Even Fiona can't get one by her, and that's saying something."

"Katie."

When she glanced at him, Luc's dark eyes were kind and patient. She knew he could tell she was stalling.

"You don't have a choice, sweetheart." His voice was gentle. "You have to convince her."

Katie took a deep breath because she felt faint. Especially after the unexpected endearment. "I know."

She dialed. It rang.

"Hello?"

"Hi, Mom." Just two simple words, but they made her want to cry. Without thinking about it, she moved away from Luc and walked into the kitchen, appreciating the fact that he didn't try to follow her. That he trusted her enough to give her some privacy.

"Katie! It's about time. Where are you?"

Katie smiled, glancing at the clock hanging on the wall. It was only nine in the morning, but her mom sounded like she'd been up for hours. She probably had been.

"What's going on?" her mother asked. "Why didn't you answer your phone at home or your cell phone? Why is the caller ID blocked? Is there a problem?"

"No, no. There's no problem." Katie tugged her wild curls out of her eyes and made herself focus. "Did you call me? My cell phone's dead, and I'm at work."

"At work? Why are you at work on a Sunday?"

"A lot of us are here." Katie breathed slowly. Keep it short, keep it sweet, keep it on target. Luc was right. The woman wasn't psychic. But she sure seemed like she was sometimes. "We were…we were told that our department is going on a corporate retreat."

"A corporate retreat?"

"Yeah. You know, one of those things where they take you out to the woods and teach you how to work together as a team? Pitch tents together. Bond. Like that."

"The woods, huh?"

"It kind of came up at the last minute. We'll be gone for a week, and we're not allowed to call anyone." Now that was a stroke of brilliance, she thought. That should buy them some time.

"Hmm. Sounds sudden."

"Oh, yeah. Nobody saw it coming. It was supposed to be a…a surprise." She grimaced. Wow, that was bad. She was going downhill fast.

Her mother was silent for a second. "When do you leave? I was hoping we could have brunch—"

"No! I mean, no, that's not possible." Katie rubbed her forehead with the heel of her free hand. "We're, uh, leaving a little later this morning."

"That was short notice." She was quiet. Katie's heart pounded. But eventually she only said, "Have fun."

"Thanks."

"Katie, please don't do anything stupid."

Katie wondered at the strange note in her mother's voice, but she didn't want to risk asking any questions. "I won't, don't worry. The bears are safe from me! Hah, hah!"

"Just remember that sometimes the consequences of your actions last longer than you ever thought they would."

Katie frowned. Her mother sounded sad. She might be a great many things, but generally speaking, sad wasn't one of them.

"Are you okay, Mom?"

"Oh, yeah. It's nothing. Just a very bad conversation with Barbara yesterday when we were shopping. She, um, well, she said that she'd seen your father…out."

Out, meaning, out with another woman. Her dad was a handsome man, and there was no trace of softness in him, even at fifty-seven. He seemed to be pure candy for women of a certain age. For most women, actually. In the past he'd let himself get slurped up a time or two.

"Bitch," Katie said, with feeling. There'd been no call for Barbara to bring that up with her mother.

"Exactly." Her mom paused. "She, uh, dated your father before he married me, you know. They were pretty hot and heavy for a while."

Katie blinked. "I didn't know that." And wasn't that just a little TMI. But it did explain Barbara's general bitchiness.

"I guess she's still jealous."

"Maybe," Katie murmured noncommittally. If Barbara knew what her father had put them through over the years, it might not have been as much of an issue.

"I'm sure the rumor isn't true." Her mother's cheerfulness sounded brittle.

"Hmm." Katie flashed back to a certain Christmas Eve a long time ago. Mom crying because she'd found out that Katie's father was having an affair with a woman they'd considered a friend. That he was with the other woman then, instead of with his family.

Katie and Melanie both just turned eighteen, listening at her parents' bedroom door while her mother wept and raged. The girls deciding to go out after him and force him to come home. The icy roads. Katie's desperate attempt to control the car when it went into a slide. The accident. Melanie's scream when her leg was trapped by crumpled metal. The blood. The fear. Her father's cover-up of where he'd been and all of the other kids seeming to buy it, although Katie knew they hadn't.

Afterwards, eventually, in spite of everything, her mother had forgiven him. Katie's own relationship with her father, already strained, had erupted into a full and bitter war. But somehow her mom had forgiven him, had knit something back together resembling a marriage.

Katie didn't know how her father felt about her

mother, but she knew without a doubt her mother loved him, deeply and desperately. He still seemed to take that love for granted, but at least he'd stopped running around after the accident. At least he'd kept it in his pants. Unless Barbara was telling the truth.

Just then the kitchen door opened. Luc stood on the threshold, watching her, his face sympathetic, but sober. He touched his wrist where he would have worn a watch to let her know that time was up.

"I have to go, Mom. I'm sorry. They're, um, calling me."

"Oh. Okay. Well, I guess I'll see you at the end of the week anyway. I hope everything goes all right on the retreat."

"Me too," Katie muttered. She paused. She knew Luc wanted her to end the call, but it occurred to her that this might be the last time she'd ever be able to talk to her mother. There was so much she wanted to say, so much she wanted to make her understand. She couldn't let her go, not yet. "Mom, I just want to tell you…" She choked.

"Tell me what, sweetie?"

Katie took a deep breath. "I love you."

"I love you too, Katie."

"Anything inside me that's good is because of you."

"There's plenty of good inside you, honey, and it's not because of me. Are you sure you're all right?"

Katie sniffed. "I'm fine. Don't worry." She cradled the phone against her shoulder, lifted her glasses and wiped her eyes on her sleeve.

"Well, okay." Her mother still sounded concerned. "Call me as soon as you get back?"

"I'll call you as soon as I can." Katie's voice was husky.

"Have a safe trip."

"Goodbye, Mommy."

Katie disconnected and walked over to Luc. She handed him the cell phone, and he took it without comment. She was blinking rapidly. She knew that if she didn't get out of there right away, she wasn't going to be able to hold herself together.

"I'd better get cleaned up," she said.

He nodded. She pushed past him and was gone before he had the chance to say a single word.

THE DREAM NET CASINO was huge, one of the biggest in Atlantic City, and Joey Silvano ran the place. So Frankie figured it was a measure of his father's affection that he'd been given an office the size of a postage stamp right next to the loading dock. Half the time he couldn't even hear himself think because of trucks idling outside. Poppa used the whole fucking penthouse and mostly he wasn't even there, but Frankie was shoved into a broom closet. Fucking old bastard.

Frankie sat behind his desk and toyed with a pencil, tapping it repeatedly. When somebody knocked on the door, he called out permission to enter. Arlo Kravitz walked into the room.

"You wanted to see me, boss?" Arlo asked. His face was placid, eager. He was a big man, far bigger than Frankie himself, with a muscular build turning to fat. A beer belly hung over the waistband of his brown trousers and there was no way the jacket would close. He'd been wearing the same suit on Friday.

Friday.

Frankie heard a pop and saw that he'd snapped the pencil in half. He threw it away with a quick gesture.

"Arlo," he said. "Thanks for coming. Sit."

"Sure, sure." Arlo sounded almost pathetically grateful. With some effort, he squeezed himself into one of the visitors' chairs. "Thanks for understanding, boss." Arlo leaned forward once he was settled. "You know, about the car."

Frankie swiveled back and forth in his chair. "You mean, the car you were driving?"

"Yeah, yeah. I wasn't sure—"

"The car you were driving when you got pushed into a quarry pit?"

Arlo looked concerned now. "Uh—"

"The car you were driving when you got me arrested?"

Arlo sat straighter, definitely on edge. "Boss—"

Frankie studied him. "I've never been arrested before, did you know that?"

"Um, yeah. Yeah, I knew that." Arlo definitely sounded nervous. Sweat beaded on his broad face.

"And the woman, the woman who was driving the other car? She's a secretary. Did you know that too?" Frankie kept his voice even, but his fingers tapped restlessly on the desk.

"Uh, no. I mean, yeah." Arlo was practically babbling now. "I think one of the guys told me after."

"Turns out she's not a Fed. Not a cop. Hasn't had any

kind of training, as far as I know. In fact, she's probably never been involved in a car chase in her life. But she pushed your car into a quarry pit."

Arlo was mute, eyes huge. He looked like he was finally grasping the seriousness of his situation.

"And I got arrested. And humiliated. She took me out with her purse. The cops, they laughed, did you know that? Laughed at me." He tamped down the anger bubbling just beneath the surface.

"I'm sorry, boss." The big man swallowed hard, his Adam's apple bobbing.

"I had to tell my father. Did you know that as well?" he continued as if Arlo hadn't spoken. That had been the worst part, really. Telling Poppa. Seeing the triumph in his eyes. The glee. Knowing that inside, the old bastard was laughing at him too.

"No. Boss, I'm sorry, I'm so sorry." Arlo struggled to get out of the chair, his breathing fast, the sweat running. "I'll fix it. I'll make it right. Whatever you need me to do, I'll do it. Just give me a chance to—"

"Too late," Frankie said, softly. He pulled a gun out of the desk drawer and fired.

Arlo jerked, gasped, his eyes going wide with shock and pain and fright. Blood blossomed on the white shirt, and he sank back in the chair. He twitched, the breath sighed out of him, and he went still.

Frankie sat, staring at the corpse that had once been Arlo, smelling the gun smoke and the blood and the urine because Arlo's bladder had let loose. Probably shouldn't have done it here because now there'd be a mess to clean up. But there were people to take care of that sort of thing, and he'd wanted to do it in his office. To show the other guys he still had power.

To show Poppa.

Frankie sat and stared at Arlo and thought about the woman, Katie McCabe. Thought about what he would do to her once he got a hold of her. So far the guys stationed at her apartment hadn't seen her, but he'd leave them there. She might go back.

Still, it seemed like either she or the Fed she was with had figured out he'd be watching her place. Only to be expected, really.

Good thing he had another angle. One they didn't know about.

One that would drown her.

FOURTEEN

"Luc?"

Katie's soft voice jolted Luc out of some rather morose thoughts. He looked up to see her standing in the doorway of the family room, watching him. He had no idea how long he'd been sitting there, but apparently there'd been enough time for her to take a shower because her hair was damp and relatively subdued. Her eyes were a little puffy and large behind her glasses, her skin so pale that the freckles stood out like tiny dots of brown sugar scattered across her nose and cheeks.

Fuck.

"Hi." She walked farther into the room, bent absently to pat Spot then moved over to him, standing so close that he could smell the clean, fresh scent of her.

"Hi," he said. "Any better?"

She nodded, absently. "What's going to happen now?"

"Now?" He shrugged, struggling to keep his face impassive. "You stay here for now."

"And later?"

He was quiet for a moment. "We'll do whatever comes next."

"I can't live like this."

"Yes, you can, because this way you will live."

"If you say so."

"I do."

She was quiet for a long time, her face turned away from him. "I can't talk to my family again, can I?"

"No." Luc forced himself to stay professional and unemotional. "Not only does it open us up to the possibility that calls could be traced and our location identified, but if Frankie finds out you've been talking to them, they'll be in even more danger."

Katie nodded. "Yeah. That's what I thought."

He watched her, feeling useless. "We'll work it out."

"If you say so," she repeated.

They were both silent for a long minute.

"Do you, ah, want some breakfast?" he asked, trying to change the subject and maybe introduce at least a hint of normality.

Katie shook her head. Her curls bobbed and weaved around her face, waking up as they dried. "No thanks. I'm really not very hungry."

He frowned. "You should—"

"I should take a walk." She looked at him with a caricature of her regular smile. "Alone."

It was ridiculous to be hurt by that.

"Stay close." It came out sounding like an order.

Her smile became more natural. "Yes, sir. Actually, I was just going to explore the Museum. I'd like to see some of the other rooms."

"Oh." He blinked. "Okay." He'd told Jane, his neighbor who watched Spot and also cleaned for him, not to bother with the parts of the house he didn't use. Since that was most of it, God only knew what Katie would find. "Take Spot with you."

Katie had turned to go, but at that she paused and looked at him. "Why?"

"So you can find your way back, of course." He smiled. "It's your turn to cook."

She laughed, which was a relief. "It seems like it's always my turn to cook. If I didn't know better, I'd say this whole thing was just a ploy to get some free domestic help."

"Never." He thought he sounded very innocent.

She shook her head, called for Spot and left the room.

As she'd kind of expected, Katie got lost almost as soon as she walked out of the kitchen, but it didn't bother her too much. First of all, she was positive that Spot could find her way back for food. And second, it was nice to get lost in the depths of the Museum, to think about something other than her own situation for a change.

Luc's personal castle really was awe-inspiring. It seemed to go on forever—room after room filled with graceful designs cut in stone and stained-glass windows, tiles and marble, antiques and tapestries. There was even a full suit of armor standing in what appeared to be an old-fashioned parlor. Wow.

Why did he keep this all closed up? Katie idly trailed her fingers over a particularly lovely cherry sideboard sitting in a massive, dusty dining room. These pieces, these rooms, should have been on display, but apparently he didn't even know they existed. His home was obviously important to him, but it looked like he only lived in one small part of it. Why was it in trust? Why had his great aunt Isobel thought he had bad blood? Obviously way more was going on here than she understood.

It occurred to her that it was a little too quiet. She looked around for Spot, but the dog had disappeared. She must have gotten bored and wandered off while Katie had been deep in her own thoughts. Great. Some guide dog.

Katie tried to retrace her steps back to the kitchen, but as usual she must have zigged when she should have zagged, because she found herself standing in a short, unfamiliar hallway ending at a pair of large, ornately carved oak doors.

Intrigued, she went to the doors and, with a little effort, pushed them open. When she peeked inside, her jaw dropped.

A ballroom. It obviously hadn't been used for a while because the trapped air was stale, but it was a real, live ballroom. She caught her breath and walked in, amazed and kind of charmed.

The outer wall of the room consisted of a series of windows and tall French doors opening onto a secluded, overgrown courtyard. The other three walls were floor to ceiling mirrors. Four huge crystal chandeliers hung from the ceiling, and the sunlight streaming in through the dust-covered windows bounced off the mirrors and the glass and the gleaming marble floor and refracted around until the whole space glittered like a jewel.

Katie clasped her hands in front of her and stopped in the middle of the room, forgetting she was lost, forgetting she was hunted, forgetting everything but the beautiful, shining place.

"There you are." Luc's deep voice interrupted her daydreams and she spun around. He limped into the room on his crutches with Spot padding softly at his side. "I got worried when Spot came back without you, so I thought we'd better come to the rescue."

"Good idea," she admitted, then smiled. "I'm not exactly sure how I would have gotten back."

He returned her smile and the brackets appeared briefly around his mouth, then he looked at the mirrors and the glass. "How'd you get here anyway?"

"I have absolutely no idea, but I sure was lucky." Katie's enthusiasm bubbled over. "Isn't it wonderful?"

"Uh, if you say so. I haven't been in this room for a while. I kind of forgot it was here." He shrugged one shoulder in a casual male sort of way. "Doesn't smell too bad."

Katie made an exasperated noise. "Way to ruin the mood, Vasco."

"Don't you think it's just a little bit over the top? Like a lot of the rest of the place."

"I think it's magical." Katie crossed her arms over her chest and glared at him.

"Magical?" He quirked his eyebrows at her. "That's strong, isn't it?"

"No." Katie shook her head firmly. "Magical."

"Huh. Well, to each their own." Luc gazed into the mirrors. A strange, remote expression crossed his face. "They say that my great aunt Isobel held huge parties in this room," he said. "All of the Broadway actors came down from New York and looked very decorative."

"That's just the way I pictured it." Katie laughed. "The ladies would have worn beautiful ball gowns, and the men would all be in tuxedos—"

Luc shot her a quick grin. "Isobel was hanging around in the seventies and eighties, so it was mostly blue jeans and cocaine. I think you have the wrong century."

"Hey, buddy, this is my fantasy. I'll picture it however I like." She glanced at him from under her eyelashes. "Were you here?" She tried to imagine a little Luc in a tiny tuxedo, standing and watching the people dance.

A shadow flickered in Luc's eyes. For a second she thought he might not even answer her. Spot whined.

"No," he said finally. "No, I wasn't here."

Katie was dying to ask why not, but a closer look at his face made her decide to change the subject instead.

"Well, I don't care what you say, I still think this would be the perfect place for a really classy party. The kind where they hire a string quartet instead of a bar band."

"Have you ever been to one of those things? They're as boring as hell."

Katie stilled. She looked around the room again, but now the ghosts of beautiful men and women did not charm.

"Hey, you okay?"

She shook her head. "Sorry. I was just thinking. Actually I have been to a party like that. Once. A couple of years ago."

"What happened?" He was much closer, moving quietly even on the crutches.

"Nothing."

"I don't think so." Before she knew what was happening, his large, warm hand touched her jaw, then slid around to the nape of her neck. He gently raised her chin until she was looking at him, then rubbed the rough, calloused pad of his thumb over her bottom lip, softly, like a kiss. He had such beautiful eyes, she thought, staring into them, her mind dazed. They were lighter in the direct sunlight, almost amber, and surrounded by long, sooty lashes.

"Tell me," he murmured, his hand moving to cup her cheek. She shook her head again. She didn't want to, but found herself talking anyway.

"My foster sister, Melanie, convinced me to go. She got me the invitation. A friend of hers was taking her, and she wanted me to come along. I was so excited that I couldn't sleep. I'd never been to a real formal ball before. It took us weeks to find the right dresses. The right shoes. We spent a lot of money."

"Did you go alone?" He had tensed. She couldn't figure out why he seemed to be getting upset over something he would probably find inconsequential.

"No. Well, I wasn't supposed to. Melanie set me up on a blind date with her brother. Foster brother," Katie amended and laughed a little. "I keep forgetting he isn't her real brother. They met at the horrible foster home where she lived before she came to us. Anyway, she thought I would like Bruce, and she'd been trying to get him to meet me." She looked away, flustered by the intensity she saw in Luc's dark, dark eyes. "So I said I'd go."

She remembered how long it had taken Melanie to talk her into it. None of her brothers had been available—or willing—to act as an escort, and Mel had insisted that it should be a real date anyway. Then Bruce had actually agreed to go with her. It had all seemed too good to be true. She'd let herself get swept up in Melanie's enthusiasm. Stories about Bruce had fascinated her for years. She could admit now that she'd been infatuated with him. Or maybe with the idea of him. She remembered her giddy excitement, her dreams of what might start between them. Like a fairy tale.

Katie turned away from Luc and wrapped her arms around her chest, almost defensively. She really didn't know why she was telling him all of this. He couldn't possibly be interested. Maybe she was just talking because he seemed to be listening.

"I walked into that party in my new dress and my new shoes, and thought I was some pretty hot stuff. I felt like Cinderella that night," she murmured. "Until the clock struck twelve."

"He stood you up?" Luc's normally smooth voice was deep and gravelly. Almost angry. Katie glanced at him, then away. She blushed as she remembered how humiliated she'd been when she'd finally realized Bruce wasn't going to show.

"Yes. Yes, he did. Oh, he called Mel the next day and made some poor excuse, but we both knew he was lying." She shrugged. "Maybe Mel pressured him too much, and he just said he'd do it in the first place out of pity."

"Maybe he was an idiot."

"Maybe." Katie looked at the endless reflections in the mirrors. "Sometimes you just don't know what's going to happen. Bruce didn't show up, but Tom was there."

"Tom?"

"My ex-fiancé."

He was quiet for another long minute. "You met him at that party?"

"I was pretty upset." Understatement. "Tom came over and asked if I was all right. He seemed so nice and was so handsome that I thought I'd fallen in love with him at first sight. He was real, you see, not just some faceless guy. He asked me out on a date. We were together for two and a half years." She laughed bitterly. "God."

Luc shifted. "And did you?"

"Did I what?"

"Fall in love at first sight?"

"No." Katie didn't know why there were tears in her eyes, but as soon as she blinked them away, more replaced them. "No. It was just an illusion. Deep down I guess I always knew that, but I didn't want to admit it until way, way too late."

"The guy who stood you up was an asshole," Luc muttered.

"Oh, it wasn't his fault that I got mixed up with Tom," she whispered. "It was mine. I'm the one who wanted the dream. I'm the one who built it. Bruce had a lucky

escape because if he'd been there I probably would have
built the dream on him instead of Tom. Stupid."

She studied the marble-tiled floor and didn't even
hear him move until his old running shoes came into
her line of vision. A gentle hand raised her chin again,
turning her face up to his.

"Melanie's brother was stupid, Katie, not you," he
said quietly.

She stared, trying to understand him. Especially since
he "sure as hell didn't want to touch her again."

"He should have shown up, Katie," Luc murmured.
"He would have built a dream on you too."

It was difficult to breathe. "I don't think—"

The words died in her throat when Luc touched her
hair softly, his fingers working into the curls at the side
of her face. His breath was warm on her skin, and she
saw that his eyes were hooded and filled with something
she couldn't name. His lips touched first one cheek,
then the other. Tasting. He lingered on the damp trail
of her tears, then his mouth covered hers. He kissed her
sweetly, deeply, passionately. Her glasses fogged up.

When he pulled away slightly, his low laugh was
just a whisper of sound. "Holy God, what the hell am
I doing?"

"I don't know." She sounded breathless, as if she'd
just run a marathon. But how could she help it when
he'd just stolen all of the air in the room? "What the
hell are you doing?"

His mouth, his wicked, wicked mouth, quirked. "If
you have to ask, I must not be doing it right."

"But you sure as hell don't want to touch me again,"

she reminded him. "It's unprofessional. David called you on the carpet for it. I'm under your protection, and you take that seriously."

He was quiet.

"And I don't want you to touch me again either," she continued, perhaps a little too quickly. "It didn't mean anything and, even though it turns out that Liza isn't an issue, it's still a big mistake."

Through the lingering patches of fog on her lenses she saw him watching her. Then, a little awkwardly because he was still balanced on the crutches, he reached up and removed her glasses. Katie's breath caught. She felt exposed, almost naked. But she didn't move away.

"You're right," he whispered, his eyes staring straight into hers. "This is completely unprofessional and a big mistake."

And then he bent his head and kissed her. This time his kiss held a kind of desperation, almost anger. His lips ate at hers, his tongue filled her mouth, and all she could do was hold on to his broad shoulders and try to anchor herself. It didn't work.

Spot barked. The sound jerked them both back to reality.

"I really am going to kill that dog," Luc muttered against her mouth. He was so close that Katie could see him without her glasses, his face soft and muted like a painting.

Spot barked again. Sighing, Luc looked down at the Newfoundland, then over Katie's head toward the outer doors. Whatever he saw there seemed to annoy him because his full mouth tensed.

"We have company." His voice was clipped as he re-leased her, the tone completely unlike the velvety rich deepness it had held just a moment ago. But he wiped the lenses of her glasses on the bottom of his T-shirt, and his hands were gentle when he slid them back on her face, hooking the sidepieces carefully over her ears. The world came into focus, and she was both more hidden and more vulnerable.

Luc gazed at her for a second longer, then moved away. "I guess I'd better go let him in."

Completely baffled, Katie turned.

She saw a familiar figure outside, lounging against the stone wall that surrounded the courtyard. Luc went to the French doors and punched some buttons on a computer keypad hanging next to them before opening one.

"David," he said. "I thought you knew the security code."

David Allen straightened and walked into the ballroom. His mouth was compressed and his eyes held an ominous sparkle.

"Hello, Lucas. I didn't want to interrupt."

Luc's face tightened. "It wasn't what it looked like," he said.

David bent down to pet Spot, who had run to greet him. "Then what was it?" he asked with exaggerated politeness.

Luc glanced at Katie, and she could have sworn she saw a flush darkening his cheekbones under his tan skin.

"Hello, Mr. Allen," Katie said, and felt a blush heat up her own face.

He turned to her and smiled, but it didn't quite reach

his eyes. Then he took her hand and enclosed it in both of his, smiling more fully. "Call me David. I don't think we need to stand on formality, do you?"

Her blush intensified for some reason. "David."

"What the hell were you doing out there?" Luc demanded, sounding harsh and irritable.

David dropped her hand and turned to face him again. His smile took on a sharp edge. "I was checking the perimeter to see if I spotted anything unusual."

"And did you find anything?"

"Not what I expected."

The two men faced each other. Katie couldn't read their expressions, but she definitely heard the warning bells. It was obvious that David was furious, and it was equally obvious that Luc was his target. Oh, for sweet Christ's sake.

"Ahem." She cleared her throat and brought their attention back to her. Both pairs of dark eyes stared at her with such intensity that she lost her train of thought briefly.

"What?" Luc snapped, the gentle lover long gone.

"You're angry," she said to David. Might as well get it out in the open.

"I am?" His voice was smooth, like butter.

"Yes, you are. You're angry at Luc because you saw him kissing me."

"Really." David's voice became, if anything, even more silky.

"Katie." Luc glared at her, but she ignored him.

"I'm going to tell you something, David. There were two of us here in this ballroom. I have a pretty good idea how to say no if I want to. I've kicked one guy in the balls and sent him to the hospital, and I'm not afraid to do it again."

Luc winced. "Katie—"

"So, I'm telling you not to worry about what happened," she said. "It was between me and Luc and is absolutely none of your business."

David remained silent for a long time, simply looking at her, his face unreadable. "It was unacceptable behavior," he said finally.

"You don't know what was going on, and you don't know what kind of behavior it was. I'm asking you to drop it. I think you owe me that much."

David considered her. "If that's what you want."

"Yes, that's what I want." She nodded her head, let out a breath and fisted her hands on her hips. "Now, I'd appreciate it if one of you fine gentlemen would show me the way back to the kitchen. I need some coffee."

Actually, what she really wanted was a slug from the bottle of whiskey she'd found in a cabinet last night when she'd been making dinner, but coffee would have to do.

Luc turned without responding and limped to the main ballroom door, Spot dashing ahead. David gestured for Katie to precede him and then fell into step beside her once they were out in the hallway. Katie stifled a small sigh.

Yeah, she thought, stick with the caffeine. She knew better than most people that sometimes what you really wanted just wasn't a good idea.

FIFTEEN

BACK IN THE kitchen, Luc and David settled down at the table while Spot sprawled underneath it like a huge black rug. Katie, willing for the moment to assume the domestic role she'd apparently been assigned, went to the counter and dug out the coffee maker and the beans, grinding and brewing and getting out mugs and spoons and milk. Anything to keep busy. Anything to stop thinking about the way Luc had touched her, kissed her. Again. And the way David had surprised them. Again.

The two men were talking quietly, mostly about business. She could tell they were both trying to ease the tension still swirling between them. They acted as if they were brothers instead of co-workers, and she knew without asking that David's disapproval hurt Luc. Which probably meant Luc really wouldn't kiss her again.

Good. That was good.

Damn it.

Eventually coffee was served and there was nothing to do but either join the men at the table or leave. Looking into David's intelligent, knowing brown eyes was hard, and a part of her wanted to make her escape and exit, stage right. But there was also the chance she might learn more about the situation in which she found herself. That possibility proved irresistible.

Katie sat next to Luc, tried to ignore the warmth of his body so close, the scent of his skin. She found herself watching him while he drank coffee, watching his throat move when he swallowed.

She forced herself to look away. God. She really had to pull it together.

The men were talking about a big case David's squad had wrapped up a few days ago when Luc had still been working on the Silvano estate.

"I just wish we hadn't been distracted by the question of whether or not Justin Némes was corrupt," David said. "When the evidence he'd compiled was called into question, it delayed everything by a good nine months."

"At least we know now that he was set up." Luc's eyes were flat and hard.

"But you wondered for a while, didn't you?"

"That was because of Liza." Luc paused and drank his coffee. "I was a little screwed up."

"I believe it. I think she's still in contact with him."

Luc sighed. "Lord."

"Who are you talking about?" Katie asked, curious.

Luc shrugged, a lazy rolling of his wide shoulders.

"Just a guy we both know. A former FBI agent. It looked like he was selling drugs when he was undercover, which threw off the whole investigation. He resigned, but the charges turned out to be bogus."

"Luc blames himself that things went as far as they did," David added. "The rumors came out at the same time he realized Némes was having an affair with Liza. Kind of got him twisted up."

Katie studied Luc. "Liza? Your ex-fiancée?"

"She wasn't an ex at the time," Luc muttered.

Katie turned to David. "Didn't Luc tell me that Liza is your administrative assistant?"

David's smile was more natural now. "I know it sounds like Peyton Place, but the woman sure can organize an office. I've thought about getting her transferred, but she's the best admin I've ever had. I just keep putting it off."

"Well, that must be awkward," Katie mused.

"We pretty much pretend we never knew each other. I stay out of her way as much as I can." Luc sounded a little desperate to change the subject. "David, Katie's mother called this morning."

David sobered immediately. "Damn." He looked at Katie, his expression all sympathetic understanding. "Did you talk to her?"

Katie's throat was very tight. She nodded.

"She had to," Luc said. "She used the secure phone." He told David about the corporate retreat story. "It's actually a pretty good cover," he said, "but we don't know if Mrs. McCabe bought it. God knows your mother wouldn't have."

David considered that for a moment. "I know someone at the company where you work," he told Katie. "I'll see what I can do to back you up if she calls there to check."

Katie blinked. "You know someone where I work?"

"Sometimes I think David knows people everywhere," Luc said.

David only shrugged. "It's part of my charm." He smiled at Katie and that charm was on full display. It was dazzling. Then he sobered. "You can't talk to her again."

She swallowed hard. "I know."

David nodded. He reached over and covered her hand with his own, then straightened away from her. They all sat silently around the big wooden table while Spot snored underneath.

"What did you do with the Corvette?" Luc asked after a few minutes.

"I had it towed, but I've let everyone think you're still on assignment. The less people who know what you're up to, the better."

"Good."

"The Nova's running okay, right?"

"Right. Hey, I forgot to tell you that it has a name." Luc smiled.

Katie saw his eyes twinkling and groaned.

"What, the car? It does?" David looked at Katie, speculative.

"Kato."

"You're kidding," David laughed. "The Green Hornet?"

Katie felt herself blush. Jeez, did everyone know the comic? It was darned embarrassing.

"That reminds me of someone." David drummed his fingers on the table and then snapped them suddenly. "I know. Your sister, Melanie."

Katie stared at David uncomprehendingly. For a moment his words did not penetrate, didn't make any sense. As if he was speaking a foreign language.

Melanie. Luc's sister, Melanie. It had to be a coincidence. Had to be.

But Luc paled, the amusement draining from his face. He glanced at her quickly. Guiltily.

"Shut up, David," he said.

David ignored him, obviously not aware of the impact of what he was saying. "You know how she always names everything after comic books? What does she call you? Dick? No, that's not it."

Katie straightened, hugging her arms across her chest without even realizing what she was doing. She went hot, then cold, then hot again.

"Bruce?" she whispered.

"Yeah, yeah. That's it. Bruce Wayne. Batman." David chuckled. "Never saw it myself."

"Shut up, David," Luc snarled.

The other man finally seemed to realize something major was going on. His smile faded, and he looked between the two of them. "What?"

Katie stood abruptly, knocking over her chair. Spot sat up and barked.

Luc. It had been Luc. How could she not have realized it? He'd known all along that Melanie called her Annie. He loved comic books, and Melanie had told her that was how "Bruce" had taught her to read. She saw the truth hiding in his carefully expressionless face.

It fit. It all fit.

"It was you." She had to push the words past the sudden lump in her throat.

"Katie—"

"You're Melanie's foster brother."

"Katie, you've got to believe—"

But Katie wasn't listening. He'd known. Oh, God, he'd known. The whole time she'd been talking to him in the ballroom, he'd known. He'd known who she was and who he was and what had happened and how he'd rejected her. And he'd just let her talk…he'd kissed her… had he laughed at her too? Had it made him think he was powerful to know how he'd hurt her? To know that he could?

She turned and practically ran for the door. She couldn't stand to be there. She couldn't stand to be with him. She had to be alone.

"Katie! Katie, wait!" Luc followed her, moving quicker than she would have thought possible without the crutches, but she was still able to outrun him. Then she took a wrong turn and got trapped in an alcove.

Sobbing, she tried to make a break for it, but Luc caught up with her and grabbed her arm, holding her.

"Katie, please listen."

"Was I an amusement? Did you find me to be terribly funny? Have you known all along?"

He held her still when she tried to twist away. She couldn't see his face because she was crying.

"I didn't know what to say," he said, talking fast. "How could I tell you?"

"By opening your mouth and talking. You knew, and you didn't say anything."

"I knew that Melanie went to live with a family named McCabe, but I didn't recognize you right away. I was certain on Friday night when you mentioned your foster sister but I didn't want to load that on you on top of everything else."

All of the blood left Katie's body and then flooded back in a rush of embarrassment so intense it was physically painful. "Friday," she said.

"I had no idea that what I did three years ago affected you so much. I swear it." He was talking even more quickly, as if he was trying to convince her. As if he thought she'd ever believe him again. "I had a...good reason not to show up at that party, but I didn't know how much it hurt you."

"You've known the whole time," she whispered. "And you kissed me anyway. What do you say about that, Luc? Or should I call you Bruce?"

"Luc. It's Luc, goddamn it. And I have nothing to say about that. I kissed you because I wanted to."

"Asshole," she spat.

He hauled her into his arms and kissed her again, but not gently this time. For one brief, helpless moment she responded. She couldn't not respond. Then she started struggling and when he let her go, she slapped him across his scarred cheek. Hard.

"Never do that again."

Luc dropped her arm and backed up. As soon as his hold loosened, she bolted for the stairs, running as if her life depended on it.

Maybe it did.

SIXTEEN

LUC STOOD, rubbing his cheek, watching Katie run away from him. His face still stung from her slap, his gut was hollowed out and empty.

Why hadn't he just told her who he was in the beginning?

Telling her on Friday would have been the right thing. But it hadn't occurred to him to do it. Hadn't even crossed his mind. He'd treated the whole situation like some sort of an undercover assignment. Protected his identity. Kept his secrets.

Even when she'd told him about the consequences of that fucking party three years ago, he still hadn't thought to tell her the truth. Instead he'd kissed her when he should have been completely open and honest.

Except he hadn't been completely open and honest since he'd been seven years old.

It was inevitable that the whole mess would come out sometime, but it had happened much sooner than he'd hoped. He'd just wanted to tease her when he'd brought up the damn car, wanted to see those blue eyes snap at him. He hadn't thought about the fact that David knew Melanie and was well aware of her penchant for the comics. He should have figured there was a possibility the other man would mention it.

He turned and went back to the kitchen, even though facing David was the last thing he wanted to do.

"Luc? What the hell's going on?" David demanded. He was standing, holding Spot's collar to restrain her. Obviously they'd both been ready to rush to Katie's rescue.

Luc didn't answer. Instead he carefully righted the chair Katie had toppled and sat down in it. He took a deep breath, then two.

David watched him for a bit, then let Spot go. The dog snuffled Luc before racing out of the room. Probably going to check on Katie.

"Luc." David sat next to him, his voice both gentle and hard. "Tell me what's going on. What just happened here?"

"She's Annie, David," Luc said. "She's Annie."

They stared at each other. Luc saw realization dawn in David's eyes, the slackness of surprise in his face. David knew about Annie. He didn't know about the photograph. He didn't know about the party three years ago. But he knew enough.

"Fuck," David said quietly. There was a strange note in his voice, one Luc could not quite interpret. "Melanie's foster sister?"

"Yes."

"And she didn't know who you are?"

"No."

"And you had figured out who she was?"

"Yes. On Friday."

David stared at him. "And you hadn't told her?"

"No."

David sighed. He leaned his head against the tall back of the chair. "Jesus, you're an asshole, Vasco. Why the hell didn't you tell her?"

Luc traced the wood grain of the tabletop with his fingertip. "I don't know."

"I wouldn't have said anything if I'd realized. I'm sorry, man."

"Not your fault."

David looked directly at him again, his dark face drawn and weary. "There's more. I didn't want to say anything in front of her, but they aren't budging on witness protection."

Luc tensed. "Why the hell not?"

"She's running, not testifying. You know as well as I do that she doesn't qualify for the program."

"Fuck." Luc closed his eyes. "Just fuck."

"I'm still looking into it."

There had to be another option. Had to be.

"So, okay," Luc said slowly. "If you can't get her into witness protection, we'll make her disappear ourselves."

"I don't think I'll be able to use Bureau funds to relocate her," David cautioned. "First of all, I don't have any Bureau funds. But even if I did, we can't risk tipping someone off."

Better and better.

"Here's an idea. How about I just fucking find Frankie Silvano and kill him?"

"Luc." David pointed a finger at him in warning. "You can't go vigilante."

Luc clenched a fist on the table and just barely resisted the urge to pound on it. "Yeah? Who says?"

"I do. Believe me, you don't even want to know what it would cost you."

Everything. It would cost him everything. Everything he'd struggled to build since he'd been seventeen and David, then a young policeman, had pulled him off the streets and, for whatever reason, decided to save his life.

He tried to think. "I'll have some money soon. We can use that." Fortunately, he'd already put in a request for the lawyers to sell a few things so he could make some much-needed repairs to the Museum.

Not for the first time, Luc fought back a wave of anger toward his great aunt Isobel. The old bitch had put so many restrictions on this place to keep him from "squandering" the family heritage he was lucky he could flush the toilet without calling someone first. The only reason she'd left him the Museum at all was because, bastard or no, son of an Anglo waitress or no, he was the last in his father's proud Basque bloodline. And since his father had died flying for the military before Luc had even been born, Isobel had apparently decided she didn't have a choice.

Oh, the relational bonds hadn't been strong enough for her to rescue him when he'd been placed in foster care after his mother died, or to make her want to help them financially before that, but keeping the Museum in the Vasco family had been important enough to force her to hold her nose and sign the papers. At least that's what the lawyers had told him. More tactfully, of course.

"Weren't you going to use that money to revamp the alarm system?" David asked. "And doesn't the Museum need a new roof?"

"It'll be fine." The Museum was the least of his worries at the moment. The money he'd be getting from the sale of those damn antiques wouldn't be enough to keep Katie hidden forever, but it was a start.

David smoothed his palms on the table. He stared down at his hands. "I have some savings we can use," he said.

"No." Luc was definite on that point. "This is my responsibility, and you are way too close to twenty years to be dicking around with your savings. You know you're looking to retire."

"That's my problem. Don't be an ass."

"You're doing enough. More than enough."

David's jaw tightened, but he seemed to sense arguing was pointless. They sat silently.

When David finally spoke again, his voice devoid of all emotion. "I want you to know that I trust you," he said.

Luc straightened, sensing where the conversation was heading. He felt himself closing up, shutting down.

"I trust you, but knowing who she is…" David shook his head. "It's not good. You're too connected."

Luc looked David straight in the eye. Looked at this man who, in a very real way, had given him his life.

"She's staying, David."

"Luc—"

"She's staying because there's no place else for her to go. She's staying here with me until we have a better alternative for her. She's staying so I can keep her safe. And if you can't trust me in this, if you don't really believe I'm going to look out for her to the best of my ability no matter what personal shit is going down, then you're going to have to accept my resignation right now."

"I don't want—"

"Right now, David. What's it going to be? Deal or no deal?"

David was silent for one long moment. "Deal." He sighed deeply. "Deal, goddamn it. She stays."

Luc nodded and stood. "Good."

KATIE PULLED her knees up closer to her chin and wrapped her arms around her legs as she sat curled in the huge armchair in Luc's bedroom. She stared out the bay window, but the scenery was a blur even with her glasses on.

She'd cried for a while after her confrontation with Luc. She didn't think she'd cried as much in thirty-three years as she had in the last three days. It was hard having your world reshaped while you were still in it.

Luc was Bruce. Bruce was Luc. She was really going to have to have a chat with Melanie the next time she saw her about that habit of renaming everyone she met. If she ever saw Melanie again.

Katie sat and stared out the window. She thought about everything Melanie had told her about her brother. Foster brother.

Bruce had already been at the foster home when Melanie had been placed there. Mr. Winston and his wife were cruel and abusive, but they'd fooled the overworked social workers for years. Melanie had been ten when she'd gone to live with them after her grandmother died in a drug-related shooting. Her mother had been a junkie and a prostitute who'd OD'd a few years before. She'd never known her father, so she'd ended up in the system. Bruce had been thirteen, already in foster care for six years. According to Mel, he'd lived in at least four other homes before that one.

Katie closed her eyes. Poor little boy.

Melanie had said that Winston and his wife liked to beat Bruce with a leather strap or a belt. They liked to hit her, too, but Bruce had intentionally put himself in front of her and taken most of her beatings. Katie was pretty sure he hadn't known about the sexual abuse, at least not right away.

Melanie never talked to Katie about what the Winstons did to her. The only reason Katie knew anything at all was because a month or two after they'd met in the cafeteria, she'd come across Mel hiding in the woods on the edge of the school property. The girl had been bruised and crying, and Katie had managed to drag some of the story out of her. She'd known then that she had to try to save her. She hadn't known about Melanie's brother; he would have been sixteen at that point and in a different school. By the time Mel finally trusted her enough to tell her about him, he'd been gone.

Mr. Winston had turned up dead after a while. A mugging in a back alley in Allentown. Katie had always wondered if that was the whole truth.

Luc was Bruce. Bruce Wayne. Batman. The Dark Knight. Katie smiled a little as she opened her eyes and looked out the window again. Well, it certainly fit. For a while there, when she'd been younger, she'd even dreamed that he might be her knight someday.

And what would he think if he ever found out she was the one responsible for the car accident where Melanie had been so badly injured?

Katie rested her head against the back of the chair. She was so tired. Now she not only had to deal with someone trying to kill her, and the prospect of never seeing her family again, she also had to face the past. It just didn't seem fair.

Her stomach growled loudly, startling her out of her thoughts. She glanced at a clock and realized just how much time had passed since she'd run away from Luc downstairs. And darn, she was hungry.

Uncurling her stiff body, Katie got up and stretched out her back, then paced restlessly around the room. The problem was, right now all she wanted to do was be a coward and stay in here forever. Which was stupid, of course. She couldn't avoid seeing Luc.

Katie sighed, stopped pacing and ran her hands through her tangled hair. The simple fact was that she didn't have a choice. She needed Luc. So, regardless of any minor—or major—humiliation she might currently be experiencing, her options were limited. She was once again going to have to just suck up and deal. Besides, if she could handle the whole "sure as hell never want to touch her again" comment, she could handle this.

She paused. On second thought, if Luc really never wanted to touch her again, he wasn't doing too good a job of it. That was encouraging. Maybe. Except now she'd spilled her guts to him about Bruce.

And he was Bruce.

She crossed her arms over her chest and stared

blindly out one of the two tall, narrow windows flanking either side of the huge bed's headboard.

Luc was still Luc. The fact that he was also Bruce didn't change him. He'd always known who she was. The real problem was that now she knew. He'd changed because now she knew him too. And he knew that she knew. And she knew that he knew. And he knew that she knew that he knew.

"Aargh." Katie smacked her own forehead hard with the heel of her hand, then rubbed it because it hurt. He was going to make her crazy. She was going to make herself crazy. If she wasn't careful, she was going to turn into the same paranoid mess she'd been with Tom and that was so not going to happen.

Abruptly, she turned on her heel and marched across the room. It just wasn't going to happen. She wouldn't let it. She was hungry, and she was going to go get something to eat. If she happened to run into Luc, well, so be it.

At the door, she took a deep, fortifying breath, opened it and stepped into the hallway where Spot immediately jumped to greet her.

"Hiya, girl," Katie murmured, rubbing the dog's large, soft head. "I'm okay. I'm all right. And I'm finished with hiding in that room. I think."

Spot whined sympathetically.

"Okay." Katie straightened and squared her shoulders. "Let's go."

Except for the click of Spot's nails against hardwood floors, the old house was quiet as they made their way downstairs, which was both comforting and unnerving.

For a few minutes, Katie thought both of the men had gone somewhere. Then she pushed open the door to the family room, intending to walk through to the kitchen, and saw Luc. He was alone, sitting on the sofa, hands clasped between his knees, body hunched forward as he stared at the carpet.

She knew that she should just turn around and walk away, but she wasn't quite prepared for what the sight of him did to her. His broad shoulders stretched his white T-shirt and his strong torso gleamed golden through the thin material. His dark hair fell over his face—he really needed to get it cut—and she could see the five o'clock shadow already darkening his chin. As she stared at him, a tremor of awareness prickled through her.

He lied to you, one part of her mind screamed. He hurt you.

He's Luc, another part answered. He's Bruce.

You can't forgive him, the first part ranted. He's a man, and all men do is hurt you.

He didn't mean to hurt me, the second part responded. And shut up.

She stood there a little too long arguing with herself because Spot walked past her and into the room.

Luc looked up, saw Katie and did a classic double-take. Any other time it would have been funny.

"Katie." He jumped to his feet, winced and shifted his weight.

"Um, hi. Sorry to interrupt." She stayed near the door.

"You're not interrupting."

"Oh. Good." She risked a glance at him to find that

he was staring at her, his eyes intense. His face looked drawn beneath the five o'clock shadow.

"How are you, uh, doing?" he asked.

"Okay." This scene was so awkward it was almost painful. She tried to relax, and looked around the room, at the chairs, the ceiling, the fireplace, anywhere but at him. "Where's David?"

"He's probably sleeping." Luc took one step closer, then another. She held her ground, but it was hard. "You learn to sleep when you can."

"Oh."

They stood for a few more minutes in uncomfortable silence.

Why? The question caught her unaware, and so did the pain. She had to bite her lip and look away so she couldn't ask him, shout it at him. Why hadn't he wanted to meet her three years ago? Why hadn't he gone to the party when he'd said he would? Why had he stood her up? Why hadn't she been worth the effort and common courtesy of a phone call?

"So, uh, do you hear from Melanie often?" she asked, just to say something.

He sighed. Katie chanced another glance in his direction. He was running a hand through his hair. The action bunched his biceps, showing off the tattoo wrapped around his arm and pulling his shirt tight against the muscles of his upper body. She hastily turned to stare at a beautiful crimson glass bowl sitting on a nearby table.

"Pretty often," Luc said finally. "She emails or calls me a couple of times a week when I'm not on an assignment."

"She'd love this place." Katie gestured vaguely around the room.

"Yeah, she does."

"She does?" Katie forgot herself in her surprise and looked at him again. Melanie had never mentioned visiting her foster brother. "She's seen it?"

"Well, sure." He seemed confused. "Why wouldn't she have?"

"She just never said anything, that's all."

Melanie had gone to see Luc and hadn't told her. Not that she had to tell her everything, but Katie had thought they were confidants. Now she realized that Mel had kept an extremely important part of her life secret. What else was she hiding?

Luc took another step in her direction. She couldn't seem to tear her gaze away from his eyes. "Mel never talked about me at all?"

"Well, uh, yes. She mentioned you. Of course she mentioned you." Abandoning her post at the door, Katie started moving through the room with nervous energy, trailing her fingers over the furniture and the items arranged on them. She paused at the fireplace to admire a painting hanging over the mantle.

"Other than when she was trying to talk you into… that party?"

Katie glanced at him, then away. He was following her as she walked around the room. Subtly stalking her. Like a big cat with a limp.

"Every so often." She touched the colorful tiles of the fireplace surround. They might have been Persian.

"Um, what about me?" She shouldn't ask, but she was dying to know. "Did she ever talk about me?"

"Sometimes." His voice was soft. "Not enough."

Her stomach jerked. She turned to face him. "Luc—"

"Katie, I'm sorry I didn't tell you."

"I'm sorry I slapped you."

"I deserved it."

"No—"

"I wouldn't have brought up the name of the damn car if I'd remembered that David knew about Melanie and the comics. Not because I was trying to hide something. I just would rather have told you in a different way."

"How did he know about Melanie anyway?" Katie asked, curious.

"David's always known her," Luc said simply.

David knew about Melanie. Melanie knew about David. Katie guessed it made sense, but it left her a little disoriented. It seemed like Melanie had been living a second life. One she'd never talked about. Katie had thought she knew her foster sister. Now it seemed like she didn't know her at all.

"Luc—"

"What's going on?" David strolled into the room and interrupted them.

"I thought you were asleep," Luc muttered.

"Always vigilant." The other man grinned, quick, bright and full. Katie blinked, a little stunned by the impact. "Katie woke me up when she crept down the hall."

"You were that close?" she asked.

"One of us should be on the same floor with you, don't you think?"

"I guess." Katie looked between the two men, aware of undercurrents she didn't quite understand.

"David's alertness knows no bounds," Luc murmured.

"Uh-huh." She really was too stressed out for this. "I'm going for a walk," she declared.

"A walk, huh?" Luc studied her. "I'd rather that you didn't go outside alone."

Katie sobered, reality intruding once again. "I'll stay in the house," she promised. "I still haven't seen all of it."

Luc relaxed a little. "Okay, but take Spot with you. She'll make sure you don't get lost."

"Right. Because she did such a good job the last time."

"Ye of little faith. You can wander while dinner is cooking."

Katie raised her eyebrows at him. "Cooking?"

Luc smiled and flicked her chin with his finger, the small contact sending a shock along her system. "Off with you, sprout. It's my turn to slave in the kitchen."

"About time."

"Get out of here. I'll come looking for you if you go missing."

She threw Luc another smile and went with Spot.

"Sprout?" David murmured. Luc cursed inwardly. He was going to have to be more careful what he said when the other man was around.

"Screw you. What do you want for dinner?"

"Food."

"Very helpful."

Luc limped into the kitchen. He was actually moving pretty well without the crutches, all things considered, but his ankle still hurt like a son of a bitch.

David followed him and sat down at the table. Luc ignored him and peered into the refrigerator. He didn't think he'd ever had this much food in the house all at one time. It was a little overwhelming. He wished he knew how to make something fancy. He'd read somewhere that women were impressed by men who could cook.

Not that he wanted to impress Katie. He was just trying to apologize. Maybe show her that he had some good qualities. Show her there were a couple of things he could do that didn't involve violence.

Okay, he was trying to impress her.

He pulled out a head of lettuce. Salad. Women liked that rabbit food shit, and it would be easy. Maybe steak? He could do steak. Had they bought steak?

"She's really not your usual type," David said from behind him.

"None of your business."

"Maybe." David was quiet for a moment. "If you're stupid enough to hurt this one, I think I'll come and hunt you down myself."

Still holding the head of lettuce, Luc turned, surprised by the intensity in his friend's voice. David pushed back his chair and stood.

"Where are you going?" Luc demanded.

"Thought I'd take a walk."

"Oh, really?"

"Yeah." David looked a little defensive. "Any law against it?"

"No." Luc was having some trouble dealing with the blow he seemed to have taken to his stomach. "Just pay attention to your own advice, David."

"I want to make sure she doesn't get lost." David turned and walked out the door.

Luc stared after him for several seconds before he put the lettuce down very carefully on the counter.

"Damn," he said. "Fucking damn."

SEVENTEEN

By the next afternoon, Katie was so annoyed with both David and Luc she was ready to spit.

She hadn't been exactly thrilled when David had joined her and Spot on their tour of the Museum, but she'd tried to be friendly. Still, it was hard not to smack the man upside the head when he talked freely about inconsequential matters and skillfully avoided the questions she really cared about—such as her future. Then, when they'd gone back to the kitchen, Luc had been all broody and withdrawn, his eyes beautiful dark mirrors.

He hadn't said two words to her the whole evening.

That morning things had gone even further downhill. Luc had remained silent. David had hung around until Katie wanted to scream. He seemed intent on putting himself between her and Luc at every possible opportunity, acting like he was her buffer, when all she wanted him to do was shut up and go away again. It had gotten so bad that she'd finally retreated to Luc's bedroom to read for a while just so she could be alone. It wasn't that she didn't like David, because she did. It wasn't that he wasn't nice, he was.

It was just that, well, he was talking to her, and Luc wasn't.

Now she sat curled in the bedroom's big armchair,

staring out the window, her book open and neglected on her lap. She'd lain awake for hours the night before, staring at the ceiling, thinking about Luc and Melanie. Bruce and Tom. Thinking about how life would have been different if only Luc had come to that stupid party three years ago. But maybe it was time to let go of the past. Forget all of the might-have-beens and get on with her life. Well, as soon as she could get on with it anyway. And at least now she didn't have to wonder what Melanie's brother was really like. At least now she'd met him.

She almost laughed at the irony of it all. Almost.

Her thoughts drifted along in that vein until she figured it was time to go downstairs and see what she could dig up for dinner. She couldn't count on Luc cooking two nights in a row and, since her lunch had consisted of a bag of corn chips stolen from the kitchen, she was hungry.

Spot had kept her company for most of the afternoon, but about an hour ago she'd padded off to destinations unknown, leaving Katie alone to make her way to the first floor. Fortunately she actually knew where she was going now.

She'd just reached the foot of the main stairs, when a hand touched her shoulder from behind. She jumped about a foot and spun around.

"Katie," David said. He had an overnight bag in his hand.

"Hi," she said with a sigh. Where the hell was Luc?

"I have to go," David said. "I have things I need to do in town. I can't stay any longer."

She almost answered with a resounding Hallelujah!

"Oh," she said instead.

David looked around the empty hall and took her hand. She glanced down in surprise, saw his big brown hand engulfing her much smaller one and let herself be led to the front door.

"Look, just watch yourself, okay?" he said. "I know this is a very stressful situation, but try to keep your perspective."

"Um, okay," she murmured and pulled her hand away, not really sure what was going on. "I'm not worried. Luc is here. And I know he can't run well, but he and Spot are pretty formidable."

"Yeah." David scrubbed a hand over his close-cropped hair. "Listen, I'm not going to be able to come out here again for a couple of days. We certainly don't want Frankie tracking you through me."

"Right," she agreed, unaccountably more cheerful.

"But I'll be checking in regularly, so you let me know if anything happens that makes you…uncomfortable, okay?"

You mean other than this conversation? Katie thought, but just smiled. He was looking at her so earnestly, his somewhat craggy features drawn and tight. A very nice man. She wasn't quite sure why she wanted to push him out the door.

Okay, she did know. In spite of any residual embarrassment, she wanted to be alone with Luc again. She wanted to get to know him now that she'd found out who he was. She wanted to know the man she had called Bruce. She wanted him to talk to her again.

"Everything will be fine," she said. "Don't worry about me."

He said nothing for a few moments. Katie was reminded of her first impression of him back at the police station. Sometimes David Allen saw far more than you wanted him to. She thought this was one of those times.

She looked away.

"Okay." He sighed, straightened. "Okay."

Katie forced herself to look back into his eyes. They were very pretty. His face was attractive and interesting and downright breathtaking when he smiled.

And she felt nothing for him but friendship. No tingle. No spark. Nothing.

Her tastes seemed to have gotten pretty specific over the last couple of days.

Great.

She made herself smile and nod. "Goodbye, David."

"Goodbye, Katie."

Then he was gone.

Katie waited until she heard David's car ramble down the long driveway before she turned and headed to the kitchen. She half feared, half hoped that she'd run into Luc, but the family room was empty when she walked through, and the kitchen stood gleaming and vacant.

At the refrigerator she paused and realized that, probably for the first time in her life, she just didn't want to prepare food. Instead she stepped out through the back door onto a small patio and let the warm summer breeze smack her in the face.

The humidity hung heavy in the air, and the afternoon sun glowed through a hazy sky. Cicadas and other bugs hummed in the somewhat weedy gardens. Birds sang as they hunted and gathered and tended their young. Out on the mown part of the lawn she saw Spot's large black bulk. The dog rolled and barked with the sheer joy of living, then jumped to her feet and took off at a gallop.

"Hey, don't run away!" she called, taking an anxious step forward.

"Don't worry, she won't go too far. She never leaves the property."

Katie drew in a breath and turned to the sound of the deep, male voice. Luc was perched on a stone retaining wall near the house, holding a mug of coffee and watching her intently. He'd been so still she hadn't noticed him until now. His dark hair, curling slightly around his ears, glistened when the sun caught it.

She swallowed. "There you are," she said, just to be saying something.

"Yeah. Here I am." His maroon shirt was faded, but it hugged his upper body in a most interesting fashion. Someday, Katie thought idly, she should probably tell him that most of his shirts seemed a little too small.

Then she bit the inside of her mouth to hide a grin. What was she? Crazy?

A vision of her own appearance popped in her head and, remembering what humidity tended to do to her hair, she tried to smooth it down a little self-consciously. When his dark eyes laughed at her, she figured it was hopeless, so she gave up.

"David just left," she said.

He sobered abruptly. "I know. He told me he was taking off."

"Oh." She fidgeted a little bit. "Um, good."

Luc put his mug down on the wall and patted a stone next to him. "Why don't you come on and sit down here for a minute? Take a load off."

Katie eyed him warily, not quite sure how to judge his mood. As she studied him, she thought she saw some tension in the set of his broad shoulders and in the firmness of his mouth. Maybe he was nervous too.

The admittedly unlikely idea gave her the courage to walk over and try to hoist herself up on the wall beside him. He watched her ungraceful attempts with some amusement, then finally took pity on her and hauled her up with one hand as if she weighed next to nothing. It was enough to give any red-blooded girl the vapors.

"Thanks," she huffed, legs swinging. His feet almost touched the ground, but hers were well above it. "Haven't done gymnastics in a while."

"And you're short."

"Yeah, thanks for pointing it out."

He laughed.

"So you're speaking to me again?" she asked.

"What? I was always speaking to you." He looked confused. Idiot.

"Oh, yeah. Right. That's why you haven't said anything to me since last night."

"I had things on my mind," Luc said, pulling back slightly.

"I noticed."

Katie closed her eyes to block him out, but it only made her more aware of him, of the warmth of his body so close to hers, the clean scent of soap mixed with faint aftershave. She took a deep breath, drew him in, thought about the way his mouth had taken hers. About how much she wished he'd kiss her again. And about how unlikely it was he would.

"You seem tired," he commented.

She jumped a little bit, startled out of her reverie. "That's because I am tired." She opened her eyes and looked out over the fields and woods surrounding the Museum, struck by how isolated they were. "How much land do you own anyway?"

"I don't own it, remember? There are about a hundred acres attached to the Museum. Why are you tired?"

"Amazing. I didn't think there were a hundred acres of land in New Jersey without houses on them."

"There are in this part. We're pretty far away from the cities. Couldn't you sleep?"

"I slept. Just not enough." Because I was thinking about you, you jerk.

"Oh." He shifted. "That reminds me. I wanted to tell you, now that David's gone and my ankle's on the mend, I'm going to move upstairs to one of the spare bedrooms. It will be easier to guard you if we're both on the same floor."

"Oh. Okay. Makes sense," she said, not quite sure what she thought about the fact that he'd only be a few rooms away. "Don't you want your own bedroom back?"

"Nah, you keep it."

"Thanks."

The silence stretched out between them.

"David's a good man," Luc said finally.

"Yes, he is." Katie agreed, wary again. "So?"

"We've known each other a long time."

"I kind of gathered that."

"He, um, picked me up off the streets after that house with Melanie. After the Winstons. I was alone and heading down a bad path, but he found me. Brought me into his family. He made something out of me."

Katie pondered that and studied his profile. It was a good profile. *He* was a good man. "I kind of think you made something out of yourself," she said at last.

"Maybe." Luc shifted, obviously embarrassed, then turned to her so unexpectedly that he caught her looking at him.

She blinked when she found herself trapped by his dark, dark eyes. God, they were beautiful. Brown and deep. She fell into them, drowned in them.

"I'm not surprised that you're, uh, attracted to him."

Katie blinked. She felt as if someone had just slapped her very hard. Her mouth opened, closed, opened again. "Huh?"

Luc shrugged. "You and David, you know? I saw how you were talking."

Katie scrambled to pull her thoughts together.

"He was talking to me, so I talked back. What was I supposed to do, mime? I would have talked to you, too, but you weren't interested."

"No, no. I mean you were talking. You know, talking. About all kinds of things."

Katie ran her mind back over the past twenty-four hours. What in the world was the man blathering on about?

"It's called small talk. You should try it sometime."

Luc pulled a hand through his hair until it stood up in spikes. "Damn it, Katie, I'm trying to say that I understand. I imagine David would attract any, um, number of women. Like I said, he's a great guy. One in a million."

She would have laughed if she hadn't been so annoyed. "You understand."

"Yeah. Who can blame you?" He looked away from her.

"You can't blame me. You understand." She wondered if she had fallen down a rabbit hole when she hadn't been looking. "Luc, I hate to break this to you, but I'm not attracted to David. I mean, I am, because I'd have to be dead not to be, but not in the way you mean."

"What?"

"I'm trying to say that I don't, uh, want him."

"You don't want David?"

"Yes! I don't want him!"

"Really?" Luc seemed genuinely shocked. "Well, why not?"

"Because I don't, okay?" Could this be any more embarrassing? "Trust me for once."

Silence.

"Is it because he's black?" Luc asked.

"No! No, it's not because he's black! God."

"Well, why not then?"

"What are you, David's pimp? You trying to get him hooked up, Luc?"

"Katie—"

"I'm sorry I said anything. You're right, he's great. He's wonderful. He's God's gift to women. I prostrate myself before him. You know, I found a bottle of whiskey the other day and it is so calling my name right now. Excuse me."

Before he could stop her, she jumped off the wall and marched inside the house. By the time he'd followed her, she was already headfirst in the kitchen cabinets digging desperately for the whiskey. She really didn't drink very much, but man, did she need it now.

"So, you're not attracted to David," Luc said from behind her. He still sounded surprised. The ass. "Wow."

She backed out of the cabinet clutching the bottle. Thank God. "What the hell is your problem?"

"Nothing."

"Jesus Christ." Katie found a glass, opened the bottle and poured herself a generous two fingers of the whiskey. She tossed back a healthy swallow of the stuff, then gasped and wheezed when it hit her stomach. Her insides were exploding.

"You okay?" Luc asked. He was closer now. Stalking her. Moving silently, his eyes intent on her face.

"Fine," she gasped out.

"Usually I add water or soda to that stuff."

"Thanks for the tip." Clutching the bottle and the glass, Katie pushed past him and strode into the family room. Without thought, she dropped onto the carpet in front of the sofa. If she'd had any sense, she'd have taken the bottle straight to the bedroom and locked the door, but now it was too much trouble to get up.

Luc came in a few minutes later and stiffly lowered himself onto the floor next to her. He had gotten his own glass and pulled the bottle away from her, pouring himself a large shot of the whiskey.

"Don't you ever sit in a chair?" He sounded both annoyed and amused.

"Sometimes." Katie took another sip of her drink and wrinkled her nose. "In my family, you just drop wherever there's room. There are usually too many people around to be picky." She drank again, really more like a gulp. Her insides weren't exploding anymore, they were getting warmer and fuzzier. It was nice. Her brothers would be laughing their asses off right about now if they could see her.

"Maybe you'd better take it easy there, slugger."

"Me? I'm a two-fisted drinker. Don't worry about me."

"Lush."

She glanced over and watched him take a sip from his own glass.

When he spoke again, his voice held a strangely wistful quality. "I can't imagine growing up with so many kids. I was in a group home once when I was about eight, but it's not the same."

"No." She had to clear her throat before her voice would work, but Luc didn't seem to notice. He was still staring off into the middle distance, obviously seeing things she couldn't. She put her glass and the whiskey bottle on the coffee table and laid her hand on his knee, trying to comfort in spite of the fact that he aggravated her no end.

Luc stared down at her hand on his leg, then deliberately leaned forward and put his own glass next to hers on the table. He covered her hand with his warm, large one.

"I meant what I said out there." He spoke quietly, but the words were distinct. "David Allen is the best man I know. I would not be surprised at all to find out that you're, uh, attracted to him." He paused. "But I'm glad you're not." He looked right into her eyes, his own dark and deep and full of secrets.

Her breath caught in her throat. She stared back at him, trapped by him again. Her hand tightened on his knee. His fingers pressed hers closer to the hard muscles under his cargo pants.

The hell with the whiskey. Luc was the one going straight to her head.

"You and David keep insisting I'm stupid," she said, her voice breathless even to her own ears.

"Never that."

"Okay, you think that I'm silly then. Naïve."

He shook his head once. "No."

"Neither of you think I know my own mind." That mind was spinning at the moment. The fire of the whiskey running through her system was nothing compared to the fire of touching him. "Neither of you think I'm smart enough, adult enough, to know how to handle myself. David spent the whole time he was here running interference—"

"Noticed that, did you?" Luc seemed to have shifted closer to her, even though she hadn't seen him move. "He was trying to protect you from—" He broke off, looked away then back at her. His gaze tracked down to her mouth and focused. Her lips tingled just from the force of his attention.

She licked them, and he actually shuddered.

"Protect me from…?" she murmured. She felt like she was looking at him through a soft mist.

"Me." He breathed the word. The air stirred on her face, and she smelled the whiskey he'd just drunk. He was definitely closer now, filling her senses.

"Did he need to?"

"Yeah," he growled. "Oh, yeah." He smiled, just a quirking of lips, and she found herself as fascinated by his mouth as he seemed to be with hers. She wanted to taste it, to bite it.

"I don't want David, Luc," she whispered. The words floated out, and she saw him tremble when her breath brushed him. It made her feel powerful. It made her feel alive. It made her feel like a goddess.

"Who do you want?" His voice was strangled.

"You."

And she kissed him.

EIGHTEEN

LUC KNEW THIS was a mistake. Knew goddamn right well he should not be doing this, but he couldn't stop himself from responding. He pulled back slightly, found her looking at him through fogged eyeglasses.

Slowly, deliberately, he removed the glasses and put them on the coffee table next to the whiskey bottle, heard her breath catch as he did so. Then he kissed her.

He tried to keep it gentle, as light as when he'd kissed her back in the ballroom, an undemanding exploration of lips, a journey of touch, of taste, even though her mouth, the warm sensation of it overwhelmed him. Maybe he could keep it to this, he thought hazily, just this. He needed to taste her. Needed to.

His good intentions lasted until Katie wrapped her arms tightly around his neck and pulled him closer. Until she acted as if she wanted to crawl inside him. Her mouth was busy on his, her tongue demanding, wordless noises coming from somewhere deep in her throat. Her hands stroked into his hair, tugged at it with fierce insistence.

And he lost it.

Somehow he had her on her back on the dense oriental carpet. Somehow he was on top of her. Their mouths met, clung, separated, came together again, wet and open and searching. Passion flared, bright and hot between them, and blew away his rapidly disintegrating control as if it had never existed.

He'd never felt like this before. He didn't know how to handle this, and he knew how to handle almost anything. He was losing his mind. His tongue swept inside her mouth, sparred with hers, pulled hers until he could suck on it. She moaned, clutching at him, and he couldn't control a little groan of his own. He buried his fingers deep in her beautiful, untamable hair and slanted her head to give him easier access.

The kiss grew even wilder. Hotter. Volatile. For long moments he ate at her as if he was starving. And he was.

Most of his blood had drained right out of his head, but a little voice of reason managed to make itself heard through the blinding throb of lust. Luc finally remembered to pull back a little.

"Katie," he murmured. He found he couldn't not touch her, and trailed his mouth over her cheek, over the freckles scattered across her nose, while his hands wandered. "What the hell are we doing?"

"Kissing." Her voice was husky and breathless as she lifted herself against him. "Boy howdy, are we ever kissing. Your mouth should be bronzed."

His laugh strangled in his throat, muffled against her ear. Then he gasped when she finally managed to yank his shirt out of his jeans so she could run her small, cool hands under it. The sublime feeling of her touching his skin made him close his eyes for a second.

"We should stop," he murmured.

"No." She pulled his head back down and whispered against his mouth. Then she kissed him again, scorched him.

And just that quickly, Luc's control shattered.

He forgot what a big mistake this was. Nothing mattered except being with her. Loving her.

Loving Katie.

He touched her hair, her face, the silky skin of her neck, then lower. She gasped when he palmed one full, firm breast, her fingers tunneling through his hair into his scalp. He rubbed his thumb across her nipple, and it hardened and swelled under the thin cotton of her shirt and bra.

God in heaven, nothing had ever been this good.

He was erect and hard, moving restlessly against her to torment them both. Digging the fingers of his left hand deep into her hair to hold her mouth where he wanted it, he went to work unbuttoning her shirt with his other hand. He was frantic with the desire to touch her, to taste all of her, to pull those sumptuous breasts into his mouth and suckle on her, to lick every inch of her body.

When her thin shirt parted, when he finally touched the incredibly soft skin of her feminine, rounded stomach, he growled and deepened the kiss further. His tongue dove, met hers, seduced as she was seducing, mated as hers was mating. She tasted of whiskey and woman. Katie.

A little voice deep inside tried to pull him back from the brink, to tell him that he shouldn't do this, but he ignored it now. He had a right, didn't he? She'd said she wanted him, and he'd waited so long. So god-damned long.

He let go of her wonderful, living hair and ran both of his hands under and around to her back, down to the rounded ass he'd craved since the moment he'd met her. Grasping her, he pulled her more tightly against him, settling himself between her thighs, letting her feel the force of his desire. He moved against her with more purpose, his legs sliding against her, entwining with hers. He wanted her to know exactly what he was going to do to her.

Oh, yeah, he was going to do all kinds of things to her.

Katie wasn't idle. Her busy hands were under his shirt again, her fingers running over the muscles of his back and chest, then sliding to clutch at his ass when his mouth finally left hers and wandered down her throat to where the unbuttoned shirt exposed her soft, beautiful breasts cupped like jewels in the plain cotton bra.

"God, more freckles," he muttered against her skin. "They drive me freaking nuts."

He had to taste the ones dancing in random patterns across her exposed skin before tonguing the upper slope of her right breast. Then he teased her by sucking her nipple through the bra. She gasped and bucked against him, which made him groan in turn and instinctively grind himself against her.

He laughed breathlessly, his hands moving to cup her, massage her until her breath came fast and light.

"Jesus, Katie. Jesus, you're so beautiful."

She wasn't. Katie knew she wasn't. But she just

couldn't bring herself to disabuse him of the notion right now. Not when he was staring at her as if he would devour her. Not when his lean brown cheeks were flushed and he was breathing hard.

Her bra fastened in the front. He dealt efficiently with the hooks before spreading the material wide.

"Look at you, Katie. Just look at you. All pink and pretty." His voice was gruff, and he ran his thumb across one of her nipples.

She gasped.

Katie looked at herself; she couldn't help looking. Her breasts were flushed and seemed bigger somehow, swollen. As if they were reaching for him, the tips a deep, dark rose that said clearer than words exactly how turned on she was. More turned on than she'd ever thought she could be. It was because of him. Because of who he was. He was Luc. He was Bruce.

"Hmm. Time to play," Luc murmured, his dark hair tousled and a sexy twinkle in his beautiful eyes. And play he did. He lapped her with his soft, rough tongue, touched her with his long, elegant fingers, until she writhed on the carpet, her head thrown back, too far gone to be embarrassed. Waves of sensation kept building and building until she thought she was going to explode. It had never been like this before. Never. She felt so wild that it was almost frightening.

He pulled back abruptly and she cried out.

"I need to see all of you," he panted.

He attacked her clothing and while he fumbled with buttons and zippers, Katie scrabbled to return the favor.

She really, really needed to touch him, to have him against her without clothes in the way.

They ended up wrestling and rolling on the carpet until Luc sat back, laughing. "Wait, wait."

In one fluid movement he stripped off his T-shirt. His chest was broad, his stomach flat. He was ripped with muscle and dusted with dark hairs. His skin was golden brown except for some lighter patches that had to be scars.

In the next moment, he was pushing down her khaki shorts, cursing when they got caught on her shoes. She toed off her sneakers, then her socks, and then the shorts were gone along with her shirt and bra.

Luc laughed again, a warm, husky sound. Standing, he shucked off his pants, underwear, socks and shoes in what seemed to be one single movement. Then he was standing before her, gloriously naked. Wonderfully aroused.

Mute, wanting him desperately, Katie reached for him. He pushed her back into the delicious softness of the oriental carpeting. And then she wasn't alone anymore.

His clever hands roamed over her body. She couldn't seem to stop touching him, the hard muscles and the rough hair and the way his skin seemed to be satin in certain places, like the back of his neck and the small of his back. The rougher patches of scars on his shoulder, biceps, thigh, spoke of a hard life. A dangerous one. The thought that he could have died before she'd ever met him froze her and had her clinging to him, her short nails biting into his skin.

And then his mouth was back on her, and she couldn't think at all. Except to get her mouth on him too.

He kissed her, tongue thrusting again and again, then raised his head and looked at her, his eyes narrowed. "I hope you're ready for me because I can't hold on much longer here."

She laughed breathlessly. "What do I have to do, hold up semaphore flags? If you're not inside me soon I'm going to die."

He kissed her and pulled back slightly, running his fingers inside the waistband of the sedate cotton panties she'd just realized she was still wearing.

Then he ripped them off her body.

She helped him.

He came down on her again, but not completely.

"Beautiful," he murmured and combed his fingers through her pubic hair, then ran his forefinger between the plump, slick folds of her most intimate place. She drew in a deep breath when he found the excruciatingly sensitive bud hidden there.

He stroked. She practically came off the floor, grabbing his biceps not so much for support, but to make sure she didn't go flying off into outer space. Her legs fell apart of their own accord, and he huffed out a breath.

"Jesus, Katie. You're so fucking pretty."

His finger sank deep. She arched again, back bowed, aching breasts pointing toward the ceiling. She moved, she couldn't help moving, riding his finger. His thumb teased her while a second finger joined the first, and she cried out, hips lifting.

Luc groaned.

"I have to… I want to…" He wasn't making any sense, but Katie didn't care because his fingers were still moving. And then his mouth, his wonderful, clever mouth, was right where she needed him the most.

She cried out in shock, in pleasure, in excitement, as he devoured her with lips and teeth and tongue. He hummed into her, the vibrations driving her insane. His tongue lapped her, worried her like a particularly juicy bone. Faster and faster. Side to side. Bringing her up and up and up…

And Katie exploded over the edge.

The top of her head almost came off, her moans flying up to the ceiling and echoing off the stone walls. Her body spasmed around his fingers while he moved them to prolong her pleasure until she finally lay limp again on the carpet.

"Oh, my God."

"Don't you dare fall asleep on me." His voice was so rough it was practically unrecognizable as he pulled his hand from her body and rubbed his fingers across his stomach, painting himself with her.

Suddenly Katie didn't feel so limp anymore. Maybe a little embarrassed, absolutely and incredibly alive, but definitely not limp.

Neither was Luc.

He grabbed his jeans and clawed through the pockets until he found a small foil packet and pulled it out. His hand was shaking. His whole body was shaking.

Katie sat up and got onto her knees, watching him. She was energized, powerful. Sexy. "No."

He froze. Stared at her with blank desperation and she smiled.

"I want to play too," she continued. "Lie down and get comfortable." She took the condom out of his unresisting fingers and pushed at his chest.

"Jesus Christ." But he fell back obediently, his arms flung wide, fingers digging into the nap of the carpet, his skin golden and glowing against the scarlet and black and navy rug.

She clutched the foil packet, but didn't open it right away. She was too busy devouring the sight of him all spread out for her. Yum.

"Katie…" His voice was gruff with warning and pleading.

She smiled. "Please. I need a minute."

His head fell back to the floor with a solid "thunk."

Katie lowered herself down on top of him. For a moment she just kissed him, gnawed on his lips as if he were a particularly tasty snack, thrust her tongue into his mouth again and again, showed him what she hoped they'd be doing soon.

When his hips started bucking helplessly, she straddled him, deliberately spreading herself wide against his pelvis so he could feel the heat he'd caused. Luc's neck and head bowed back, veins standing out as he let out a loud, inarticulate noise that was somehow more than a groan.

He reached for her, but she leaned back to avoid him.

"No," she said. "I'm not ready to stop yet."

He looked at her, his lean brown face and throat flushed a deep red, his pupils so dilated that his eyes looked like black pools. "Then you'd better hurry the hell up." His voice was hoarse and barely recognizable.

Katie felt a wave of giddiness wash over her. She'd done this. She'd done this to him.

She licked her lips and his head fell back again.

"Shit," he said.

Katie laughed and leaned over him, rubbed her nipples through the hair on his chest to tease both of them. She stretched farther out, heard the frantic rhythm of his breathing, saw his fingers clench the carpet until his knuckles turned white. She kissed him. His mouth, his jaw, his neck.

He groaned.

She laved his throat with her tongue, nibbled on it, on the strong cords and sinews. Who knew she was a neck person? Eventually she moved to his collarbones, his pecs. Learning the taste of him, the scent of him, taking extra care to love every scar she found—and she found quite a few. Cataloging them as her hands moved over him.

"What are these from?" she breathed, letting her tongue trace the ragged edges of two round scars in the meat of his muscled shoulder.

"Gunshot— Jesus, Katie!"

"Oh." She loved the scars with her tongue, trying to draw out the pain, the memories.

"God." He moaned and threw his head back farther, strong throat working until she had to taste it again, had to draw that brown, salty skin up against her teeth. Had to mark him.

No other man had ever offered himself so freely to

her before. No man had made himself so vulnerable. Noises were coming out of his mouth constantly now, helpless groans and gasps that made her writhe on top of him, even as she circled one of his flat nipples with her mouth, pulled at the nub with her lips.

She slid off him and looked at him, lying there. He was so excited. He was so beautiful.

"Oh, what a piece of work is man," she murmured and found herself wanting to try something she'd never have done with Tom. Or anyone else, for that matter.

"Katie?" He groaned, then bucked when she grasped his sex in her hands.

Before she lost her nerve, she licked him from stem to stern as if he were a lollipop.

He reacted as if she'd put an electric charge on the thing and his control finally broke. With one fluid movement, her threw her onto her back, leaned over her, panting. "I can't take it. I can't fucking take it." He snatched up the condom from where she'd dropped it and had it open before she could blink. He sheathed himself quickly and positioned himself between her thighs, entering her just a little bit before he stopped and braced himself.

"Now. Please now." It was her turn to gasp, her turn to struggle. She tried to force him to come down but he didn't move. He just looked at her and smiled, the twist of his lips halfway between pleasure and pain.

"Katie," he said and sank in up to the hilt. Then all bets were off.

He was wild for her and that was okay; she was wild for him too. He thrust again and again, harder, deeper, faster. She tried to meet him, tried to encourage him. He twisted his hips and she gasped when he rubbed against a particularly sensitive spot deep inside her. So he did it again…and again…and again…and again…

Then the pressure broke, and Katie's orgasm rolled through her. She spasmed around him. He thrust into her even harder, which brought her all over again.

"Bruce," she groaned. "Bruce."

"What?" he asked, breathing labored.

She didn't answer because she couldn't. His hips slammed into hers, and with a shout he followed her over into oblivion.

LUC THOUGHT HE MIGHT have fainted. The only thing he knew for sure was that there was an extended amount of blank happy time before he swam back to full consciousness. He considered it a tribute to his training that he had any strength left at all after that session. Katie McCabe had worn him out.

He pulled out of her and rolled over on his back. Katie murmured in protest and then curled up against his side like a very sleepy, very satisfied kitten. He rubbed her shoulder. Grinning foolishly at the ceiling, he smelled the sweat and the sex and the woman and thought that he had never in his whole life been quite this content.

"Holy Jesus," he muttered.

His brain was like mush. Sluggish mush. But as he lay there trying to work up the energy to get up and dispose of the used condom, he started to think again.

Something had been wrong. Something there at the end hadn't been quite…

He frowned. What had she called him?

For a moment his mind refused to work. Then memory snapped in.

Bruce. At the end there, it sounded like she'd called him Bruce.

Katie curled closer into him and grumbled.

He forced his lazy muscles into action, slipped off the condom and hoisted himself to his feet. Katie protested louder when he left her, then she stretched languorously and settled back down.

He pulled an afghan off the sofa and covered her with it before heading to the bathroom to clean up. A few minutes later he was back, looking down at her.

Bruce. She'd called him Bruce.

He bent and pulled on his pants. He zipped them, but didn't bother with the button.

It might have been funny if it wasn't so fucking pathetic. Almost like that old Monty Python routine. "Everyone's name is Bruce."

Luc almost smiled at the irony of it all. Almost. She'd called him by another man's name. The name of the man she thought he was. A man who didn't exist. Who had never existed. Who never would.

Absently he rubbed his stomach, wondering how someone could be so physically sated and emotionally empty at the same time.

Too bad, Vasco, he thought. Just too goddamned bad.

As he watched, Katie's eyes opened, the blue deep and blurred with spent passion.

"Mmm," she murmured. "Hi, sailor."

"Soldier." He didn't smile. Couldn't really. "You

called me Bruce. Earlier." Instantly he was sorry he'd said anything, hadn't meant to bring it up at all. His tone made her stiffen, that lush body still and wary.

"What?"

"Nothing." He turned away and pulled on his T-shirt.

"No, it's not nothing." She sat, tucking the afghan carefully around soft, naked skin that was still much too tempting.

"Forget it." He gathered up her clothes from where they'd tossed them around the room, but he couldn't help watching her out of the corner of his eye. He saw when she remembered, saw the frown of confusion crease her forehead.

"I did call you Bruce, didn't I?" She smiled a little tentatively. "Well, that's embarrassing. Sorry."

He turned to face her, her glasses in his hand.

"My name is Luc."

"I know." Katie sobered instantly and shrugged. "I'm not quite sure why I called you Bruce. Sorry about that."

Luc looked down at her glasses. Made an effort and didn't snap them.

"Sure."

"Luc, what's wrong?" Katie climbed to her feet, still careful to keep the afghan wrapped around her, which was kind of ridiculous considering what they'd just done.

"It's nothing. Really." Luc handed her the glasses. He wouldn't have been able to explain it to her, even if he'd had the inclination. "We should probably try to get some sleep," he said.

Without waiting for her reaction, he turned and limped out of the room.

FRANKIE SILVANO SAT in a chair in his father's penthouse office, heel resting on the opposite knee, foot bouncing restlessly. He looked through the bank of windows that made up most of one wall and saw brightly colored lights from the casino reflected in the Atlantic Ocean. It was nearly three o'clock in the morning, but the Dream Net Casino never slept.

Poppa did, though, and Frankie had been forced to wait while the old man was rousted from his comfortable bed. He wished he hadn't needed to take the time, wished he hadn't had to drive all the way to Atlantic City, but he wanted to use a few of the more seasoned guys for this job, and good old Dad was spending some time at the casino this week. He could recruit fuckhead hired muscle like Arlo no problem, but the regular guys wouldn't take a shit without the big boss's okay.

His foot jiggled faster as excitement and impatience coursed through him. He'd found her. He'd found the little bitch who'd humiliated him. Katie McCabe. Now he'd make her pay.

The office door slammed open. His father strode in, a thick robe belted around his thick waist. He shut the door, turned to face Frankie, the expression on his face reminding him that the old man might look a lot like a stuffed sausage these days, but he was still one tough son-of-a-bitch.

"What the hell d'you want?" Poppa's voice was sleep-roughened and harsh. It was obvious he hadn't appreciated being woken at this hour.

Frankie smiled. "I know where she is." His father would know who he meant.

Poppa tightened the belt of his robe and studied him as he settled his bulk behind the desk. "Jesus, the guy she's with is a Fed, Frankie," he said. "You know that. I don't want to get any more involved with the Feds than we already are."

"I know where she is." Frankie repeated. "I'm only telling you because I want to take a bunch of the guys with me to get her. So give your okay and I'll be gone."

"Just like that?" His father's voice rose. "Just like that. You're going to fricking go get her just like that. What the hell—"

"I'm going for her," Frankie said. He rose from the chair. "Either lend me the guys or don't."

Poppa didn't say anything for a moment, but he didn't toss him out of the office either. Frankie had noticed his father tended to walk more carefully around him these days, treated him like he was a snake who could strike at any time. Not like when he was younger and old daddy-o would beat him until he couldn't walk. Trying to toughen him up, he'd said. Trying to teach him a lesson.

Yeah, he'd fucking learned a lesson.

If his father only knew the real reason they were losing so much ground to the Colombians, why Carlos and his crew were always one step ahead, why the organization was now in trouble to the point that the don himself was coming here to personally review accounts, well then he'd know exactly what lesson Frankie had learned. He'd know what kind of a snake Frankie was—a deadly one. Poppa was going down because Frankie, the 'idiot' son, the whackjob, had pulled the supports right out from under him.

God, just thinking about it was enough to get him off. But that was going to have to wait. Right now he needed the guys and he needed to deal with Katie McCabe. First things first. He knew how to fucking prioritize.

"Give the okay, Poppa," he said, and his voice was cold.

His father watched him for a few more minutes and whatever he saw in his face made his own harden. Slowly, very slowly, he nodded his head. "Sure. I'll tell Tito."

Frankie smiled, a peeling back of lips over teeth. Then he turned and left the office.

Time to get busy.

NINETEEN

KATIE SAT CURLED up in the big armchair in Luc's bedroom, staring out through the bay window and watching the sky gradually lighten with dawn.

She hadn't slept especially well. Not too surprising, she supposed. She'd showered, changed, even gotten into bed and tried to sleep. Useless. Her mind just kept chewing over the events of the prior evening. Luc. Their passionate lovemaking.

His sudden, cold withdrawal.

He'd walked her upstairs to the bedroom and left her there. He hadn't said anything, hadn't even tried to. Instead he'd gone farther down the hall and disappeared into another room. She'd watched him go, suppressed the urge to call him back, ruthlessly strangled her need to follow him, to confront him.

Alone, she'd turned and gone into his massive bedroom. Then she'd spent the rest of the night trying to figure out what in the hell had happened to screw up something that had been so right.

Except she knew perfectly well what had happened.

She'd called him by the wrong name.

Katie buried her face in her hands and then pulled at her own hair. She just could not believe she'd been so stupid. It had probably come from the shock of actually having an orgasm.

She would have expected anger. Anyone would get pissed at being called the wrong name in that sort of a situation. Anger she could have handled. What she didn't get was the layer of hurt she'd sensed just beneath the surface. The withdrawal. The closing off. In spite of the intimacy they'd shared, he'd shut her out as efficiently as if he'd been slamming a steel door. What was the big deal? Luc was Bruce. Bruce was Luc. It wasn't like she'd yelled out the name of another lover. They were the same.

But it was more than apparent that it had mattered to him. A lot.

Lifting her head, Katie looked out at the brightening sky and sighed deeply. Okay. Okay, so she'd royally messed up. She'd hurt him, and she had to make it right. Somehow.

What if he never let her get close to him again?

As she sat brooding over the problem, Katie gradually became aware of a sound just on the edge of her consciousness. It was muffled, so she couldn't place it at first, but then realized it was a dog barking outside.

A dog.

Outside.

Barking.

Spot.

She'd never heard Spot bark like that before, Katie mused. Not with warning and violent intent. Not like she was trying to wake them...up...

Katie's eyes widened as the implications of what she

was hearing hit her. She vaulted out of the chair, stood quivering while fear leapt and clawed at her insides.

"Holy crap."

Now the faint, urgent noise sounded ominous. Dangerous. Oh, God, Frankie Silvano had found them. He might be breaking into the house right now.

"No. Don't be silly. Don't panic," she told herself. "There's nothing wrong wffith a dog barking. They do it all the time."

The barking grew wilder. Then there was a sudden, loud yelp.

The dead silence that came after was more terrifying than all of the noise before.

"Okay, then. Panic." Katie made it to the bedroom door in two jumps. Where was Luc? For one horrible second she couldn't remember which way he'd gone. Right. No, left. That's right, left. Okay, left. Please God, left.

She swallowed, opened the bedroom door and stepped cautiously out into the hallway. For once in her life she actually chose the correct direction, because a few minutes later she found Luc passed out face down across a bed in another room. He was only wearing khaki cargo pants slung low on his hips and some old sneakers. The empty bottle he had clutched in one hand looked suspiciously like the whiskey from the night before. Apparently he'd gone back downstairs to get it at some point during the night.

Katie sprang to the bed.

"Luc!" She pulled the bottle out of his hand, put it on the nightstand and shook one of his bare, powerful shoulders. "Luc, wake up! There's someone here. I think there's someone outside."

Luc rolled over onto his back and put his forearm over his eyes to block the light. "Ow. What?"

Katie wanted to punch him. "Listen to me, you moron. I think there's somebody outside."

"Outside?" Luc's arm dropped and he sat up in one swift motion, then his head fell forward. "Oh, shit." With obvious effort, he hauled himself off the bed and looked at her through dark, bloodshot eyes. "Talk to me."

"I heard Spot barking outside," Katie told him. "It went on for a while before it stopped. Then I heard someone scream. That's what it sounded like, anyway."

"Shit," Luc said again. He pulled on the old maroon shirt from yesterday. With his scar and his midnight dark hair tousled around his face and his chin shadowed with an overnight growth of beard, he looked like a grumpy and hung-over pirate. "The building is alarmed," he said. "A sensor on Spot's collar lets her come and go as she pleases, but nobody else should be able to get inside the house without us knowing about it. I need to get you someplace safe so I can take a look around."

"I can help—"

He stopped her by the simple expedient of putting his big hand over her mouth. "No. You are not going to argue with me about this, Katie. Your safety is the most important thing."

She could tell by the hard look on his face that even if she argued, he wasn't going to listen to her, so she nodded reluctantly.

He stared at her for a moment longer, then released her and headed for a connected bathroom.

"Where are you going?" she demanded.

"Hey, I drank almost a whole bottle of whiskey last night. Where do you think I'm going? Some things just have to take priority." He closed the door behind him.

A few seconds later, Katie followed Luc out into the hallway. She had to make an effort not to burrow into his back like a rabbit.

"We need to get back to my bedroom," he told her softly over his shoulder. "I have some weapons stored there."

"You do?" She wasn't sure how she felt about the fact that weapons had been stored in the room she'd been using. "Where's your gun?"

He glanced at her. "I left it downstairs. I kind of... forgot it."

"Oh." Not too much to say about that.

The Museum was almost eerily quiet, even its usual creaks and groans seemed muffled. Like a morgue, Katie thought with a shudder. Maybe she had only been imagining things. Had she really heard what she'd thought she'd heard? What if there was a perfectly reasonable explanation for everything? God, she hoped so.

But when they drew near to his bedroom, Luc came to an abrupt stop. She ran right into him.

"What?" Her question was a mere whisper of sound, but he turned and clapped his hand over her mouth again.

Then she heard it. Light, rhythmic footsteps on the stairs. A low murmur of voices. Voices? As in more than one?

Luc rushed Katie the last few steps, pushed her inside the room, then very gently closed the door behind them and locked it.

"Give me a hand," he murmured. She helped him lift a heavy chest of drawers and move it in front of the door.

"They're inside the house," she whispered, fear itching over her skin.

"And they got in without setting off the alarm," Luc muttered, rubbing his forehead.

"Luc?"

He ignored her and went over to the bay window, peered out, then quickly pulled his head back inside again.

"Well, we sure as hell can't get out this way. There are at least ten guys down there."

"Ten? Besides those men we heard coming up the stairs?"

"Yeah. They think they've got us trapped in this wing of the building."

Katie tried not to giggle hysterically. "Are they wrong?" She rubbed her arms, trying to get warm as shiver after shiver ran through her body.

"Maybe. Maybe not."

Luc went to one of the closets, hoisted out a long, flat box then carried it to the bed and opened it.

Katie peeked over his shoulder and felt her eyes go wide. "Holy cow, you've got an arsenal in there."

"I'm just prepared."

"Yeah, for a world war, maybe."

Luc ignored her while his hands moved smoothly over the weapons. He chose some and rejected others, worked quickly and with a sureness that spoke of long familiarity and experience.

"We have to get out of here," he said in a rough whisper. "We're sitting ducks in this room."

Katie didn't know how to respond to that, so she just nodded.

He looked like he wanted to say something else, but they heard a voice out in the hallway. It sounded calm and cold. And familiar.

"Search the rooms. They're supposed to be on this floor somewhere."

Luc's face tightened and he held Katie's eyes with his own.

"Frankie Silvano," he whispered.

Katie felt the terror that had been growing inside her flash. Somehow over these last few days, she'd managed to push Frankie Silvano to the back of her mind, even though he was the original reason for her situation. He'd seemed like a shadowy figure, an imaginary threat. Not quite real, sort of like the bogeyman. In an essential way she'd forgotten about him.

What a mistake. Stupid.

"He found us," she gasped.

"No shit."

"But how? And how did he know which floor we'd be on?"

Luc's expression was grim. "I have absolutely no idea."

"What are we going to do?" Her voice shook.

Luc watched her for a moment, then put his hand

under her chin. His palm was warm against her skin. She almost hated that she found it comforting.

"What do you think? We're going to get out of here."

"Get out of here?" Katie echoed softly as he dropped his hand. She could hear doors opening and closing. The men were getting closer. "How?"

Luc didn't answer. Instead he went up to the fireplace and ran his fingers over the stones.

"You're nuts," she muttered. "Murderers are out roaming the halls and you're mauling the fireplace."

"Just get your purse," he said, a little sharply.

Still convinced he was insane, but willing to go along because she didn't have a better option, Katie grabbed her purse and threw it over her shoulder.

Frankie's men reached their room. When they found it locked, they battered at the door. The noise reverberated through Katie's head, but the door held. "She's in there." Frankie's voice was right outside now. It was muffled, but shrill. Excited. "The bitch. Shoot the lock."

There was the sound of a gunshot, the shattering of metal, the thunk of solid wood.

"Luc." He continued to ignore her, his fingers still moving swiftly over rock and mortar. "Luc, we have to do something now!" Katie didn't bother to keep her voice down.

Luc turned, and smiled at her with keen satisfaction. "Got it." His hand slid under a stone and the entire fireplace swung away from the wall exposing a small hidden alcove.

Katie could see a flight of stairs leading off into darkness. It was a secret passage. In the wall. "Holy shit."

"Come on." Luc grabbed her arm and pulled her with him into the opening. He jabbed a finger at another hidden switch and the fireplace moved back into place just as the chest of drawers they'd pushed across the bedroom door fell forward. The door itself exploded inward under the combined force of at least six men.

Standing pressed close against Luc in the tiny, dark compartment, Katie heard the muffled shouts of the men entering the room.

"Where'd they go?"

"Jesus, the fireplace moved."

"Quiet!" That was Frankie's voice. Then Katie heard muffled beeping. A cell phone?

Luc's hand tightened on her shoulder, holding her in place, keeping her still in the complete, cool darkness.

"What?" Frankie sounded clipped and irritated. "What the fuck do you mean, you've got the girl?" Katie stiffened. Luc's grip tightened until she knew she'd have bruises. "Where? Her apartment?" Pause. "Then who the fuck…forget it. Take her to the place." Another pause. "What the fuck do you mean, which place? Atlantic City, asshole. The Dream Net. You know where." He abruptly ended the call.

"Who—?" Katie whispered to Luc, but he squeezed her shoulder again, and she fell silent.

"Stupid fucking morons!" Frankie wasn't quite shouting, but it was close.

"Boss?" one of the other men asked, sounding tentative. "Um, what do you want us to do here?"

"Do I have to think of fucking everything?" Frankie

really was screaming now. "You just told me you saw them go into the fucking fireplace."

"Uh, well, I saw it moving when we broke in—"

"If they went in there, they've got to fucking come out somewhere, don't they? You two! Stay here and get this thing open. The rest of you assholes cover this place inside and out. Kill the guy, but if he has a broad with him, I want her. I don't care who she fucking is! Just fucking find them!"

"Come on." Luc spoke slow and close to Katie's ear. "We need to get outside."

Katie wanted to protest, to wait and see if they heard more about the person Frankie had apparently kidnapped, but she knew Luc was right.

She felt him shift, and then there was a dim light and the blackness around them lifted just a little, precious, bit. Luc was holding a small flashlight.

"Definite boy scout." Her voice was almost embarrassingly weak. She didn't realize how much she'd longed for some light until she had it.

Luc just smiled and took her hand. "Come on."

Slowly, carefully, they descended the narrow stairs. Katie tried to keep her breathing even, but she suspected it was a lost cause. The light from the flashlight was a comforting glow, but it really did little to penetrate the shadows around them. Cobwebs brushed her face unexpectedly, and she aged a thousand years every time one touched her softly and without warning. She gulped at the stale air and tried to remember she wasn't claustrophobic.

Her foot brushed something soft and unidentifiable.

When she jumped away from the squishy object, she tripped and fell into Luc's broad back.

He staggered, the flashlight flew out of his hand, and as it clattered down the stairs they were plunged once more into utter blackness. He grabbed her arms. They teetered on the tread for one horrifying second.

"Jesus! Be careful, would you?" Luc growled after they'd gotten their balance. His voice was tight. She spared a second to wonder if he'd hurt his ankle again, but the dark was pressing in on her, driving all other thoughts from her mind. It was so…blank. So close. She wondered if she was going to have a panic attack right then and there.

"Hold on to me. We've got to keep moving," Luc said.

She obediently put her hand on his shoulder. She forced herself to breathe, to concentrate on putting one foot in front of the other while he felt his way along the wall and started back down the stairs.

They seemed to go on that way for hours, Luc picking his step, Katie following, their breath loud in the silence. Then, at last, she searched for another stair beneath the sole of her sneaker and there wasn't one.

"We're at the bottom," Luc said softly.

"Thank God." Truer words had never been spoken.

"There's a door here somewhere. I just hope the hinges aren't rusted shut."

"Don't say that." Katie shuddered.

More minutes dragged by while Luc's hands moved slowly over a surface she couldn't see. She could only sense his arms lifting, muscles shifting, the tension spinning out, pulling taut, driving her insane.

"Ah," Luc said.

"What?" She'd clutched at the back of his shirt while she'd waited. Now she twisted the material in her fists.

"I found the latches and the handle. Doesn't need a key, thank Christ."

"Will it open?" Katie's heart was pounding.

"Let's find out."

Katie forced herself to let go of him. Made herself get out of the way. It was one of the hardest things she'd ever done, but she knew he needed room to maneuver. Still, when she wasn't touching him, she was lost. Adrift. He had been the only real thing there in the darkness with her. Her only point of reference.

She heard some scuffling noises, the sound of metal rasping against metal, and knew Luc was fumbling with the latches.

"Cross your fingers," he muttered and she did. All of them. Toes too.

Katie heard him curse with strained effort. For a few blood-curdling seconds nothing happened. Then she heard him take a step backwards. Then another. He was pulling the door.

With no noise other than Luc's labored breathing, no indication at all that there was movement, blessed light began to outline a rectangle in the blackness. Luc shifted again. It grew brighter, wider, until she had to close her eyes against the glow. Fresh air flooded the chamber, and she gulped it like food.

"Good enough," Luc grunted. "Shit, I'm too old for this."

Katie opened her eyes and, as they adjusted, saw

that now there was a thick panel open at an angle and a space in the wall large enough for a person to squeeze through. Outside, the opening was covered by a loose green hedge. Camouflage, she thought, but not so much that it blocked access. She could see the grass and trees beyond the branches and the sun shining through.

"Remind me to check the mechanism on this door when this is finished," Luc said. He peered out, then took a gun out of the waistband of his jeans. "I think I gave myself a damn hernia."

"O-okay." Katie stammered, shocked at the casual implication that they would be talking after this whole thing was over. She'd never even thought about the future.

Luc seemed to realize what he'd said because he cursed, checked the clip on the gun and glared at her.

"Stay here."

"Your ankle—"

"Forget my damn ankle. I said to stay here."

"Sir, yes, sir," she muttered. But he was already gone.

Katie pressed her body up against the cold stone wall and looked after him.

He'd disappeared.

Just that quickly he'd blended into the land around the Museum as if he'd never existed. As if he'd become a part of the beautiful, weedy gardens.

She was alone with her worry for him, her worry for the unknown person Frankie Silvano had kidnapped. Whoever it was, they'd kill her when they found out they had the wrong woman. She knew it.

A man carrying a machine gun strolled into view.

Katie hastily slid back into the darkness. He didn't yell or give any indication that he'd seen either her or the door, so she had to assume the hedge was doing its job.

She inched forward again. Where was Luc? Was he okay?

Noises echoed from the stairs behind her, making her jump and whirl to stare up into the blank emptiness. A loud crash. Shouts. Rushing footsteps reverberating strangely around the long, narrow stairwell.

Katie's breath stilled.

Oh, God. The men must have broken through the fireplace.

She looked back through the door. Some of the sound had carried outside to the man with the machine gun, because she saw him staring at the hedge, weapon held ready. He took a step forward.

Katie never knew where Luc came from. One minute he was nowhere in sight, the next he'd tackled the man with the machine gun down to the ground, ripped the weapon out of his hands and was mercilessly taking him apart with some well-placed punches, with thick, wet thuds of fist against flesh. The thug never even had a chance to react.

After his opponent lay still and crumpled, Luc jumped to his feet and gestured to Katie. Shaking, she scrambled out of the door and through the hedge.

When she got closer to him, she got a better look at the man on the ground and swallowed. "Wow."

Luc wiped his hands on the bottom of his shirt and slung the machine gun over his shoulder by the strap.

Then he looked at her, the scar tight across his face, his eyes flat.

"I did what I had to do," he said.

"I know."

There were more sounds from the dark staircase she'd just left. The men must almost be at the bottom.

"Come on." Luc held out his hand. Katie took it.

He dragged her behind him, around the side of the house, out to where the Nova was parked. As they came around the corner, Katie saw a large, black shape lying still in the driveway.

"Spot!"

"Those bastards." Luc's gait was lopsided, favoring his hurt ankle, but he dropped her hand and ran faster, skidding to a stop beside the dog. Kneeling, he pressed his head to her side.

"Is she alive?" Katie panted when she caught up. There was blood, but she couldn't tell if it was Spot's or somebody else's.

"She's breathing," Luc said. "I can't leave her here. Help me get her to the car."

Each of them grabbed a handful of fur, dragged the heavy dog over to the Nova, and stuffed her into the backseat. They had just finished when there was shouting from the house.

"Give me the keys." Luc held out his hand. "I'll drive."

"Keys." Katie stared at him, her mind blank. She frantically rummaged through her purse. "God, keys." She stopped and looked at him again, her eyes wide as a wave of sheer panic broke through her. "Luc, they're in the kitchen. I left them on the counter in the kitchen."

"The counter?"

"Habit. After we got back on Saturday." Why, oh, why hadn't she listened to her father and put a spare key in her purse? Probably because her father had been the one who'd told her to do it.

"Perfect. Absolutely fucking perfect. Cover me." He shoved the confiscated machine gun into her hands.

"Cover you? Cover you? Are you crazy? I don't know how to shoot this thing!"

Luc muttered something she wasn't entirely sure she wanted to hear and grabbed the weapon. He made sure it was loaded, pulled back the safety and shoved it at her again.

"It's got a full clip, and I took off the safety. Just point it away from me and squeeze the trigger."

"I don't want to kill anybody!" she wailed.

"You're probably not going to hit them."

Before Katie could respond to that, he jumped in the car, sprawled across the seat and yanked the covering off the steering column, presumably to hotwire something. She didn't have time to argue with him anyway because about six or seven men were running toward them from the castle.

Okay. "Well, here goes nothing."

Katie lifted the nose of the machine gun over the hood of the car, aimed in the general direction of the men, closed her eyes and squeezed the trigger. The weapon kicked back violently, and she lost control for a moment. Glass shattered all over the front of the Museum.

"Oops."

"Not the windows!" Luc cried as the Nova roared to life.

Katie didn't respond. She just dug in her heels more firmly and pelted the trees and bushes around the house with a hail of bullets. Men who had been advancing shouted and leapt for cover.

She laughed. Served them right.

"Bitch! Whore! I'll get you!" Frankie's voice screamed across the yard and Katie's nerves jumped. "You can't get away. You can't get away from me." The little man detached himself from the side of the house and ran at them, firing his gun, apparently berserk with rage.

Katie froze.

"Get in! Get in!"

Luc was there next to her. He grabbed the gun, pushed her into the passenger seat then sprayed the area with bullets.

Frankie went down with a sharp yell. Luc scrambled around to the driver's side, pausing only long enough to rake shots over the five or six cars scattered in the parking area, ripping tires and metal. He jumped into the driver's seat and thrust the machine gun at Katie.

She took it with shaking hands and he threw the car into gear.

The Nova spun gravel, then sped up the long driveway. When they had reached the end of it, Luc looked in the rearview mirror and cursed.

"Shit, I didn't get them all," he said.

"What?"

But she heard other cars and knew the chase was on.

TWENTY

"I CAN PROBABLY figure out how to make the machine gun work now if you want me to," Katie told Luc. She tightened her death grip on the door handle when he swung the Nova onto a small country road. Three black sedans followed a minute or two later. Why was it always black sedans, she wondered. Why not blue Mini-Coopers? Or silver SUVs? The Silvanos must be traditionalists.

"Should I shoot at something?" she asked.

"Thanks for the offer, but no. The farmers in the area would probably like to keep their cows alive."

"Ha, ha. Very funny. I'm just trying to help."

Luc glanced in the rearview mirror and then over at her. "With the way you handle a gun, I'm not sure it's safe to even have you in the same car with one."

Katie gasped at the unfairness of that. "Hey! I told you I'd never shot one before."

"I know, I know." He looked over at her again briefly and scowled. "But why in hell did you have to take out those stained-glass windows? Do you have any clue how much they're going to cost to replace?"

"No." She squirmed. "You noticed that, huh?" Some gunshots whizzed by, but the road was bumpy and the Nova was sending up great clouds of dust, which helped to obscure them from view.

"The gaping holes in the front of the building were kind of hard to miss." He made a sharp turn, and the tires spun. "If you keep your head down, do you think you can you see if Spot's okay?"

"I'll try." The Nova didn't have a big opening between the seats for a center console or arm rest or anything fancy like that, but there was a split in the middle so they could recline separately. With a little maneuvering Katie was able to slide her arm through that. She ran her hand over as much of Spot as she could reach from that awkward angle, then turned to face the front again.

"There's some blood, but I can't tell where it's coming from," she told Luc. "Why isn't she waking up?"

"I don't know." He sounded worried. "But I don't have time to think about it until I lose these guys." He made another turn and sped down an even smaller dirt road that trickled haphazardly between two cornfields. In fact, Katie didn't think it was a road at all. She suspected it was just a lane the farmer used to move his equipment around.

She glanced back through the rear window and ducked when more shots were fired. "We're not going to get away this time, are we?"

"Oh, hell, sure we will." Luc's voice sounded strained, but almost cheerful. "Here, hold the wheel for a second."

"What?"

Instinctively, Katie grabbed the steering wheel when Luc let go. He reached over and got the machine gun, opened his window, twisted around and shot back at the sedans.

"What are you doing?" she shouted at him as she struggled to control the car.

"What do you think I'm doing?" He kept his foot jammed on the accelerator, his upper body turned out of the window, firing more shots. Tires squealed behind them. "Just try to drive straight."

"Drive straight?" Katie looked out of the windshield and gulped. She could see curves up ahead through the rows of green corn stalks. Really, really sharp curves. With banks of rock and dirt on either side.

And the car was going way too fast to handle them.

"Luc!"

He ignored her, continuing to shoot at their pursuers. The cloud of dust behind them had reached epic proportions, which made the Nova harder to hit, but also kept Luc from getting a good shot at anything. Or so she guessed from his very imaginative cursing.

But to tell the truth, Katie wasn't paying much attention. She was too busy watching those curves in the road getting closer.

Taking one hand off the wheel, she pushed at Luc's leg to try to get him to ease up on the gas pedal.

"Luc, slow down!"

"What?" Irritated, he turned and finally saw what she saw. "Holy shit." Spinning fully into the seat, he shoved the weapon at her and grabbed the steering wheel.

"Don't shoot anything," he ordered.

"But—"

"I mean it, Katie."

Grumbling a little, but glad that the car was back in Luc's capable hands—and out of hers—Katie carefully put the safety back on the gun and propped it on the floor. Luc braked, Kato screeched, and they hit the first curve.

When the car swerved violently, Spot woke up. Barking.

"Jesus Christ. Be quiet!" Luc shouted at the dog. "Sit!"

He'd managed to slow the car down a little, but they still whipped through the turns like a roller coaster ride while stones and clods of mud and dirt spat out around them. The Nova veered into a deep gully on the edge of one of the embankments, but with brute strength Luc wrestled it back into the two ruts passing for the road.

There was a horrendous sound of crunching metal behind them.

"What happened?" Katie looked up over the seatback.

Luc took one hand off the wheel long enough to push her back down. "Damn it, you sit too."

"It looks like they crashed or something." She spun to face him. "We got away!"

"Not quite," Luc replied grimly, glancing in the rearview mirror. "They've already straightened themselves out. All we got was a little time." He made a sharp turn onto another farm road and Katie pitched sideways into his shoulder.

"Would you give me some warning before you do that?" she snapped at him.

"Sounds familiar."

"Funny."

Now that Spot was up, she was easier to reach. Katie ran her hands over the dog again, looking for an injury.

Spot didn't show any sign of pain until Katie touched the back of her head, then she yipped and pulled away. Katie frowned and faced forward again as the car jostled and bumped and bottomed out and finally hit smooth pavement.

"There's a wound on her head, but it doesn't seem too bad."

"Good." Luc sounded a little preoccupied.

Katie saw that they were now on a nice, straight, empty asphalt two-lane road. The black sedans had fallen behind, thank God, and hadn't made the turn yet, but she knew they would. They would.

Luc grabbed her arm. "We need to switch drivers."

"What?" She stared at him. "Are you crazy?"

"Yes. Look, those assholes will be behind us any minute. We need to take them out—"

"I told you I could shoot the machine gun thing."

"—and you can't hit the side of a barn—"

"I can so hit a barn! Didn't you see what I did at the house?"

"—so we have to switch."

"You couldn't think of this before we were driving eighty miles per hour?"

"Ninety."

"Whatever." There were the sounds of squealing tires behind them. Frankie's men had made the turn. "We can't just, like, stop."

"No. We can't." He glanced at her.

She stared back at him, hardly able to believe what she thought he was suggesting. He couldn't be thinking...he couldn't mean...

He was. He did.

"You want to switch drivers while we're driving?"

"Yeah. The advantage of an, um, vintage car like the Nova is that it's big." His eyes moved over her and even under the circumstances she felt herself grow unaccountably warm. "And you're short."

"Petite."

"Exactly. So it should work."

Katie restrained herself from punching him because he was still driving. A bullet whizzed by, and one of Kato's new side mirrors shattered.

The one on her side of the car.

"Okay, then. What do you want me to do?"

"Get in my lap."

"Excuse me?"

More gunshots sounded behind them. Something "pinged" off the trunk and somewhere glass shattered. They both ducked instinctively.

"Don't argue with me!" Luc shouted. "Just come on and do it. Once you have control of the car, I'll slide out from underneath you."

Katie still wasn't sure about this whole thing, but she edged closer to him on the seat. "Well…all right…"

She wasn't prepared for the way his arm snaked out and pulled her over and up into his lap. Luc blew at her hair and she shivered.

"Katie, I can't see around your hair. Will you take the wheel already?"

"Oh, yeah. Sure. Sorry." She blushed.

Once she had the wheel, he shifted his legs, somehow switching so his left foot was on the accelerator instead of his right one, then slid out from under her, his body rubbing against hers intimately as he moved. All of those bullets shooting past the windows didn't seem to matter so much.

Well, they didn't matter until one of them caught the already broken mirror on the side of the car and Katie realized just how high her head was above the back of the seat.

"You should have just let me drive in the first place," she said.

"I didn't think about it, okay?" He sounded irritated. "I guess I'm only human, after all."

"Sorry, sorry."

"Put your foot over mine on the gas pedal," he directed. Katie obeyed and he slipped his foot out from under hers while he slid over into the passenger seat. With barely a bobble, she was now driving the car. Katie shook her head. Amazing.

"Thank Christ there's no center console in this thing. That would have hurt," Luc muttered.

Katie giggled. Giggled! She really must be hysterical.

He grabbed the machine gun she'd propped against the door and rolled down the passenger window. Then he took a minute to pin her with a dark and steely glance. "Now drive fast."

"Yes, sir."

Katie stomped her foot even harder on the gas pedal, although it was already pressed down to the floor. Kato shuddered, but he truly was a mountain cat at heart so he didn't stall.

Luc leaned out the window and shot in earnest at the

cars following them, his concentration complete and his skill with the weapon evident. But hitting something moving at almost a hundred miles an hour while you were doing the same was difficult at best, and since the Nova shook with effort, it kind of stacked the odds against him. He shot, missing and cursing, until there was a squeal and loud crash behind them.

Katie looked in the rearview mirror. One of the sedans had made friends with a telephone pole, and was now smoking and crumpled by the side of the road.

"You got one!" she cried out.

"About goddamn fucking time." Luc ducked back inside, then put his hand to his head and winced. "Sorry. Christ, my head hurts."

Katie glanced over at him. "Are you going to throw up?"

"No."

"Good." She shivered. "Because here they come." The two remaining black sedans were bearing down on them again.

Spot barked and lifted her head, but Luc shoved her back down. "Stay."

"Will she listen?"

"Probably not. Don't worry about her, just drive."

"I'm trying to."

Luc checked the ammunition clip then turned to lean out the window again, methodically pulling the trigger. A second later, the front window of one of the sedans chasing them shattered, the car veered wildly off the road, flipped and exploded into fire.

"Two," Luc said.

The Nova practically flew up a steep hill until, almost too late, Katie realized the road was a dead end, and they were at the intersection of a busy crossroad.

"Oh, God." She eased up on the gas without really even thinking about it.

"What are you doing? Why are you stopping?" Luc yelled at her. "They're right behind us."

"I know that!" Katie shouted back at him. Taking a deep breath, she punched down the accelerator and sent Kato jolting out onto the cross road, making the cars already there scatter for safety. A moment later the one remaining black sedan followed.

"Shit," Luc muttered.

"I'm doing the best I can." Now that they were on a flat, straight road again, Kato's engine was cranking. Katie frowned over at Luc.

"It's not that I don't appreciate… Jesus Christ, look out!" he shouted

Katie jerked her attention back to the road and realized they were coming up behind a long line of traffic moving very, very slowly for no obvious reason. She slammed on the brakes while Luc braced himself against the dashboard.

The Nova drew to a shuddering halt, gently kissing the bumper of the car in front of it.

"What's going on?" she asked.

"How the hell should I know?"

The sedan was coming up fast behind them. There were so many cars around them now, so many innocent people who might be hurt or killed by a stray bullet. Katie knew that she had to act quickly. This was no time for common sense.

"Hold on," she yelled to Luc.

"What?"

Without answering or even stopping to think about what she was doing, Katie swerved out into the lane for the opposing traffic and sent Kato right up the middle of the road. They forced the drivers coming toward them over into the shoulder while horns blared and tires squealed.

The black sedan followed without hesitation.

Luc, who'd been taken completely by surprise, rapped his head on the window frame when the car jerked and swerved.

"Ow. Shit. What are you doing? Are you crazy?" he shouted.

"I hope not."

While Luc muttered curses and prayers beside her, Katie clung to the steering wheel. They crested a rolling hill. As they started down the other side she finally saw what had caused the backup. A huge crane was lumbering slowly along at the head of the line of traffic, doing fifteen miles per hour at best.

But what caused the breath to die in her throat was the vehicle she could now see coming at them.

"Oh, crap," she whispered.

She couldn't believe it. She didn't believe it. It was a house—a house for sweet Christ's sake. Well, half a house. Half a double-wide trailer, to be precise. The oversized truck pulling it was already running in the shoulder and it still took up more than the width of its own lane of the road.

Katie's heart pounded heavily. The road now dropped off sharply on their left, cars were on their right and murderers were behind them. They were boxed in. She heard Luc cursing, low and violently.

"You have to keep going now. Get past that crane."

Katie didn't bother answering because she knew he was right. She demanded even more speed from the Nova, and its wheels practically left the ground.

The truck pulling the house had seen them and stopped, but the crane still continued its slow pace forward, its operator apparently blissfully unaware of what was happening behind him. Katie was praying out loud now as she watched the gap between the two large vehicles narrow. The Nova had nothing left to give.

She held her breath. They drew even with the crane. There was a horrible stretch when she was sure they wouldn't make it. Then, at the last minute, she swerved around the crane and missed the house by inches.

"Holy shit." Luc's voice sounded reverential and just a little weak.

Behind them there was the sound of horns, of squealing brakes, of crashing metal.

"Are we alive? Are we still alive?" Katie asked. She tried to control the trembling of her hands on the steering wheel.

Luc leaned out the window to look behind them. "That crash must have been the guys chasing us. I don't see them and the crane's stopped now. Nobody's getting through."

"Thank God. Oh, thank God."

Luc turned to face forward. "You can say that again, sweetheart. Talk about stupid luck."

"You said you were sure we'd get away."

"I lied."

For a few minutes the only sounds in the car were the whine of Kato's engine and their own heavy breathing.

"Did you get Frankie? When you shot at him back in the Museum?" Katie asked. There wasn't any traffic now, the way clear.

"I think so."

"Do you think he's dead?"

"I doubt it."

"Oh."

Silence.

"I wonder who was kidnapped," Katie said, voicing the question that had been haunting her since they'd overheard Frankie's conversation back at the Museum. "Who's being taken to Atlantic City?"

"Yeah, I've been thinking about that myself," Luc admitted. "Whoever she is, she's in some serious trouble."

"We have to help her."

"I'll help her after you're safe."

Katie started to protest, but just sighed when she saw the firm set of his jaw.

"I wish I knew who she was," she said instead.

"It sounded like somebody was at your apartment. Or close to it."

"I wasn't expecting anyone."

"One of your neighbors? Checking up on things?"

"I wouldn't think so." She tried to picture her neighbors in her mind.

"Whoever she is, she has to look enough like you to fool Frankie's guys. They had to have a description."

"I'm not sure…" Her voice trailed off as a sudden, horrifying thought struck her. Her stomach pitched and dropped. "Oh, no. Please God, no."

Her mother.

"What?"

"It could have been…" She pulled her purse up from the floor and tried to rummage through it one-handed, digging frantically for her cell phone. "It might…please don't tell me…"

"Jesus! Don't tell you what? Would you just drive? And don't use that thing." Luc handed her the small cell phone she'd used earlier. "If you have to call someone, use this one."

Katie grabbed the phone and, eyes flickering from it to the road, punched in her parents' phone number. No answer. She tried her mother's cell. No answer. There were other explanations, of course. Of course there were. But she knew. She just knew.

She gave the phone back to Luc, hand shaking.

"Katie." His voice was a low growl. "Talk to me."

"I think they have my mother."

"Your mother?"

"You know how I told you the other morning that I wasn't sure she'd completely bought my story about the retreat? She was depressed and antsy. And she's so stubborn. She said she didn't think I sounded right, and… She doesn't normally check up on us. She always says that we're all adults and are entitled to live our own lives without her interference." Katie knew she was babbling, but she couldn't seem to stop. "She told me once that she never wanted to be like her own mother, that she wanted us to have our privacy. She never wanted any of us to think we couldn't trust her—"

"Katie."

"—but we look a lot alike. Mom and me. Well, she's prettier, but we're the same height and we have the same build and her hair's red like mine. Most of the other kids took after my father, but not me. Mom put her stamp on me—"

"Katie," Luc said again. He put his hand over hers on the steering wheel. She realized she had a death-grip on the wheel, that her knuckles were clenched and white.

"Darren always says that I'm a chip off the old Mc-Creary, which Mom hates because she hates being called 'old' anything. Anyway, she has a key to my apartment." She swallowed. "She doesn't sneak and or spy on me, but if she thought something was wrong, if she didn't believe the story I told her and stewed about it for a couple of days and decided to go see for herself…if she was worried about me, she might have gone to the apartment. She might have gone, Luc. And it would have been so easy to mistake her for me…" Katie ran out of breath and she just panted for a moment.

Luc didn't say anything for a long time.

"Maybe," he finally agreed. "Maybe."

Katie's heart pounded. She clenched the steering wheel even tighter under his warm grip. For once she wanted him to argue, to tell her that she was an idiot, that her idea was stupid.

"Luc, my mother! What are we going to do?"

He sighed and squeezed her hand before he released it.

"We'll figure out something."

TWENTY-ONE

THEY SWITCHED DRIVERS again, this time the old fashioned way—by pulling over to the side of the road. Then they drove on without speaking for quite some time. Luc seemed to know where he was going and eventually farm and country turned to suburban sprawl, the two-lane road to a busy highway.

Katie thought about her mother. Maybe she wasn't the person being taken to Atlantic City. Maybe it was somebody else.

Maybe.

She shifted her gaze to the scenery flashing by the window. The day had turned hot, almost stiflingly so. Kato's air conditioning worked, but the compressor was as old as the rest of him, so it didn't keep the car what you could call cool. She rolled down her window and lifted her face to the warm, humid breeze.

She didn't want to believe that it was her mother, but if somebody who looked like her had been in her apartment, who else could it be? Had they realized yet who her mom was? Had they hurt her yet?

Katie swallowed and instinctively looked to Luc for reassurance. His face was drawn into harsh lines, the scar slashing tightly white across his cheek. He met her eyes when he sensed her watching him, and his own were dark and deep under his brows.

"It will be okay," Katie whispered, compelled for some reason she couldn't explain to be the one who comforted.

He turned away without speaking. They were both quiet while the wind whistled and Kato hummed along the road and Spot snored in the backseat loudly enough to be heard over both.

"I have to stop for a minute," Luc said.

"Stop? Why?"

"I have to make a phone call, and I don't want to risk using the cell phone." He smiled, a small shadow of his normal grin, as he turned the car into the parking lot of a convenience store, drawing to a stop under the shade of a scrubby tree. "Besides, I need to get some aspirin."

Katie realized that her own head was pounding. "Better make that enough for two," she told him.

Luc nodded. "Do you need to, uh, use the facilities?"

Katie couldn't quite control a blush. "No, I'm good."

"Then why don't you wait here? I'll leave the car running."

"Okay."

"Maybe if you close the windows the air conditioner will work better."

She laughed a little. "Trust me on this one. The only thing that will make the air conditioner work better is if I get another car."

He smiled again, got out and opened the back door. Spot let him run his hands over her, even let him push aside fur to look at the wound Katie had found earlier. When she finally pulled away, Luc let her go.

"Looks like someone shot at her and creased the back of her head. Must have had a silencer," he added. "Since we, uh, you didn't hear a gunshot. It knocked her out. "

"And they didn't make sure they'd killed her?" Katie wondered. "Not that I wanted them to," she put in hastily.

Luc shrugged. "Who knows? Maybe they thought she was dead. I'm just glad they were sloppy." He slammed the door shut, then leaned in the open window. Spot tried to lap his face, but Luc ignored her and stared at Katie with a fixed intensity.

"I'm going to find the woman who's been taken to Atlantic City, Katie."

She saw the resolve in his face and smiled. "I know."

He hesitated, then nodded and, after a quick pat for Spot, strode off in the direction of a bank of pay phones.

Katie watched him go, his long legs eating up the ground, his old cargo pants riding low on his hips. On the other side of the parking lot, he leaned against the side of one of the phone boxes, balancing the receiver between his chin and shoulder as he dialed. A few minutes later he was talking. He seemed angry, his hand moving in the air as he spoke.

She wished she knew what he had in mind. She wished she knew how to help him. They'd have to talk about it so she could convince him to let her be involved in whatever he did. Then she could tell him she was sorry she'd upset him last night. Maybe he'd tell her that it was all right.

Luc hung up the phone and, as if he knew she was watching him, turned and held up one finger before striding into the store. Presumably for the aspirin.

Katie sighed and rested her head back on the seat, trying to ignore how Spot nuzzled her hair.

She hated the fact that Frankie was after her. That her mother was very likely in danger. That she had been thrown into a terrifying situation and didn't know which way to turn. She even hated the heartache and pain she could see coming not too far down the road when Luc walked away from her. She hated all of that and more. But she didn't regret last night. She wasn't sorry about Luc.

What was killing her was the sneaking suspicion that he had a different opinion on the matter.

She closed her eyes.

This was a fine mess she'd gotten herself into, wasn't it? A fine state of affairs.

She was still sitting like that when Spot woofed in greeting. She looked up and straightened as Luc walked up to the car. He was holding a surprisingly large paper bag in one hand and a couple of bottles of water in the other.

"Whatcha got?" she asked, striving for a casual tone.

"Supplies." He handed her the bottles of water through the open window, then put the bag on the driver's seat. He drew out a large plastic cup, took one of the bottles back from Katie and poured most of the water into it. She held out a hand, expecting him to give it to her, but instead he opened the rear car door and offered the cup to Spot, who slurped at it with mad enthusiasm. Katie sighed and opened another bottle for herself.

After Spot had finished drinking, Luc used the rest of the water and a paper towel to clean the back of her head before smearing on what looked like antibiotic ointment. Finally, he pulled a container of aspirin out of the bag, then stored everything except it and the last unopened bottle of water behind the driver's seat. Spot snuffled at the bag with a distinct lack of enthusiasm, which meant there probably wasn't any food, darn it. Katie was starving.

Luc closed the door on Spot and slid into the car, then struggled with the childproof cap on the aspirin.

"How is she?" Katie asked, breaking the silence.

"Seems okay. The wound isn't very deep. She probably has a headache, though."

"She should join the club." She watched him wrestle with the cap until she couldn't stand it anymore, then took the bottle away from him. Efficiently, she dealt with the cap, the safety seal and the cotton stuffed in the top before dumping out two tablets for herself and handing it back.

Luc glared at her before he dumped four of the aspirin into his hand and tossed them into his mouth, chasing them down with a drink of water.

"Who did you call? It was David, right?" she asked.

"No."

His answer caught her by surprise just as she was swallowing her own aspirin, and she coughed and sputtered until he started to whack her on the back.

"I'm fine. I'm fine," she choked, afraid he was going

to send her sailing right through the windshield. She coughed a little more, eyes watering, and finally got the aspirin down. "You didn't call David?"

"Didn't I just say that?" He put Kato into gear and backed out of the parking spot.

"Well, yes, but why not?"

Luc turned the Nova onto the highway. "You were right. Somebody had to tell Frankie where we were."

Katie gaped at him. "You think it was David?"

"No. Maybe. Hell, I don't know." Luc rubbed a hand through his hair. "I've just been wondering, that's all. About how they found my house. And how they knew what section of the house we'd be in. And how they got through the alarm system, although any half-rate break-in guy probably could have cracked it."

"Well, it was the leak, right? The mole at the Bureau. Whatever you call someone like that. What are you trying to say, anyway?"

Luc glanced at her. "Look, maybe it was the mole. Or maybe they just lucked out and found you through me." He hesitated. "Or maybe it was David."

She stared at him. "You really think he's the mole?"

His mouth was grim. "All I'm saying is that we can't risk letting David know where we are, and we can't tell him that Frankie Silvano's guys probably have your mother. We can't be sure word won't get back to the wrong people." He glanced at her, then away. "We really are on our own now."

Katie watched the highway unfold in front of them as she listened to Spot snore in the backseat. She looked over at Luc again. "But won't David wonder where we are? He said he was going to call today."

"Yeah." Luc's eyes were focused on the road. He guided Kato through the traffic, his face set. "He'll try to find us when he can't get us on the phone. I don't even want to think about what's going to happen when he sees the Museum. After you and your mother are both safe, I'll get in touch with him. Then he and I will talk." There was stark promise in the words.

Katie tried to listen to what he wasn't saying. "If David told Frankie where we are, what else has he told him?"

"Shit." Luc ran a hand up the side of his face and then around to massage the back of his neck before gripping the wheel. "Frankly, I'm so goddamn tired I don't even know what to think anymore. I can't think. David Allen pulled me off the streets and took me into his home when nobody in their right mind would have even given me a second look. He taught me how to be a human being instead of some kind of an animal. He's a good man, Katie. The best."

You don't trust him, she thought, and it's killing you.

"I'm sure there's an explanation. There's got to be," he continued. Katie knew he was talking as much to convince himself as her.

But what had David Allen been doing for the past couple of days, she wondered. How could they know for sure?

Without saying anything, she edged across the seat and leaned against Luc. He tensed, but didn't move her away. She put her head on his shoulder and slid her arm around his waist. She didn't really know what she was doing, she just wanted to let him know she was there. But she found that the warmth and scent of his body comforted her as well.

Luc relaxed a little. Almost hesitantly he took one of his hands off the steering wheel, put his arm around her shoulders and pulled her closer.

Katie sighed. She might not have him forever. He might push her out of his life at any moment. After the way she'd called him Bruce last night, he might think the only thing she felt for him was a leftover, childish crush. He might never see who she really was.

But right now he needed her just as much as she needed him. Right now she was important to him. Right now she could hold him.

That had to count for something.

LUC THOUGHT SOMETHING inside of him shifted when she touched him. She felt good up against him; his arm felt good around her. He let himself briefly savor the sensation of her body next to his, her head on his shoulder, the softness of her breasts pressed to his side, the way her hair smelled like his shampoo. He breathed deeply, letting her nearness ease him on some deep level. It was too bloody hot in the car to hold her this way, but he wasn't going to let her go.

The traitor had to be someone else. David more than likely didn't have anything to do with it. Hell, David had been almost like a father to him, for all that he was only seven or eight years older. He trusted him.

But the little voice of suspicion just kept whispering.

His arm tightened around Katie. Nobody else had known where they were.

Luc shook his head slightly. No, he was being stupid to even suspect David.

He was pulled out of his reverie by a strange, low, grumbling noise. After a moment he realized the source was Katie's stomach, and he glanced down at her with more than a little amusement. She looked embarrassed. She looked adorable. He wanted to kiss her, to touch her again. To say the hell with whatever she thought of him, and lose himself in her body for just a little while. To say the hell with the consequences.

"Sorry." She moved away slightly and cleared her throat. "You, um, didn't happen to pick up any baked goods when you were in that store, did you?"

He grinned. It was good to smile. "We're going to stop in a few minutes. You'll be fine."

"Easy for you to say," she muttered, but her head found his shoulder again. Her wild red curls brushed his chin.

His smile broadened for an instant, then he sobered as he turned his attention back to the road, absently stroking Katie's upper arm, her soft skin. Frankie Silvano was undoubtedly still alive, and if he was, he'd be on their trail again soon. Katie had to be kept safe. She wasn't going to suffer any more because of him. That was non-negotiable. And if her mother had been kidnapped, well, he'd rescue her. He'd fix things. He'd make things right.

She thought he was Bruce.

Yeah, he would right all of the wrongs he'd done to her, just like some kind of a fucking superhero. And then he'd do her the biggest favor of all and disappear.

TWENTY-TWO

LUC'S FEW MINUTES actually turned out to be closer to an hour. Katie returned to her own seat after a little while and fell into a light, exhausted doze, waking only when the car came to a stop and the engine died. Disoriented, she raised her head and blinked when she realized they were in a large parking lot attached to a series of sleek, modern buildings.

Spot put her big, shaggy head over the back of the seat and looked at them, eyebrows wriggling soulfully as she rolled her red, drooping eyes from one to the other. She was so pathetic Katie couldn't help but laugh.

"Poor baby." She rubbed the dog's jowls and was rewarded with a blast of dog breath potent enough to make her cough and quickly turn away.

"Our secret weapon," Luc chuckled. She was glad to see a gleam of humor back in his dark eyes.

"You can say that again." Katie studied the buildings. "Where are we anyway?"

"A popular South Jersey convention center."

She stared at him. "For Pete's sake, why?"

"I have to meet a guy. He's going to help us."

"You are? He is? Who?"

"Someone I know," Luc said evasively.

Katie watched him quietly. "Someone you trust?"

"For this, yes. He, uh, thinks he owes me."

She nodded, accepting the explanation for now. "And you're meeting him here?" She looked at the buildings again. One of them, she assumed it was the hotel, stood five or six stories tall, with another long, low structure spreading out at a right angle from the side. There must have been a convention or meeting in progress because the parking lot was packed. She could see men and women in business suits coming and going through large glass doors.

On a brighter note, it looked like the complex boasted at least one restaurant inside, in addition to the normal sprinkling of chains on the periphery. Maybe there was some food in her immediate future, after all.

Her stomach rumbled loudly in anticipation at the thought.

"So, it's safe to stop?" she asked.

"Safe enough." Luc smiled. "Besides, you need to eat. Your stomach's singing an entire opera now."

"Well, sorry. I'm not a camel. You know, storing food in my humps or something."

Luc's eyes ran over her and she felt warmer. "Yeah. I like your humps the way they are."

Katie blushed. "Jerk."

The word "food" had caught Spot's attention, and she nuzzled the back of Luc's head with a fair amount of enthusiasm. The nudge would have broken Katie's neck, but Luc just laughed and reached back to fondle the dog's ears.

"Yes, yes. I said the 'F' word. Don't worry, we'll get you a side of beef to gnaw on." He looked at Katie. "Let me take Spot for a quick walk before we go inside, okay? It's been a long morning for her, too, and she probably needs to, uh, take care of business. You might as well stay here for a minute."

Fond as she was of the Newfoundland, Katie had absolutely no desire to participate in Spot's bathroom activities, so she nodded and relaxed back against the seat, watching Luc get out of the car and walk off with the big dog. Spot ran obediently beside him and, when she discreetly slipped behind some well-kept shrubbery to do her business. Luc looked back at Katie and grinned. That smile, the sparkle she could see in his eyes even from where she sat, hit her like and unexpected punch to the stomach.

Oh, God. She even found him attractive while he was waiting for his dog to poop. This was bad.

He winked at her and turned away, whistling with elaborate casualness, hands tucked in his front pockets. The breeze stirred his hair and whipped it around his head. His T-shirt stretched across his shoulders and his stance stretched the light material of his cargo pants across his butt. God, he had a nice ass. She wanted to take a bite out of it.

Katie groaned.

Bad.

Really bad.

Man and dog loped back to the car after the completion of an apparently successful mission, and Katie got out to join them.

"Whoever finds that isn't going to be happy," Luc chuckled.

Katie sighed. "You're not even going to try to clean it up, are you?"

He arched his eyebrows at her. "With what? A napkin?"

"Okay. Valid point."

"Let's go in and get something to eat."

"Who could resist after such an appetizing moment." She gestured to the dog. "What about Spot?"

He grinned at her. "She's coming with us."

Katie stared at him. "They're not going to let you take a dog into a restaurant. Especially not a dog approximately the size of a bus."

"Don't worry. It's all been arranged."

"Arranged? How? When?"

"When I made the reservations."

"Reservations..." Katie shook her head to clear it. It didn't work. "What are you talking about?"

Luc opened the car door and took out the mysterious paper bag he'd brought from the convenience store. He pulled out a dog leash that seemed much too small and laid it on the roof. "This is where the guy wanted to meet me," he explained patiently. "The restaurant only accepts reservations, so I called and made one after I talked to him. Get it?"

"I guess." Katie was still a little dazed. She felt even more so when, without any modesty or concern, he stripped off his shirt right there in the middle of the parking lot, all of his smooth brown skin glistening in the sunshine. Her fingers itched to touch, to stroke. Her mouth longed to taste the tanned flesh, the paler scars, the dusting of black hairs... Her whole body clenched.

Luc didn't pay any attention to her. He just tossed the T-shirt onto the backseat of the car, then reached into the bag and pulled out a white polo shirt with "Welcome to New Jersey" embroidered across the pocket. The muscles in his arms and chest bunched and flexed as he pulled the new shirt over his head and tucked it into his jeans.

"There. Now for you." That got her attention.

Her eyes snapped to meet his. She saw that he was smiling slightly, as if he'd known very well what he was doing to her. Jerk.

"Me?" she asked suspiciously. He wasn't going to ask her to strip down in the parking lot, too, was he? Talk about frightening.

"Do you have sunglasses?"

"Sure."

He nodded. "They should be okay as long as they're dark. I got you a pair at the store, but you'll probably be more comfortable if you wear your own glasses. Put them on, and let's see how you look."

Still not quite sure what he was up to, Katie got her purse out of the car and dug out the shades. She switched them with her regular glasses, and everything went dark and muted. It was almost comforting.

Luc looked her over critically. "Fine. Now wrap this around your hair." He reached into the bag again, pulled out a bandana and held it out to her.

Katie looked at it, looked at him and then pushed up the sunglasses so she could see the thing without the dark lenses. She was sorry she had.

"It's purple," she said.

"So?"

"It's a really bright purple."

"And I repeat. So?" He pushed the bandana closer to her.

She backed away. "How shall I put this delicately? Um, no."

"Katie—"

"Nope. No way. Not in this life or any other. I am not putting that purple thing on my head."

"You have to."

"Obviously you weren't listening when I said no."

"Katie, I love your hair, but it does tend to stand out in a crowd. This should cover most of it."

Her jaw dropped and she stared at him. He loved her hair? He loved her hair?

Loved. Her. Hair.

Does. Not. Compute.

She was so floored by the information she couldn't even protest when Luc finally got tired of waiting for her to take the bandana and tied it around her head himself like a scarf, his long fingers grazing her neck as he stuffed as much of her hair under it as he could. When he was done, she felt like a housewife straight from the fifties and guessed that she looked just about as bad as she'd suspected she would. Hey, Luuuuuucyyyy!

"Perfect," Luc said and snapped the ridiculously tiny purple leash onto Spot's collar. "Here. Take this."

"Why?" Katie's fingers twitched. Even the fact that he loved her hair wouldn't keep her from throttling him if he didn't answer at least answer one question.

"You're blind."

She blinked behind the glasses. "Excuse me?"

"You're visually impaired, and Spot is your Seeing Eye dog," Luc explained patiently. "That was the only way they would let us bring her into the restaurant without causing a scene. And if anybody asks about us later, I want people to remember a blind woman in a purple bandana and her dog. Not the sexy redhead."

Katie stared at him and absently took the leash. "Are you telling me that you did all of this just so Spot could come into the restaurant with us?"

"Well, I also wanted to change our appearance a little bit in case Frankie manages to find our trail, but yeah, I guess I did. It's too hot for her to wait in the car. Besides, she saved our lives and she's hungry. She's coming in."

The man was insane. Just insane. The hair comment had made her suspicious, and this clinched it. Her heart, already a puddle, melted a little bit more. He was doing this for his dog. Awwww.

"You're nuts."

He took her arm. "Thanks."

Katie tried to act sightless as Luc, with his usual calm assurance, shepherded her and Spot to the *very* fancy convention center. Everything went okay until Spot spied a fountain near the main entrance and made a beeline for it, dragging Katie along behind her as if she were nothing more than a bothersome flea.

Ignoring the stares of passersby, the dog waded right into the fountain's shallow pool and slurped water as if she was trying to drain the thing. Katie tugged desperately at the ridiculous leash and was completely disregarded by the dog until Luc stopped laughing long enough to help her.

Eventually Spot obeyed…something, either Luc's commands or Katie's muttered oaths, and climbed back out of the fountain, but with such a longing backwards glance that Katie tugged even harder on the leash in case the big monster decided to take another swim. But she was a little sorry she was standing that close when Spot shook herself and sent a shower of water all over her and anyone else unfortunate enough to be nearby. Which Luc wasn't, Katie noticed. He'd taken shelter behind a shrub, obviously anticipating what the dog was going to do. Jerk.

Spot looked up at her and wagged her tail, dripping a little and jowls happily a-drool.

Katie sighed.

Still chuckling, Luc took her arm again, pulling her and the dog into the convention center.

Once they were inside the building, Katie found that her blind act wasn't all that far from the truth. Her sunglasses were pretty dark and the place was dimly lit, so it really was difficult to see. Luc's hand was warm and strong on her elbow as he led her around obstacles and people with apparent care and concern. An act, she reminded herself. It's all an act. Don't get all excited about it.

Sexy redhead? Please.

Even through the dark glasses, Katie could tell that the restaurant Luc was steering them toward was posh and expensive to the max. They probably didn't even have prices on the menus.

And she was wearing a purple bandana on her head. A very bright purple bandana.

Did he honestly think she wouldn't stick out?

She shook her head, but carefully so as not to dislodge the hideous monstrosity covering her hair. Maybe sticking out was the point. If they were asked later, the people inside were definitely going to remember her, but they'd remember this…uh, disguise, not her as she normally looked. So that was a good idea, right?

All right, it was, she admitted to herself a little sulkily. But when she glanced over and saw Luc next to her, all handsome and confident in his very nice white polo shirt, it just didn't seem very fair.

Luc brought them to a halt in front a lectern placed just inside the restaurant door and waited for the maître d' to notice them. Spot immediately sat at Katie's side, looked around with great interest and dripped on the dense carpeting.

The maître d' had been standing in the middle of the restaurant talking to one of the waitresses, but with the sixth sense of a good host he turned to them, smiling broadly in welcome. The smile faded immediately when he saw Spot sitting at Katie's foot, tongue lolling.

The little man rushed forward, hands waving wildly. "Oh, my God! Oh, my God! Get that…that…thing out of my restaurant!" he sputtered.

Luc looked around blankly until his gaze fell on Katie. "Her?" He jerked his thumb at her. "I realize she's a little short, but it's hardly fair to call her a thing."

"Hey!"

"Not her." If Katie had been able to see the maître d'

without her sunglasses, she was sure that his face would have been a very lovely shade of red. "That." He pointed a shaking finger at Spot. "Get that…that…that bear out of here!"

"Ohhhh." Luc smiled cheerfully. "We have a reservation. Smith. Party of three. The bear is one of the three."

"But—"

"I called earlier today. Remember? My wife is blind, and this is her Seeing Eye dog."

Wife? Katie resisted the urge to stare at him, but only barely. Wife?

The maître d's eyes roamed over her. She knew he had taken in the full effect of her purple bandana when his mouth twisted into a painful grimace of superior disdain. He sniffed. "Humph. Well, I don't believe it. I've never in my life seen a Seeing Eye dog like that."

Katie gripped Luc's arm tighter. "We tried for a Labrador, but they were all out," she said. "I didn't realize it mattered to the restaurant what breed of dog I owned," she added with an icy politeness. Hey, two could play that game.

Katie could see people at nearby tables listening to the conversation.

The maître d appeared to notice it as well, because he glanced around and rubbed his hands together nervously. "Well, uh, no. It doesn't. Of course it doesn't. It's just that the animal is shedding. And dripping all over the carpeting. The very expensive carpeting."

"Excuse me." Luc's voice was not loud, but it was cold and it carried. "Are you telling me that my blind wife cannot bring her Seeing Eye dog into this restaurant?"

People started to whisper.

The maître d's hands rubbed together faster and faster. Katie expected him to start a fire in a moment. Or maybe start humming like a locust.

"No! No, no, no." The little man broke under the pressure of so many eyes and grabbed some menus. "If you and your, uh, wife, will follow me."

They were led to a table at the very back of the restaurant right outside the restrooms. The maître d' waited until they were seated, then put the menus in front of them. "We're only serving lunch now," he warned. "The choice is limited."

"That's fine," Luc said.

"All right." The maître d glanced at Spot, who was making herself comfortable beside Katie's chair and swallowed. "What about the, uh, animal? Food...?"

"I'll order for both of the ladies," Luc told him gently.

"Oh. Good." The little man seemed to remember Katie was supposed to be blind. He started to pick up the menu, then hesitated, decided to leave it and scurried away.

Luc watched him go. "Asshole."

"Why did you tell him I was your wife?" Katie blurted out, and then bit back a groan. That was the last thing she'd wanted to ask.

Luc turned to her, and his frown faded into a small smile. "Because I wanted to."

"Oh." Well, there didn't seem to be too much to say to that one. She sat in silence for a minute while Luc

watched her with evident amusement and maybe just a
hint of something else. She wished she could take off her
sunglasses so she could see him clearly. She tugged at
the scarf around her hair and tried to adjust it so it was
more comfortable. "Can I take this off?"

"No." His smile broadened.

"Great." She tugged at it some more. "Why in the
world did you pick purple? I always look like a dead
woman in purple."

His eyes roved over her face. "You look great. I
thought purple would be a good girly color. It brings
out your eyes."

"I'm wearing dark glasses."

"I know what your eyes look like."

"Oh." Katie sighed deeply and let her gaze slide over
his face. Before she realized it, she had reached out her
hand and put it against his cheek, his growth of beard
rough against her fingertips. "Luc, what are we going
to do?"

He held her palm against his face. "The waitress is
coming. So right now, we're going to eat. I sure hope to
hell they have some real food here."

They did, although it took a minute to figure out that
the 'marinated lean ground beef on a Kaiser roll' was
really a hamburger.

After about ten, Spot fell to the floor with a happy
sigh and promptly started snoring. Katie felt some moisture on her foot and discreetly moved it out of the way
of any slobber.

"Well, that bump on her head certainly didn't hurt
her appetite."

Luc paused in the middle of stuffing a third hamburger into his own mouth. "She's had a rough day."

Katie folded her arms on the table, watching him eat. Her stomach was full, and her worries had returned full force.

"My mother knows karate. She's a black belt."

"She was taken by surprise, outweighed and outnumbered. If she knew how to fight, she probably fought, but these guys are rough. They know what they're doing."

Katie swallowed. "I hope she's okay."

"She will be." He smiled at her, although she could tell it was just a pathetic attempt to be supportive. "It could be worse, right? We know exactly where they took her. I'll get her out of this."

"So, when do we leave?" Katie leaned forward, eager to be up and doing.

Luc wiped his mouth with his napkin. Then he grabbed her hands, holding them gently down on the table. "We're not going anywhere. I'm going. Rescuing your mother, assuming it is your mother, means walking right into the middle of Silvano's organization. I'm not putting you in that kind of danger."

"But—"

"I'm not going to do it, Katie. I got you into this mess and I'll get you out, but I'm not going to let you walk into that…that pit with me. It's not going to happen."

Katie read the stubborn determination on his face. She knew, knew she was playing this wrong, but she couldn't seem to keep her mouth shut. Her spine stiffened. "You're not going to keep me out."

"I have to."

"I'm not going to sit around somewhere twiddling my thumbs while you go and risk your life. I can help. You need me."

"No," he said, "I don't. You'd only be in the way."

Katie felt that if she got any stiffer, she'd turn to stone. In the way. He didn't need her and he thought she was in the way.

She pulled her hands back and he let her go. The sudden pain inside her made her want to lash out.

"Yeah, you're right. I guess it is the least you can do. After all, this is all your fault. We wouldn't be in this mess if it wasn't for you."

"Like I said." His voice was calm now. Emotionless. "Wait here. I've got to make arrangements."

"What are you going to do, lock me up?" She was pushing him and she knew it, but if she didn't she was going to cry and that would be really embarrassing.

"Katie..." Luc said her name, stopped and stood. "Just stay here." He turned and walked quickly away.

She watched him go, watched him weave his way through the room. She even forced a smile for the openly curious waitress who'd come over to remove their plates. Shaking off the offer of dessert, she tried to ignore the moisture in her eyes and failed miserably. So, this was it, then. He was going off to play the big hero while she sat all alone and worried. Probably going to get himself killed.

And even if he managed to stay alive, she suspected that he'd never come back to her again. Not really.

But then, she'd never expected him to.

LUC IGNORED THE MAÎTRE D and walked to a small table tucked away in a corner near the bar.

The man who was its sole occupant looked up and met his eyes over a newspaper, then sighed, folded it and put it down on the table. "Vasco."

"Némes."

Luc studied Justin Némes. It had been about a year since they'd last seen each other, but the other man hadn't changed much, except now his dark hair was so long that he actually had to tie it back to keep it out of his face. That would have driven Luc nuts.

Némes's expression was blank as he returned the stare. "Is she really blind?"

"No." He pulled out a chair and sat without being invited. Although they hadn't been assigned together on the case that had destroyed Némes's career, this man had been his partner off and on for four years. They'd depended on each other, fought for each other. Saved each other. He'd thought they'd been friends. Almost family.

Until Liza.

"She isn't your usual type," Némes commented.

"Didn't know I had one." Luc leaned back in his chair, watchful.

"Of course you do. Leggy blondes with big tits. Liza." Némes smiled but it wasn't a pleasant sight. "Too bad we have the same taste."

Luc kept his face expressionless, but it took some effort.

"Is that the excuse you used to rationalize sleeping with her behind my back?"

Némes shrugged, a lazy roll of shoulders. "It just

kind of happened. One of those things. Spontaneous combustion."

But I trusted you. Luc shook off the thought. He knew what instant attraction did to a guy. Made him think with the little head instead of the big one. And Liza hooking up with Némes had shown him what she really was. Shown him what he really wanted.

And now there was Katie. Maybe if he hadn't been screwed over by Liza, he wouldn't appreciate Katie as much.

Némes was watching him, eyes lit with an ironic amusement. "So, how's David doing these days? Rumor has it he misses me."

Somehow Luc managed to hold on to his patience.

"He finally broke the Central American trafficking ring. Now we're rounding up the girls they'd already sold and trying to get them some help."

"Good. Very good." For a moment there was genuine emotion in Némes's hard face, then it was gone.

"You can't blame David for being pissed off."

"He wants me to pay because he had to rebuild the case from scratch." Némes smiled again, tightly. "Believe me, I've paid."

Luc nodded in silent acknowledgement of the part he'd played in that. They'd heard the rumors that Némes was pushing high-quality coke about the same time he'd found out about the man's affair with Liza. Finding out about his friend and his fiancée had rocked him hard.

So when the accusations of drug dealing surfaced, Luc had let emotion cloud his better judgment. He'd been the one to lead the criminal investigation that had forced Némes's resignation from the Bureau. It was only later, when he'd been able to think rationally, that he'd realized he might have acted too hastily. Whatever he'd done to clear Justin Némes had been too little, too late.

"So, tell me why you're here," Némes said. "I understand you gave my assistant quite a hard time until she handed out my cell phone number. I'm scheduled to lead a seminar on international taxation in a few minutes."

"Jesus Christ, you really are an accountant."

"I got my C.P.A. before I joined the Bureau." Némes smiled again, but it didn't reach his eyes. "Contingency. The work's a lot less stressful. Except at tax time, of course. And the pay's better, which I grant you isn't saying much. So. Talk to me."

"You've always said you felt like you owed me for your sister. I'm going to give you a chance to make it even." There'd never been a debt as far as Luc was concerned, but he knew Némes believed there was. And he knew that as long as Némes believed he was discharging an obligation, he could be trusted.

Luc was willing to say anything, do anything, use anything to keep Katie safe.

Something flared in Némes's face, but it was quickly gone. "Sara is alive. I owe you for that."

"Help me with this, and you'll never see me again. All debts canceled."

"Enticing beyond belief. What can I do for you?"

Luc leaned forward. Right now he didn't care about the past. He knew Justin Némes. He'd seen what the other man was capable of, had seen it firsthand. He could protect Katie.

"The young lady I'm with is a witness against…some very bad people. They're trying to kill her."

"Hmm."

"I have to go straighten out a few loose ends. While I'm gone I want you to watch out for her."

"Me?" For the first time, Némes's expression was less than contained. "Why me? Why not David?"

Luc shifted position. "I can't go to him," he said quietly.

Némes was silent for a few long seconds, digesting that. Luc didn't say anything else. Instead he sat back and waited, unwilling to give any more information than was absolutely necessary.

"Interesting." Némes pinned him again with his cold, blue stare. "And if I watch out for her while you're gone, we'll be even. Closed."

"Yes." Luc bit off the word, hoping to God that this time his instincts were sound. But what choice did he really have? He couldn't leave her without any protection at all.

Némes's smile was broad, feral. "What do you want me to do?"

TWENTY-THREE

KATIE LET LUC usher her and Spot into a room in the hotel that was attached to the convention center. She dropped her purse on a table and, as soon as Luc closed the door behind them, took off her sunglasses and put on her regular ones. Unable to stand the hideous bandana a second longer, she unknotted it and ripped it off her head. Her hair sprang free into a million bouncing curls, the follicles practically singing as she massaged her scalp. God, it felt good.

Spot, being a curious soul, wandered around the room sniffing at the rug and the air conditioner. Katie followed her, pretending to look out the window when she was really watching Luc from the corner of her eye. He stood just inside the door like a big granite statue—feet braced apart, arms folded across his chest.

A tall, cold stranger wearing Luc's face.

He was leaving. He was actually going to leave her.

Turning, she trailed a finger over the spread on the king-sized bed before facing him fully. Okay, she thought. One last chance. One last try.

"I want to come with you, Luc. Please take me with you."

She knew she'd failed to sway him when his face remained composed. Unmoved and uncompromising.

"No. You can't come." Final.

"I'll follow you," she threatened.

"No, you won't. Not if you ever want to see your mother alive again."

"But I—"

His composure cracked and fell away. "Would you just let me do my fucking job, Katie? I can't fucking find your mother if I'm worried about you all the time."

Katie looked away, refusing to admit he was right.

"You are staying here. End of argument. No discussion. I don't want to leave you alone, but I can't afford to wait. I have to get on the road. Némes will be here as soon as he's finished running his damned tax seminar. Jesus, I can't believe he's really an accountant."

Katie thought about the man Luc had introduced her to before they'd left the restaurant. He was probably as tall as Luc but not so heavily muscled, which gave him the impression of a sinewy grace. Like a big cat. His dark, silky hair was long and tied in a queue at the back of his neck, and his cold eyes were clear blue and empty. She didn't think he was an accountant either.

She sighed. "Yeah, yeah. I'm staying here, okay? I'll wait for Justin Némes. Satisfied?" What the hell was the point of arguing? He was leaving. No way would he take her with him. She'd be lucky if he didn't tie her up first to make sure she didn't move.

He studied her for a moment before nodding slowly. Now that he had her compliance, he seemed a little reluctant to go. Maybe he didn't trust her to keep her word. Maybe he shouldn't.

"I can't stay," he repeated.

"You said that. So go already." She tried to keep the bitterness out of her voice and failed.

"Némes will take you somewhere safe."

Safe. Yeah, right. No place was safe.

"You'll hear from me within three days." Luc hesitated. "If I'm not in touch by then, I won't be in touch at all."

Her eyes flew to his face. "Why—"

"Because I'll be dead. I won't leave you hanging otherwise."

Dead.

She couldn't control a violent shudder. In a couple of hours or days, Luc could be dead. This vital, caring, alive man standing across the room from her could be dead. He could die, and she would never know what happened, who killed him.

Katie put her hand to her chest because her heart was heavy. Numb.

"Here." Luc stepped forward to hand her a little card. She stared at it for a minute or two before she realized there was a name and telephone number printed on it. "This is Némes's cell. If anything happens before he gets here, you call him right away. I mean it, Katie, right away. We should have time before Frankie tracks you, but still…" He let the words trail off.

"Sure." Katie tucked the card into her pants pocket.

"I've rented a car for myself, and I'm leaving Spot here with you."

Recognizing her name, the dog walked up to him. He knelt, ruffling her large ears and stroking her head affectionately with his long fingers.

"She'll take care of you, won't you, girl?" Spot yipped and he straightened again.

"Luc...you'll be careful, right?" The words ripped out of her.

"Of course." He started to turn, to go, then hesitated. "I'll make sure your mother's safe."

"I know." She was crying, she realized, and wiped her cheeks with the backs of her hands like a child.

The reality of what was happening swept over her. The loneliness of it. The irrevocability of it. He was leaving. She might never see him again. He might die trying to save her and her mother. And even if he came back, she knew he would put aside the days they'd spent together.

Katie took a couple of steps toward him.

"I have to go," he murmured, backing away. For a moment there was a glint of something like desperation in his eyes. "I have to set up my cover."

"Yes. I understand." She smiled at him through her tears. Knowing this was the end gave her the courage to reach up to him, to take his face in her hands and pull it down closer to hers. She kissed him, kissed him with everything she felt, everything she was, tried to tell him what he meant to her without burdening him with words. And maybe she was just a little afraid to say the words anyway.

His hands stayed at his sides, but his lips parted, soft against hers. For one endless breath, he responded, mouth moving, tongue dancing with hers as he'd danced with her in the mirrored ballroom so long ago. In that instant he gave and she gave and they were both giving and receiving at the same time. The sensations spiraled around them and through them until she took that last step closer, molded her body to his and clung.

He let her hold him, then, abruptly, grabbed her shoulders and pushed her away. They stared at each other, lungs heaving, breaths mingling. Katie licked her lips and tasted him.

"Don't do this," he growled. "Just…don't."

"Don't do what?" She could barely talk. She wanted his mouth again. On hers. On her.

"This isn't right. You don't really want me."

"I don't?" Katie met his gaze and was trapped by the haunted expression in his beautiful eyes. "I think I do. I want you. Didn't I prove it last night?"

She leaned forward again, but stopped when his grip tightened to the point of pain. His sudden anger was unleashed and boiled against her skin as his fingers dug into her.

"You think you want me? You think you even fucking know who I am? I'm not fucking Bruce Wayne, or whatever else it is you think you see. I'm not even close. Isobel was a bitch, but she was right about me."

"Luc—" She reached for him, but he abruptly released her and spun away, one hand raking through his thick, dark hair. Then he turned to face her again, a sneer distorting his mouth.

"Between the Army and the Bureau, I've killed so many people that I've lost count. Do you know how much blood I've spilled in my life? A swimming pool full of it. A lake full of it. Enough blood to drown in." He laughed without humor. "But it doesn't mean dick.

War still happens. The creeps are still out there. The terrorists still attack innocent people. People still die when they should be alive."

She found her voice. "You're wrong if you think that's all you are."

He didn't seem to hear her. He was prowling, pacing back and forth, back and forth. "I couldn't stop those bastards from hurting Melanie at the foster home," he growled. "I couldn't stop them from hurting me. Then, after everything was finished, I finally managed to do something. Want to know how Winston died?"

"Luc, you don't need—"

But he didn't let her finish. His face was strained, his eyes wild. Katie knew it was all going to come out now whether she wanted to hear it or not. "I took off when Melanie went to live with you, but he still tracked me down. Fucking living on the streets like an animal, but I look up, and there's Winston standing at the end of the alley, smiling. I don't know how he found me, but the gang I'd been trying to join let him come. My initiation." He laughed again, a bark of sound.

"He wanted to teach me a lesson, but I'd learned a few tricks. I knifed him. Slit his throat. My first corpse, but not the last one, that's for damn sure. The gang was impressed."

"Luc—"

He stared at her, dark eyes blank. "I was glad I'd done it. Glad I'd been the one to off him. But it didn't help Melanie, did it? It was too damn late for that. I was too much of an idiot to know what was going on when it was happening. Too much of a coward to help her."

"You helped her." She sensed that he wouldn't welcome her touch right now, so she curled her fingers into her palms to keep from reaching for him. She wanted to cry for him, but she wouldn't let herself do that either.

"Oh, yeah, right. Sure. Like I've helped so many other people. Okay, then, let's talk about Marie, shall we? She was an informant. Just someone I was playing because I knew she had feelings for me, and she was helping in an investigation. I lied to her and I didn't—wouldn't—stop lying to her. I let her believe what she wanted to believe until she jumped in front of a bullet and saved my life."

He turned away. "When she died she touched my face and told me that she loved me. I lied to her even then because I told her I loved her too."

"Luc, listen to me—"

Without any warning, he took two strides over to her and grabbed her shoulders again. She couldn't control a wince when his fingers curled into her skin.

"I should have stayed as far away from you as I could get, Katie. You were under my protection. Someone I was supposed to be guarding for fuck's sake. But who could protect you from me?"

"I don't want to be protected from you, you moron."

"Shut up. Just shut the hell up."

Then he kissed her, hard and harsh and desperate. His mouth forced her head back; his lips were fierce and ravishing, as if he was trying to prove to her that he was what he believed himself to be.

But his hands gentled as his fingers slipped up to her hair and through it. As he removed her glasses and put them on a table. As he cradled her head in his large palms. As he cradled her.

Even if she'd been reluctant, Katie couldn't have helped responding. Her mouth opened under his, moved on his as his moved on hers. His tongue came to dance with hers, and she tasted his warm, rich flavor. She couldn't resist nipping at his bottom lip, then sucking on it.

He groaned deep and husky in his chest. The nature of the kiss changed, becoming less about force and more about passion. Excitement.

Katie lifted her arms, wound them around his neck and held on, her fingers caressing the soft skin above his collar.

He twirled in one of those swift, graceful movements and backed her up against the nearest wall, moving against her in a heart-stopping, fully-body caress that made her stomach flutter and her thighs clench. He ran his wonderful hands all over her body, his mouth wild on hers. He smelled so good, all wild and spicy, and she fought him for control of the kiss. The bulge of his erection rubbed high on her stomach. She loosened one hand from where it tangled in his hair, and cupped him, exploring his firmness with her fingers.

Then his clothes were loose and so were hers, her pants down around her ankles. He pressed her back against the wall, his fingers under her panties, on her skin, inside her, and she came so quickly, so violently that she cried out.

"Katie."

She had her hands on him, too, running under his

shirt, then digging his erection out of his pants, caressing him, pulling more strongly as he groaned in her ear.

"God, Katie. We need to stop. I need to…"

"If you won't take me with you, then leave me with this. Don't just walk away from me as if I don't matter," she whispered. "Please."

He shuddered, his hands warm and so strong on her skin. "Condom." His voice was guttural. "God. Need condom."

She blindly grabbed for her purse on the table. Her mouth fused with his, their tongues twining, as she searched through it, unseeing and one-handed. Finally, finally, she touched the little foil packet Darren had given her and pulled it out.

She wrenched herself back an inch and pressed it into his hand. "Condom."

"Jesus." The word was halfway between a laugh and a prayer before he was kissing her again.

They fumbled him out of his pants and her out of her underwear. Katie groaned as he massaged her breasts through her shirt, under it, as he tweaked her sensitive nipples. Her head fell back against the wall with a thud. His teeth were on her throat, his hand leaving her for one painful moment to outfit himself with the condom.

Then he was inside her. They both moaned at the sensation of him filling her, stretching her. He shifted and she gasped. The slide of it. The heat. Skin against skin.

"Luc."

Her fingernails dug into his shoulders, through the polo shirt. His thick muscles shifted as he lifted her, adjusted her into a better position. He moved, the rhythm of his hips quick and desperate. As if he would drill her through the wall. As if he would plant himself so deeply inside her that he would never come out again.

"I. Am. Not. Bruce," he growled in time to his thrusts.

Her answer was a groan.

Pictures rattled next to her, her back slapped against the drywall, and she came again with a shocked and startled cry. "Luc!"

A second later, he followed her over the edge, his own groan reverberating around the room.

They stood, grasping each other, knees trembling, breath shuddering, until Katie gradually became aware of another noise in the room. A slight whining. She opened her eyes, looked over Luc's shoulder and saw the black blob that was Spot lying on the floor, watching the proceedings with apparent confusion.

"Oh," Katie said. "God."

They separated. While Luc stepped into the bathroom to clean up and deal with the condom, she tried to put herself at least partially back to rights. The world came into focus when she put on her glasses again, but her brain refused to function. Satisfaction and pleasure and sadness and fear all swirled around inside of her until she couldn't think.

She heard water running, the toilet flushing. After a moment, Luc stood on the threshold of the bathroom, staring at her while he zipped up his pants and buckled his belt. The expression in his eyes was so bleak she could hardly stand it.

"Luc—"

"I have to go. I can't stay." He walked to her and

stopped close enough that she could feel his body heat, smell his sweat and the residue of their recent lovemaking.

"I didn't mean for that to happen," he said.

"I know." She gulped, trying not to cry. He studied her then scrubbed a hand through his hair.

"I'm no fucking hero, Katie." His voice was weary and resigned. "Don't forget that. Don't make more of me than I am. Don't think I'm something that I'm not. Don't—"

He broke off when she moved closer and smoothed her fingers over his cheek. She felt him swallow, felt the bristles of his beard, traced his scar. He let her touch him for a second, then jerked away as if she had burned him.

"I have to go. Wait for Némes." Then he was gone, slamming the door behind him, leaving her to stare at the blank wooden finish.

"You're too late warning me off, bud," she whispered. "Way, way too late."

What had just happened? She'd never acted like that. Had never been like that with any other man.

Ignoring Spot, she walked into the bathroom and got cleaned up. She could still smell him on her skin. Taste him.

When she came back out into the bedroom, she stared again at the door he'd slammed shut behind him.

"Idiot. Stupid idiot. Moron. Jerk!" Her voice got louder with each word. "Asshole!" She shouted at the door. She didn't know if she was yelling at him, or at herself. Didn't know which one of them deserved the names more.

Spot whimpered and Katie stooped to comfort her, then sat on the floor next to the dog and wrapped her arms around her thick neck, burying her face in warm fur.

"I'm sorry we had sex in front of you, baby," she said. "But you could have closed your eyes." Spot grumbled and shoved her nose into Katie's armpit. Katie hugged her tighter.

Luc was gone.

What she felt for him was so different than what she'd felt for Tom, or any other man. So much deeper that it was frightening. Tom didn't mean anything to her anymore, nothing at all.

But, Katie thought with a sudden insight, maybe if Tom hadn't been in her life, if she hadn't spent that time with him, she wouldn't have been able to recognize what she saw in Luc. Maybe she wouldn't have been able to forgive him, wouldn't have been able to see the goodness that lay at the heart of the man.

Tom, creep though he was, had helped her to grow up. Because now she knew what honor looked like.

Honor looked like Luc.

She smiled. Yes, she thought. The unknown Marie had been right. Lucas Vasco was infinitely worthy to be loved.

The knowledge hit her then and stopped her breath and her heart. Her stomach rolled and she grabbed it, hoping she wouldn't throw up.

Oh, God. It was real. She knew that it was real. She was in love with Lucas Vasco. She was so incredibly in love with him, loved every contradictory, stubborn, idiotic inch of him. Even the parts that he hadn't shown her yet.

The jerk wasn't going to let her do anything about it, of course. After all of this was over, assuming he managed to live through it, he was going to walk away, still struggling to redeem a soul that had probably never been lost.

And even then, she'd still love him.

She could see now that she'd hurt him worse than she'd realized when she'd called him the wrong name in bed. Because he'd been right, and she'd been stupid. Luc was not Bruce. Luc had nothing to do with Bruce.

Luc was Luc.

And she loved him because he was.

For several more minutes nothing else penetrated as the knowledge that she loved Luc unfolded inside her, growing larger and larger until it filled her. Then she thought about what he had gone to do, how he was risking himself to try to save her mother. She thought about the very real possibility that she wouldn't see either of them again.

"No."

Luc was wrong. About this, he was wrong. He was trying to protect her, but he was wrong. She couldn't sit in a hotel room alone with Spot while two of the people she loved were in danger. She had to go to Luc, had to try to help. She had to participate, even if there was a risk. It was the only way she could respect herself, and her self-respect had been reclaimed at far too high a price to just let it drift away now.

Luc was strong enough to push her away, to go do

what needed to be done. But she was strong enough not to let him do it alone. Maybe she was strong enough to hold on no matter what he did.

"See, the fact of the matter is, I've always hated being told what to do," she said to Spot, who lifted her head and listened attentively. It was nice to talk to a sensible female for a change. "But I've always been a good little girl. Didn't want to rock the boat. Didn't want everyone getting all upset. Where has it gotten me?"

Spot snorted.

"Right. Nowhere."

Katie got to her feet. Even if she could have caught up with Luc, and she was pretty sure she couldn't, she'd have to follow him without him knowing about it. Otherwise he'd just send her back here. He'd be angry when he realized what she'd done, but it didn't matter. Nothing mattered but getting to him and helping him rescue her mother. And keeping him alive so that even if he walked away from her later, he would still be breathing somewhere on this planet.

A little voice whispered that he had trusted her to stay at the hotel. That he would never have left her alone if he'd thought he couldn't trust her. But Katie silenced the doubts and focused on the task at hand. Luc was alone, he was in trouble and he needed her.

Frankie Silvano had told his men to take her mother to the Dream Net Casino, so that's where Luc was going. Atlantic City.

"Yup," she told Spot, "I'm thinking it's time for the Hornet to leave the nest."

Spot barked.

"Okay. You can be Underdog if you really want to be." She smiled. "But neither one of us is going to be Sweet Polly Purebred. It's about time someone helped save the hero for a change."

Spot wagged her tail and stood.

TWENTY-FOUR

Now that her decision was made, Katie was desperate to get moving. Justin Némes would be finished with his tax seminar soon, and she really didn't want to be in the hotel room when he came to collect her. The chances that he would agree she should go to Atlantic City were between slim and none. She imagined he could throw up some pretty significant obstacles if he had a mind to. She didn't have time to deal with him.

Moving quickly, she clipped the ridiculous purple leash back on Spot's collar, then tucked the equally ridiculous purple bandana into her purse. It made her feel stupid, but she knew she was always going to treasure the thing just because Luc had given it to her.

She opened the hotel room door and looked cautiously up and down the corridor. There was no sign of a tall man with long black hair and ice-blue eyes. Maybe she'd actually be able to pull this off.

Tugging the leash, Katie urged Spot out of the room and into the elevator. When they emerged from the cab on the main level, she pulled the dog away from the lobby and out a side entrance, thereby minimizing the risk that they'd run into Justin Némes coming from his seminar. She hoped.

Luck, fate, God, whatever, was with them and, as

they slipped through the door, Katie realized that not only were they in the parking lot, but she could actually see Kato parked under his tree not too far from where they stood. That was a good omen. With her sense of direction, she'd been kind of afraid that she'd wander around for hours looking for the car.

She tugged on Spot's leash again. "Come on, girl."

They made a break for it, Katie running and Spot ambling agreeably along beside her. They'd almost reached the Nova when a cool, masculine voice called out behind them.

"Going somewhere, Ms. McCabe?"

Katie skidded to a halt, spun around. Spot spun, too, barking at the new game. They watched as a tall shadow separated itself from the deeper shadows of some shrubbery and walked to them.

Justin Némes.

Crap.

Katie lifted her chin, trying to appear calm. "What are you doing here?" she demanded. Némes stopped and raised an eyebrow at her inquiringly.

"What am I doing here? I'm following you, of course. Here I was, innocently leaving my seminar room when I spotted you and your, um, companion, trying to appear inconspicuous and heading for a side door. Oh, and FYI? Nobody's inconspicuous when dragging around a dog the size of a grizzly bear."

"Well—"

"You're supposed to be tucked safely away in a hotel room." Némes moved closer until he was only a few feet from where she stood. "I shudder to think what

Vasco would do to me if so much as a single hair on your head was harmed." His eyes lingered on her wild corkscrew curls.

Katie put up a hand to smooth them before she realized what she was doing. He was making her feel like the entrée of a particularly tasty meal. Which had been his intention, of course.

Spot sat, shifted her bulk and lay down on the pavement next to her. Apparently Némes did not make her feel like a tasty meal.

"What's going on, Ms. McCabe?" Némes purred. "Out for a stroll? Dog need a potty break? It can't be that you were thinking of leaving. You can't be that stupid."

Katie's temper flared. God damn it, she was sick and tired of not being taken seriously. Throwing back her shoulders, she met his gaze. "I'm going after Luc."

"You are, are you?" He stood, hands in pockets, one hip cocked, looking dangerous and in control. No way in hell was he an accountant. "Know where he's heading?"

"Yes." She spat the word at him and had the satisfaction of seeing both surprise and annoyance flash across his face.

"And you're going to him."

"You can't stop me." As soon as she issued the challenge, it occurred to her it hadn't been the brightest thing she'd ever done.

His eyes grew colder, if possible, and he glided a step closer.

"Are you sure?" His voice was as frigid as his gaze, but she refused to let herself be intimidated.

"Yes. Luc needs me and I'm going to help him."

"Fearsome to contemplate. If he needed help, he would have asked me for it when we were talking."

Katie snorted. "Luc? Please."

Némes waved that off. "Ms. McCabe, I must tell you that, for reasons I won't bore you with, I have promised to protect you. And you will be protected. You are certainly not going after Vasco."

"I don't—"

"If I have to, I can put you in storage so fast it will make your head spin. Trust me, it won't be pleasant. Vasco told me to look after you, but he didn't tell me how to do it." He tilted his head. "Are we clear?"

Something in his face made her take an involuntary step back. Then, angry at herself, she stepped forward again.

"If you touch me," she said, quietly and with great menace, "this dog here will rip your lungs out."

Némes glanced down at Spot. Spot yawned.

"Uh huh."

Katie had had enough. "I'm going," she said. "Every minute I stand here arguing with you is a minute Luc could be getting killed in Atlantic City."

Némes started to speak, then paused. She saw a flicker of surprise in his eyes. "Atlantic City?"

Crap. Luc hadn't told Némes where he was going, and now she'd spilled the beans.

"Yes," she angled her chin. "Atlantic City."

"Where?" There was a hint of emotion in his voice that hadn't been there before.

"Why should I tell you if Luc didn't?"

"Tell me where." He took another step forward.

She studied him. "You know something."

"I know lots of things."

"You know something about this that you're not telling me, and I think it's important." In fact, she was sure of it.

Némes thought for a bit longer, then shrugged. "It's nothing. It's just that Liza said she was going to be in Atlantic City today."

"Liza?" Katie stared at him blankly. "Liza, as in Luc's Liza?"

Némes's face hardened. "She's not Luc's Liza anymore."

"No, but his former fiancée? That Liza?"

"Yes." Némes snapped. "We keep in touch. She mentioned she was going to Atlantic City. It just seems odd, Vasco going there, that's all. It's nothing."

"Liza," Katie murmured and her head spun with all of the implications. "Liza." Liza, who was David's admin. Who in the role of assistant would be privy to all of the comings and goings of Luc's squad. Who was in Atlantic City on the same day Katie's mother was being taken there. On the same day Frankie Silvano would be there.

It could be a coincidence, of course it could. Probably was. Lots of people went to Atlantic City for lots of reasons. There were probably a lot of people there right now.

But still…

"Nobody ever notices the administrative assistant," Katie murmured. "Believe me, I know. People treat us like we're a part of the office furniture, but we see everything that goes on in a place."

Némes looked at her as if she were nuts. "Good for you."

She met his eyes, her feeling of urgency growing. Yes, there could be other explanations, but this felt right. This made sense. And if it was true, Luc would be walking right into a trap.

"It's Liza," she breathed. "Liza is the leak."

"What?" Némes sounded thoroughly confused now. "What the hell are you talking about?"

"I have to go." She turned, tried to move to the car, but he grabbed her arm and jerked her back.

"Oh, no, you don't."

"Listen to me." She struggled to free herself. Spot had gotten to her feet, but she was just watching them and not doing anything useful like ripping Némes's lungs out. "There's a leak at the Bureau. I think it's Liza."

"What?" He shook his head and then he shook her arm. "No."

"Yes!" She yanked and finally managed to break his grasp. "Why do you think I'm here and not in some safe house? Why do you think Liza went to Atlantic City right when something big is going down there? She knows. She's always known. She's the leak."

"No," Némes said again, but it lacked conviction. She saw the thoughtfulness in his eyes and hoped. Maybe she had a chance, after all.

"I'm going, and I'm going now."

"To help Luc."

"Yes."

"You're in love with him, aren't you?"

Katie threw up her hands in exasperation. "Well, freaking duh!"

He was silent for a full minute, then two, studying her. "Okay." He nodded slowly. "Okay, okay, okay. But this is against my better judgment."

A knot in Katie's stomach loosened and she turned to the car. "I don't care."

"And I'm coming with you."

She stilled, blinked at him. "What?"

"I'm coming with you. I'm sure as hell not going to let you wander around Atlantic City by yourself."

Wary now, she took a step back. "I don't think—"

"Listen up. We are only doing this if I go with you, and you agree to do everything I say."

Katie considered that. Having Némes along could be useful. He seemed like he might know what he was doing, while Katie most assuredly did not. So maybe she shouldn't argue too much about him tagging along. But doing everything he said? No. She'd have to keep him under control, and that wasn't going to be easy.

"I think—"

"First, you wear a disguise. Sunglasses. And a wig." He looked at her hair again. "Yeah. Definitely a wig."

"But…" Katie frowned and touched her hair with one hand, not sure whether or not to be offended. Then she stiffened. He was doing it already. He was already trying to push her aside, to smother her. She tilted her chin and managed to look down her nose at him even though he towered over her.

"You can come with me, and I'll wear a wig, but we're using my car and I'm driving."

"No."

"Yes."

She could actually see him make the decision to let the little woman have her way. That was okay. Time was ticking, and she was burning with the need to get on the road.

"Fine, fine," he grumbled.

"Come on." Trying to appear powerful and decisive, Katie turned and strode to Kato, Spot at her heels. Némes followed. But when he got a good look at the Nova, he stopped abruptly.

"Oh, hell no."

"What?"

"Oh, hell no we are not leaving in this piece of shit. My car is—"

"We don't have time for this." Katie wrestled Spot into the backseat and slammed the door shut before turning to face him. "This is my car, and I'm driving it. Now, for God's sake, get in and shut up."

Hopped up on outrage and frustration and fear, Katie jerked opened the driver's door and started to slide inside. That was when she remembered an important little detail she had until now forgotten. A minor inconvenience.

Keys. No freaking effing keys.

Taking a deep breath, she spun to Justin Némes again, since the idiot man was still hovering behind her. "You can hotwire a car, can't you?" she demanded, her voice as cold as the North Pole. Never let them see you sweat.

"What?" Némes looked totally bewildered, but Katie didn't have time to enjoy it.

She stepped aside and gestured imperiously. "Luc had to hotwire the car. I don't have keys. Get it started. Now!"

Fortunately, and even rather miraculously, Némes obeyed, starting the car as easily as Luc had. As soon as the motor caught, Katie grabbed hold of his belt and pulled him out of the front seat, slipped behind the wheel and hesitated just long enough for him to scramble around the car and get in the passenger side. Then they were off, squealing down the access road and out onto the highway.

Once the conference center had disappeared from her rearview mirror, Katie glanced over at Némes. She stiffened when she saw he had a gun in his hand. He pulled a thingee out of the grip, checked it—presumably to make sure it was loaded—and slapped it back in.

"You've got a gun," she said.

"I always have one." He shifted around and the weapon disappeared again.

"So you could have shot me."

"Tempting as the thought was, it wouldn't have exactly been protecting you, now would it?"

"Right." She stared out at the road and the traffic. They drove in silence for a few minutes. Spot was already snoring loudly in the backseat.

"So, why did Vasco go to Atlantic City?" Némes asked.

She pondered the question, trying to decide how much to tell him, then mentally shrugged. In for a penny...

"My mother was kidnapped because the bad guys thought she was me. He's going to rescue her."

"Of course he is." Némes was watching the road too. "Take that tu— Okay, we'll go another way."

"Well, give me a freaking clue before I get to an exit, will you? Should I turn around?"

"No. There's another ramp we can use in about three miles." She felt his eyes on her face. "If you don't even know where Atlantic City is, how in hell did you think you'd get there by yourself?"

"I'd have found it. Drive until you hit the ocean, then go up or down until you hit the city. Easy."

"Easy," he murmured.

"Besides, I wasn't about to sit around with my thumbs up my butt while my mother and Luc are both in danger."

"Right. No thumbs up your butt. Where are we going anyway?"

"Um, Atlantic City," she answered, confused.

"No." Némes practically shouted the word, before he calmed himself. "I mean, where in the city are we going? Which casino? I'm assuming it's a casino."

Katie hesitated. "Why do you want to know?"

"Jesus Christ, woman!" She could almost hear him grinding his teeth. "Don't you think I'm going to figure it out when we get there?"

"Oh. Yeah." Katie took a deep breath. "The Dream Net Casino."

For a moment, Némes made no response. "Really," he finally said softly. Dangerously. She glanced at him.

"What?"

"That's where Liza was going. She told me when I talked to her. Very, very interesting." He glanced at her. "I can't believe in this much coincidence. Maybe you're right, after all."

Katie gripped the wheel tighter. Frankie Silvano. Liza. Her mother. Luc. Liza was working with Frankie. Had to be. She had to warn Luc. She had to help.

"Maybe I'm right," she whispered.

The rest of the trip passed in relative silence, broken only by the occasional argument about which roads to take, and the sound of Spot's snoring. Némes spent most of the time staring out the side window, his jaw hard and his features unyielding. Katie spent most of it worrying.

Némes spoke again just as they entered the Atlantic City limits.

"Change your mind yet?" The sound of his voice in the stillness was so unexpected that Katie jumped.

"No," she said, although the butterflies in her stomach had morphed into airplanes.

"Better be sure, because there it is." He gestured at a sign glittering and blinking on the horizon. The Dream Net Casino.

Katie drew in a deep breath, rolled her shoulders. "I'm sure."

He shrugged. "So, let's get you fixed up."

She followed his directions to a small costume shop where he left her in the car and eventually came back out clutching a black wig. A few minutes later she was parking the Nova in the underground garage of the Dream Net Casino itself.

Némes reached over and did something and Kato's engine fell silent.

"Last chance to back out," he said into the stillness.

"Stop trying to scare me because it's not going to work." Her hands were trembling. "We have to warn Luc."

"In the dictionary they have a picture of you as the definition of stubborn." He sighed and held up the wig. "Well, let's see if we can jam this thing on your head."

Pulling the wig over Katie's hair was far easier said than done, especially when Spot woke up and tried to help. After it was finally on, Némes sat back and looked at her. He didn't say anything, but the corners of his mouth twitched.

"If you laugh at me, I'll cut you right now," Katie warned.

He laughed anyway, then grabbed her wrist when she tried to punch him.

"Such violence. I'm shocked."

She jerked her hand away from him. "Yeah, well, you don't have to walk around in a public place looking like a doofus." What she could see of her reflection told her that the black wig was shaped like a pyramid. "An Egyptian doofus."

"You look like Cleopatra with freckles."

"Great. I knew I should have gone into that costume shop with you. Why did you have to pick this one anyway?"

"Just lucky, I guess." His light blue eyes were twinkling, and Katie realized he would probably be attractive if he let himself loosen up a bit. He didn't do anything for her, of course, but it was nice to know he actually had a human side.

"If it makes any difference, you certainly don't look like yourself," he said. "I don't even think you need to wear the sunglasses."

"Wonderful. Then I'll actually be able to see the people running away in horror." She got out of the Nova, trying not to hyperventilate. Némes slipped out of the passenger side and watched her over the roof of the car.

She licked her lips. "Maybe Spot—"

"No. The dog stays here unless you want to get us all killed."

"But it's going to be hot—"

"She's not in the sun. We'll leave the windows open partway. We can come and check on her in a little while, but she is NOT coming into the casino with us."

"You're just hoping you'll be able to stuff me into the car with her when we come back out."

"That too."

"Yeah, well, you can always try it, buddy." She shrugged. "But I guess that you have a point." A Newfoundland would likely draw attention, even if they could pretend that she was a Seeing Eye dog again.

Spot whined. Katie leaned over to give her a quick hug through the half-open window.

"Okay, girl. Guard the car. And wish me luck." She closed her eyes briefly, then let go of the dog, threw back her shoulders and grabbed her purse out of the car. "Come on," she told Némes. "Let's get this done. I already have a headache."

"Is the wig too tight?" he asked politely. She really did want to smack the smirk off his face.

"I'm irritated, I look like a pyramid, and my hair can't breathe." She glared at him and slung her purse over her shoulder. "Let's roll."

They took the elevator from the parking garage up to the casino's main lobby. Even though Katie knew the wig made a dramatic difference to her appearance, she found herself sticking pretty closely to Justin Némes as they were swept along with the crowd to the casino floor.

Looking up, she stared at the garish gold and silver fishing nets suspended from the ceiling three stories above her. They appeared to be catching huge coins cascading from the sky in an endless, blinking stream. It was hypnotic. Must spend money. Must spend money here.

When she realized she really was going under, Katie let her eyes drop. The room was cavernous, cloaked in perpetual twilight. Slot and poker machines rang and clanged and flickered with strange neon colors. Spotlights pooled on the floor at blackjack and dice tables, highlighting the tense, hopeful faces of the people clustered around them. Music blared. Colored lights flashed.

She tugged on her wig again.

"Stop that." Némes pulled her into a corner. He looked down at her with amusement.

"It hurts."

"We should probably have shaved your head." He ignored her snort and swept the casino floor with his eyes. "Do you have any idea what Luc's cover was? Any idea at all?"

"No." She shook her head and grimaced when the wig pulled her hair. "This is going to be like looking for a needle in a haystack, isn't it?"

"Try looking for a needle in about a hundred haystacks."

Katie sighed. "So, I guess we'd better get started."

TWENTY-FIVE

"FRANKIE," JOEY Silvano said. "What the hell's going on?"

Frankie Silvano met his father's hard, black-eyed stare. Once again he sat in front of Joey's big oak desk in the penthouse office at the Dream Net Casino. He'd gotten sewn up from where the FBI guy had shot him, but the wounds still fucking hurt. Plus, the pain meds made his head spin, he had bulky bandages on his thigh and upper arm, and he had to use a damn cane to get around. When his father's doctor had suggested crutches, he'd almost shoved them up the guy's ass.

Frankie was fucking pissed off. He looked at his father, sitting there like a smug little king, and his jaw ached with tension. The anger, humiliation swirled inside him, and all he wanted to do was hurt and maim and kill and take everything out on Poppa. He wanted to tear the old man's heart out and feed it to him. He wanted to slice at the old bastard until he was ripped and bleeding on the floor. Maybe that would work off some of the rage eating at his insides.

But Carlos had said it would be a mistake to take his father out now, and Carlos was one of the few people Frankie actually listened to.

With an effort, he wrestled his fury back into a box, leveled his breathing. "Nothing's going on," he said.

"Nothing? What the fuck do you mean, nothing?" Poppa lumbered to his feet. Frankie realized his father was angrier than he'd seen him in quite some time. "First you get arrested when you chase after the FBI agent nosing around the big house, now you get shot up chasing the same fucking FBI agent. And the guy gets away again!"

"Yeah." The woman had gotten away too. Katie McCabe. The woman who had caused all his embarrassment, all his humiliation. She had to pay. Had to.

Poppa was still talking. "—and now I fucking find out you have some fucking broad in the fucking basement. Here in this fucking basement. And it's not the broad who was helping the FBI agent, it's another broad. What the fuck is going on?"

"Some of the boys caught her at the woman's apartment. I had them bring her here so I could talk to her."

"Talk. Right." His father's eyes traveled over him. Frankie saw them linger on the way his suit hung on his slight frame, on the bandages and the cane. Watched the old bastard's lip curl with undisguised contempt. "Frankie, that broad in the basement is trouble. Fucking trouble I don't fucking need, you fucking moron."

"I need her," he said.

The old man's face grew red, and his barrel of a chest expanded until the buttons on his shirt strained. Frankie wondered idly if Poppa would just explode into a thousand pieces.

"I don't care what you need!" his father practically

screamed the words. "Get rid of her. I want her gone or I want her dead. Just get rid of her before the don finds out what's going on and goes fucking ballistic. Jesus God, I can't believe you're so fucking stupid!"

Frankie didn't bother responding. He watched Poppa pace back and forth. Back and forth.

"And for fuck's sake, watch out for that FBI guy. All we'd need would be for him to show up too. I feel like I'm running a fucking zoo."

"I doubt the FBI guy will come here now." Frankie kept his voice flat. "He's probably still holed up with his little slut." The slut Frankie was going to enjoy bringing down a notch or two. He'd play with her a little bit before he killed her...

"Watch for him anyway. I don't want him in the fucking place." His father turned back to face him and now his voice was cold and deadly. "You made this fucking mess, Frankie. You fucking clean it up. Now!"

Frankie rose, bowed ironically. "Certainly, Poppa."

He limped out of the room, his father's curses following him into the hall.

Obviously one of the guys at the house this morning had run right to dear old Dad and told him everything that had gone down. Maybe more than one of the guys had squealed. Maybe all of them. He couldn't trust them.

When he took over the organization, when Uncle Roberto finally got fed up and iced Joey, he'd get rid of all of the guys who used to work for his father and bring on a whole new crew. Carlos would help him. Carlos wanted him to be in charge. Carlos felt like Frankie was his own son—he'd said so.

But that was the glorious future. In the meantime, there was only one person Frankie knew he could trust. One person he was sure he owned.

Liza.

Tall and blond, built and beautiful. His first love. Really, his only love. Ever since the day when he was sixteen and she was fifteen and Poppa had brought her home and told him that she was his half-sister. In the beginning he'd tried not to want her, but it hadn't taken long before he'd realized they were inevitable. She'd been so beautiful then. Was so beautiful now.

His.

They'd handle things themselves, just like old times. She'd watch his back while he talked to the woman in the basement, found out what she knew. His father could go fuck himself.

Leaning on the cane, Frankie walked down the corridor, rang for the elevator and headed to the next floor down. To the room where Liza was staying.

LUC VASCO WAS MORTIFIED.

Sure, he'd gotten into the Dream Net Casino without tipping off any of the Silvano goons. And yes, he had a cover. An excellent cover, come to that, one nobody would even think of examining, but...

Lights came up, blinding him. He felt like a bug pinned on the small stage. Thank Christ he was wearing a cheesy Zorro costume. At least the thing came with a mask.

Music started playing, a slow Latin tango. Awkwardly, clumsily, Luc began to dance, calling on whatever recessive Latin rhythm gene he might have inherited from his father. The Zorro costume was so tight he almost castrated himself.

An exotic dancer, for sweet Christ's sake. A stripper. A stripper! What if David heard about this? What if the other guys…what if Némes found out? He'd never live it down. Never. He was glad the mask covered most of his face, because he was sure as shit that he was blushing. Thank God Katie wasn't there to see him.

Not once, not when he'd been a scrawny, malnourished and mistreated kid, not when he'd survived on the streets and in the shadows, not even when he'd left the Army and hadn't known how he was going to get by, had Luc imagined this day. His nightmares had not even encompassed the merest possibility. And once it was over, he was going to kill—fucking kill—John Carter. The man might have been one of the best officers he'd ever served with, he might be a valuable contact at the casino, but as of right now, he was officially dead. Dead man walking. Deceased. Take your bow, Carter and exit, stage right. You little shit.

Why was the crowd so fucking quiet? Yeah, there were some screams, but the women had practically molested the other dancers. They were just kind of…staring at him. Maybe he was boring.

He deliberately thought about Katie, how the two of them had "danced" in the hotel room and back at the Museum. His pelvis shifted from side to side and he let his backbone slip, so to speak, moving with thoughts of her in his mind. Her wild red hair. Her freckles. Her lush body. Hell, yeah. Then he had to quickly think about something else before he grew too aroused. Inspiration, good. Erection, bad.

He couldn't actually see the crowd of women beyond the light, but he heard them breathing, smelled the combination of alcohol and perfume and sweat hanging heavy in the air. This was like one of those dreams where you go to work naked, only it was worse because it was real. The stage he was on was in the middle of what looked like a cattle pen and he was the prime bull. The focus of all of the attention in the room.

It was fucking humiliating. Which Luc was pretty sure had been Carter's intention all along. But shit, it had been years since he'd stolen the man's girlfriend. Surely the guy couldn't be that anxious for revenge. Hundreds of eyes watched him, waiting for him to start peeling off.

They were so goddamn quiet. The people who said men were the aggressive sex had never been to one of these shows, that was for damn sure. When he'd seen the crowd's reaction to the other dancers, he'd just barely resisted the urge to cover his privates and make a break for it. But they weren't mauling him. He wondered what he was doing wrong. He hoped he wasn't making a complete ass out of himself. He hoped they wouldn't all just start laughing.

He'd been concentrating on holding onto as much of his clothing as he could for as long as possible, but finally he couldn't delay any longer and untied his cape fastening. Kind of proud of himself for the timing, he whipped it off to coincide perfectly with the music. And the place just…erupted.

Luc thought he must have jumped about ten feet at

the sudden noise. He paused, a little bit frightened by the deafening screams and all of the women waving money. He just barely resisted the urge to bolt for the nearest door.

Okay. Man up, Vasco. You can do this. You survived a whole hell of a lot of bad stuff in your life, you can survive this.

Maybe.

He started to dance again, but a little more hesitantly. Then he realized that slowing the steps down had put him into a kind of bump n' grind rhythm that served to emphasize his, uh, attributes. The screams intensified. Bills wove wildly like little green flags. Women leaned over the fence so far that they were in danger of falling into the pen and out of their shirts.

Unless somebody had an electric cattle prod, he was probably within seconds of being mobbed.

He realized he was supposed to be kissing people, so he ran around and grabbed one or two of the bills, twisting away when arms came out to clutch him. He tried to keep his tongue in his own mouth, but those of the women kept invading his personal space. Panting, he scrambled backwards, out of the kill zone.

Time to take off more clothes. He unbuttoned his black shirt, stumbling a little in his dance as he worked on the buttons.

He wondered if he'd be able to keep on his jockey shorts.

TWENTY-SIX

KATIE AND NÉMES searched for about an hour with no sign of Luc. Between the main gaming floor and all of the smaller side rooms and alcoves that fed off it, there were too many people, too many lights, too many nooks and crannies where a person could hide. Discrete questioning of the casino employees turned up no leads. Katie was beginning to see why Némes had tried to discourage her from coming here.

"Are we wasting our time?" she asked finally. Némes didn't answer as they weaved through the throngs of people.

"Let's check the showrooms," he said instead.

"He could be anywhere. Be anyone."

"Where's my little Amazon?"

"Back in the car with Spot."

"Don't tell me you're giving up so soon." Némes stopped and turned to face her, his well-formed mouth drawn up in a sneer. "I thought you said you loved him."

"I do love him." She said it quietly because she sensed an undercurrent in his voice that she didn't quite understand. "I'm not giving up."

Némes looked over her head and froze. His hands gripped her shoulders, fingers digging into her muscles.

"Hey!" Katie squeaked and tried to wriggle free. "You're hurting me."

"Shut up." He grabbed her arm and pulled her after him. She followed because she didn't have a choice.

"What's going on?" she demanded, although it was a little hard to talk and wheeze for breath at the same time.

"Frankie Silvano," he said shortly. "Back by the elevators."

"Oh." Katie discovered she could move faster, after all. "Did he see me?"

Némes turned to stare down at her. "Why do you care if he sees you?"

"Well, hello! He's trying to kill me. It would probably be good if he didn't know I was here."

"Frankie Silvano?" Némes sputtered and he swung her forcibly into an alcove. "Frankie fucking Silvano is the person you're hiding from?"

"Yes." She studied him in the dim light. "Luc didn't tell you that either?"

"Fuck no! Do you think I would have fucking let you come to the fucking Silvano family's fucking casino if anyone had told me that Frankie fucking Silvano was trying to kill you?"

"Keep your voice down." Katie shoved at him. "He'll see us. If you didn't know he was after me, why are we running?"

Némes was breathing hard and his face had turned a dull red. It couldn't be good for him. "Because Frankie Silvano is a sociopathic whack-job, and I thought it would be a good idea to stay out of his way, that's why!"

"Oh."

Némes cursed, took her arm again and dragged her to a dark hallway. He pressed her into a corner.

"I think he's working with Liza," Katie offered, trying to see around him.

"What?"

"I've been thinking about it, and it's the only thing that makes sense. If Liza's the one who told the Silvano family that Luc was working undercover on their estate, then she's probably the one who told Frankie I was hiding out at Luc's house. So they're working together. That must be why she came down here today. She knew Frankie would be here."

"Oh, my fucking God." Némes ran a hand through his hair. "I'm going to kill Vasco the next time I see him. I am going to fucking kill him."

"If you don't shut up, you're not going to get the chance." Katie elbowed Némes until he gave her a little space and she could look out onto the gaming floor. There was a bank of elevators across the room. Frankie Silvano stood in front of them, looking worse for wear and even more dangerous because of it. He had turned and seemed to be staring over at them, as if he was trying to see them.

Even though she knew they were protected by the relative darkness of the hallway, she shrank back.

"Why is he staring at us?" Katie whispered.

"Well, if he's trying to kill you, maybe he recognized you," Némes said dryly.

"Maybe," she admitted, but it didn't seem right. If he'd recognized her, he wouldn't still be standing at the elevators.

"You," she said suddenly, looking up at Némes. "He recognized you."

"Don't be ridiculous."

"No, listen. Frankie saw me for what, five seconds? And I had my back to him. With this wig, there's no way he could have known who I was. He must know you."

"He doesn't. I never went anywhere near the Silvano's when I was with the Bureau. I only know what he looks like from mug shots."

"It's the only thing that makes sense."

"Shit." He looked around. "Okay, maybe you're right. Jesus Christ, I am so going to kill Vasco for getting me into this." Grabbing her hand again, he pulled her farther back into the labyrinth of service corridors that fed the casino's maze of showrooms and restaurants.

And Katie worried about Luc. And her mother.

FRANKIE SILVANO HAD BEEN standing near the elevators, waiting impatiently for Liza to show. Since she'd only just gotten out of the shower when he'd gone to her room, he'd known it could take a while. So he'd been waiting for her on the main casino floor, muttering and pacing with restless energy, absently cataloging the faces, people. Then he'd focused on one guy, tall in the shadows, talking to a short, dark-haired woman, and everything inside him had gone still.

Justin Némes. Former FBI agent. The guy Carlos hated. What the fuck?

Frankie had known he'd been made because Némes had grabbed the arm of the woman he'd been with and hustled her away. Which had been pretty damned interesting. The guy'd had no good reason to run.

Sure, Frankie had followed the former Feeb around for a while a year or two ago. Carlos had asked him to set Némes up as part of some kind of a revenge deal. He'd rather have just killed him, but Carlos had insisted so he'd had to settle for getting him kicked out of the Bureau instead. He'd even gotten Liza to fuck him, used her to add a final layer of suspicion.

But Némes didn't know they'd even seen each other before. Frankie had been practically fucking invisible.

Pondering that, he'd turned his attention to the woman Némes was propelling through the crowd. She was short, wore glasses and there was something off about her hair. Something not quite right. Well, something other than the fact that it was cut like a freaking Egyptian princess. It looked almost lopsided. She tugged at it, and he thought it shifted.

Was she wearing a wig?

While he'd watched, Némes pulled her into an alcove, then, a few minutes later, into one of the dark service corridors.

A wig. Frankie had contemplated that for a moment.

Then the most ludicrous, most improbable thought slammed into him.

Her.

The woman. Katie McCabe. Here in the casino. No. Couldn't be. But…

Short. Glasses. Wig. With Némes. Némes who'd been partnered off and on with Vasco for years. Vasco, who'd gotten away from him—twice—with the help of a woman.

This woman.

It had to be her.

As realization struck, Frankie cursed violently and started to follow them.

Just then the elevator door behind him opened and Liza stepped out. She took one look at him and raised her eyebrows. "What's wrong?"

She could help him, he thought. She knew what Némes looked like, so she'd be able to help track him, find him. And the woman.

Katie McCabe.

"Némes is in the casino," he told her shortly, grabbing her arm.

Liza looked at his hand with surprise. "Justin? So? I thought we were going to talk to some woman you're holding in the basement."

"He's not here alone. He's with the bitch."

Liza let him drag her a few steps before she dug in her heels and pulled them both to a stop. He practically howled with impatience and rage.

"The bitch? What bitch? What the hell are you talking about?"

"The bitch who humiliated me."

"I repeat. So?"

Frankie dragged in a deep breath, then another. He reminded himself that Liza was useful to him, that he trusted her, needed her. And he knew exactly which buttons to push to make her do what he wanted her to do.

He smiled up into her mocking brown eyes. "The

woman is also the whore who's been shacking up with
Vasco, Liza baby," he purred. "The slut he's been fucking for the last couple of days. The one he's protecting.
He's probably told her all about you. Would have made
an amusing story."

Liza's eyes darkened, chilled. Her pretty face went
hard and sharp. "Luc? She's the woman Luc's been hiding at his house?"

"The same," Frankie said, still smiling.

Yeah, he knew her. Knew all of her obsessions and
desires. Knew exactly how she felt about Vasco. Still
felt about him, even after all of these months, even after
he'd dumped her. Maybe because he'd dumped her. He
knew her better than she knew herself.

Liza was staring blankly down at him.

"I want her," he said. "She's mine."

Slowly, Liza nodded. "Yes," she agreed, her voice
like ice. "She's yours."

"We'll split up," Frankie ordered, quickly now.
"They're somewhere in the service corridors. Maybe
they'll try to get to one of the emergency exits or duck
into a showroom. Send word if you catch anyone."

Liza nodded again and strode off on her long, long
legs. One of the guys who'd been hovering on the out-
skirts of the room followed her. Frankie jerked his head
at the remaining men and went to the right, toward the
hallway where Némes and the woman had disappeared.

The bitch was his. He could almost taste it.

TWENTY-SEVEN

IN THE END, Luc had done something he'd sworn he'd never do.

He'd run.

He'd been dancing, actually getting into it a little bit, until he couldn't delay stripping off his pants any longer. He'd ripped them away, the velcro fastenings giving easily on the breakaway pants, and stood before God and man clad only in black jockeys. If he'd ever been more embarrassed in his life, he couldn't remember it.

Actually, the jockey shorts were a step up from what Carter had wanted him to wear, but the man had relented after Luc had practically stuffed the black sequined thong down his throat.

When he'd ripped off his pants, the women had gone even more ballistic, which was kind of gratifying. But then, as he'd stared out into the screaming faces, watched the waving money, heard the pounding rhythm of the music, he'd…frozen. He hadn't been able to move, couldn't even wiggle a little bit. He'd just stood there in black jockeys while hundreds of women looked at him. Then he'd thought "the hell with this," turned and walked off the stage.

Back in the dancer's dressing room, he quickly shrugged into his real non-breakaway pants, a T-shirt and his running shoes. He was checking his gun when John Carter, the bastard, burst into the room. His light brown hair stood out from his head in tufts, as if he'd been pulling at it. He was wearing a tuxedo because he acted as the host of the 'show,' but his bowtie was undone and the cummerbund askew. He looked like he'd been mugged.

"What the fuck are you doing?" Carter barked. "Get the fuck back out there! Jesus, can't you hear them yelling?"

Luc holstered his gun, stepped forward and smashed his fist into the other man's face. It hurt like hell, but watching the shithead go down on his ass was so worth it.

Carter sat up, shaking his head, his hair hanging in his eyes. "What the hell was that for?"

"That was for actually making me strip, you asshole."

"Sorry. But Vasco, listen to those women!"

"Go to hell, Carter. And if this was because of Susan? You got your payback."

"Luc, please. I'm begging you. Just swivel those hips for five more minutes—"

"I told you to go to hell. Or better yet, go out there yourself. Wear the damned thong."

Luc dodged when Carter tried to grab his ankle and headed for the exit.

"Bastard," Carter spat, lurching to his feet.

Luc nodded. "Back at you." He opened the door, scanned the corridor then turned. "Thanks for the cover."

Carter was still cursing him when he slipped out into the service hallway.

Luc moved quickly, anxious to continue his search for Mrs. McCabe or whoever the hell Frankie Silvano had captured at Katie's apartment. And, he had to admit, just as anxious to get away from the screaming, cheering, chanting women.

He edged toward the main gambling area, moving quickly and quietly while he tried to come up with a plan of action. Frankie could have stashed a person anywhere. He should probably check out Joey's penthouse and Frankie's office first, but getting into either place was going to be a bitch. There were way too many people who knew what he looked like, and both Silvanos were well guarded.

He was frowning over the problem when he took a turn and saw two people ahead of him, a man and a woman. They were arguing. He stopped, faded back into the shadows and waited for them to move on.

Then the man turned his head, and Luc saw his face clearly in the dim light. All of the breath left his body, like he'd been punched in the gut.

Némes. Justin Némes. Here. And that meant...

Luc looked at the woman, took in the fact that her hair was dark and shaped like a pyramid. She was short. She was gracefully rounded. Her hands moved when she tried to make a point. He knew she'd be beautifully freckled and that her real hair was wild and free and auburn.

And he was going to kill her. He was going to fucking kill them both.

Pushing away from the wall, he stalked over to them.

Katie wanted to punch Justin Némes right in his cold, handsome face. If she could have reached it, she would have.

"No," she said for the thousandth time. "No, I am not going back to the car." She tried to keep her voice down, but it was difficult.

"If you think I'm..." Némes trailed off, looked over her head. "Oh, fuck me," he muttered.

"What in the HELL are you doing here?"

The voice was deep, familiar and very, very pissed.

Katie whirled around. "Luc?"

He was standing about two feet away, a little sweaty, a lot angry, and looking absolutely wonderful. She wanted to throw herself into his arms, except from the way he was glaring at her, she thought he'd sidestep her and she'd end up on her butt.

"I'll just go see what I can see," Némes said and slipped away. Coward.

"What the hell." Luc's entire attention was focused on Katie. He kept his voice low, but it rolled over her with the force of his anger. "What the hell. Do you want to explain yourself?"

"Listen, Luc—"

"Be quiet! Why don't you tell me why in the hell you are here in Atlantic City when I specifically told you not to come?"

"I'm here to help you, you jerk. What do you think I'm doing?"

"Shit, shit, shit." Luc ran his hands through his hair and tugged hard as he paced in a tight circle.

"Oh, well put. You can't keep me out of this, Vasco. I want to help you, and I'm going to. First of all, Liza is the leak you've been looking for."

"Liza?" He sounded astonished and stopped pacing to stare at her as his arms fell to his sides.

"Yeah." Katie tried to keep the satisfaction out of her voice, but she felt vindicated by his reaction. "Liza is the leak, and she's here in the casino now."

Luc's face grew tighter. "Are you telling me you figured out Liza was involved and she was here, and you came here anyway? Are you completely insane?"

"Hey!" Now her anger rose to match his. "If I hadn't come here, you wouldn't know. You'd be a sitting duck."

"Katie, I'm HIDING! Liza doesn't know I'm here." He was pacing again, back and forth in front of her. "I can't believe I trusted Némes, and I can't believe that I trusted you. I should have known better."

The hurt in his voice calmed her as nothing else could.

"I couldn't sit back in the hotel, Luc." Katie reached out for him. She caught his arm, felt the warm skin and the rigid muscles beneath it as she pulled him to a halt. "I had to do what I thought was right."

Luc stared down at her, obviously struggling for control before he spoke. "I understand that, and I respect it, but you didn't think, Katie. You didn't think about what your showing up here might do to your mother."

"My mother?" She was stung by the accusation. "Of course I thought about her. I'm going to help you find her."

"Katie," Luc grasped her shoulders and shook her

slightly, but his touch was more or less gentle. "Think, okay? If they find out you're here, what reason do they have to keep your mother alive? They were using her to get to you, remember?"

Katie stared at him as his words penetrated. As she understood what they meant. And she knew that Frankie Silvano had seen them. If he'd figured out who she was...

Her mother.

Her heart really did stop beating this time.

"Oh, my God," she whispered with dawning horror.

"Katie..." Luc hesitated, then grabbed her hand. "Come on."

"Némes—"

"Will find us."

He tugged her after him. Eventually they ended up back at the main gaming floor. It seemed like it was a different part of the room from where she and Némes had exited, but she couldn't be sure.

Abruptly Luc pressed her up against a wall, shielding her with his body. "Frankie Silvano," he whispered.

Katie looked around his shoulder, through the maze of slot machines. Frankie was leaning on a cane near the cashier's booth looking both angry and annoyed. He was talking to some other men, ranting, gesturing wildly.

"I don't think he's seen us," Luc said.

"He saw us before." Katie was having a hard time thinking. Her mind was numb. "At least I...I think so. I think he might have seen Némes."

"Are you telling me Frankie Silvano might already know you're here?"

"I...he might."

"Christ." Luc growled. "I can't believe this."

"I'm sorry," she choked, the tears very near the surface now. She forced them back ruthlessly, knowing she didn't have time to fall apart.

Luc looked down at her with something other than anger in his beautiful dark eyes. It might have been tenderness. It might have been pity.

He caressed her cheek with long, gentle fingers. "Katie," he whispered.

"I'm so sorry, Luc. I do trust you. I do. And I didn't mean to let you down. I just wanted to warn you. To help you. I couldn't stand back and watch you die or get hurt without trying to do something. I just wanted to be with you, but I didn't think. I never do. I'm so stupid."

"Hey." He tapped his forefinger against her lips. "Stop that."

"I'm such an idiot. I'm such a stupid, fucking idiot."

"Katie." He paused, then leaned down and kissed her softly on her mouth. "Come on, Hornet. We need to get you out of here. There's an employee exit nearby. No alarms."

"Frankie—?"

"We'll be careful. He won't see us."

Not giving her the chance to argue, he took her hand. He pulled her across the casino floor, sticking close to the wall where the darkness was deeper. His free hand was under his shirt, probably holding a weapon he had tucked in his waistband. Or else he was injured and hadn't bothered to tell her. But he didn't seem to be in pain. He was urging her along at a pace that was brisk without obviously rushing, expertly maneuvering her through the crowd.

Then he pulled her around a corner in the thick forest of slot machines, cut it a little too close and ran smack into an old woman. She bounced off his chest like a shriveled rubber ball and dropped her bucket of quarters with a resounding crash. The coins rolled and skittered across the floor while she cursed Luc with the fluency of a sailor.

Until she saw the gun in his hand. Katie figured he'd probably drawn it reflexively, without conscious thought. Maybe he didn't even know he'd done it. The old lady stared at it, stared at them.

And screamed.

She sure had a set of lungs on her. Her screech had the piercing quality of a smoke alarm. It sliced through the dense noise of the casino, attracting the attention of everyone within a hundred feet. Beside Katie, Luc did some creative cursing of his own.

Katie turned, had a clear view of Frankie Silvano still standing next to the cashier's booth. She saw the astonishment, the recognition flash across his face, saw him shout and point. Saw men running in their direction.

"Come on!" Luc shouted. He yanked Katie's hand and they sprinted through the web of tables and machines. He pushed people out of the way or simply mowed them down, dragging her after him. Katie could hear the men behind them. Luc still had his gun up and ready, but she knew he wouldn't use it and take the chance that he'd hit an innocent bystander. She hoped Frankie and his men had the same opinion.

They rounded another corner, and someone grabbed Luc's shoulder. He lashed out. Katie heard a thick thud when his fist connected.

"Shit," a familiar voice said. Justin Némes stepped forward, rubbing the side of his face, his own gun dangling at his side. "Christ, Vasco. I've been trying to catch up to you two."

"Yeah?" Luc punched him again and the other man staggered. "That's for bringing her down here."

"Hey, if I'd known what the hell was going on, maybe I wouldn't have. But you didn't tell me, did you?"

"Uh, boys?" Katie could hear the sound of running footsteps getting closer. "We don't have time for this."

The men glared at each other.

"We're going to have to split up," Luc said.

Katie gripped his hand tighter. "I don't—"

"It's our only chance. They'll follow me. You get her out of here." Luc's face was fierce as he looked at Némes. "I'm trusting you again."

"Got it."

The sounds of the pursuit were very near now.

Luc freed himself and flicked a finger down Katie's cheek. "Be careful." He slid away. Then she heard shouts and knew the men were chasing him.

"Come on." Némes grabbed her arm and before she knew what was happening, Katie found herself dragged off in the opposite direction. He towed her into a narrow hallway with a door at the far end. She thought it was probably either the employee exit Luc had mentioned or a fire exit. It didn't matter. The end result was that she was leaving Luc.

They were leaving him. Alone.

Then somebody grabbed Katie's free arm from behind. Her shoulder wrenched in its socket when Némes, unaware, kept running, pulling her. She screamed in pain. At the sound Némes whipped around, eyes widening as he looked past her.

"What the fuck?"

He started to lift his gun, but a man holding something that looked like a board stepped out from the shadows and slammed it across the back of his head. There was a loud cracking noise. Némes went down in a heap on the floor.

Katie fought the hold on her arm, struggling to pull away. A tall, blonde woman with dark brown eyes and a thin face stepped around her, tightening her grip so that her long red nails pierced the skin.

In one smooth motion, she held up a small gun and pointed it at Katie's forehead. "Just give me a reason," she whispered.

Katie stopped moving. The man who'd hit Némes ripped her purse away from her. She grabbed for it, but he jumped back out of reach.

Panting, Katie studied the woman who held her. "You must be Liza," she guessed.

"And you're the bitch. The one with Luc," Liza said. She stared down at Katie, then used two fingers of the hand holding the gun to yank off the black wig. Katie couldn't control her gasp of pain when it pulled and ripped at her hair. Liza continued to stare.

"He's with you?" she asked, incredulous. "He could have me and he's with you?"

Well, now Katie might be upset and terrified, but she really couldn't let that one go. "I guess I'm better in bed," she said.

For a moment, unexpected pain flashed in Liza's exotic dark eyes. Her body went rigid.

"Don't hurt her," the man who had hit Némes warned. "You know Frankie wouldn't like it."

Katie wasn't sure Liza was going to listen. Then the other woman smiled. The sight of that smile scared her more than the gun.

"That's right. Frankie wants you for himself. Frankie always gets what he wants." Liza tugged her arm. "Let's go wait for him."

Katie couldn't control a shudder. She tried to break away, but Liza's fingers dug like claws.

"Hey, what about the guy?" the man asked, nodding to Némes, crumpled on the floor. "Want me to off him?"

Liza studied Némes. "No," she said, and Katie could hear regret in her voice. "Someone Frankie knows wants him alive. But it might be kinder if we killed him now."

"Why?" the man asked, clearly mystified.

Liza rounded on him, dark eyes flashing, and he backed up a step. "None of your goddamned business!" she shrieked, then calmed herself. "Besides, he's not going anywhere for a while."

"Sure, sure," the man said hastily.

"Just go find Frankie. Tell him that I have the bitch he's looking for and I'm taking her to the basement. Do it now!"

The man rushed off to do her bidding.

"Idiot," Liza murmured. She turned to Katie and smiled again. "Now. You. Come with me."

LUC HOPED TO ALL HELL he'd drawn most of Silvano's men away from Katie. He vaulted over a blackjack table, raced through yet another buzzing, clanging jungle of slot and poker machines. God, please let him have bought Némes enough time to get her out of the casino. He varied his pace, let the men chasing him get a little closer. It wouldn't be good if they got so impatient that they started shooting up civilians. On the other hand, he didn't want Frankie Silvano to notice that he was alone and Katie had disappeared.

Luc rounded a corner, hit a patch of polished marble floor at a dead run and slipped. His semi-healed ankle, already aching like a bad tooth, finally gave up, gave out and dumped him unceremoniously on his ass. He hit the floor hard and cursed as pain flared up his leg. He scrambled quickly to his feet and took off again at a hobbling run. When he glanced behind him this time, Silvano's men were a hell of a lot closer. It was time to get serious about getting away.

Ignoring the now nauseating pain in his ankle, he dove for the nearest stairwell, praying there wouldn't be a guard on the other side of the door. There wasn't. He flew down the stairs, his injured ankle throbbing darkly, his feet barely touching the treads. He'd lose his pursuers in the parking garage. He didn't have much of a choice.

Silvano's guys burst through the door above him, shot at him, and Luc realized he'd made a serious mistake. Bullets ricocheted around him, bounced endlessly off the narrow cement walls. He felt a sudden, sickening pain in his shoulder. Another farther down on his side. He stumbled, almost lost his balance, but somehow stayed on his feet. He fired a few shots back at the men chasing him.

Luc practically fell down the remaining steps. Panting, hurt, his entire body on fire, his leg dragging, he ran out into the parking garage and ducked behind a row of cars.

WALKING STIFFLY ON HIS bad leg, Frankie Silvano finally made it down the stairs to the garage and looked around at all of the parked cars. His anger was a living, breathing thing, a creature he didn't even want to control.

"Where the fuck is he?" he demanded of the men. "And where the fuck is the woman?"

"We didn't see no woman, boss," one of the guys answered. "Leastwise there weren't no woman on the stairs. Just a guy."

"Fuck!" Frankie screamed with rage and frustration. "Fuck! Go get him!"

His men melted into the garage, spread out among the cars. Frankie panted, trying to calm himself down. Okay. Okay. There was no way the woman would get away from him this time. No fucking way.

If she wasn't down here, then Frankie would make the Feeb talk. Yeah, he had lots of ways of getting people to talk. This was his turf. He was in control here, and—

"Boss."

Snarling, Frankie turned and saw the guy who'd gone

with Liza. The other man was breathing hard, as if he'd been running.

"What?" Frankie snapped.

"Liza has the woman you're looking for." The man's brow creased. "At least, I think that's what she said."

Joy, hunger, anger exploded in Frankie's chest, filled him with excitement and power. "Where?" he asked, softly now.

The guy had backed up a couple of steps, as if the force of Frankie's exultation had pushed him.

"Uh, the basement."

"Good," Frankie said. "Very, very good." He turned to his men in the garage. "When you find him," he shouted, "kill him."

The pain of his wounds forgotten, he headed to the room where he knew Liza had gone. To the woman. To Katie McCabe.

TWENTY-EIGHT

LIZA MUSCLED KATIE into a service elevator, then down several floors to a hallway lit with industrial fluorescents, the harsh light reflected against bright white walls. Katie could hear the roar of heavy-duty machinery and smelled heating oil, and maybe a little garbage. Quite a contrast to the carefully constructed luxury just a few stories above them. Then again, basements were basements.

She struggled as they came off the elevator, dragged her feet, looked desperately for some way to escape. Liza's grip tightened painfully and the other woman's small gun dug into her back as she urged her forward.

No chance. But surely Liza would let down her guard once they got where they were going. Katie would have to wait for an opening. Because she didn't think Luc was going to be able to ride to her rescue this time.

Several doors lined the hallway, some open, some closed. A big man stood in front of one of the closed ones, looking bored. He straightened away from the wall as they drew nearer.

"Unlock it," Liza commanded him, and he hurried to obey. The door opened to a small, square room with the same hard light and white walls as the hallway.

Another man was standing inside. He turned, gun

drawn, when Liza propelled Katie across the threshold. Katie ignored him, her full attention caught by the figure tied to a chair in the middle of the room, arms behind her back, bright hair an unruly mess around a bruised face.

"Mom?"

"Hey, honey." Her mother shook back her hair and smiled a little apologetically. "Looks like I've got a problem."

"You both do." Liza shoved Katie, and she landed hard on her hands and knees on the concrete floor.

She scrambled to her mother, touched her arms, her face. "Mom, are you all right?"

"Fine, but honey—"

"You're tied so tight." Katie whirled on her knees to face Liza. "She's tied too tightly. She's not going anywhere. Can't I untie her?"

"No." Liza turned to the man who'd been in the room. "Go outside and wait for Frankie."

He swallowed. "Frankie?"

"Yes." She smiled. "He'll be here in a few minutes."

The man hurried out and closed the door behind him.

"Mom," Katie's hands trembled when she ran them over her mother's face, her arms and legs, trying to make sure she was okay. "What are you doing here? What happened?"

"Well, I'm not exactly sure," her mother admitted. "I was worried about you. I knew something was wrong after that phone call—"

"I tried to tell them you wouldn't believe me—"

"—and it just preyed on my mind, you know? So finally I couldn't take it anymore, and I had to go check it out. I called your work—"

"You called where I work?"

"—and they told me that you really were on a retreat, but I, well, I had a feeling."

"You're psychic."

Despite everything, her mom's bright blue eyes lit with amusement. "Hardly. But I couldn't shake it, so I, oh, honey, I went to your apartment."

"I figured you had."

"And those two guys knocked me out." Her mouth twisted in disgust. "So much for karate."

"They took you by surprise."

"And outweighed—"

"Would you both just shut the hell up?" Liza demanded.

"—me. But Katie," her mother said. "What in the world is going on? What kind of trouble are you in?"

"Bad trouble, Mom," Katie said. "Really bad." She got to her feet and faced Liza. "You have me now," she said. "I'm the one you want. Let my mother go."

Liza shrugged. "That'll be up to Frankie." She smiled. "He might find her useful."

"Don't hurt her." If they wanted her to beg, she would. "She has nothing to do with this. She doesn't know anything about this. You can let her go. Please."

"Shut up, slut." Liza stepped forward and backhanded her, hard.

Katie reeled from the force of the blow, put her hand up to her now throbbing cheek and tasted blood where her lip had gotten cut on her teeth.

"Slut?" her mother asked. "Seriously?"

"Mom—"

"You shut up too, old woman, or I'll gag you both," Liza snarled.

"Old woman?" Her mom murmured, sounding a little put out. Katie could understand her annoyance, but all the same she hoped she wouldn't piss Liza off any more than she already was.

After they'd been silent for a few minutes, Liza relaxed. She still held the gun steady on Katie, looked at her intensely.

"I just can't believe you're the one," she said finally. "I can't believe you're with Luc. And I can't believe you're the one who took down Frankie." When Katie met the woman's dark eyes this time, she thought she saw some reluctant admiration there.

"Why are you doing this?" Katie ventured, not wanting to make her angrier, but wanting to know.

"Why am I doing what?"

Katie gestured vaguely. "Why are you selling out the Bureau? Why are you selling out Luc and David? Why team up with Frankie Silvano?"

"I'm not selling out anybody." Liza took a deep breath. "Especially not Luc. I put myself on the line for him. I kept quiet to try to protect him. I didn't say anything when he went undercover on the estate until I had to."

"Until you had—"

Liza moved restlessly, pacing in the tight space. "I didn't have a choice," she said, more to herself than to Katie. "I did what I could to keep him safe. He'd broken off our engagement, but I still did the best I could. I was supposed to report on everything. But I didn't say anything until I found out Luc was going to break into the office. Then I had to tell. I had to."

"Why?" Katie asked gently. She put a hand on her mother's shoulder in warning, but Mom was too smart a woman to say anything that might break the mood. "Why did you have to?"

Liza turned to face her and the gun came up again. "I had to protect my family. They come first. They have to come first."

"Your family?" Light dawned. "Joey Silvano? He's your—"

"He's my father." Liza's full mouth twisted. "My mother was his mistress for a little while. He didn't know about me right away, but when he found out he came and brought me to live with him. I'm important to him. I owe him everything."

"How in the world did you get a job with the FBI in the first place?" Katie asked, glad that Liza seemed inclined to talk. Liza talking meant less chance of Liza shooting. "They have to run extensive security checks, especially since 9-11."

Now Liza looked amused. "Do you honestly think Daddy and Uncle Roberto don't own people at the Bureau? Believe me, not everyone there is as pristine as David."

Katie blinked. She guessed she hadn't thought of that. "But still—"

Liza lifted her shoulder in an elegant shrug. "Frankie thought it was important to have somebody inside, and

Daddy agreed. I was the best choice. They arranged for me to have a new name and background. I...I had some surgery..."

Her smooth voice, which until now had sounded almost robotic, faltered, and she reached up to touch her cheek. "Not much. There weren't that many pictures of me around." She stared at a point over Katie's head.

Katie felt her mother stir and tightened her hold on her shoulder. "But surely David checked you out, didn't he?" she asked.

Liza shook herself slightly and focused on Katie again. "David has an organized crime squad, but he's really not that high on the totem pole. Besides, once you're inside, it's easier to move around. Especially if you have skills." She smiled, and it was ugly. "I do."

Somehow Katie knew she wasn't referring to her ability to organize an office.

"So you got engaged to Luc and everyone was just," Katie waved her hand, "okay with it?"

"I never told Daddy we were engaged. If I'd told him, he would have been angry."

Katie wondered how Liza had expected to keep it a secret once she and Luc had gotten married, but she didn't think it was a good idea to ask. Pointing out craziness wasn't exactly smart when the other party had a gun.

"I didn't tell Frankie either," Liza continued, "but he found out. He always does." Something flickered across her face. Something hurt and hard and terrible. "We've been...close since I was fifteen."

"Close." Katie wondered what it had been like to be 'close' to Frankie Silvano at the age of fifteen.

"Yes." Liza smiled again, one of her bright, frightening smiles. "And you don't even want to know how angry he is with you."

"I've kind of got an idea," Katie muttered.

"I don't think so. Because if you did you wouldn't be here. You'd have kept as far away from this place as you could."

"Well, then, we'll just go—"

"Don't get cute." Liza bit off the words. "I don't want to hurt you and spoil Frankie's fun. God knows what he's going to do to you. He'll probably chop you up and eat you or something sick like that."

The door to the room opened and Frankie Silvano walked in. "Always good to know what you think of me, Liza," he said. But he didn't look at the other woman. His entire focus was on Katie.

She swallowed, although her mouth had gone dry. All at once the threat that he'd chop her up and eat her actually seemed possible.

"Jerry," Frankie called over his shoulder. "You and Paul go to the parking garage and see if you can help the boys nail that guy. Liza and I have this covered."

That guy, Katie thought. Luc. Oh, God, Luc.

"Uh, sure boss," the man who must have been Jerry said and shut the door. Katie heard the muffled sound of footsteps as the men hurried away.

"So. Katie McCabe." Frankie's hot eyes wandered over her like fingers. He limped across the room toward her, leaning heavily on a cane. He had an obviously bulky bandage wrapped around his thigh, and she thought there was another around his arm under his shirt. Each thump of his cane against the concrete sounded threatening, his injuries somehow making him more frightening, not less. Angrier. More dangerous. Like a rabid dog.

Katie licked her lips. "Mr. Silvano."

Frankie smiled, showing small, pointed teeth. "Hey, call me Frankie, huh? We're gonna be friends, you and me."

"I don't think so."

"I do." He laughed, and it chilled her all the way to her bones. "You're gonna be screaming my name by the time we're through."

Katie tried not to shudder and failed miserably. "Yeah? What do you think you're going to do anyway?" She wanted to sound brave and unconcerned, but she failed at that too.

Frankie laughed again. This time it was with real amusement. Joy, even. The sound traveled up Katie's spine like fingernails on a blackboard, like he had run his hand over her nerve endings and pulled. For the first time in her life she understood sheer, unadulterated terror.

"I'm gonna play with you," he said, still in that joyful voice. "And then I'm going to kill you. And then I'm gonna play with you some more. And then maybe I'll mail what's left of you back to what's left of your family."

An emotion so far beyond fear that it was almost unrecognizable flashed through her. She struggled not to let him see it, not to give him the satisfaction of knowing he practically had her on her knees and he hadn't even touched her yet.

She felt her mother's shoulder grow tense and tight beneath her hand. Her mom was wise enough to keep quiet, but Katie knew she was on high alert.

They had to give Frankie a bigger target, Katie thought. Had to make it harder for him to get both of them. And she had to give herself room to maneuver.

It was hard, but she forced herself to let go of her mother's shoulder, to take a step to the side. Ignoring her quick, questioning glance, Katie continued to sidle away until they were separated by a few feet.

"Where you going, huh? There's nowhere to run and I have some things to…discuss with you." Frankie smiled broadly.

She stared at him, mesmerized by the lack of something in his eyes. The lack of something human.

"You're gonna pay for everything," he told her, his smile fading until it was replaced by rage. "Everything that's happened. I'm a laughingstock because of you. I got arrested because of you. I got shot because of you. You're gonna pay."

"No!" With one powerful thrust of her legs, her mother launched herself, chair and all, sideways into Liza, who had been so caught up in what was happening that she'd come a little too close.

Liza shrieked. Her gun went skittering across the floor as the two women landed in a tangle of arms and legs and chair.

Frankie glanced at the melee, distracted, and Katie

saw her chance. She leapt at the little man, kicked his gun up just as he turned it on her mother. He pulled the trigger, but the bullet discharged into the ceiling. Frankie snarled, spun quick as a snake. This time she punched, like her brothers had taught her. She caught him right where she suspected he'd been shot in his arm.

He howled, and his gun flew out of his hand. He hit her with his cane, but she twisted so that the blow glanced at her kidneys instead of breaking ribs. The pain was powerful, but she kept her footing and ducked his next lunge. She kicked again, this time into the bulky bandage wrapped around his thigh. He screamed, his leg buckled, the cane went flying. She kicked him in the balls. Hard. Hard enough to jam them up into his throat.

He made a wet sound deep in his chest and finally went down, hands cupping his groin.

Katie dashed forward, got his gun, skipped back and turned to her mother. She and Liza were still grappling on the floor. Liza, flailing around, grabbed Katie's mom's hair and yanked it hard. She gasped in pain, but her eyes lit with fury, and she brought her head forward abruptly, smacked it into the other woman's face. Liza cried out and jerked back.

Katie raced forward. She brought the butt of the gun she held down hard on the other woman's head. Liza cried out again, and fell back, unconscious.

"Jesus." Her mom wheezed. "Jesus. I've never really done a head butt before. That freaking hurt."

Katie rushed to her, dropping down beside her on the floor. "We have to get you untied. We have to get out of here."

"The ropes are too tight," her mother said. "It's going to…" Her voice trailed off, her eyes moving over Katie's shoulder. "Katie."

Katie spun around on her knees.

Frankie Silvano, face white with pain, was sitting up. He was holding Liza's gun. It was pointed at her. His anger was a living thing, filling the small room. Insanity swirled in his eyes, making him seem inhuman. Demonic. He didn't even seem to notice that she held a gun too.

"Bitch. Whore." He didn't scream now, he hissed. Then he smiled, turned the gun slightly. "Say goodbye to Mama."

"No!"

Katie shot him.

Frankie's whole body jolted as the bullet plowed into him. Katie would never forget how he shuddered and twitched, how blood and other fluids slapped against the stark white wall. How half of his face was suddenly just…gone.

His body jerked, his gun fired, but the bullet went high. He fell back on the floor.

Frankie Silvano really was dead this time.

Deafened by the twin gunshots in the small room, Katie sat, shaking, the gun slipping from her limp hand, the acrid smell of gunpowder strong and stinging. Oh, God. Oh, God. She'd killed someone. Oh, God.

There wasn't time to fall apart. They had to get out of here. They had to leave before Frankie's henchmen came back or Liza woke up. She shook her head to clear it, turned to her mother and struggled with the ropes that bound her to the chair.

Her mom was saying something, but Katie couldn't hear her past the buzzing in her ears. The knots were small and tight and impossible to loosen, but she fought them doggedly until it occurred to her to look for a knife. The room was empty, no handy place where the bad guys might keep some tools. She looked at the two people sprawled on the floor, and swallowed hard against the bile that rose in her throat. Frankie had been a killer. Maybe he'd had a knife as well as a gun. God.

It was probably one of the most difficult things she'd ever had to do, but she made herself go to Frankie's body. Made herself touch it, search it. She found a knife in an ankle sheath and scurried quickly back to her mother. The blade was sharp and she made short work of the ropes. Then her mother was free.

Katie's hearing was coming back, so she heard her mom cry out when she gingerly brought her arms back around to the front of her body, rubbed them. Katie helped, massaging up and down her mother's arms, feeling the cramped muscles held too long in one place. She realized she was crying, felt the moisture on her face, especially when her mother couldn't choke back sobs of pain as the circulation returned.

Her mom took the bottom of her own T-shirt and stuffed it in her mouth to stifle screams as waves of agony crested, grew almost unbearable.

"Crap," she gasped, spitting out the shirt after the worst had passed. "I knew that was going to happen. Too tight for too long." Then she pulled Katie into a power-ful hug and they clung to each other, shaking.

"Mom. Oh, Mom."

"We have to get out of here," her mother said. "Give me another minute, and I'll try to stand up."

"I'm sorry, Mom. I'm so sorry."

"Not your fault, honey. Whatever's happening, it is not your fault."

Katie's laugh was watery. "Don't count on that." Her mind went to Luc. He was alone. He was being chased, she was sure of it. No way would Frankie have called off his men when he'd been summoned to this little room. Luc was too big a prize.

"Come on," she said to her mother, trying to control her sense of urgency. "We have to go." She'd get her to safety, and then she'd call David. He could send the po-lice. He could help. Then she'd try to find Luc herself.

And Némes, she remembered belatedly. Némes too. But Luc first.

Katie helped her mother stand. She stretched, turned then nodded.

"Better than expected. Guess all that time at the gym paid off. Let's go."

"I'm going to drop you off at the car," Katie told her as they started to the door. "Then I have to go try to help Luc."

"Who the heck is this Luc?" her mother demanded.

"It's a—"

The door crashed open, and several police officers burst into the room. Justin Némes, gun drawn, head bleeding, face determined, staggered in after them.

"You," he pointed at Katie, paused, shook back his wild hair and pointed at her again. "You're okay?"

"Um, yes," she said.

"Good. Now, don't MOVE! Get it?"

"Got it," she said because he looked more than a little crazed.

"Good!" He turned to Katie's mother. "You're the mother, right?" he asked. Her mom nodded, her eyes gleaming with silent amusement. "Yeah, well you stay put too. I'm going to try to find Luc."

"I wish somebody would tell me who Luc is," she murmured.

Némes was still looking at Katie. "David will be here any minute," he told her. "He'll get things sorted out."

"David?" Katie said with surprise.

"Who's David?" her mother asked.

"I called him as soon as I came around. Turns out he'd become suspicious of Liza and was on his way over here. He's the one who convinced the Atlantic City police chief to send people just on my say-so. Now DON'T MOVE!"

And then he was gone again.

"Who was that?" her mom asked.

Katie ignored her. She felt her face flush with irritation. Némes had talked to her like she was a kid or something. Hadn't she just gotten herself and her mother out of a very dangerous situation? Hadn't she just shot a man?

How dare he push her aside and try to ignore her.

Her mother was watching her closely and must have noticed the telltale signs of the legendary McCabe temper rising, because she pulled Katie away from the corpse and the police officers swarming all over it and Liza. The room was small, but nobody seemed to be paying attention to them, so they slipped outside into the hall.

"You know," her mother said in a low voice, "I hate being patronized."

"Yeah," Katie agreed fervently.

"And we *did* take out those two all by ourselves."

"Without any help at all," Katie said with a nod. "Damn it," she added for emphasis.

"If there's somebody still in danger, we need to try and help."

"That's what I think."

They looked at each other.

"Let's go," Katie said.

"Just tell me who this Luc person is," her mom said as they walked away, unnoticed in the chaos.

"Later. I promise."

"You always say that, but this time, you're actually going to do it. While you're at it you can tell me who you shot, who that blonde woman is and what the hell is going on."

Katie looked at her mother and realized she meant it. "Yes, ma'am."

"And there's no way I'm sitting in a car waiting. I'm in this now, and I'm coming too."

Katie looked into her mother's set face and had a small inkling of how Luc and Némes must have felt over the last couple of days. Stubborn McCabe women.

She smiled. "Come on."

TWENTY-NINE

So FAR Luc had managed to elude the men chasing him, but they hadn't given up. He could hear them walking around the garage and knew they were looking for him row by row. He just couldn't seem to find the strength to move.

He huddled in the shadows between two cars, his shoulder and his side throbbing unmercifully. Taking those hits from the ricocheting bullets had really fucked him up, plus his damned sprained ankle was swollen again and hurt like a son of a bitch. He hoped he'd be able to run soon, but he kind of doubted it. He was getting lightheaded. He wondered if Katie was all right. In spite of everything, his lips twitched into what might have been a smile.

She'd come to help him. Because she wanted to be with him. Because he was important to her.

He was important to her.

He shook his head slightly with self-disgust. God, Vasco, bleeding to death is turning you into some kind of a damn romantic sap. Even so, he couldn't stop thinking about her, couldn't help remembering how back in the hotel room she'd clasped his head in her hands, put her soft mouth on his and breathed something special right into him.

Something that was only Katie.

The voices were closer. Luc made himself get up, forced himself to ignore his body's screams of pain and move. Maybe he was going to die, but he sure as hell wasn't going to make it easy. Fighting was what he did best, and he'd do it until they blew him off his feet.

He managed to scuttle like a big crab to the end of another row of cars before he collapsed again. Twice more he moved, avoiding the men, listening to their increasingly frustrated voices echo in the garage. As he blinked the sweat out of his eyes and tried to look through the maze of parked cars, something caught his attention. He turned his head, then stopped, stared.

It was an old car, battered in the overhead lights. Dark green. Bullet holes scattered up the side.

Kato.

"Hell," Luc muttered.

Calling on a reserve of strength he hadn't thought he still had, Luc half ran, half crawled over to the Nova and tried the door handle. It was unlocked. He slithered into the driver's seat and closed the door behind him as tightly as he could without slamming it. There was a loud snort behind him, a sudden rustle, and something cold and wet prodded the back of his neck.

Luc almost went through the roof. Weapon up, he twisted around as best he could and, to his shock, found himself staring into a large, furry and very familiar face.

"Spot?" The dog woofed and snuffled at him again. "Spot." He touched the Newfoundland's broad nose almost tentatively in case she vanished. She drenched his finger with a single lick. "What are you doing here?"

He probably shouldn't have been surprised. What else would Katie and Némes do with a dog the size of Texas except bring her along on this moronic trip? Of course. Completely logical.

Spot bathed his face and licked his ears, then sniffed his wounded shoulder, obviously wanting to leap into the front seat with him.

Luc pushed her away. "Later, honey, okay? Later. We've got to get out of here first."

He tried to shake off the faintness, but a black cloud was creeping farther into the sides of his vision.

"I have to draw them away. I have to save Katie." He didn't let himself focus on anything but that. He had to save Katie. He had to save Katie's mother. He'd promised. He'd given his word.

Although his breathing was harsh in his ears, he heard the footsteps echoing on the cement floor outside and knew Silvano's men were close. Time to go.

He fooled around with the ignition and although the motor made a grinding noise, it didn't turn over.

"Come on, you fucker," Luc muttered.

There were shouts as the men in the garage realized what was happening, and then some wild shots.

"Down!" he yelled at Spot. The dog sank obediently into the backseat just as another shot cracked. The Nova's rear window exploded.

And Kato roared defiantly to life.

"Holy shit." Luc pulled himself straighter in the seat and threw the car into gear. "If I get out of this alive, she's going to fucking kill me."

The Nova leapt out of its parking place. Silvano's men shot after it then went racing for their own cars.

He sent Kato spinning up a nearby ramp. They burst out of the garage and onto the street, rocketing down the boulevard that ran in front of the hotel. A minute or two later, he heard loud screeching noises and looked in the rearview mirror. A bunch of black sedans erupted out of the parking garage like a horde of angry wasps.

Not enough time, goddamn it. Not enough of a lead.

Spot sat up and barked.

"Get down!" he shouted.

She dropped to the seat.

He dodged through the traffic, a rush of adrenaline giving him momentary clarity. He couldn't shake them. No matter what he did, he couldn't shake them. There were too many of them. They shot at him without reservation. They'd hit an innocent bystander. If they got one of his tires, he'd be dead meat.

He swerved through the streets, narrowly avoiding other cars. His wounded arm hung useless at his side. His head spun from pain and the loss of blood. He struggled to hold on, to think, but it was no use. His ears buzzed, flashing lights danced in front his eyes—red and blue and gold.

The sedans were right behind him. Then one pulled even with the Nova. Luc looked over. He saw an Uzi pointing at his head, ducked as a series of shots shattered the side windows.

High above the street the Dream Net Casino's sign flashed on and off. He almost laughed out loud when he realized he'd come back to where he'd started.

He'd gone in a circle. Come full circle.

Instinctively, he yanked the steering wheel. The pain of the movement made him feel like he was being ripped apart, but the Nova obeyed. It veered with a sickening scream of tires, crashed through a barricade and launched into the sand under the pier that stood across from the casino.

Luc struggled to control the fishtailing car. He settled for forcing it toward the packed sand at the edge of the water. The other cars were still close behind him.

Fog was rolling in off the ocean, shrouding the beach in a mist that grew thicker the closer they got to the water line. Luc couldn't see any farther than his windshield. Silvano's men kept shooting at him anyway, even though they couldn't have had any better visibility. Just literally shots in the dark. Probably hoping they'd get lucky.

Then they did.

One of the tires blew. He lost control of the car in the sand. The Nova spun wickedly round and round, finally stopping when it faced the way he had just come. The engine, clogged with sand, sputtered and died.

A large dark object that appeared to be a tower of some sort loomed up out of the thick air nearby. Probably a first-aid station. One of the cars chasing him burst out of the fog and plowed headlong into the structure. It must have hit a supporting leg, because there was a loud splintering noise. The whole tower came crashing down, smashing the sedan under its weight, spraying wood and debris everywhere.

Luc ducked, as if that would have helped, but the

Nova had been far enough away from the tower to escape serious damage. He wasn't trapped. He needed to get out.

He was opening the door when a second car, apparently not realizing what had happened to the first, hurtled out of the fog. It hit the remains of the structure at full speed, flipped end over end several times and came to a halt balanced on its roof.

Shouts and curses rolled across the sand.

Every particle of his body was screaming with pain. Luc crawled out of the Nova and stood, weaving on his feet, clutching his gun. Men scrambled out of the second overturned car. Other cars had arrived, and he could see the shadows of more people getting out of them. He shot at them, but he was weak, his hand was shaking. He missed. Only the fog and the cover it provided saved him now.

He sank down on his knees in the sand beside the Nova, not able to stand any longer, and pulled the door handle to let Spot out of the backseat. She jumped to him, stood protectively in front of him. Her growl was a low, almost subsonic warning that lifted the hairs at the back of his neck. It sounded otherworldly as it echoed weirdly through the fog.

Dimly, he saw Silvano's men pause. He heard them yelling at each other.

Somehow he lifted his gun again and shot, just to try to keep them back, but they were advancing anyway, albeit cautiously. The world around him was receding. He was flowing like the blood flowing out of his body and into the sand.

Katie, his mind whispered. Katie.

Luc thought about her blue, blue eyes and wild curly auburn hair and delicious freckles. He thought about how she had looked leaning over him and yelling at him and wearing his clothes. And not wearing anything at all. He thought about how it had been to hold her, how she'd tasted, how it had felt when he'd slipped inside her. How good she was, how sweet. All of the years he'd wasted because he'd been afraid and run away from that damned party.

And now it was over. It never should have begun. Maybe this was the best thing, after all.

Spot's whole body was stiff. Silvano's men were close. Too close. The dog wouldn't leave him. They'd probably shoot her as soon as they could see her well enough to make sure they killed her. He didn't think he'd be able to stop them.

Another life gone. Another life he couldn't save.

"I wouldn't." The voice rang out, bounced through the fog. Unexpected. Masculine. Hard and cold. Familiar.

Luc was confused. He realized the man was talking to the men surrounding him when he spoke again. "I said, I really fucking wouldn't, assholes. This beach is crawling with cops, and I've got one hell of a headache. Just give me an excuse to shoot, you bastards."

Cops? Luc wondered if maybe some of the flashing lights he'd seen on the street in front of the hotel hadn't been his imagination, after all.

There were some shouts, some scuffles. A few gunshots that didn't seem to hit anything. Luc didn't really know what was happening anymore. He didn't want to know. He closed his eyes and let himself fall on his face in the welcoming sand, let it cradle him. The voice would handle things. He thought it might belong to Justin Némes.

"Luc! Luc!" A small female form fell onto the beach next to him.

Luc turned his face to the side. He couldn't open his eyes, but he smiled. "Katie." It wasn't more than a whisper, but there was a wealth of satisfaction in saying her name.

"Where in the bloody hell did you come from?" He heard Némes shout the words and frowned. Némes shouldn't talk to her that way.

"We followed you, you asshole. We saw you chasing the cars when they turned onto the beach." Luc felt her small hands on his arm, his side, and groaned with the pain. "Luc! Oh, my God, Justin. He's hurt. He's bleeding." Her voice was higher, louder with panic.

"Shit. I'll be right there. Put pressure on the wounds," Némes said. "I have to make sure these guys are tied down."

"We need to turn him over." This voice was older and female. She sounded like she knew what she was doing.

"Mrs. McCabe," he murmured.

"Yes, it's my mother. She's okay," Katie said.

Hands touched him and carefully rolled him onto his back. Luc choked back a scream as agony lanced through his shoulder and side.

"Luc, shhh. It's okay." He realized Katie was practically lying next to him, her face pressed close to his. He breathed her in and was comforted by her scent.

He didn't even mind it when hands that felt like steel pressed against the places that hurt the most.

He swallowed and tried to open his eyes. "Katie, I think I killed Kato."

"I don't care." She was crying. He could hear it.

"Katie?" It was getting very difficult to talk. He wanted sleep. Just sleep. He was so tired. He was really hurt and about to scare the hell out of her and faint. Jesus, how wimpy. But maybe he wouldn't wake up again, so he had to make sure she knew something. It was important that she knew.

"Yes?" Her voice was a whisper. Choked.

"They say that you see your life go by. At the end."

"Stop it." Katie feathered a kiss along his scar. It felt good. "Save your strength."

"But I didn't see my life," he whispered. He had to tell her. She had to know. She deserved to know. He opened his eyes and looked right at her. "I saw you." Her eyes were shiny with tears behind the glasses.

"I love you." She said it into his ear, her breath soft and warm against him.

Those were the last words he heard as the blackness finally, finally won.

Katie watched Luc's head fall back into the sand. "Mom!" she screamed.

"The ambulance will be here in a minute, Katie. Keep pressure on that shoulder."

"I am, I am."

"I need to get a better grip on his side." They jostled around a little, fought for position. "Talk to him, baby.

Make him want to stay. He needs to fight. Make him want to fight."

Katie lowered her head down next to Luc's. She kept pressure on the horrible wound in his shoulder. While his blood flowed over her fingers, she put her lips right up against his ear and whispered all of the hopes and dreams she'd held buried in her heart since the day Melanie had set her up on a blind date with her foster brother. The dreams she'd had almost since the first time Melanie had mentioned him.

She pleaded with him to fight, to be alive in this world somewhere, even if it wasn't with her. Over and over again, she told him that she loved him, that he was important, that he was wonderful. That he was a good man.

She was dimly aware of the chaos raging around her. Her mother shouted at Némes that they needed an ambulance, NOW! All at once David Allen was there, his face dark and strained. He took over applying pressure to Luc's shoulder, his deep voice joining the plea that Luc fight, that he live. The genuine emotion she heard when he spoke to his friend confirmed for her that he was one of the good guys.

Then more police came, then Némes's face joined David's, then the ambulance finally arrived with spinning lights and the loud siren. People. Hands. Voices. Shouts. More hands trying to drag her away. Her resistance.

And all the while she kept telling Luc that she loved him. She tried to force her strength into him. She begged him to hold on.

David pushed Spot into his car, although she did not want to leave her master and cried pitifully.

No one tried to keep Katie out of the ambulance. She continued to whisper to Luc while the technicians worked around her and spoke with stark, emotionless voices.

They arrived at the hospital. Luc was whisked away by men and women in white coats who shouted orders at each other and handled metal equipment.

And then she was alone.

Katie sank to her knees in the middle of the reception area and covered her face with her bloody hands. A nurse saw her and helped her over to an uncomfortable settee in the waiting room. Then somehow her mother was there again, sitting next to her.

Katie turned her face into her mom's shoulder and sobbed like a child. "He can't die," she cried.

"The doctors will do all they can, honey," her mother said softly.

The next hours were hell, filled with nothing but waiting. Waiting for word that Luc was in surgery, waiting for word that the surgery was over.

Eventually, Katie cleaned herself up in the restroom. She told her mother about Luc, what had happened over the last few days and why she had been kidnapped. Mom seemed to take it all pretty well, but then Katie wasn't really paying attention. Her mind was with Luc on the operating table, with him while the surgeons tried to piece together his damaged body.

He had to live. But time trickled by, and there still

wasn't any word. He had to live. He had to. It wouldn't be fair if Luc died.

Then again, life was seldom fair.

When Némes and David finally joined them in the waiting room, Katie's mom was pacing, her legs still stiff after having been tied up for so long. At some point during the last couple of hours, she'd been examined and was as well as could be expected.

Némes, a white bandage gleaming against his dark hair, stopped to talk to Katie's mother. David moved over to sit next to Katie in a chair positioned near the settee, a paper cup of horrible hospital coffee clasped in his big, capable hands.

For a bit they were both silent, Katie staring at the floor, David staring into his cup of coffee.

"Némes told us you were already on your way to the casino when he called you," she said finally, more to distract herself from worrying about Luc than anything else.

"I was." David stirred. "I was getting suspicious of Liza." He shrugged. "Nothing major, just little things. And I was looking at everyone on the squad, even the admin. If I'd been smarter, I would have looked at her first."

Katie blinked. "Really?"

He shrugged. "Sure. Admins know all kinds of things, but they tend to be ignored."

"Most people don't realize that."

David smiled slightly. "I'm an FBI special agent, ma'am. I'm not most people." The smile faded. "I just wish I'd put things together sooner."

Katie looked down at her hands. "Liza said Frankie and her father really went all out to make sure she got past the background checks. She even had some surgery in case there were pictures."

"It had to be a coup to have her placed in the Bureau. When she was assigned to my squad, they must have been ecstatic," David said. His expression was wry. "We're organized crime. They must know we have them on our radar. With her as my admin they could find out everything we were doing."

"But they didn't know how she felt about Luc," Katie said.

"Joey didn't." David agreed. "Frankie, well, Frankie was one messed-up dude. Just based on what little I know at the moment, I'd say he was playing her."

"Probably." Katie shivered. She did not want to think about Frankie Silvano. "All of this doesn't explain why you were headed for Atlantic City."

David settled farther back in his chair, long legs stretched out in front of him. "I tried to call you guys this morning, but Luc didn't answer the cell and I couldn't get anyone on the house phone. I went out to the Museum and found it all shot up with some dead Silvano guys in the front yard. It was not...good." The restrained emotion in his voice had her putting her hand on his arm. He met her eyes. "I was a trifle concerned."

"I'll bet. We couldn't call you." She didn't tell him that they'd suspected him, but David, being David, didn't need everything spelled out.

His dark eyes twinkled a little ruefully. "Couldn't or wouldn't?" When she would have protested, he put his hand over hers and squeezed it. "I know, Katie. I know that I had to be on the radar after everything went down. I don't fault you or Luc for not trusting me."

"It ate him up," she said. "It was killing him."

David nodded. "When I calmed down," he said after a moment, "I thought about how Liza had called in and taken a few days off from work for a family emergency. I thought about how often she's mentioned Atlantic City over the years, and how the Silvanos controlled a casino there. I didn't have a better lead and I was already in New Jersey, so I figured I might as well go see what I could see. All I could do was hope I'd turn up something or that Luc would contact me. I was almost at the casino when Némes got a hold of me. The rest you know."

"David—" Whatever she'd been about to say flew from her mind when a nurse entered the waiting room and came striding over to them.

Katie jumped to her feet.

Her mother stepped quickly over to stand beside her and took her hand. Katie stared at the woman in her crisp scrubs, willing her to have good news, to have some news. She must have looked a little desperate, because the nurse smiled at her compassionately.

"He's alive," she told them. "One of his lungs collapsed during surgery—"

Katie gasped.

"—and his condition is critical, but barring any complications, we expect him to make a full recovery."

Katie let go of her mother, sank back down onto the uncomfortable settee and hid her face in her hands.

Thank you, God. Thank you, God. Thank you, God. Luc was alive. Luc would live.

THIRTY

LUC'S PRIVATE HOSPITAL room was dark and quiet when Katie walked in. She paused briefly in the doorway, struggled to hold back more tears and just looked at him. His skin had lost all color, his big body still for once, his face more vulnerable than she'd ever seen it. The only noises were the beeps and whirrs of the equipment they'd hooked up to him; the antiseptic odor of the hospital made everything seem impersonal and maybe somehow horrible. But even from across the room, she could see his chest rising and falling as he breathed steadily in and out. He really was alive.

Moving silently forward, Katie dragged a chair over to the bed and sat as close to Luc as possible in the cramped space. She touched his hand on his uninjured side, careful of the IV and other tubes going into his arm, then threaded her fingers through his and gripped him, holding on tightly. With her free hand she brushed his dark hair away from his forehead, trying not to worry about how drawn and haggard he looked.

"Jerk," she whispered. "Stupid jerk, getting yourself all shot up like this."

Staring at him, touching him, the reality of the last couple of hours, the last couple of days, slammed into her.

She'd killed a man, shot him dead. Watched his face disappear. Watched his blood spurt and his body jerk because she'd pulled a trigger on a gun.

Yes, it had been Frankie Silvano, and yes, he'd been threatening them, but still. She'd ended his life.

God, how she wished Luc was awake so she could talk to him about it, so he could soothe her with his deep, smooth voice. So he could hold her until she stopped shaking inside.

She ran her fingers through Luc's too-long hair, loving its silky texture, then let her fingertips trace over his scar, over his firm mouth, ran her thumb over his lips. They parted and for a moment, she stopped breathing, thinking that he was going to wake up, but he just whispered a sigh against her skin.

She'd fallen in love with this man, deeply in love. Fallen so far in love that she'd been insane from the need to be with him.

It had happened so fast. It had taken years. She didn't know him at all. She knew him better than anybody. It was the best of times. It was the worst of times.

She smiled slightly and sat, holding his hand, watching him sleep. For the first time in her life, she understood how her mother felt about her father. That understanding terrified her.

Because the truth she saw inside herself as she stared into Luc's pale face was that she wanted him to be with her. But more than that, she desperately wanted Luc to want to be with her.

She needed him to love her back.

And what scared her the most was the knowledge that maybe he never would.

Time meandered by, the machines hummed and clicked, and Katie sat, staring into Luc's face, thinking.

David seemed to materialize beside her. Katie had been so focused on Luc that she jumped, startled. He was carrying her purse under his arm like a football and he smiled at her, but his sharp, dark eyes missed nothing.

Katie felt a little awkward and nodded at the purse. "I was wondering where that was," she lied. Actually, she hadn't even thought about the thing until now, but it was something to say.

"I just got it from one of the uniforms. He found it at the casino."

"Thanks."

David shrugged and moved next to the bed. "My pleasure. But if I'm going to have to rescue it on a regular basis, I'll have to go back to the gym to build up my strength. It's like carting around an anvil."

"Smart aleck."

"They want me to convince you to go away now."

"No." Katie had waited hours to get into this room. She wasn't leaving.

"Yeah, I told them you'd say that. I also told them to let you stay. You're not hurting him, and you're probably helping."

Katie looked at him with some surprise. "Thanks again."

David pulled another chair over to the bed and sat down beside her, dropping her purse to the floor with a thud. He leaned back and stared at Luc, brooding.

"Did Mom ever get a hold of Melanie?" Katie asked. She'd finally remembered to tell her mother that Melanie was Luc's foster sister and that she should be called.

"Oh, yeah." David smiled at her. "She also got in touch with your father and brothers."

Katie gulped. "She did?"

"They're on the way, like the proverbial cavalry. And one of your sisters is coming too. Brenna, I think she said."

"Jeez."

"They all want to meet Luc."

"I'll bet they do."

David laughed again. "Don't worry. Maureen is working on calming the troops." He hesitated. "She's quite a woman."

Katie studied him, wishing she could read what was going on behind his calm mask, wondering if she needed to tell him to keep his hands off her mother, wondering if the situation would get even more surreal.

They sat in silence for a few minutes.

"Am I in trouble for shooting Frankie?" she asked. It had belatedly occurred to her that the law tended to frown when you killed someone.

"No. It was obviously self-defense. You'll have to give a statement to the police about what happened, but nobody's going to shed any tears over the fact that you offed Frankie Silvano. In fact, the cops might give you an award. I know I want to. Hell, Joey Silvano might give you an award for getting rid of Frankie. He hated the little bastard, but I think his wife wouldn't let him do anything about it."

Katie looked down. The thin, cruel face melting away. Red blood splattering the white wall. Please. No award necessary.

"What about Liza?" she asked.

"She's in the hospital. Another hospital," he qualified. "Her injuries are minor, but she needed to be stitched up. There's a chance she has a concussion."

Katie squirmed, remembering how hard she'd hit the other woman with the butt of that gun.

"Once she's been released she'll be a guest of the fine state of New Jersey," David continued.

"Will my mother and I have to testify or anything?" She dreaded the possibility, but she had to know.

"Well, I just spoke to the agent I put in charge of cleanup at the casino. They think they've found a journal on Frankie Silvano's computer. It clearly implicates Liza in all kinds of things. That, combined with Némes's statement, and the fact that her records were doctored to get past the Bureau's employment checks should be enough for us to put her away for quite a while without your testimony. Maybe not for attempted murder, but one way or the other she'll go down." He glanced at her. "I'd like to keep you and your mother out of it if I can."

"That would be nice," Katie murmured.

"You can certainly pursue charges against Liza if you want to—"

"No."

David smiled sympathetically. "I thought you might feel that way. In that case, I think you'll be free to go after you give the police your statement."

Katie closed her eyes. It was over. It was finally over.

She and David listened to the hum of the machinery for a while.

It was over. Now what?

There was a slight rustle. The hand clasped in hers twitched, the fingers tightening briefly.

"Katie?" The voice was weak and a little slurred, but it came from the bed.

"Luc." Everything else was immediately forgotten as she clutched his hand in both of hers and bent over him. "Luc, are you awake?"

"I guess," he said. Then his eyes opened and he blinked up at her. "Unless you're an angel."

"Not bloody likely." Katie laughed and cried at the same time. She kissed Luc beside his mouth, just barely restraining herself from kissing every inch of his tired face. "You're awake."

"A very perceptive woman," Luc whispered.

Katie turned back to David, smiling broadly. "He's awake."

"I can see that." David laughed and stood. "Soon he'll be able to start on all of the paperwork he's going to have to fill out."

"Go to hell, David." Luc moaned.

David grinned. "I'll get the nurse." He squeezed Katie's shoulder and left the room.

"Don't go, Katie, okay?" Luc murmured. He looked like he was trying to focus on her face, but the painkillers and the aftereffects of the anesthesia were obviously still bothering him. "Don't leave."

Katie just couldn't stop herself. She leaned forward and let her lips trail over his cheekbone, moving up the long scar in a soft caress. "Never," she promised in a whisper.

She sat back abruptly when David re-entered the room followed by a nurse, who took Luc's vital signs with calm efficiency.

"Mr. Vasco needs to rest," the woman announced when she was finished. She eyed Katie with ill-concealed hostility. "I think you should go now, Ms. McCabe."

"But—"

"No!" Luc's eyes popped open. "No, she stays." His tone was low but firm, and Katie thought she heard an undercurrent of desperation that surprised her.

"Luc." She shifted under the nurse's stare. "Maybe it would be best—"

"No. I want you to stay. You said you'd stay."

"But—"

"You stay," he insisted again, gripping her hand tightly, obviously fighting against unconsciousness. "Please. Please stay."

Katie stroked back his hair, felt the softness against her fingers. "Of course I'll stay."

He smiled at her, just a little, and his eyes closed again. After a couple of minutes she knew he was asleep.

From a distance, she heard David talking quietly to the nurse and muffled footsteps as the woman left the room. Then he let out a soft sigh, and the other chair scraped against the floor as he settled down beside her again.

"I think he's going to be okay," he said.

Katie felt her face stretch into a wide smile. "Yes."

David sat, silent. "You're going to get hurt, Katie," he finally said.

She hesitated, but decided that she wouldn't pretend not to know what he meant.

"You can't be sure."

"Maybe," David admitted. "I love Luc like a brother, but I've known him a long time." He paused. "Long time. He hates hospitals. Always has. When he was six or seven his mother got sick and ended up in the hospital. Next thing he knew his mom was dead and he was alone."

Katie stared down at Luc's sleeping face but didn't say anything. Poor little boy.

"Don't take the fact that he asked you to stay too personally. He would want somebody here with him watching his back until he's more in control. Don't read more into it than's there."

"Then why didn't he ask you?" Katie said softly. "Why me and not you?"

David sighed again. "You're not going to listen to me, are you?"

She didn't bother to answer. She knew David was trying to help her. He was a good man. Maybe he was right, and she would get hurt.

Or maybe David didn't know Luc, after all.

THIRTY-ONE

LUC SLEPT. Time crawled. Darkness and light shifted outside the window. Katie sat in the chair next to the bed, so tired that she wasn't feeling or thinking or dreaming or anything. The nurses came and went, and David showed up periodically to bring her coffee and food, but Katie had no idea how long she'd been sitting there or even what day it was. She only knew that Luc's condition had improved. He was still asleep, but he was going to be all right.

Finally, unable to hold back her own exhaustion any longer, Katie lay her head down on the bed beside him and slept too.

She woke in the fluorescent half-light with no idea where she was or how long she'd been there. Oh, yeah. Luc's room.

She had a truly severe crick in her neck. Her face felt smushed from lying so long on one side, and she knew her hair must be a sight to behold.

A little painfully, she looked up and realized with a large internal leap of joy that Luc had his eyes open, that he was watching her.

"Luc." Her own discomfort forgotten, she smiled and grabbed his hand in both of hers.

But instead of smiling back at her or making any gesture to indicate he was glad to see her, he just looked at her, his expression remote.

Katie's smile slipped as a bubble of panic bobbed to the surface. Maybe he was in a lot of pain. Maybe she should call the nurse…

"Katie?" Well, at least he knew her name. His voice was much stronger than it had been, and his dark eyes seemed alert. "What are you doing here?"

"You…" The word sounded rusty and she had to clear her throat and start again. "You wanted me to stay with you."

His brow creased as he frowned at her. He was definitely still pale, Katie thought, studying him anxiously, but he really did look a lot better. In fact, he probably looked better than she did. Good. That was good. So why was he acting weird?

"I asked you to stay? That was stupid," he said.

Katie drew back a little. She shook her head, trying to clear it. "What?"

Luc's eyes flicked down to where her hands held his. "It's all a blur," he said. "I guess I was really out of it because of the medicine. Sorry about that."

"Oh." Katie didn't know what to say, how to act. The man who had clung to her on the beach, who had begged her not to leave him at the hospital was gone, and the cold stranger was back. She didn't know this man.

"I, uh, didn't want to leave you alone," she said.

Luc shrugged his good shoulder slightly and winced at the movement. "Oh, well, you didn't need to worry."

Katie let go of his hand and sank back in the chair.

Self-consciously she tried to smooth down her hair and wondered if she had sheet marks on her face.

Okay. Okay, so he was pushing her away again like he'd tried to do before. He felt vulnerable, and now he was retreating.

Katie rubbed her sore neck, put her palms over her gritty eyes. If only she could think.

Luc pressed some buttons and raised the bed until he was sitting. He held his breath and sweat dotted his forehead, but otherwise he didn't acknowledge that he was in pain, although she knew it must have hurt like the devil.

"Are you sure you should do that?" she asked.

"I heal fast. I'm okay."

Silence.

A nurse came in and scolded Luc for sitting up as she lowered the bed. Of course, he raised it again as soon as she left.

While Katie was thinking of a way to break through the strange new tension, a very familiar woman burst into the room, limping a little, but still graceful. Her brown hair hung long and straight like satin, her hazel eyes wild with fear.

Melanie Grant. Her foster sister. Luc's foster sister.

"Luc! Luc, are you all right?"

"Melanie." Smiling, he held out his good hand to her and she ran to him, took it.

"Mom called…" Melanie was breathless, both panic and relief in her voice.

Katie stared at her, at the emotion in her face. Emotion Katie had never seen there before.

"I've been trying to get into your room forever. They said I couldn't come in until you woke up, but that Katie was here." Mel finally turned and stared at her. "Katie, Mom told me Luc has been protecting you."

Katie blushed, unaccountably embarrassed, and tried to smooth her hair down again.

"It's a long story," she muttered.

"We'll talk later." Melanie dismissed her and turned back to Luc. "I'm just so glad you're alive." She gave him as big a bear hug as she could manage around all of the tubes and sensors. Katie knew it had to hurt, but he didn't complain. Instead his uninjured arm curled around her sister's waist. He pulled her closer and kissed her gently on the cheek.

Katie stood and moved aside so Melanie could sit down. Then she backed farther away from the bed. Luc and Melanie didn't seem to notice. They were too busy talking and answering each other at the same time, totally involved in each other. Katie watched them. And felt isolated. Cold. Outside the secret life Melanie had never shared. Outside the life Luc wouldn't let her enter. Didn't want her to enter.

She took a deep breath in and pushed it out. Looking at them, it was so obvious that Melanie was in love with Luc that she wondered why she hadn't even considered the possibility before.

Katie breathed. In and out.

Damn you, she wanted to scream at both of them. What about me?

Before she could even hope to decide what to do next, Justin Némes strolled into the room. He was elegantly dressed, his dark hair tied back into a queue, bandage at a rakish angle, his blue eyes mellow until he caught a glimpse of Katie's face. Then they narrowed, became a little dangerous.

She looked away.

"Némes," Luc said from the bed. "An unexpected pleasure."

Melanie nodded at the other man. "Némes," she murmured.

"Hey, this is a red-letter day. You actually called me by my real name," Némes said.

So, Melanie had met Némes before. Had another secret.

Melanie's lips tightened. She turned away, her long hair swinging to hide her face. Hiding from everyone. Except Luc.

"I could think of a few other things to call you," she said shortly.

"I'll bet." Némes faced Luc. "I just came to tell you that I have to take off. Now that you're on the mend I need to get back to work."

Luc shifted and obviously zinged himself. He panted for a moment through the pain, then grinned. "Poor slob."

"Tell me about it. David's trying to talk me into coming back to the Bureau, and I'm so far gone that I'm actually considering it."

"You should." Luc took Melanie's hand and intertwined their fingers, holding her close to the bed.

"Eh." Némes shrugged his broad shoulders. "We'll see. There's a certain allure to international tax laws."

"If you say so." Luc paused. "Thanks, man. For everything."

Némes shrugged again. "I owed you."

"You didn't owe me anything for your sister. Nothing at all."

"Not for my sister." Némes hesitated and shifted on his feet. "For Liza. For the way I didn't think. Or rather, for the way I thought with the wrong part of my anatomy."

Luc shook his head. "Forget about it."

"I understand that after you launched your initial investigation into the drug charges, you didn't believe I was involved and worked behind the scenes to clear me," Némes said. "It looks like I've wasted a lot of time hating a man who didn't deserve it."

"I wasn't able to do too much."

"Maybe not, but you did all you could." Némes turned and then he was standing in front of Katie. "Well, kid, it has been extremely…real."

"Thought you'd say that." She forced a smile, but of course it didn't fool him.

"Anything wrong?" he bent closer to her and asked in a lower voice.

She turned her head away, knowing he'd probably seen more than she'd wanted him to. "Nope. But thanks anyway."

He leaned down, brushed her cheek with a chaste kiss and left.

And Katie was alone again.

"Just who does he think he is?" Melanie demanded of the room at large.

"An accountant," Luc said.

"Oh, right." Melanie didn't sound like she believed it. Frankly, Katie didn't either.

"Well, it's what he thinks he is," Luc said. "Sometimes that's all that matters."

FOR THE FIRST TIME IN HIS LIFE, Luc actually wanted to be left alone in a hospital room. He needed to sort things out. To get back on an even keel. To start rebuilding some boundaries between himself and Katie. Katie with her wild red hair, freckles and blue, blue eyes.

On the beach, she'd said she loved him...

Christ, she fucking terrified him. And what she thought she felt for him scared him even more. He wasn't what she needed. Hell, he wasn't what anybody needed.

Katie deserved a better man. Someone kinder. Less damaged. Less cruel. Someone who was more like Bruce Wayne and less like, well, Luc Vasco.

Look at what he was doing to Melanie. He loved Mel like a sister, but he'd known for a while that she wanted more. And here he was using that knowledge without hesitation, using her to drive Katie away. Because even now, all he wanted was for Katie to stroke back his hair with her gentle fingers and kiss him with her soft lips.

And he hated himself because he wanted it. Hated himself because he was using Melanie. And hated himself because he was going to hurt both of them. All of them. But he didn't have a choice.

"Katie," he said, interrupting Melanie without even realizing it. "Why don't you go?"

"Go?" she repeated the word uncertainly.

"Go get some rest. You look beat." He paused, despising himself, and forced a smile. "Besides," he said, "Melanie's here, and I'd like to be alone with her." He released Mel's hand and deliberately drew it through her silky brown hair.

Katie watched his hand and an expression of pain passed through her eyes. Then anger flashed.

"I can take a hint. I was just going anyway. See you later, Mel." She picked up her purse and walked out of the room without looking back.

Luc dropped his hand and clenched his teeth. He tried to tell himself the pain ripping at his chest was from the bullet wounds. Shouldn't have moved like that.

Liar.

Her body smooth and pale and soft as she rose over him in the yellow lamplight.

Her mouth on his skin...

Intensely weary, he glanced at Melanie and saw her staring at him as if she'd never seen him before.

She pushed away from the bed, walked a few paces across the room. "What the hell was that all about?"

"What do you mean?" He didn't meet her eyes.

She fisted her hands on her hips. "Oh, come off it, Luc. You tried to hurt her deliberately."

"Don't be stupid," Luc said, inwardly cursing. Mel always had known him too well.

"But why? Why Katie? What's she ever done to you?"

"She annoys me." He said it loudly, as if volume would make the words true.

Melanie folded her arms across her chest. "Bullshit."

"Drop it, Mel." God, he was tired. Tired of himself. Tired of the whole fucking mess.

"No, I'm not going to drop it. Katie is my sister, and I love her. I'm not going to sit back and watch you hurt her again."

"She'll get over it." Luc absently picked at the hospital sheets.

Melanie studied him. "You care about her, don't you?"

He kept silent.

"For God's sake, don't hide it from me, Luc. If you have feelings for Katie, then why are you pushing her away?"

Luc pressed his lips together so he wouldn't yell at her.

"You're scared." Melanie said it slowly into the silence, as if she was working something out. "And if I know you, and I do, you're probably telling yourself you're doing this for her own good." Realization dawned in her eyes. "You're using me, you creep!"

"I'm not."

"Tell me the truth."

"Okay, here it is," Luc said a little desperately. "Katie's just confused right now. She thinks she feels things, but she doesn't, and she'll figure it out after this all calms down. Besides, she deserves more than I can give her, that's for damn sure. I'm just shoving her out of the nest, that's all."

"In other words, you're running away."

"I'm not running."

Melanie walked back up to the bed, grabbed his chin

and forced him to look directly at her. He stared into her clear hazel eyes, saw them glaze with tears.

"Yes," she said. "You are."

"I am not," he whispered.

"You shouldn't be afraid, Luc." She smiled, small and bittersweet, then shook her head twice. Her hand left his chin to stroke his face, the scar. "Don't be afraid to hold onto something for yourself. You deserve so much. So much more than you've had. You need someone warm and real and loving."

"Someone like Katie?" He tried to sound cynical and sarcastic, but knew that he failed miserably.

Melanie drew in a deep, deep breath and let it out slowly. "Yes," she said, smiling as the tears shimmered on her eyelashes and trailed down her cheeks. "Someone like Katie."

THIRTY-TWO

WHEN KATIE STUMBLED into the hospital waiting room, all she wanted to do was make good her escape. If she was alone, she could try to deal with the emotions tearing and whirling inside her. She could check into a hotel and sleep. Maybe then she could decide what to do next. How to go on. But as soon as she entered the room, three large men jumped out of chairs that seemed barely able to support them and descended on her en masse. Their big bodies hovered around her and blocked out the light until she felt like she was in some sort of a cave of testosterone.

Oh, God. Her brothers.

"Katie."

"What the hell's going on?"

"Are you all right?"

Darren, Brandon and Michael each hugged her in turn, and she was a little comforted by their obvious strength and by the knowledge that they, at least, loved her.

"Leave the girl alone, you behemoths," a female voice scolded. Katie found herself caught up in another hug as a tall, round woman practically squeezed the life right out of her.

"Jesus, Brenna, she's not a tube of toothpaste. Leave off," Brandon said, but his twin ignored him.

Katie looked at them and wished they would all go away. She just didn't have the energy to deal with them. Besides, she had to get out of the hospital before she saw Melanie again. Melanie, who loved Luc. Melanie, who, on whatever level, Luc obviously loved back.

Her father was standing off to the side with her mother, but he didn't move to come over.

She turned her attention back to her siblings. "Fancy meeting you guys in a place like this. Come here often?" She tried to joke, but it fell flat.

"Tired sweetie?" Darren asked, his deep voice gentle. He was the oldest and tallest of her brothers, taller even than their father, his shoulders broad and muscular from years working in construction. His bright blue eyes were concerned as he surveyed her from head to toe.

She turned away from his too-knowing gaze.

"Yeah, I'm pretty drained." Mentally, emotionally and spiritually. Her thoughts drifted back to Luc and Melanie in the hospital room.

"That David guy booked us all rooms at a hotel a couple of blocks away," Darren said. "I was thinking I'd wait for Mel, but Michael can take you over." He punched their youngest brother in the arm.

"Ow!"

"Wimp. Can't take a hit 'cause you're a loan shark."

"Stockbroker, you jackass."

"Whatever."

"I'll take her," Brenna said. "All of you can wait for Mel. You know you want to meet Luc anyway."

Darren's face hardened. "Yeah," he said. "We want to meet Luc." Katie saw her brothers exchange glances.

Oh, great. "Look, you don't have to—"

"How is everyone?" David Allen walked into the waiting room.

Katie bit back a groan. If she didn't get away soon she was going to lose it, just completely lose it. She closed her eyes.

"Katie?" David prompted. "You decided to leave?"

She forced herself to look at him. "Melanie's there," she said simply.

"You're pale." David said. "I think you need to go to the hotel."

Yes! Yes! she wanted to scream. I need to go to the damned hotel. Everyone just shut up so I can get there.

"I'll—" Brenna started, but her mom finally stepped forward.

"I'll take her," she said. "All of you stay here and wait for Melanie. She probably won't be too much longer."

Katie kind of doubted that, since Mel and Luc obviously had a lot to talk about. Melanie might want to sit beside Luc while he slept. Watch over him. Maybe Katie had just been a stand-in until she got there anyway.

She shook her head, hoping to dispel the thought, but it stuck and buzzed around with the rest.

She tried telling everyone that she could find her own way, but her mom, as usual, wouldn't take no for an answer, and shepherded her to the parking garage. Katie was a little shocked when her father fell into step behind them.

"What?" He frowned, noticing her stare. "You want to walk?"

"Uh, no. I mean, thank you." Any strength Katie had left was draining rapidly. She just wasn't up to arguing with her father. It took a minute before she realized those were the first words she'd exchanged with him in months, and their first relatively civil words in longer than that.

None of them said anything else as they climbed into her father's huge gas-guzzling pickup truck, her dad driving, Katie plastered against the passenger door and her mother in the middle. Once the big truck was humming with subtle power, her father drove out of the garage and onto the highway, his elbow crooked out the open window while he steered one-handed through the traffic. He exuded the confidence of a man who was used to finding his way with only the skimpiest of directions. Another trait he hadn't passed along to her.

Katie stared out the window and tried to think of something to say to him. She didn't want to hate her father anymore. She didn't want him to hate her. She was so tired of hate. Of uncertainty. Just once, she wanted to feel like his daughter. Just once, she wanted it to be okay to need him. Just once, she wanted him to love her too.

Taking a deep breath, she turned and looked over at him, big and strong and handling the truck as if it was an extension of himself.

"I'm glad that you're here, Dad," she said finally.

Her father glanced at her quickly. She thought she saw an echo of her own panic in his eyes.

Her mother sat silent between them, watching but

not trying to help, her body a living conduit, connecting them somehow.

"Um, thanks. I'm glad I'm here too," he said.

They were silent again. Katie's heart sank. She stared down at her hands and gripped her fingers together.

Her father cleared his throat. "Uh, the cabin's the same. The guys were all having a good time. Well, at least we were until the owner of the local grocery store came tearing up the mountain with your mother's message," he said. "There's no phone in the cabin, you know, and cell phone service sucks."

"The message got a little garbled," her mom explained. "They thought you were the one who'd been hurt."

"Oh," Katie murmured. She couldn't think of anything else to say.

They drove in silence for another stretch before her father sighed. When he spoke again, his voice was huskier than she'd ever heard it.

"Jesus Christ, I aged about twenty years getting down off that damn mountain," he said. "I don't think I've ever seen Brandon move so fast, and I still had my boot up his ass."

Katie smiled in spite of herself. Brandon was by no means lazy, but he had an easy way about him that drove their father crazy.

"I'm okay," she pointed out, and chanced another look at him. He didn't seem to have heard her. He was staring straight ahead, both hands gripping the wheel now.

"I drove like a maniac to get here. The boys had trouble keeping up. The whole way I kept seeing you in my mind. How perfect you were when you were born. How much you look like your mother."

Katie stared at him, not quite able to believe what she was hearing.

"I kept thinking about what I'd said to you, how much I've hurt you when all I wanted was to—"

"Dad, stop. Please." She really couldn't handle this on top of everything else. She was going to bawl if he kept it up. "It's okay, really."

His jaw tightened, and he kept his eyes on the road, but he didn't say anything more. She drew in a shaky breath.

They pulled up in front of a very nice looking little hotel, not one of the big casinos, thank God. Her father cut the engine.

"You're already checked in," he told Katie, not quite meeting her eyes. "Why don't you let your mother get you settled and I'll just stay here out of the way."

Katie and her mother slid out of the cab of the truck, but when her mom started to lead her into the hotel, Katie disentangled herself and walked around the truck. She wasn't going to leave it like this. Not this time.

Her father was sitting, staring out through the windshield. He looked alone.

"I'm sorry, Dad," she said through his open window. She wasn't sure what she was apologizing for. Maybe nothing in particular. Maybe everything.

He turned his head to look down at her. Katie was shocked to see tears standing in his eyes.

"I'm sorry, too, baby. For so, so much."

Katie gaped at him. She'd never, ever thought that

she'd hear those words coming from her father. Never thought she'd see him show so much emotion. Never thought that emotion could be directed toward her.

"Dad?"

"I'm so glad that you weren't hurt. I… Oh, shit, I love you, honey."

Katie launched herself up onto the running board and through the open window at him, twisting her arms around his thick, weather-roughened neck. He wrapped his strong arms around her as best he could and lifted her until her feet were dangling. She buried her face against his shoulder.

They clung to each other for several long moments. Then he gently pulled back and combed her hair with his blunt fingers as if she were still a little girl.

He smiled, his eyes crinkling at the corners, the laugh-lines deepening. "You're worn down to a nub-bin, honey. Go on with your mother and get some rest. After she settles you in, we'll go back to the hospital and make sure the rest of the crew get tucked away into their safe little beds."

"But Dad, I want to—"

"We'll talk soon, baby, I promise." His big hand cupped her face. "But you're not up to it now. We've got all the time in the world."

She tried to protest some more, but he just shook his head and leaned out of the window, gently lowering her feet to the asphalt as if she weighed nothing at all. He patted her cheek again before he let her go.

"Go on, now," he said.

Katie swallowed. "I love you, Daddy."

He turned away abruptly, and she smiled for the first time in ages. Then she followed her mother into the hotel.

The room was dark and cool and anonymous, with two neatly made double beds, a horrible still-life painting and a door leading to a modest bathroom. The air conditioner whirred in the background and the air smelled antiseptic and clean.

"Okay, Katie. Spill it," her mother said almost as soon as the door had closed behind them. "What else happened?"

"Dad's waiting—"

"And he can wait a little bit longer. I'm not leaving here until you tell me what's going on. And I'm not talking about the gangsters either."

Katie sat on the side of one of the beds. She dropped her head into her hands, willing her mother to leave, to please leave. "I'm just tired."

"I can believe that. How much sleep have you had anyway?"

Katie glanced up and sighed. "Not nearly enough."

She gave Katie a tilted-head look. "But there's more to it than that."

"No there's not."

Her mother sat on the bed beside her, patting her clenched hands. "Katie. I'm not leaving until you tell me. And you know how stubborn I can be."

Katie laughed a little and looked down at the industrial grade blue carpeting between her feet. Well, why not? She was going to find out eventually.

"Melanie's in love with Luc, and it seems as though Luc's okay with the idea."

Her mother was silent for a full minute. "You're sure?"

"Yes."

"Did she tell you that?"

"No. I mean, not exactly, but I saw them. Together. The way he acted with her. The way she acted with him. I've never seen her look like that before. And Luc was, well, he was so open with her. He loves her too. I think he was trying to tell me that it was, um, over."

"Honey." Her mother draped her arms around her shoulders and pulled her close. "I don't know what to say."

Katie laughed again, although this time it was a little watery. "Just don't say I told you so."

"Who, me? Such words would never cross my lips."

Katie clung to her mother and rested her cheek against her shoulder, closing her eyes for a second as she breathed in the comforting scent of her. Then she pushed away. "I'll be okay. I just need a little time alone. You know."

"Oh, yeah. I know We can talk tomorrow." Her mother's voice sounded sad. She stood, and Katie thought that she probably did know. Better than almost anyone else in the world.

"I'm, um, I'm thinking that I'll leave tomorrow." Katie looked at her hands again. "I'm pretty sure David will be okay with it."

"You don't want to stay?"

"It's for the best."

"You're not going to fight for him?" Her mother sounded like she did not approve.

"How can I fight Melanie? She's had such a rough life. And then after what I did to her…"

"Katie! Melanie has had a good life. Yes, the beginning of it was terrible, more terrible than any child should have to endure, but she's made something good out of herself. And you, well, you did nothing to her. Nothing but give her love and a chance. The accident was just that. An accident. It was her decision to go with you. You don't have to turn your back on Luc because you're trying to make up for something that wasn't your fault."

"I know." Katie sighed. And maybe on some level she did know her mother was speaking the truth. Accepting it was the problem. "Okay, then how can I fight for a man who doesn't want me enough to admit that he wants me?"

"I actually followed that." Her mom walked to the door, then stopped and turned back to face her again. "I know you're upset right now, but don't forget that you cared enough about that man to put yourself in some real danger to come to Atlantic City for him."

"I came for you."

Her mother shook her head. "Don't try to rationalize it, dear. We both know why you came here. I'm sure I played some part in the decision, but I wasn't the only reason."

"I was stupid."

"Maybe. Maybe not. You're just tired and not thinking clearly. I don't think you can judge anything right now. All I'm asking is that you remember that you were willing to come here. Remember that he almost died trying to save you."

"Mom, please." Katie couldn't take any more. She really couldn't.

"Just don't do anything too rash, Katie," her mother said. "Give yourself time. Give him time. After all, he's been shot and practically died. I'm sure he's not up to par yet. And he's a man, so that means he's emotionally stunted anyway. And maybe you need to go a little easier on yourself too."

Katie didn't answer.

Her mom sighed. "But I know how you feel. I understand what you're saying." She hesitated, then came back and sat next to Katie on the bed again. When she spoke, her voice was a little dreamy, her eyes focused on something only she could see.

"I've loved your father from the first time I saw him. He'd been friends with my brother. Same unit in the Army. After Billy was killed…" She drew in a deep breath. "After Billy was killed and Sean got out of the service, he stopped by the farm to pay his respects. Maybe ask for a job. He knew Daddy was in construction." Now she smiled. "I was seventeen, and I opened the door when he knocked. Daddy wasn't there, and Mama wouldn't answer the door anymore. Not after they told us about Billy. Anyway, I opened the door, and there was this young man, all big and handsome and wearing his uniform." She smiled. "And I just fell in love. I actually felt myself turn into a puddle at his feet."

"Mom—" Katie tried to interrupt. She'd heard this

story before, but now it just grated painfully across her raw emotions.

"A few days later, we were naked in the old apple orchard—"

"Mom!" She really didn't want to hear about that.

"—and a few weeks after that, I realized I was going to have Darren. Your Grandpa McCreary went after Sean with a shotgun and forced him to do the right thing, but Sean was pissed. I understood. Here he was, twenty-one years old and just out of the Army. His whole life was ahead of him. Now he's tied to some young girl he doesn't even know."

Katie was silent this time when she paused. Her mom stared at the floor then looked up at her, eyes blue and clear and drenched with tears. "He doesn't love me."

"Mom, you don't—"

"He doesn't love me, Katie. A woman does an awful lot of thinking when she's been through what I've just been through. Sean has never once told me that he loves me. I've made excuses for him when he's hurt me, forgiven him when he played around, but he…he just doesn't love me. He cares about me, but he resents me too. Resents me after all of these years." She paused. "He called Barbara."

"What?" Katie asked, confused.

"He told me before you came back into the waiting room that he'd called Barbara when he was on his way out here. He didn't have time to call me, but he called her. Talked to her. She told him I'd caused a scene when we went out to lunch. Didn't tell him what it was about, of course, but he's taken her word for it. He takes her word for everything. Never mine. I've always wondered whether they...well, it doesn't matter."

Katie put her arms around her mother. For a moment they just held each other.

Then her mom stood with a small and weary sigh. "I'm sorry. I shouldn't have gotten into all of that. I didn't mean to. I guess all I'm trying to say is that you're right. You are absolutely right. No matter what I think, if Luc loves you, he has to be willing to tell you, to commit to you. You can't go through your whole life wondering, making excuses, believing, and then find out you were wrong after you've been married to the man for almost thirty-six years. He has to say the words. You have to know."

"Mom—"

"I'll go now, honey, and leave you alone. Just try to sleep. Try to rest. You can think another day."

"I love you, Mom," Katie choked the words out.

"I know you do. And I love you too, baby." Her mother walked to the door and opened it. "I'll talk to you tomorrow before you go."

Then she was gone. Back to the big red truck parked outside. Back to the man she loved with all of her heart. The man who did not love her.

Katie buried her face in the thin hotel pillow and cried.

THIRTY-THREE

AFTER SPENDING MOST of the next morning answering questions for the FBI and the police, Katie drove the rental car David had provided back to the hospital. She parked and stared at the ugly square building, her grip hard on the steering wheel.

What was she doing here?

When they'd spoken earlier, her mother had told her Melanie hadn't come back to the hotel, which meant that she'd probably stayed with Luc all night. Katie wasn't sure how she'd feel when she saw her foster sister again.

But she hadn't slept much the night before. She'd spent a good deal of the time thinking. About Luc and Melanie. About her mom and dad. About Tom. About everything that had happened and what would come next. About her life as it was and would be and could be. About guilt and fear and how one could be used as an excuse to mask the other.

And at the end of the long, sleepless night she'd known she couldn't leave without talking to Luc one more time. She needed at least that much…closure. She had to give him the chance to change his mind. She couldn't walk away without making one more attempt. But, God, she just didn't know if she was brave enough to go through with it.

Her fingers tightened on the wheel until they hurt, then she forced herself to let go, to open the door, to get out.

Melanie was indeed in Luc's room, sitting at his bedside, talking earnestly, hands waving. Luc was watching her, beautiful eyes hooded and brooding.

Katie's courage failed. She paused in the doorway, but she must have made some noise because Luc's head jerked around, and she found herself trapped in his dark gaze.

Melanie turned, saw her, and stood and rushed to her. "Katie! Come in. Come in."

Katie let Mel take her arm and urge her across the room, while she took the time to study Luc. He seemed better. That was a relief. He was too pale, of course, the lines on his face too deep. The tubes running into his wrist and the hospital gown he wore were reminders of what he'd just been through. But he was awake and alert. And he was looking at her without any expression whatsoever on his face.

"Listen," Melanie said, a little too cheerfully. "I really need a cup of coffee. Why don't you two chat while I go down to the cafeteria?"

"Mel—" Katie tried to protest, but Melanie ignored her and almost ran for the door.

"Back soon!" she called.

Startled, Katie stared after her. Whatever she'd expected from Melanie, this was not it.

"Subtle," Luc murmured.

Katie turned to face him, awkward now that they were alone. After a tense pause, she sat in the chair next to his bed and tried to think of what she wanted to say. Hi, are you trying to push me away because you're an emotional cripple who can't deal with your own feelings? just didn't seem like a good opener.

"Were you able to sleep?" she asked instead.

"Some." His deep voice curled through her insides and made her stomach clench.

Silence.

"How are you?" She wanted to touch him, but didn't dare.

"Okay."

Silence again. Luc's face was shuttered against her, his mouth a straight, unsmiling line. The scar stood out starkly against his cheekbone.

"I just came to say goodbye," she said finally. "I'm leaving this afternoon."

"Already?" Well, at least he was finally showing some emotion, even if it was disapproval.

She forced herself to shrug. Casual. "They said I could. I gave my statement to the police this morning."

His dark brows drew together in a frown. "David agreed to let you go?"

"Did you think he was going to arrest me?"

He made a noise that was something like a growl. "No. But we don't know if you're still in danger."

"Please." She snorted. Better to snort than to cry, she always said. Better to do anything than cry in front of him again. "No one other than Frankie ever made a direct threat against me and he's d…dead. David is sure that Joey Silvano and his uncle, the don, won't bother with me. Liza's in custody. Did you think I was going to hide under a rock forever?"

"No." He didn't say anything else, and Katie held her breath, wondering if he would suggest that she come back with him to the Museum. But he didn't, of course.

When the silence lengthened again, she spoke to fill it. "So, all's well that ends well," she said brightly. "You got your mole, Frankie's gone and I get to return to my boring little life."

"Katie—"

She interrupted him, the words coming in a rush. "Actually I owe you big time for a lot of things. You might have gotten me into this mess, but you didn't just leave me there. A lot of other people would have."

"Yeah, well—"

"You saved me." *And you made love to me in ways I'll never be able to forget.* "Thank you."

"Thank you?" He laughed bitterly. "Thank you? What the hell are you thanking me for? For coming into your life and ruining it? For ripping you away from any security you've ever known? For almost getting you killed?" He sounded so bitter and self-mocking that she couldn't stand it.

"No," she whispered. "Just thank you for coming into my life." She leaned over and feathered a kiss along his cheek, along the scar.

He flinched.

She stood, pretending that she hadn't noticed his re-action. Pretending he hadn't just cut her deeply enough to make that scar look like a scratch. "Well, I guess I'd better go," she said.

She waited.

He didn't say anything.

She backed up a step.

He still didn't say anything.

Katie stared at him for another long, silent time. Then she turned and walked to the door. He didn't try to stop her and her heart broke all over again. Even if he wanted to, he wasn't going to reach out to her. Even if he felt something for her, he was letting her go. No, he was pushing her away.

So this was really it. This was the end.

In the doorway, she paused, looked back at him, gave him one last chance. He was quiet.

"Go with God, Luc," she said at last. "I know He'll watch over you."

"How do you know that?" His voice was just as soft as hers had been, just as strangled. Good. Make it hard. Make it awful for him too.

She smiled, and her lips quivered. "Because I'll ask Him to."

She left the room, walked down the hall, around a corner. Then she sagged into the wall, her arms wrapped tightly around her chest. Feeble protection against the hurt.

Things would get better. She knew they would. The pain would dull. Maybe it would never go away completely, but someday it would become bearable and she'd get on with her life. Someday she'd be able to look back at this last week as an adventure, as a memory. It just wasn't today. And it wouldn't be tomorrow. Or the day after that. But all she had to do was endure. To exist. One step at a time. One day at a time. And it would get better.

Someday.

"Katie?"

Melanie.

Katie straightened and turned to face her foster sister. Melanie was standing close by, watching her with a concerned expression on her face.

Katie cleared her throat. "Hi, Mel." That sounded normal. Good. Normal was good.

"Are you okay?"

She wasn't quite sure how to answer that one. "I'm leaving."

Which pretty much said it all.

Melanie's pretty hazel eyes widened. "You are?"

"The police have released me so I can go home. I don't have any reason to stay."

Melanie looked down the hall, then back again. "You don't?"

"No."

"Aarrgh!" Mel threw her hands up in the air. "What an incredible asshole!"

Katie blinked. "Excuse me?"

"Not you. Him." Melanie shook her head, and Katie watched the silky-straight brown hair flare around her shoulders. If she closed her eyes, she could see Luc's hand touching that hair, caressing it.

She pushed the memory aside with an act of will. "I have to go." She couldn't stay here.

"Wait." Melanie clutched at her arm. "Wait, okay? I have to talk to you."

"Not now."

"Yes, now." Her sister looked around at the busy hospital corridor. "But not here."

Without waiting to hear any arguments from Katie, Melanie pulled her over into a little alcove where upholstered chairs had been set up for family visits. Mel pushed her into a chair and then perched in another next to her. "I don't know where to begin."

"This isn't going to stop me from leaving," Katie warned.

Melanie heaved an exasperated sigh. "Okay, okay." She fidgeted. "God, this is harder than I thought."

Katie stared at her, purposefully not helping.

Eventually Mel sighed again and looked right at her. "Okay. First of all, Luc doesn't love me. Or, I should say that he does, but only as a sister. It's nothing compared to how he feels about…you."

Katie swallowed. "So?"

"So, Mom seems to think you might have gotten a different impression."

Katie stared at her. "You've talked to Mom about this?"

"Well, of course I did. I'm not stupid. I saw your face when you left yesterday, and I was worried. She told me you might think Luc doesn't care about you and that you need to step back because he's in love with me. And he's…not."

Hey, thanks a lot, Mom.

"Man, this is embarrassing." Mel's voice lowered, and she cast a furtive glance around as if to make sure no one could overhear them. Her hair slid forward to hide her face a little bit more. "Okay, here's the whole truth, and you'd better listen up because I only plan on saying this once. I've…I've been in love with Luc forever. He always tried to protect me when, well, you know, and he was so nice to me. After I moved in with your family we kept in touch, but I wanted to, uh, keep him a secret, I guess. He was mine, the only thing I had. I didn't want to share."

"Then why in the world did you try to set me up with him on a blind date for that party three years ago?" Katie asked, curiosity getting the better of her.

Melanie blushed bright red and stared at the floor, then looked at her again. "Oh, boy. Well, it was because…because I was desperate. I wanted to see him. Dance with him. Or something. Maybe get him to see me as someone other than a little girl he'd protected. Not a sister. You know, vamp him." She squirmed on the edge of the chair. "I knew he wouldn't go on a date with me—he'd always been clear about how he felt about me—so I thought I'd see if he'd go with you. He kept asking me about Annie and how she was doing, so it sounded like he wouldn't mind meeting you. But I was a little surprised when he said yes right away."

Now it was Katie's turn to look at the floor. "I get it. You used me."

"No." Melanie flapped her hands and then folded them tightly in her lap. "I thought it would be good for you too. You needed to get out more, and I knew he could be so charming…oh, hell, I don't know. Things got all messed up, and I felt so bad that he stood you up like that, but then you met Tom and everything seemed to be okay. And when Luc didn't show up, I thought maybe he'd changed his mind about me, about how he felt or something. That he was afraid of his feelings. Oh, I don't even know what sort of romantic bullshit I was thinking. Even when he got engaged to Liza, I just saw what I wanted to see." She chewed on her lip. "Right up until you left the hospital room yesterday. That's when I finally understood what was going on."

Katie shook her head. "What are you talking about?"

Melanie stared down at her feet. "That's when I saw that Luc was in love with you."

Katie let out a huff of air. "Yeah, right."

"And he's scared of you."

"Oh, sure." Katie laughed, but it was without humor.

Melanie grabbed her hands. "It's true, I swear it. I was…jealous last night. Of the way he was looking at you. He's never looked at anybody like that before. I hurt you with the way I acted, and I'm so, so sorry, but you have to believe me."

"Melanie," Katie sighed and squeezed her sister's fingers. "What about you?"

"Me?" Melanie clung to her. "I'll be okay. I always am. Like I said, I've known the score for years, I just didn't want to admit it. You're really not leaving because of me, are you? Mom said you might. Don't walk away from him because of me, Katie. I swear I'm fine and I never had a chance anyway and Luc—"

"Melanie," Katie said again, cutting her off. "I'm not walking away because of you. I don't want you to be hurt, and if he loved you back the way you love him, I'd dance at your wedding." She hoped. She held Mel's hands even tighter. "I'm leaving because of him. Honey, if you're right, if he feels something for me, then he has to tell me. And he hasn't said a word." And she knew he never would.

"See, he's not very good at talking about things like that." Melanie's face was eager.

"Don't apologize for him, Mel. Don't try to make excuses for him. Either I'm important to him, or I'm not."

"Katie—"

"Please," Katie interrupted. "Just let it go for now, all right?" Her heart felt like ragged shards of glass rattling around inside her chest, and she couldn't take any more.

Before Melanie could say anything else, Katie hugged her, this person who'd been such an important part of her life for twenty years. How strange to realize there was so much more to Melanie than she'd ever suspected. They'd have to talk, but not now. Not now.

"Just let me go, honey." Her voice choked.

"Katie—" Mel clutched at her.

"It hurts, okay? I have to go, sweetie. I really do."

Neither of them said anything.

"Okay," Melanie whispered.

Katie squeezed her sister one last time, then got up and walked out of the hospital. A few minutes later she was in her rental car heading home.

LATER, A LONG TIME LATER, Luc lay in his cold, sterile hospital room and stared at the faded photograph. Two girls still smiled at the camera, but the picture didn't bring him the comfort it once had. It never would again.

Katie was gone. She'd left him. He'd pushed her away. He sighed. Well, it was for the best.

Melanie had been pretty angry with him. She'd stomped around the room for a time, then thrown up her hands and left him alone. He was glad.

Knowing that he only did what he had to do didn't make it hurt any less. He felt as though someone had carved out his insides and left the shell to rot.

"You're an asshole."

"Yeah." Luc didn't look up from the photo as David Allen entered the room and dropped into the chair next to the bed. Instead, he traced Katie's young face with his fingertip. "Any particular reason you bring it up now?"

"Melanie told me you let Katie leave. You're throwing away the best thing that's ever happened to you, you shithead."

Jesus, wasn't it bad enough that Mel had completely shifted gears and was now devoting herself to getting him to hook up with Katie? Did she have to bring David into it too?

"Lay off." He didn't want to discuss Katie with anyone, not even the man who was as much of a brother as anyone he'd ever known.

"I don't know what kind of guilt trip you're on this time, Vasco, but it's getting kind of old. The girl loves you. Even you should be able to see that."

"She'll get over it."

"Oh, yeah. Right. Bullshit."

Luc looked up from the photo and noted with dull surprise that David really was angry. Angry like he hadn't seen him in a long time. "She deserves better than me," he said. The explanation sounded weak, but then he wasn't particularly strong at the moment.

David leaned forward, his dark face tight and drawn, his eyes haunted. Full of pain and memories that Luc could not guess at, not even after all this time. "You listen to me, Lucas Vasco. You are rejecting the greatest gift life has to offer. No matter why it happened, no matter how quickly it happened, somebody loves you. Really, truly, deeply loves you. And you're flushing it down the toilet."

"No, I—"

"I know you've done some terrible things. Hey, join the club. I know you think you're doing what's best for her, or some other shit like that. But let me tell you, buddy, most people live their entire lives, their entire fucking lives, and never have the chance to experience one tenth of the love Katie McCabe was prepared to give you."

Luc's whole body was tight and sore. "You don't know that."

"Oh, you think so, huh? Listen up, bright boy. I saw her leaning over your body on the beach. I heard her scream when she thought you were going to die. So don't tell me what I don't know. Believe me, I know more about this than you can possibly imagine."

Luc didn't reply, just couldn't.

The other man stared at him, took a deep breath, another, then abruptly stood and walked over to the door. He glanced back over his shoulder.

"If you throw this away, you're going to regret it. You'll always wonder what might have happened if you'd had enough balls to take a chance. Love like Katie has for you, and you have for her, is…well, it's a miracle. And most miracles only happen once." He paused. "You think about that before you just give it up."

"David—" Luc finally found his voice, but it was too late. David had already gone.

Alone again, Luc looked at the photograph. This time he saw Katie as she was today superimposed over the face of the girl she had once been. New over old.

He'd hurt her. He knew he had. He'd meant to. But in the process he'd hurt himself too. Now his life seemed gray. Lonely. David was right, because every time he looked at this photo, he'd see Katie and think about what might have been. What could have been if he'd only reached for it. Why shouldn't he…?

No. He shook his head, denying the voice that whispered he was making a serious mistake. No, it didn't matter how he felt. It was better they go their separate ways now. Better for her. He'd just go home to the Museum with Spot. He'd let Katie get on with her life while he got on with his. While he forgot about wild red hair, blue, blue eyes and freckles that tasted like specks of brown sugar.

The soft, pale skin in the yellow lamplight.

Who was he kidding? He'd never forget her. Never.

So, okay.

Okay, maybe he wouldn't forget. But he'd try to continue.

THIRTY-FOUR

Weeks after Atlantic City, Katie was still trying not to measure everything in relation to Luc. It wasn't working. Her family was worried. Again. And who could blame them. The woman currently reflected in her bedroom mirror had large dark circles under her red-rimmed eyes. She looked like she was sick.

Katie shook herself like a wet dog. Like Spot after she'd climbed out of the fountain at the hotel and Luc had laughed…

Stop it! She was being pathetic, and she was tired of it. She had too much to do to waste time moping around like this. She was in the middle of packing up her apartment because she'd decided to move in with Brenna and save a little money. Next week she was going to start looking for a new job, even though David had worked his magic so she still had her old one. She desperately needed a change because she couldn't concentrate, couldn't focus. She knew she was making mistakes, that there had been talk around the office. Once she was at a new place, she'd be able to forget.

She'd never forget.

Katie grabbed a tissue and blew her nose with determined ferocity. Lucas Vasco had had his chance, and he'd blown it. Now it was time for Katherine McCabe to get busy and get on with her life.

She snapped her fingers at her reflection. Her life, damn it. Her life.

Without Luc.

Her shoulders sagged.

Boy, she missed him.

Sighing, she grabbed the box of clothes she'd gone into the bedroom to get and went back to the living room where her mother was industriously packing books. Her mom and Brenna had both offered to help today, but Brenna had been called in to work, so Katie and her mother were alone.

Her mother glanced up when Katie entered the room. "I'm almost finished here," she reported. "What's next?"

"Well, I guess the kitchen—" Katie was interrupted by an unexpected knock on the apartment door.

She and her mother both jumped and stared at each other.

"Jeez, we're a couple of cowards," Katie laughed. "I, uh, I'd better go see who it is."

"I'll be right behind you," her mom assured her.

Together, tense, they walked to the door. Katie peered through the peephole. She let out a squeak of surprise at the sight of her father standing in the hallway.

"Who is it?" Her mom asked.

Katie ignored her, unlocked the deadbolt and threw open the door. "Dad?"

Her mother went very still behind her.

Katie studied her father. She saw wildness in his eyes and he had a piece of paper crumbled in one massive fist.

"Hi," he said to both of them, although Katie's mother was the one he looked at. "Can I come in?"

"Um, okay." Katie stood back, and her dad stepped past her. She closed the door and turned. "Is everything okay?"

"Sure." Her father gave her an absent one-armed hug, just like he did it every day. "Give me a minute with your mom, okay?"

"Okay," Katie said again. She looked between the two of them, but they weren't paying any attention to her anymore, they were watching each other. She left the room, but the apartment wasn't exactly spacious so she couldn't help overhearing their conversation.

"Sean," her mother whispered.

"Maureen," he said, just as quietly.

"Where did you get that?" She must have been referring to the paper he was holding.

"I...uh, found it. It was on the floor. Behind the desk." There was a pause. "I thought you were writing again. I wanted to read it. And then I found...this."

"It's a draft. I didn't know what to say." Her voice was soft, but Katie heard the sadness. Heard the pain.

She stood in her bedroom, staring at boxes and packing paper. Staring at the blank walls.

"You didn't know what to say?" Her father's voice rose until even the neighbors could probably hear him. Katie winced. She knew that tone. "We've been married thirty-six years, and you're going to leave me with a 'Dear John' letter?"

"I...I..." She stuttered.

Katie's breath stilled, her stomach clenched. Suddenly she was a little girl again, hiding in her bedroom, listening to her parents argue, wondering if her father would leave. Wondering if her mother would stay.

"I love you," her mother said at last.

"You love me? You love me?" He laughed, but it was a harsh and brittle sound. "Well, you've got a fine way of showing it, don't you, Maureen?"

"Yes." Her mother's voice rose now, too, trembling with emotion. "Yes, I do have a fine way of showing it, as a matter of fact. I gave you six children and was mother to seven. I forgave you when you ran around with another woman."

Katie took a deep breath. She should not be hearing this. This was not something meant for her.

"I cared for you, nursed you when you were sick or hurt. I stood by you in richer and in poorer, when you were being kind or when you were being an ass. I never, ever cheated on you. I've never even wanted to look at another man. Not since that first day. I loved you then, Sean, and I love you now. I've loved you all of these years."

"Maureen—"

"But you never loved me."

Katie put her hands over her ears, but she could still hear them. She could still hear Luc. She could still see him looking at her, turning away from her.

"What are you talking about? You've got to know that I care about you." His voice was confused, and Katie knew he didn't understand. He really didn't. Maybe Luc didn't understand either.

"I know you care," her mom said. "That's what makes it so hard. But it's not enough anymore."

"What the hell does that mean?"

"I want to be more to you than your wife and the mother of your children."

"Sweet Jesus, you know I'm not good at interpreting this kind of emotional shit. Just tell me what you mean, damn it."

"I want to be vital to you. Not just someone who makes your lunch and washes your underwear."

Yes, Katie thought. That's what she wanted too. She wanted to be vital.

"What the hell?" Her father roared. "Woman, you are driving me crazy. I can't believe we're even having this conversation. You're coming home with me now, and that's final."

Katie turned and opened the bedroom door so she could see them. Her father sounded so angry, so hurt. She didn't think he would ever strike her mother, but she had to make sure.

Her mom was standing, staring at her husband, her arms wrapped tightly around her own waist. She didn't look afraid, just sad. Worn. Fragile. She was never fragile.

"No," she said. "No, I'm not coming with you."

Her father's face grew red, and his eyes went hard. He pointed a finger at her mother. Katie took a step forward, ready to intervene. "You listen to me, Maureen McCabe. Either you come home with me now, or you don't come home at all. Do you hear me?"

Her mother nodded. "Yes, I hear you."

"Well, then—"

"No," she said. "No."

They just stared at each other.

"Fine. Good." Her father ripped up the letter and threw it at her mother so it rained down on her head like confetti. "Have a nice life. Forget about getting any of your things." He stomped to the door and pulled it open so violently that it banged into the wall. Then he paused on the threshold, his head turned slightly. "I didn't mean that, Mo. Send one of the kids over to get your stuff. But you never set foot in my house again."

"It was always your house, Sean," she whispered, choking. Katie saw the tears streaming down her face. "It was never ours."

He just nodded and slammed the door shut behind him.

As soon as he was gone, her mother sank down on the floor and covered her face with her hands.

Katie rushed over to her. "Mom? Mom, are you all right?"

"No. No, I'm not."

Katie knelt beside her and held her tightly while she cried.

"He'll feel terrible about yelling like that," Mom said finally. "He always does. He doesn't think before he talks."

"Are you going back?" Katie asked.

"No," her mother said softly. "I'm not going back."

"You're going to leave him? Divorce him?"

"I don't know."

"What will you do?"

"I don't know that either."

Katie hesitated. "So you weren't, uh, planning this?"

Her mom gulped back a sob. "I was trying to figure out what to say to him. I thought I'd have more time. Maybe ease him into it a little." She glanced at Katie and sighed. "I hurt him, honey. That's why he lashed out at me. I hurt his pride. But he's hurt me too. More than he even knows. Or cares."

Then Katie and her mother both wept for a while.

LUC STRETCHED OUT on the sofa in the family room at the Museum with Spot snoring gently next to the empty fireplace. The wide-screen television droned in the background. He barely heard it.

He was still on medical leave, but David had called to tell him that Liza had escaped from custody. They'd traced her to a plane heading for Rio, and David was certain she was out of the country. The authorities had been holding her for a psych eval, which took for freaking ever, especially since she was all lawyered up. Apparently she'd seduced one of the guards at the facility, then brained the idiot with his own gun and walked out.

Luc didn't care. As long as she was gone and Katie was safe.

Katie.

Jesus, she was everywhere. Everywhere he looked. Everywhere he went. Standing outside on the patio. Sleeping in his bedroom. Dancing around the kitchen table. Laughing up at him with blue eyes. Lying here on the crimson Oriental carpet, where she'd kissed him so sweetly. Where they'd made love…

He jumped off the sofa as if it had scorched him, stalked to the kitchen, grabbed his car keys and headed for the door. Spot immediately woke and padded after him, but he ignored her. He wasn't really supposed to drive yet, but he didn't give a shit what the doctors said, and he had to get out of here. Had to drive and drive and drive until he left everything behind. Until he left her behind.

He practically ran for the car.

Luc drove for hours. Anywhere. Nowhere. It didn't matter where he went, he couldn't shake the memory of Katie sitting next to him, touching him. The roads snapped by in a blur. Trees and sky and buildings and asphalt. Pain in his shoulder as he followed a curve, reminding him of bleeding on the beach in Atlantic City.

She'd said she loved him. She'd said it, and he'd heard her.

And he remembered that, as he'd been running from Silvano's thugs, he'd thought that fighting was the one thing he'd always been good at. But he hadn't fought for Katie.

Katie, who loved him.

All of this time he'd been certain he was doing what was best. For her. But was David right? Was he throwing away a miracle?

He drove, and he brooded.

And as he brooded, as he contemplated his empty, angry life, he finally understood something else. He needed her. Whatever happened in the future, he wasn't going to make it without her. She was his center.

He might not be the best guy in the world, but she

was his. His, damn it. And she always had been. Right or wrong, he just couldn't let her go.

Jesus Christ, he couldn't let her go.

He loved her. He loved Katie McCabe.

And he'd shoved her away. Hurt her.

He drove blindly, thinking of her face as she'd left the hospital room, thinking how set and pale it had been. Thinking of the anguish he'd seen in her eyes.

She'd never forgive him.

Fear gripped him, churned in his belly. Had he completely fucked things up? Was he too late? Had he thrown away his one chance?

No, he decided. No. He wouldn't let himself believe it. If she turned him away, turned him down, he'd be left with nothing.

He'd tell her how he felt. Tell her what she meant to him. He'd grovel. He'd beg. She had to forgive him.

What if she had changed her mind? What if she'd turned to somebody else in the last couple of weeks?

He'd kill the fucking son of a bitch.

Luc gripped the steering wheel hard, until the pain shot through his still healing muscles. She'd forgive him, he assured himself. He couldn't be too late.

Maybe he should romance her, woo her. Lord knew he hadn't given her any softness during their time together. He could charm the ladies, he knew how. Surely he could charm the one who really mattered.

Luc turned the car back to the Museum. The germ of an idea took root in his mind and grew, developed. Yeah, romance her. Make it special. Let her know that he treasured her. As long as he wasn't too late. Dear

God, he couldn't be too late. He pushed harder on the accelerator, and the old Volvo practically left the road.

Flipping open his cell phone, he hit the speed-dial for Melanie.

THIRTY-FIVE

ON THE SATURDAY afternoon following her father's confrontation with her mother, Katie was alone in her apartment. Brenna, Darren, Brandon and Michael had all gone to their parents' house to pick up her mom's things. Katie would have gone with them, but she wasn't sure she'd be able to hold her temper around her dad, so Brenna had insisted she stay home.

Her mother was out looking for a place to live. She had some money of her own, and they'd arranged for her to take over Katie's apartment until she got on her feet, but she'd wanted to see what else was available. Fiona hadn't gone back to school yet, but she'd been conspicuously absent, content to stay out of the family drama. Since her younger sister never liked drama unless she was the center of it, Katie was just as glad she wasn't around.

She didn't know where Melanie was.

Katie's own packing was finished. This was actually supposed to have been her moving day, but Brenna and the boys had thought it more important to get her mother's stuff out of the house, and she agreed with them. Her apartment was paid through the end of month anyway.

The big problem was that now she didn't have anything to do. And it was easier, so much easier, to keep busy.

She was idly clicking through channels on the TV when she was interrupted by a knock on the door. Glad for the interruption, she jumped to answer it. She found Melanie standing in the hallway, smiling, even though Katie hadn't heard a word from her in days.

"Mel?" Katie was a little confused, but happy. "Come in. Come in. I'm so glad to see you." She stepped back from the door.

"Hi, there." Melanie gave her a quick hug, then walked into the living room. She gave it an assessing glance. "You're all packed."

"And if everything comes together, Mom is probably going to move in."

"Yeah." Melanie's smile faded and her face grew troubled. "I can't believe she's leaving him after all this time. I just can't believe it."

"Neither can I. What's up, Mel? Do you need something?"

"I came to get you."

"Get me?" Katie blinked.

"Yeah. David wants me to take you to pick up Kato."

"He does?" Katie was surprised. "Well, why can't he just bring him here?"

"Please. Do you think he has time to deliver cars? He's an important guy. Besides, Liza Anderson escaped."

"What?"

"Don't worry," Melanie assured her hastily. "David

found out she jumped a plane for Rio. He's tracking her, but he's sure she's out of the country."

"Oh. That's good, I guess." Melanie had a lot of information. Had any of it come from Luc? Did Melanie talk to him? Of course she talked to him. Katie shook off her thoughts. "Okay, well, let's go."

"Go? You can't go looking like that."

Katie glanced down at herself. "What's wrong with how I look?"

"Katie, those sweats are older than God and your hair. I mean, I love you and all, but come on. Take a shower at least. Phew!"

"I'm not that bad."

"Shows what you know. I'm the one who's going to be stuck in a car with you for hours."

"Jeez. Okay, okay, I'm going," Katie grumbled and headed for her tiny bathroom. She sniffed herself delicately. Come to think of it, Melanie might have a point. She did seem to be a little...ripe. There just hadn't been much of a need to clean up on a weekend when nobody else was around.

"Wear something pretty," Melanie called after her.

Katie stopped at the bathroom door and turned around to stare at her. "For God's sake, why?"

Melanie picked up the remote for the TV and settled down on the sofa. "Hello! Because we might run into Luc. Do I have to tell you everything?"

"What?" Katie's heart gave one hard thump, then pounded a little faster than normal.

"He's out on medical leave for another couple of weeks, but you never know if he'll be checking in at the office. I know it's Saturday, but David will be there, and we'll probably have to get him to sign something or other, so we might see Luc. Now get moving."

Katie frowned and went into the bathroom. She wasn't sure how she felt at the prospect of seeing Luc again, however slim that chance might be.

Thoughtfully, she stripped off her clothes and climbed into the shower, letting the warm water pound her.

Part of her wanted to tell Mel to forget the whole thing, but that was just stupid. She needed her car, after all. Maybe she could ask Mel to spring Kato while she waited outside, except that would just be avoiding the issue. Now that the relationship between Luc and Melanie had come to light, chances were good she'd run into him sooner or later. It might as well be sooner.

Besides, he probably wouldn't even be there. She didn't know why she was worrying about it.

Still, she took a little extra time with her appearance and, after some debate, put on a new skirt and blouse set her mother had talked her into buying.

When she finally made her way back into the living room, she met Melanie's grin with a defiant tilt of her head. "I'm ready."

"Nice." Melanie laughed, stood and turned off the television.

"Shut up."

"Sure, sure. Let's get going. I don't have all day."

Melanie dragged her out to her little Honda, and soon they were on the highway.

Katie looked around with some surprise. She knew she didn't have a great sense of direction, but she just thought they weren't going the right way. "Isn't Kato in Philadelphia?" she asked Mel.

"I'm just taking a back way. I hate traffic."

"Okay." Katie was dubious, but Melanie seemed certain, so she let it go.

Sometime later they passed a big sign that said "Welcome to New Jersey."

Katie's entire body went rigid. She spun in the seat to face her sister. "What the hell is going on? Where are you taking me?"

But she knew. She knew where they were going.

Melanie bit her lip. "Don't be angry."

"Don't be angry? You're taking me to the Museum, aren't you?"

"Yes, but—"

"Melanie, what are you doing?" Katie wanted to cry, wanted to scream. Wanted to jump out of the car and run away.

"No, no, wait! It was Luc's idea," Melanie said quickly. "All of this was Luc's idea. Everyone else knew about it. That's why you were alone today."

Katie drew in a deep breath, not sure she'd heard correctly. There was an incredible pressure in her chest. Like hope struggling to grow when it had been chopped down to the roots.

"What? What did you say?"

"Luc. He planned this. He wants you to come to the Museum. It's like a date. But he didn't want to come himself to get you because he wasn't sure how you'd react. And he said he wanted to give you the chance to stand him up." She glanced at Katie and grinned. "Although I'll admit I was supposed to get you as far as I could before you figured out where you were going."

Katie stared at her sister. "He wants me to come to him?" she whispered. "After all of this time?"

Melanie glanced at her again, then away. "He wants you." Katie thought there might have been some pain in that quick look. But when Melanie smiled, the smile was real. "He wants you, Katie. I know he's a pea-brained, terrified idiot, but are you going to hold his mistakes against him? Or are you going to let him tell you how he feels?"

Katie thought about it for a moment. Did Luc even know how he felt? Did he really know what he wanted? Would she be able to believe anything he said to her? Would she ever forgive herself if she didn't at least listen?

She swallowed, hard, and took a deep, shuddering breath.

He'd sent Melanie to get her. She had to find out why.

"He's such a jerk. I'm going to kick his sorry ass and then feed it to Spot."

Melanie laughed. "There you go."

Katie looked at her. "Melanie—"

"Don't." The word was sharp. Melanie clenched the steering wheel. "Just don't go there now. You and Luc are the two people I love most in this world. He was worried about asking me for help, but I insisted. I want you both to be happy." She looked away from the road to meet Katie's eyes. "I want that."

"I love you, Mel. If this—"

"No." Melanie smiled, bright and sad and calm. "No. This is right. This is good."

Before Katie knew it, they were driving down the long and familiar driveway leading to the Museum. The building stood among its guardian trees, looking regal and solid and out of place in the twenty-first century. A dream.

Then she saw boards nailed over windows where stained glass had once been, and she knew it was also reality.

The tall and handsome man dressed in a crisp black tuxedo stepped out of the front door as soon as Melanie pulled her Honda to a stop in the parking area. He walked toward them. A dream. A reality.

Luc.

Katie's stomach clenched almost painfully. She didn't think she'd be able to stand it if he was just playing with her, if this didn't mean what she thought it meant.

Luc bent down and opened the passenger door. He looked so good. He looked so damn good. God, her hands were shaking.

If he broke her heart again, she would never survive it.

Melanie gave her a little shove. "Go on."

Luc held out his hand. She put hers into it, felt his warm skin, let him draw her out of the car. He shut the door behind her and then they stood, just staring at each other.

Katie dimly heard the rattle of gravel as her sister's little car sped back up the driveway.

"Hi." She sounded breathy even to her own ears.

"Hi," Luc answered. His dark eyes were fixed on her face, as if he couldn't quite believe she was there.

"Um, where's Spot?" Katie asked, realizing the dog wasn't around.

"In her kennel. This is my date, not Spot's." Luc tugged at her hand. "Come on. We have to talk."

His face was so serious that it made her pulse spike with anxiety. But surely he wouldn't have gone to all of this trouble, wouldn't have had Melanie lure her out here, wouldn't have gotten dressed up in a tuxedo for God's sake, if he was just going to tell her goodbye again.

No. No, he wouldn't have.

She gripped his hand tighter. "Okay."

He relaxed, just the slightest bit, and she realized he was as tense as she was. Somehow the knowledge gave her more confidence. She smiled at him.

He pulled her to the house.

"Where are we going?" she asked.

"Shh. Surprise." His stark, beautiful face split into a grin that brought out the dents beside his mouth. She stared at them, at him. His smile faded, his gaze intent on her own mouth. "But first…" he murmured, then he dipped his head and kissed her.

And just like that, she was alive again. Just like that she was ravenous for him again. For his taste, his touch, and even though they hadn't talked, hadn't resolved a single damn thing yet, she grabbed him, held on to him. Loved him.

"Hello, Luc."

The voice that rang out behind them was shrill and close and female and familiar.

It was Liza.

Luc jerked away from Katie and whirled, instinctively putting himself between her and danger.

Liza looked terrible. Her skin stretched tightly over her cheekbones and was so pale it was almost translucent. Her exotic dark eyes were sunken and held a wild, crazy glint. But the Browning 9 mm in her hand was steady.

He took another step forward.

"Stop!" Liza aimed her weapon at his forehead.

Luc froze. The woman might have gone completely batshit insane, but she was more than capable of pulling that trigger.

"Liza." He tried to keep his voice soothing while sweat trickled between his shoulder blades. "What are you doing here?"

"I know you're carrying," she snapped. "Put it on the ground."

He hesitated. They were too far away from the buildings to make a run for it, and if he tried to jump Liza, she'd shoot him. Still, he had to do something...

Liza smiled, lips curled back from even, white teeth.

"Don't piss me off, Lucas. Put your gun on the ground like a nice boy, or little bits of your head are going to be missing."

Jesus.

"Okay, okay. Take it easy." His weapon was under his jacket at the small of his back. Moving carefully, he pulled it out, and in the process palmed a small knife he kept in his belt. It probably wouldn't kill her, but maybe it would distract her. Assuming he ever got close enough to use it.

Hiding the knife behind his hand, he placed his gun carefully on the ground and straightened, arms out to the side.

Liza licked her full, red lips, eyes glittering as she watched him.

"What are you doing here?" he asked again.

Katie stood silent behind him and he willed her to stay that way, to let him handle this.

Liza smiled, a horrible little smile, and drifted closer. That's right, babe. Keep on coming.

"I've been watching you."

That made him pause. "What? What are you talking about?"

"I knew I should come today. I knew she'd be here. I heard in town that you'd bought a lot of flowers and champagne and arranged for caterers. You even hired a jazz trio."

Luc felt Katie jerk with surprise. He thought about the three guys he'd left warming up in the ballroom, jamming softly amidst the flowers and the perfectly prepared meal and the iced champagne. They wouldn't come looking for him for a while because they knew this was a special deal. They'd probably figure he and Katie were talking or, more likely, rolling around in the sheets upstairs.

"David thinks you're in Rio," he said to Liza, just to keep her talking.

"David's an idiot. It wasn't hard to leave a false trail."

She took another step closer, then another. "I escaped. I came here. And I've been watching you, waiting. I knew sooner or later your little whore would pay you a visit. I wanted the two of you to be together."

"Why?"

"You were mine. I love you, but you want her. I got into so much trouble because of you." She shook her head. "Daddy didn't like it when he found out you were at the estate and I hadn't told him. He didn't like it at all. So much trouble..." She trailed off.

Luc was silent, watching for any opportunity to act. Katie stirred behind him, but he kept his attention on Liza.

Liza stared into his face, her brown eyes large and haunted. "She killed Frankie. She has to pay for killing him, don't you see? Then Daddy will like me and you'll come back to me again. It will all work out."

Luc shifted to the balls of his feet. "Liza, baby, listen—"

"No!" Liza's voice was shrill. The gun quivered. Behind him, Katie drew in a sharp breath. His own breathing was shallow and forced. "No, don't you call me that. Don't you call me anything nice. I protected you. I went out on a limb for you. Daddy would have killed me if he'd known I was keeping things from him. But I never told him about you. I love you."

There'd been a time when Luc had believed Liza really did love him. Now he knew that whatever sick emotion she felt, it was a far cry from love. Now he'd seen love, obvious and glowing in eyes as blue as the sky.

Love was Katie.

"Come on, Liza," he said as gently as he could. "Put down the gun. We'll go talk. Just you and me. We'll talk and figure things out."

Liza stared at him and licked her lips again. For a second he thought she would do it. The Browning even dropped a little. Then she shook her head and her hand steadied. "You left me for her," she murmured. "You could have me, but you want her."

Yes, Luc thought. Yes. He wanted Katie. She was everything.

"What happened between us doesn't have anything to do with Katie," he said desperately.

"I think I'm going to make you watch me kill her," Liza told him, taking another step forward. She was getting close now. She smiled again. "Frankie taught me how to play too."

"No!" Katie leapt out from behind Luc, grabbed a handful of gravel from the driveway and threw it into Liza's eyes. She was too far away to do much damage, but the action, the bite of the small stones distracted Liza, and she turned instinctively.

Luc threw his knife.

The small blade caught Liza in the forearm. She cried out in pain and frustration. She shot her gun, but the bullet went wild.

Luc was already moving. He grabbed Liza, getting her in a chokehold while he twisted the weapon away from her. She clawed at him. Finally he knocked her legs out from under her and smashed her face-down into the dusty stones. He sat on her, twisted her arms behind her back and held them there.

Liza bucked and screamed and cried. Then she lay still, weeping into the earth.

Luc looked at Katie to make sure she was okay and found her standing, her breath coming in sharp gasps, her wild hair a curly red mass around her face. She had his gun and it was pointed at Liza.

Luc grinned. "You'd better call the cops."

Katie nodded and dropped the weapon to go back to where she'd left her purse. "If that food goes bad," she said, "I'm really going to be pissed."

Luc laughed. He just couldn't help it.

What a woman.

His woman.

His.

THIRTY-SIX

AFTER THE POLICE had come and taken away the still-sobbing Liza, after statements had been made and the crime scene investigated, after a startled jazz trio had been sent home with apologies and a substantial tip, after the irate Spot had been released from her kennel to roam free on the grounds and make sure all was well, Katie sat alone with Luc in his kitchen, sipping champagne. He'd rescued the food and drink when he'd sprung the jazz trio, and what looked to be some very nice chicken florentine was heating up in the microwave.

Katie was quiet. She didn't know what to say to him now that the frenzy of the past couple of hours was over. She didn't know what he wanted to say to her. She sipped champagne, sparkling bubbles tickling her nose and throat. He'd brought a vase of delicate pink roses back with him from the ballroom. They were sitting on the kitchen table, their sweet fragrance filling the room.

"Some date, huh?" Luc said finally.

"You do know how to show a girl a good time," she agreed, trying to keep her tone light.

"Yeah." He downed about half his glass in a single pull. "Freaking romantic."

"Frankie and Liza were quite a pair, weren't they?" she said.

"I guess. Both of them were totally screwed up. Probably screwed each other up too."

"Yes." Her eyes travelled over him. He'd lost his tuxedo jacket and bowtie somewhere along the way, and his pleated shirt no longer gleamed white. It was filthy and ripped. He'd rolled it up to show strong forearms sprinkled with dark hair, the little snake tattoo wrapped protectively around one of them. His scar stood pale against the dusky gold of his cheek.

Dear God, she loved him.

Luc looked up, caught her staring and smiled just a little, more with his eyes than with his mouth. He put down his glass, stood up abruptly. "Come on."

Katie set her own glass on the table and took the hand he offered, palm sliding against palm, skin against skin. "The ballroom?" Her voice sounded wispy and she swallowed.

"Another time. Mood's ruined."

"Not necessarily."

He smiled at her again, and the grooves on either side of his long, delicious mouth put in a brief appearance. She let him lead her out the back door into the evening, to the terrace where once they'd talked on a hot summer day.

To her extreme disappointment, he dropped her hand as soon as they were outside and stepped back, dark hair gleaming in the light that fell through the open kitchen door.

"Did you call David?" she asked eventually, just to be saying something.

"Yeah. He's pissed off that Liza gave him the slip. It won't happen again."

"Good."

They were both silent. Luc massaged the back of his neck. Katie linked her fingers together, not sure what to make of his sudden apparent awkwardness.

"Did Melanie tell you that Vinnie in the motor pool fixed Kato?" he asked finally, shifting on his feet, hands in his pockets, then hanging down at his sides, then back in his pockets. As if he didn't quite know what to do with them.

"That's what she'd said. I assumed it was an excuse to get me out here."

"No, it's true. He looks like a brand new car. We'll go pick him up sometime so you can turn in the rental."

"Oh. Okay." We'll go pick him up. What did that mean?

The silence stretched out between them again, so long this time that Katie thought she was going to go insane. Or scream. Or bash him over the head with a blunt instrument.

"Luc—"

"Katie—"

They both started talking at the same time, then stopped.

"Me first," Luc said. He took a deep breath, let it out and looked at her.

Katie froze, mesmerized by what she thought she saw in his eyes.

"I tried to stay away from you," he said. "I meant to stay away from you."

"And yet you sent for me. Asked me out on a date. I didn't stand you up."

"No." He moved until he was standing very close, staring down at her, his breathing harsh and difficult. "Katie. Damn it, you could have died today. Liza could have shot you and you could be dead and I'd never... never have—" He broke, pulled her hard into his arms, buried his face against her hair. She felt him shuddering. Felt him holding her as if he would never let her go. "Christ, Katie. You could be dead! You could have died in Atlantic City. You could have died today."

Katie clung to him, let her hands roam over his broad shoulders, his strong back, let his scent and heat seep into her pores until she could hardly think for wanting him. "But I didn't," she pointed out.

"I love you," he whispered right into her ear.

And her heart simply stopped.

He laughed softly, a little nervously. "Breathe, why don't you?"

She obediently gulped for air.

"What?" she gasped. "What did you say?"

He pulled back slightly, looked down into her face, and smiled.

"I love you."

"Oh." The words. The beautiful, beautiful words.

Luc watched her, obviously concerned. "That's it?" he asked, his face tight. "Have I, um, left it too long? Have you changed your mind about me?"

"No." Her laugh was more like a sob. "No. I love you too."

Luc grinned, relief and love and pure male arrogance dancing across his face.

"I know," he said, just like he'd never doubted it. "I heard you on the beach."

He kissed her before she could tell him that he was a jerk. Deep, hard, wet, their lips blending, tongues searching and finding.

"But you were going to walk away from me. You tried to push me away," she said when he let her up for air.

"Yes."

"Tell me why, goddamn it!" She shoved at him, angry.

"You deserve a lot better than me," he said, sincerely. "I was going to let you get on with your life."

"Gee, thanks a lot." She tried to pull away from him, but he held her tighter. "You've got some weird picture of yourself in your head, Lucas Vasco, you know that? I don't need you to be noble. How many times do I have to freaking tell you? I just need you."

"I'm sorry that I hurt you."

Katie rolled her eyes. "Do me a favor and lose the guilt, okay? You sent for me." She smiled as the wonder of her own words dawned on her and her voice was softer when she continued. "You sent for me. You want me." She felt like her face was one big smile. "You love me. And you told me so." She looked around. "On your beautiful terrace. Outside your beautiful house. After your ex-fiancée tried to kill us."

He grimaced. "Yeah, sorry about that."

"We have something to remember. It'll make a great story," she said, giddy. She had a great story. With Luc.

"Wonderful."

They kissed some more. His hands roamed over her body, one crept up to massage her breast and she moaned. Then he kissed her again, gently now, just like she was precious and fragile, when she knew perfectly well that she wasn't.

"I was afraid," he whispered the confession into her neck. "I am afraid."

"Afraid of me?"

"No." He took a deep breath, pulled away to look at her. "I'm afraid of us. 'Us' terrifies me."

Katie laughed, but it was a little shaky. "Me too," she admitted.

"I'm no prize," he warned. "I'm sure I have deep psychological problems that are going to come out at the most inopportune moments."

"Hmmm. Good thing I'm perfect, then."

She reached up, traced his jaw, the grooves that lay dormant beside his mouth, his lips. He kissed her finger, then took her wrist and kissed her palm.

"Maybe it's the wrong thing to do, maybe it's stupid, but I swear you'll never regret loving me, Katie."

"I know." Her voice was soft and he kissed her again. They were both breathing hard when he stopped.

"I can't believe this has happened so fast," she said.

He laughed. "Fast? Hell, no. I've loved you for twenty years."

"Oh, I'm so sure. You didn't even know me twenty years ago."

Luc reluctantly took a step away from her and reached into the pocket of his tuxedo pants. "I knew you." He pulled out an old dog-eared photograph and handed it to her.

She dragged her eyes away from his face to look at it, and her mouth fell open with shock.

"Hey, I remember this picture. Someone took it at school before Melanie moved in with us. It was the last photograph she ever let anyone take of her. How did you get it?"

"She gave it to me when I skipped town. And I fell in love with the little imp standing next to her grinning out at me."

"I can't believe you kept it all this time."

"Yeah." He took it from her and slipped it back into his pocket before grabbing her again. "Stupid and pathetic, I know, but I could never let it go."

Katie looked at him and a deep sadness swirled through her.

"Melanie loves you."

"I know." His eyes were sad too. "I've always known."

"I have to tell you…you have to know," she took a deep breath. "I was driving the car the day the day she got so hurt…"

"I've always known that too. It was an accident."

Katie stared at him. "You knew?"

"Mel told me when it happened. She never blamed you."

"I blamed myself. I…" She hesitated, started again. "When she came to you, back at the hospital, I thought maybe I should just go, leave her with a clear field. She'd been so hurt, and she obviously loved you and I owed her so much."

Luc held her slightly away from him. "It's you I want, Katie. Not Melanie. You."

"I'm glad. I'm sorry for Melanie, but I'm so, so glad."

His eyes moved over her hair and he touched it, smiling when the curls tugged at his fingers.

"I think I fell in love with your hair first," he murmured. "Your wild, exuberant hair."

She wrinkled her nose. "I'm glad one of us likes it."

"So much life. There's so much life in you. In your hair. In your smile. How could I not fall in love with you?" He drew in a deep breath. "Marry me?"

Katie smiled up at him. "I'm afraid my family comes with the package," she warned him.

"A daunting prospect."

"My brothers will want to meet you officially."

"Are you trying to scare me off?"

"And my parents are separating. It's bound to be a little weird for a while."

He was beginning to frown. "Are you going to marry me or not?"

"Well, of course I am. You may be stupid, but I'm not. Now kiss me again."

"Yes, ma'am."

"Hold me."

"Always."

"Can we have our reception in the ballroom at the Museum? With a string quartet instead of a jazz trio?"

He winced. "Jesus. Okay. Sure."

She laughed at him, her joy bubbling like the champagne. "I love you, Lucas Vasco," she said, almost shouting it. Somewhere in the distance, she heard Spot bark.

"I love you too, Hornet."

"Then kiss me, you fool."

So he did.

And in another minute, Spot exuberantly tackled them both down to the ground.